. . . as the story kept peeling away, like a snake dropping away its skins, it was I who held it wriggling and twisting and darting out. The truth, when such extreme efforts are made to conceal it, develops a peculiar life of its own . . . The Truth dies hard. Maybe it never dies at all, but lies sleeping, waiting for someone to find it, decipher its code . . .

My name is Paul Cavanaugh. This is what happened.

THE CAVANAUGH QUEST
Thomas Gifford

"Occasionally, but very rarely, there comes along a mystery you literally can't put down . . . far above average, better than the best you've read in years. Such a mystery is *The Cavanaugh Quest*."

—*Daily Press,*
Newport News

Also by Thomas Gifford:

THE WIND CHILL FACTOR

Published by Ballantine Books

THE
Cavanaugh
Quest

Thomas Gifford

BALLANTINE BOOKS • NEW YORK

Library of Congress Catalog Card Number: 75-37083

ISBN 0-345-25653-0-195

This edition published by arrangement with
G. P. Putnam's Sons

Manufactured in the United States of America

First Ballantine Books Edition: March 1977

For my mother and father

I am not I;
he is not he;
they are not they.

quest: a chivalrous enterprise in medieval romance usually involving an adventurous journey.

—*Webster's Third New International Dictionary*

Prologue

DURING the latter part of this past summer and the early autumn several people I knew were murdered in the most publicized and bizarre crime wave in the history of Minneapolis. It didn't last long but things like that don't have to be lengthy to do the damage. Some lives were blown to pieces which were terribly difficult to reconstruct; others floated soundlessly off into eternity like space garbage. Violent death has a way of attracting money and power and media. Having written a previous book about a crime and a trial, I was commissioned by my publisher to write an on-the-scene journalistic investigation of the murders. I was even expected to do some detecting myself, an expectation smacking of another era altogether. As it turned out, it would have been much too close to autobiography for me to give it the proper treatment. So I returned the advance and retired to lick my assorted wounds. No book was ever written and the whole matter remains so shrouded in inconclusiveness that I seriously doubt if there ever will be one.

Lovers of crime fiction and, even more so, followers of true-life crime stories have a weakness: They want the story to come to a satisfactory climax and denouement which finds justice being evenhandedly meted out, the guilty punished, the innocent freed to resume their normal lives. Neat 360-degree affairs rounded off with legalistic tidiness. In the case of the murders in Minneapolis there just wasn't that happy, convenient set of conclusions followed by the lights coming up, THE END hanging in limbo as the curtain rattles closed.

The fact was, the murderer was never brought to

1

justice or even revealed; identified by some of us, yes, but never quite brought to heel. The motive remained hidden from the public and the murders remain officially unsolved. And the innocent would never return to the lives they had once found quiet, comforting, normal.

My life was one of those which exploded. I was no writer, no observer, no reporter. I was a participant. And as the story kept peeling away, like a snake dropping away its skins, it was I who held it wriggling and twisting and darting out. The truth, when such extreme efforts are made to conceal it, develops a peculiar life of its own. It struggles to make itself known, to receive the credit it deserves, to achieve the capital T. The Truth dies hard. Maybe it never dies at all, but lies sleeping, waiting for someone to find it, decipher its code.

This, then, is a story about the search for an elusive truth.

The truth exists independent of us all, for its own sake. It has no moral validity. It reminds me of Melville's white whale. Captain Ahab was wrong: Moby Dick was not evil, he simply *was*. And so it is with the truth. There it sits, expressionless, a disinterested party. I am what I am, says the truth, and the rest of us are stuck with it.

When you have finished with what I've decided to say, you will know the truth and only you will be able to decide if it was worth learning. Worth it for the people involved, worth it for you, and most of all if it was worth it for me.

My name is Paul Cavanaugh. This is what happened.

1

SUMMER frequently ends abruptly in Minneapolis, where the natives speak of the Theater of Seasons with a pride not unlike that they take in the Guthrie Theater and the Minnesota Vikings. It can be there one August day, the summer, and be gone the next as the clouds sift down over the lakes and the beaches go grainy and lonely beside the whitecaps. I knew such a day was coming, had to be coming, but the August warmth was still hanging in the trees and I was sufficiently optimistic to buy some new Slazenger tennis balls the day Hubbard Anthony and I played our monumental world class five-setter. I hadn't lost the weight I'd promised myself that summer. I was still struggling into my Fred Perry shorts and shirt with the distinctive marking; snug, yes, but I wear them on principle, proving a point which recedes each summer. I was freshly forty and not prepared to make concessions to time.

The day of the five-setter was also the day Larry Blankenship blew his head inside out against the green-and-gold-flocked wallpaper in the main lobby of the building where I lived. I'd played three hours of sweating tennis with Hub at the Norway Creek Club and my ass was dragging. He was sixty years old, hard as the judge's bench he sat on, and possessed of an infernal stamina which wore me down over five sets.

The temperature hung entrapped at ninety but huge oaks left the clay courts shade-dappled, playable; but Hub craftily used the shadows. After winning the first and third sets I began to go a trifle rubbery in the face of his great, awful cannonading serves. They rock-

3

eted down like V-2's, blurring in and out of the sun
and shade, and he took the final two sets, 6–2 and
6–1. I'm a rather boorish loser, but I had to admire
the way he'd paced himself.

We stood at the net, Hubbard looking as if he'd
been out for a pleasant Sunday-afternoon hit. He was
grinning at me, spinning the sixty-dollar Arthur Ashe
carpet beater in his large tanned hand.

"I'm sure you cheated somehow," I said. "Come on
back for a drink. Tell me your secrets." I was puffing.

"It's only a game," he said as we walked back to
the clubhouse, past the pool with the kids shouting
and splashing and the mothers looking eighteen in
their bikinis and tans. "But it's more fun to win than
to lose." Everybody was looking too young, too vig-
orous. It made me nervous. Hubbard was talking while
I watched all the breasts struggling to slip out of
their bikinis.

"What?" I said. "I missed that."

"Zen tennis," he repeated in that patient, judicial
way. "I've been playing it for years and now this fellow's written a book about it. You've got to let yourself win, he says, Paul, as opposed to making yourself
win."

"Cutting it a bit close, don't you think?"

"Well, your body knows how to hit the shots.
You must simply let it do what it already knows how
to do." He twirled the racket again.

"My body weighs twenty pounds too much. Twenty
pounds larded in between knowing and doing."

"All you have to do," he went on, "is let your mind
make a picture of how the shot should be hit, how
you've seen Laver or Rosewall hit it, and *let it happen.*" He chuckled apologetically. "Of course, I'm
oversimplifying. . . ."

"Of course," I said. Sweat was burning nasty little
holes in the corners of my eyes. "Let it happen. . . ."

Hubbard Anthony was too good for me, a fact which
I discovered all over again each summer, but I was
counting on time as my ally. In ten years I'd be fifty
and he'd be seventy and then, by God, I'd show the
old bastard.

Showered and dressed and exhausted, I flung the Porsche around Lake of the Isles Boulevard with a childish daring which I equated with the great Fangio behind the wheel of his Ferrari or whatever it had been. Fangio dated me, of course, and the Porsche looked as old as I felt but driving it fast helped me regain the self-respect I'd labored so long that afternoon to lose, to squander.

I wheeled it up the driveway to the guest's parking area since I'd have to take Hubbard home later and it was obvious that something was happening. There were two police cars, an ambulance, and a rescue-squad van cluttering up the driveway and a nattering wave of curious tenants lapped at the edges of the red carpet under the canopy. Reflexively I looked up the twenty-five-story façade with its geometry of redwood balconies and sharp angles. It looked as if it were gnashing its teeth at the world. Somebody finally fell off; that's what I was thinking as I walked toward the apparent disaster area. The pathetic little fountain in the middle of the glaring concrete squirted faintly, tiredly, as if the long day were just too much for it.

"Somebody took a header," I said. "It was bound to happen, sooner or later."

Hubbard followed me past the ambulance, between the rescue van and a cop car, and through the delivery entrance tucked in behind a screen of decorative concrete blocks. There was no point in using the front door: Two uniformed cops were blocking it off. There wasn't a big splotch in the driveway after all. Whatever had happened had happened inside.

The door to the manager's office was open and the room was empty. The swivel chair behind the desk lay on its side. Someone had gotten up in a hell of a hurry and kicked it over. I used my key on the mailroom door and went through it, out the other end into the lobby with its green thick carpet as soft and yielding as a dune. There were several people standing in a kind of awkward, anticipatory silence and a few more speaking in self-conscious undertone. Bill Oliver, the manager, and his wife, Pat, were standing by the fireplace with its fake fire flickering cheerily behind the plastic log. They were talking to a plain-clothesman in a business suit and white shirt while another cop stood staring at something in the corner beside the enormous, sparse, split-leaf philodendron. Two men in white medico costume were bending over the something which appeared to be a pile of green army blankets. Two highly polished penny loafers with virgin tan soles protruded from the bottom of the pile of blankets.

Fritz, one of the caretakers, was standing near the bank of elevators looking past the small crowd, sizing up the situation with soft, pained eyes which looked out from behind a well-creased face that had once been hard and maybe even mean. He was the kind of material they made fiftyish caretakers from: too much booze, too little luck, and a life gone a bit sour.

"Mr. Cavanaugh," he said hoarsely, dropping his cigarette into a gleaming cylinder of white sand. He looked as if he expected to be blamed for whatever had happened.

"What's going on?" I asked. Fritz was sweating, per usual. "Who's under the blankets?" Just looking at Fritz always made me feel peculiarly guilty, as if I'd done something unspeakable to him.

Hubbard couldn't quite tear himself away from body watching. His long bony arms were resting on his angular hips and he looked very calm. He'd been around, after all.

"I don't know for sure," Fritz said apologetically. Under stress his German accent surfaced. He was always apologizing; he acted like a friendly old dog who expected to kick square in his fidelity. "I've been up on the roof working on the dehumidifier system, see, and I come down here to check on the lobby vents—people been complaining, see, about coming in outa the ninety degrees and not feeling no big change like they oughta. So Bill ast me to get on it. . . ." He wiped his grease-stained hands across the olive-green work shirt, eyes flickering softly past my shoulder.

"So, I come outen the elevator and I'm heading through the delivery hallway toward Bill's office and this guy comes by me, going the other way, goes into the mail room and I go into the office. Bill's at his desk there tearing open this here envelope and he looks up and I start telling him about the goddamn vents which are finally putting out cool air—see, nice and cool now—and he's kinda half listening to me and reading this letter, at the same time like, and —sumbitch, he says, 'Holy shit!' and he jumps up from behind his desk, the chair falls over, and there's a hell of a noise . . . gunshot, I guess, from the lobby area, loud as a bastard, we can hear it through the glass door of the office and the glass door into the lobby, and Bill's out from behind the desk, through the office door, then he's gotta fuck with the lobby door, which is locked, naturally." Fritz took a breath and swallowed. Nothing had changed over by the fireplace, but Hubbard had joined us, smelling of Vetiver and looking cool in his seersucker slacks and Izod shirt. He was watching Fritz and listening carefully, like a judge.

"By the time he got his key out and got into the lobby there," Fritz continued, "I could see old Mrs. Hemenway come into view and she's got those little white gloves she always wears, well, she's got her hand up over her mouth and she's looking at something. . . .

"Guy fuckin' shot himself right in the lobby!" Fritz concluded abruptly.

"How long ago?"

"Half an hour, maybe."

"Did you know him? Was it the guy who passed you and went into the mail room?"

"I guess so . . . but, hell, he smiled at me, nodded, when he went by me. Seems funny as hell. I didn't see the dead guy close up, y'know, but he had one of them light-blue summery suits on and so did the guy I saw go past me. . . ." He shook his head. "But the guy said hi, nodded, real friendly. Then he goes out in the lobby and shoots hisself. . . ."

"Did you recognize him?"

"Well, yeah, not by name—but I seen him before, going up and down in the elevator." Fritz wiped sweat off his forehead and left a bar of grease in the horizontal wrinkles of his supplicant's brow. "Bannister? No, something like Battleship but that's not it." He looked around as the elevator door opened. Margaret, one of the cleaning ladies, got out in her green smock and blue shorts.

"Marge," he said, "what is the guy's name? The dead guy? Something like Battleship. . . ."

Margaret looked like a dowager even when she was on the trash run, stopping at every floor. She had iron-gray hair swept back and wore glasses on a chain around her neck and was always calm. Her costume was completed with blue tennies, yet she always appeared to be going to or coming from the Symphony Ball.

"Blankenship," she said. "Larry Blankenship."

Hubbard Anthony whisked in a sharp breath and said, "Oh, Jesus, not Larry!"

But there wasn't time just then to investigate the slightly glazed, uncharacteristic cast in Hubbard's eye because the little group by the still-warm remains of Larry Blankenship was breaking up and the well-bred inhabitants of the building were backing away, trying to look as if they weren't really interested in such an unseemly business. Bill Oliver's gaunt face looked pale and his mouth was clamped shut; a great many rich, elderly people lived in the building so he was used to an occasional death, but guns going off in the lobby was something else, something you didn't get used to.

The plainclothes cop turned out to be Mark Bernstein, a homicide dick I'd spent some time with while I was writing a book about a celebrated murder investigation and trial a few years before. He was forty-five or so, powdered and cool, neatly barbered with a fringe of hair over the collar and a long handsome face. He always reminded me of Craig Stevens, who used to play Peter Gunn on the tube. He nodded when he saw me and gave a tight-lipped grin.

"No book in this one, Paul," he said. He nodded to Judge Anthony, who was still distracted, ashen-faced. I suppose Hub's sudden pallor was the first thing that struck me as peculiar about the whole Blankenship story, other than Blankenship's manner of departure. The corpse meant nothing to me but Hub was a friend.

"Low marks for neatness, though," I said.

"Nobody cares about neatness anymore," Bernstein said.

"What actually happened? Why are you here?"

"I was in the office, that's all. Slow Sunday afternoon. The call came in and I figured what the hell, I'd go out myself. All we had was a guy'd been shot. . . ."

I followed along beside him. Bill Oliver was heading on into the office and we went with him. Bernstein looked at my tennis racket. "You win?"

"Nope, the judge here did it to me again."

"I never get a chance to play tennis anymore," he said.

"You're too damned busy trying to become mayor in your spare time. Dumb priorities. Tennis you can play all your life, being mayor is a sometime thing."

"Bullshit," he said. He was sensitive about his political ambitions and I didn't really think he was wrong. Anything is better than being a homicide dick, even being mayor.

Nobody said we couldn't tag along so Hub and I went on into the office. Pat Oliver had gotten there first and was putting the desk chair in place. She looked worried, her deep-set eyes downcast and hiding. She sighed heavily and leaned against the filing cabinet and watched the lads in white with stretchers go in to wrap up their bundle.

Bernstein said, "May I see this letter, please?"

Oliver picked it up off the neatly arranged desk and handed it to him. "Goddamnedest thing I've ever seen," he said. His jaw was rigid and his pale blue eyes flickered nervously from Bernstein, who was reading the note, to me. "He comes in here, Paul, and says hi to Pat and me, just as normal as hell, all dressed up like he's going out to dinner or something, fresh clean suit, tie, like all he's got on is brand new. . . . I could smell the Old Spice. He says he's got this for me, hands me the envelope, and I figure it's rent or something. Rent's the only thing people come in here with in an envelope, and I don't even give it a second thought.

I took it from him, said, 'Okay, Mr. B.,' and he just smiles and goes back out. Fritz is coming in at the same time and he's going on with some song and dance about the goddamn air conditioner and I'm opening the envelope and I read the note and I can hear Fritz talking, at first it doesn't take—and then, holy shit, I get the point and right away the gun goes off. . . ."

His voice was shaking and he was short of breath. He shrugged his square farm boy's shoulders and took off his bifocals. He grabbed a Kleenex from the desk dispenser and began polishing them. "Christ, I hardly knew the guy, but still, it hits you when a guy does that to himself in your goddamn lobby. . . ." He turned to look out of the window where the sun's waves jumped and quivered on the cars.

Hubbard sat down in a straight-backed chair. He hadn't said a word since his quiet little exclamation in the lobby. I knew him well enough to know that he was getting himself under control by an expenditure of will; I'd seen him do it on the tennis court, counteracting a bad shot or a miscalculated placement I'd returned for a winner.

Bernstein bit his lip and said, "Funny, very funny, this one," and shook his head.

"So what does it say?" I asked.

He handed it to me.

"Read it out loud," he said. "Slowly, conversationally. I want to hear what it sounds like."

It was written in green Flair ink on cream-colored stationery of high quality. His name, Lawrence Blankenship, was printed in simple, unexaggerated capital letters across the top of the sheet, centered. No address, no occupation. Just the name. Very classy.

" 'Dear Mr. Oliver,' " I read. " 'I'm very sorry to cause you the inconvenience of doing this in your lobby but I do have my reasons. As you know, I live alone. It bothers me to think that my body might go undiscovered for several days and suffer the unhappy effects of hot weather. Particularly with this lousy air conditioning. So accept my apologies and my good-byes to you and Mrs. Oliver. Sincerely, Larry Blankenship.' "

Nobody said anything and I read it again to myself.

Bernstein went to the window facing into the entranceway and the lobby. They were bringing the stretcher out, all covered up, and that was the end of Larry Blankenship.

But of course it wasn't. It was only the beginning.

I built us a pitcher of Pimm's Cup No. One with brandy, apples, cucumber slices, and lime wedges, sloshed over a seventy-nine-cent bag of sanitary ice cubes, all in a silver pitcher that had long ago been a wedding present and which I had stolen from what had once been my own home. Hubbard was sitting in an Italian deck chair with his feet tilted up on the rim of a flowerpot. I put the pitcher on a little plastic cube between us, poured two glass mugs full, and sat down on a porch swing I'd stolen from my father's garage. The best things in life are quite frequently the things you steal.

He sat staring into the evening sky, the sun slanting across the skyline of Minneapolis to the north, a view set off by the towering glass monument to Investment Diversified Services. The lake below us in Loring Park was green and ducks paddled about in geometric precision which you could see only if you were far enough above. The breeze on the shady side of the building almost made you forget the heat. Hub's face looked as if it had melted from the cheekbones downward, forming a pouch of jowls where his chin was tucked back against his long throat. At just that moment I figured I could have taken him, 6–0, 6–0.

"So who the hell was he?" I finally asked.

Hubbard sighed and sipped his Pimm's Cup. He wiped his lank white hair back straight, the way it was combed. I'd seen pictures of him up north in the thirties with my father, the two of them standing grinning at opposite ends of a string of bass or whatever it was they caught up there. He was tall and thin then, wearing a white shirt with the sleeves rolled up above his elbows, and he hadn't changed much in nearly forty years. His hair had been black then, shining in the sunlight that hid his eyes in dark shadows.

"Larry Blankenship was an innocent, an authentic innocent. A victim." He paused, looking off the balcony, sipping, trying to sum up a man's life to someone who'd never met him. "It was almost a pathology, his instinct for finding a way to be hurt in any given situation, by everyone he became involved with. . . . The way some people are looked upon as being trouble, trouble for everyone else, well, Larry was always trouble for himself. Maybe he wanted to be hurt. I'm sure a two-bit psychologist would say he was self-destructive. . . ."

"That theory looks pretty good right now," I said.

"Perhaps, but I don't really believe he was that complex, at least he never struck me as a deep person. He just wanted everything to turn out all right but it never seemed to. I'm sure he was an identifiable type. But saying he was a loser wasn't quite fair."

"Who said he was?"

He stuck a cigarette into his inconspicuous little holder and lit it, beginning to relax and move death a convenient distance away. The inner vista was fading but I'd never seen it before, had never known he was prey to such things.

"His wife, for one. She wasn't being unreasonable either, not from her point of view. He must have seemed a loser to her. At least when she said that." He shook his head.

"You knew him well, then?" I wasn't following very well and from inside my apartment I could hear the Twins game on the radio. They were in the twelfth inning at Oakland and Carew had just laid down a bunt and beaten it out. Rollie Fingers was pitching for Oakland and Larry Blankenship was nothing to me. He was a dead guy and I was just trying to provide some company for Hub. Larry Blankenship was just a name and two penny loafers under a blanket and an eccentric suicide note.

"Off and on, I kept running across him. Larry and his wife just kept turning up at the edges of things. His wife was the kind of woman who makes a strong impression on people. But that didn't work out for him either—they're separated or divorced by now. And they had a child who didn't turn out right. A mongoloid, something wrong like that, put away in a home somewhere. I don't believe I ever actually knew the details. Just things I heard. . . . Larry and Kim weren't ever at the center of things and of course they were much younger, your age or even a bit younger, she was younger, I'd think. Maybe thirty-five now. And Larry must have been forty or so. I'm not at all sure my figures are right. But I couldn't be far off.

"Larry was in sales at the beginning, had a job working for some people I knew. He was a fair-haired lad who was making it on his own, went over into the marketing end of things . . . but there was always a problem of some kind that would come up. I don't think I ever heard his name come up in a really happy conversation. There was always a soap-opera quality about him." He crossed his ankles on the flowerpot, drained the Pimm's Cup. I filled his mug again.

Darwin struck out on a Fingers change-up and Hisle hit a long fly to center. Two out and Killebrew was up, the designated hitter. Fingers got a quick strike on the outside corner away from his power and I longed for the summers of the Killer's youth when there wouldn't have been enough left of Fingers to clog a drain. Strike two.

"And then I heard his name down in the lobby and it hit me rather close to home. I wouldn't have thought he meant a thing to me, Larry Blankenship, just the name of a troubled man . . . but when I saw him dead, then the circle of his life seemed so sadly complete. Such a bitter waste. Maybe the tennis wore me down, made me susceptible. Maybe I'm just getting old. How the hell should I know?"

Fingers made a mistake with a fastball, let it get inside, and the old man pulled the trigger. Reggie Jackson was going back, back, and the announcer was screaming that it might be, it could be, it was. The Twins suddenly had a 4–2 lead and Hubbard Anthony hadn't noticed. I controlled my enthusiasm but it was there, the summer joy of a man who wasn't

young anymore. Me and the Killer. Without giving it
a thought, I wondered if Larry Blankenship had been
a baseball fan.

"Coincidence always has interested me," Hub went
on, his voice oiling up with the drink. "I'm always
amazed at how much of it I'm asked to believe in when
I'm sitting on a criminal case. A met B by sheer coincidence and was observed by C, who put an incorrect
interpretation on the meeting—it happens all the time
and the problem is you never know when it's true and
when it isn't.

"Last week I saw Kim Blankenship at Norway
Creek. She was playing tennis with the pro, McGill,
and I was having lunch on the porch with your father,
as a matter of fact. A very nice Rhine wine, I think,
with the Dover sole *amandine,* my treat, and your
father said he thought that was Kim Roderick down
there on the courts—Roderick, that was her maiden
name, of course. So there she was, playing just as well
as ever—"

"How the hell did *my father* know her maiden
name?"

"Oh, Kim had been a waitress at the club when she
was in her teens, used to bring lemonade down to the
pool, and eventually she became lifeguard, then Mc-
Gill's assistant, giving lessons and working in the pro
shop. . . . I said she was the sort of person, both as a
girl and as a woman, who made a strong impression
on you." He leaned his head back, eyes squinting shut
to give himself a better view of the past. "You'd never
see Kim Roderick loafing. She was always busy, being
helpful, making herself useful. Self-improvement was
what my generation called it, always bettering herself . . . talking about her correspondence-school
courses. . . ." There was admiration in his voice as if
he were a boy again with long black hair all shined
back with Brilliantine, stuck on a girl from the wrong
side of the tracks. On the radio Bill Campbell shut out
the Athletics in the bottom of the twelfth for the win
but my boys were still also-rans.

"Upwardly mobile," I said. "That's what they'd call
it now. Chronic overachiever."

Hubbard stood up and ejected his cigarette stub into my Cinzano ashtray.

"Well," he said, "there were those who thought she was a little pushy. Never could see it myself." He shrugged. "Let's go. I'm bushed." He looked it.

By the time I got back a wind with wetness in it had come up and the old wooden swing on my balcony was moving by itself. I kicked off my tattered penny loafers and padded out to watch the storm coming across the western suburbs. The purple clouds reflected darkly in the face of the IDS building and the downtown lights glowed yellow. It was still hot but I could see the rain like a frail curtain hanging on the outskirts of the city.

I was thinking about Larry Blankenship and his wife, Kim, the sad little pile of lifeless flesh which had been the sum of what he'd left behind. Hubbard Anthony had called him a natural victim, a man determined to be a victim, and his wife had called him a loser. That was all I knew about Larry Blankenship and even that clung like a scab on the side of my consciousness. It was seeing the body that did it; take away the body and it would have bothered me no more than any of a thousand other sad stories you're always hearing somewhere.

Lightning walked across the horizon like a regiment of stick soldiers and I flinched at the crack of thunder. Then the rain began to swish past the balcony and I took a deep swallow of Pimm's Cup. Headlamps probed at the swirling rain below me and I went inside and put an old Freddy Gardner saxophone record on and went back to my chair hearing the lonely, elegant, sad music. I suppose the music was a stupid idea because it only deepened the mood which had grown so steadily since the sunshiny afternoon of tennis.

But what the hell. I was giving up to it, the sense of reflection, more and more lately. Closing in on forty, I'd decided that life was no longer quite the endless parade of possibilities it once had seemed. Every time I turned around I caught sight of another option being shot to pieces. Still, I was better off than Larry

Blankenship. As far as options went, Larry Blankenship was fresh out.

Unhappy marriages are all alike. I wondered if all marriages are unhappy. Probably not, but then you never knew. Kim and Larry, in their upwardly mobile way, had tried to make it on their own. She'd made herself useful at Norway Creek, where no one was upwardly mobile because no one in Minneapolis had found anything higher to aspire to. They must have served as wonderful models for Kim Roderick as she made her move from waitress to tennis instructor. How many passes had the rich made, how many by the sons of the rich? How many tennis lessons had turned into something else?

I'd finished the pitcher and I was thinking like Scott Fitzgerald in his "Winter Dreams" period. Freddy Gardner kept playing, now "Roses of Picardy," and I was withstanding a mixed-media assault. A woman on another balcony was laughing, a woman who sounded like Anne, from whom I'd stolen the wedding-present pitcher. I hadn't seen her in several weeks but the laugh was like hers and she had hated my Freddy Gardner saxophone records. Thank God, we'd had no children. Maybe I was lucky, not a victim; Larry and Kim had had a child and naturally there'd been something wrong with it. Naturally. And it had been stuck away somewhere. And his wife had called him a loser and had left him and a while later he blew his brains out in my lobby. It was the saddest story I'd ever heard and the wind had changed, shifting to blow across the park toward me. I was getting wet so I went back inside and left the sliding door wide open to keep me in touch with nature. I was a romantic; Anne had hated romantics. But then she was one of those from the Norway Creek Club who had nowhere left to go, at least not upward. Those people, by and large, are not romantics, are not so afflicted with what is clearly a condition of the middle classes. Kim and Larry probably had had fairly advanced cases. I'd have bet on it.

I didn't much like the way my mind was running. The thunder was smashing steadily at the city like artillery trained on the enemy campfires and lightning kept going off like rocket fire. I went down the dark hallway, hung a left, took off my clothes, switched off the telephone, turned on the old wicker lamp by the bed, opened the windows, which sent the curtains billowing, and lay down on the bed with *The Baseball Encyclopedia,* which meant that I was afraid of the night.

Two of the most important treasures anyone can find in life are, one, something which can effectively take your mind off yourself and, two, something which can put you to sleep when the nighttime is your adversary. For $17.95 *The Baseball Encyclopedia* does both and consequently, dollar for dollar, it is the most valuable object ever devised by man. On page 687 I began rummaging through the career of one of my favorite players of the forties, Bill Nicholson, also known as Big Swish, who played the outfield for the Cubs from 1939 until 1948, when, almost sacrilegiously, he was traded to the Phillies, where he ended his career in 1953.

When my father had been a professor at the University of Chicago I had frequently gone to Wrigley Field, where the green vines grew thick on the outfield walls. Nicholson had been a six-foot, 200-pounder with a reputation as a home-run hitter, though his totals don't realize that World War II baseball was sort of a make-do-with-what-you-could-find proposition. When I was ten years old, in 1944, and when Nicholson was thirty he led the National League with 33 home runs, 116 runs scored, and 122 runs batted in. I'd never heard of anybody quite like Bill Nicholson before and one day while I stood watching some teenagers play baseball on a vacant lot I heard one of them refer to the one who was batting as Big Bill Nicholson. I felt my heart jerk and I swallowed hard, inconspicuously edging around the sun-bleached grass until I could see if this guy really was Bill Nicholson; after all, the Cubs had an off day before Brooklyn came in and maybe this was how he spent his spare time. But it wasn't Bill Nicholson, of course. It was a big muscular kid with boils on the back of his neck and he could hit hell out of the ball. But he was a long way from being Bill Nicholson.

It was thundering again and rain was spraying through the window onto my bare feet. The huge volume had slipped down on my lap and my eyelids felt as if somebody were rubbing sand into them but my brain hadn't cut out yet. I was still thinking about Larry Blankenship and wondering why it all works out for some people and doesn't work out at all for others. It was a train of thought which could drive you crazy and maybe nothing really worked out for anybody. Maybe that was why everybody got so tired.

2

I HAD showered but was still in my underwear and gaping robe when I went to fetch the morning *Tribune* from the hallway. Her voice came like the muffled caw of a bird; everything about her was birdlike, the sharp darting nose, the gray feathery hair, the overquick jerks and snaps of her head. "Why, Paul"—quick breath, mouth snapping shut between words, eyes poking about in a random pattern, flighty—"how are you this morning?" It was her perfunctory way of getting to whatever was really on her mind. She was rubbing her nose with a Kleenex, ready to begin the next remark.

"I'm fine, Mrs. Dierker," I said, "just getting my paper."

She always looked as if she'd only just that moment come across a conspiracy of some significance. I'd known her all my life, through my parents. The Dierkers had recently sold their elaborate Lake of the Isles mansion and moved into the building, waiting for the end. Harriet Dierker looked as if she had a way to go.

"Well, I'm so upset I don't know what to do. . . ."
She twisted her hands, an elderly woman acting like
a child, tailoring the performance to her audience.
"Tim just sits there and eats his Rice Krispies, dribbling cream on his Pendleton robe, telling me to calm
down—it's so frustrating, so upsetting. And he's not at
all well, you know. There's been something particularly bothering him lately."

I looked bland. She always sounded the same,
whether discussing the weather or a natural disaster.

"You've heard about what happened yesterday,
haven't you?" Her voice eased out in a long phony
chord of consolation, exaggerated. She didn't really
care, I'd always thought, but pretended that she cared.
She was the Spirit of Gossip; she would have fitted well
into *The School for Scandal*.

"Ah. . . ." My mind wasn't really connecting yet. I
was trying to hold my robe together. "I don't
know. . . ."

"In the lobby, Paul," she said accusingly, "Larry
Blankenship killed himself!" She found another Kleenex in her alligator bag. She was wearing a striped
Peck & Peck knit, lime green and yellow and blue,
with matching blue shoes. She always looked like that,
perfect in a rather hideously premeditated way.

"That, yes, I heard about that."

"Such a tragedy," she said reprovingly, as if I
weren't properly saddened. "He couldn't have been
more than forty and he had every reason to live. . . ."
She was edging toward my doorway, and it was inevitable. I asked her if she'd like to join me for my morning coffee. She said she certainly would and she could
use a few minutes, sitting down, ignoring for the moment her own doorway not more than thirty feet away.
But her husband was behind that door, dribbling
cream on himself.

I'd put the fresh-ground coffee into the top of the
Braun Aromaster before my shower and it was steaming and ready. I poured two mugs and we went out
onto the balcony, where the morning sun had dried the
green Astroturf. The world looked fresh and clean.

It was nine o'clock and Minneapolis was moving below us.

"Shot himself in the head, poor man," she began again, determined to get on with it, and I didn't stop her. It was all coming back to me and I was curious. She repeated what I already knew about the circumstances of the suicide, item for item; she always had her sources. Her sorrow, her pity, they were all on the surface, in gestures and movements of her eyebrows and vocal intonations which conveyed another strong message: Somehow Harriet Dierker was above and impervious to the problems of lesser mortals. She sorrowed for them as she would for a dog struck by a bus.

"What made it all the worse is that he'd just started his new job, he'd just moved in here, oh, my . . . and he had that lovely new Thunderbird, the green one parked down by the fountain. Everything seemed to have finally gotten all straightened out for him." She pursed her lips. "And he was finally free of that woman!" The expression on her face reminded me that birds are killers. Only a few days before, I'd stood by the bird sanctuary at Como Park and watched a graceful, terrible swan rip a baby duck to pieces while the mother stared frantically, helplessly on.

"Which woman is that?" I asked, sipping my milky coffee and watching the morning duck inspection far below in the pond.

"His wife, of course, that Kim person—oh, she was lovely to look at, beautiful, but, Paul, she was the sort of woman the word 'bitch' was invented for. . . ."

"Really?" There was no need to prod her. She was moving ahead under her own power.

"Worse, Paul, worse—you wouldn't understand, no man could unless they'd known such a woman. A hellion. A witch!" She was working herself up to some pinnacle of ladylike disgust but words failed her and she made an alert, quick face of undisguised revulsion.

"Hub Anthony said some people thought she was a little pushy, maybe," I said, "but he couldn't see it himself. Said she was always making herself useful—"

She shivered as if Hubbard's frailty made her flesh crawl.

"Oh, Hubbard Anthony should know! He certainly should know!"

"What do you mean? What are you implying?"

She clammed up; she always did when someone stood up to her line of accusation, innuendo, half truth. She knew she'd gone too far and switched back to the subject of Kim Blankenship with awesome, practiced ease.

"Did you know her, Paul?"

"No. But I understand my father did, and your husband, as well as Hub. I never knew her. I never knew Blankenship, for that matter."

"Well, you were away much of the time, weren't you?" She dabbed the corner of her mouth with a paper napkin. "And Larry's world was quite different from yours—business, accounting, the sort of thing you never got involved in. Larry wasn't sophisticated, no big college, none of the advantages," and she went on in the Horatio Alger vein while I wondered why she was being so defensive about him. She sounded as if she had a stake in him, as if he were something like a son and I was the enemy who had cast some near aspersion on his background.

"But he was a good boy and when he came down to Minneapolis—let's see, it must have been 1952 or 1953, I'd think—he showed up at the plant asking Pa for a job, wanted to go on the road and learn the business by selling paint." She cocked her head like an aging parrot, watching a memory scurry along the edge of time like a mouse behind the sideboard. "I remember Pa coming home that day and telling me about this young man with white socks and a blue suit —that always appealed to Pa, that the boy dressed the same unfashionable way he did himself. He'd come in and looked around the offices and it was lunchtime and the secretaries all happened to be out and Larry saw Tim's name on the office door, Timothy Dierker of Dierker and Company, and he figured this must be the fellow to see, the big mucky-muck, he called him. . . ." Her eyes were developing shiny tears and I supposed she really was remembering. "He walked right in on Pa and Pa was so surprised and impressed that he gave him a job. Oh, if Dan Peterson hadn't finally come into the office off the road, there wouldn't have been a job but Pa always said he'd have found him a job, he liked him that much." She sighed spitefully. "Oh, he'd never met her at that point . . . but, you know, Paul, it must have been foreordained even then because it was just about that time that Ole Kronstrom began giving Helga problems—Helga was his wife, one of my best friends, and Ole was Pa's partner in Dierker and Company." She was turning it over in her mind, like a marginal worm. "Yes, it was just about the time that Larry Blankenship came to work for Pa that Helga told me that she thought Ole was going through the change—she thought he was running around with girls; she saw him winking at the waitresses out at Norway Creek . . . it was hard for me to believe at first because Pa had never been one to engage in that sort of smutty thing. But wives know their husbands best, Paul"—she touched my arm to underline her contention—"and it turned out that she was right, Ole was beginning to chase. . . ." She sniffed righteously. "Working his way up, or down, if you see what I mean, to that Kim Roderick, who was just nothing, nothing but a waitress herself at Norway Creek, a waitress out to catch a rich man." It was difficult to tell which upset her more, Ole's infidelity or the fact that it had been committed with a waitress. The Dierkers had never really gotten used to having a lot of money, even though they were the second generation in paint, but while Tim never took it very seriously Harriet was self-consciously moneyed—unsure of her grammar and schooling and antecedents but sure of her power over underlings, all those who didn't have as much money and were defined in their own minds by the lack of it. Largesses, noblesse oblige—she loved to take those poses but only if you were well behaved and knew your place. Larry Blankenship had but Kim Roderick apparently hadn't.

The story Harriet Dierker told me about Kim Roderick was a honey, filtered through a mesh of venom, hatred. I couldn't quite imagine why she was so virulent about it but then I remembered that Blankenship had done himself in only the day before and her grief, real or imagined, was at least new and raw.

According to Harriet Dierker, Kim had come down to Minneapolis from some backwater up near the Canadian border, one of the desolate places that made you feel that you were treading the line between life and death, balanced in the darkness between the blue-black forests of pine and evergreen and fir and the flat, strip-mined wastes where the Mesabi had been slit open and its innards pulled out for the good of the steel companies. That part of the country remained an impenetrable, sorrowful mystery to me. Anyone who'd come from there, it seemed to me, must have had to try a little harder. But people I knew who'd come south to the lights of the Twin Cities said I was wrong: Anything, they said, was easy after growing up on the Iron Range. Anyway, the Norway Creek Club must have seemed like heaven to Kim Roderick in the late fifties when she'd gone to work as kitchen help.

Mrs. Dierker wasn't sure if Kim had known Billy Whitefoot from up north or if she met him at the club, where Billy ran the tractor with the eight lawn-mower assemblies splayed out behind it, back and forth, every day all summer long across the golf course. Billy had been a very handsome black-haired, black-eyed Indian boy, who had done well at the club, lived over the pro shop, and gone to Dunwoody Institute in the fall and winter to learn the baking trade. Anyway, she thought so; after all, it had been more than fifteen years ago and she couldn't expect to remember the details.

She did know that the members' golf committee had allowed Billy to live in the room over the pro shop because they were convinced that here was a boy who just wasn't like all the other Indians who didn't give a damn about anything but getting drunk. By saying that, Harriet Dierker believed she was showing her own open-mindedness, her willingness to judge people individually. And Billy had been just fine for a while. Then there had been Kim Roderick. "Billy, my God—

he looked like an Indian god, Paul, like a real-life Hia-
watha!"—Billy hadn't had a chance. By the end of the
summer Kim was pregnant and she and Billy got
married. After all, even though he was an Indian, he
was a bright boy, well-liked, doing well at Dunwoody,
a serious boy. . . . And apparently he really fell for
Kim Roderick. Harriet allowed as how you couldn't
blame him: a temptress, she'd been, always bending
over and stretching and showing her legs and her
bosom. "I'd never say anything but several of the
club members used to make sure they were around
when she'd help clean the pool late at night and take
a dip," she said. "I saw her and I saw the men watching her."

The baby was due in the late winter, to the best of
her recollection, and Billy Whitefoot didn't live that
winter in the pro shop. The couple dropped out of
sight, maybe went back up north for the winter, but
when spring came there was a letter from Billy wondering if their jobs were still open. They were and the
first week in April they drove up in an old station
wagon, Billy and Kim, no baby; everyone assumed
it must have been left with a grandmother or an aunt
up north and no one really wanted to know. There
were rumors that summer about Billy. People said
he'd been drinking; just like an Indian, some of them
said. Several mornings he didn't show up for work and
the gigantic mower stood along with the other equip-
ment in the shed. Kim never missed a day, though,
refused even to discuss Billy, almost as if he weren't
there anymore. She was working as a waitress in the
evening and as a pool girl during the day, but every
free moment found her on the tennis courts with Darwin McGill, the pro, learning the game.

That was where Ole Kronstrom first really paid any
attention to her.

The sun was warm and the wind scurried blissfully
in the rich green crowns of the trees in the park. Mrs.
Dierker showed no signs of letting up so I went
inside and warmed four brioche, which were actually
flown in several times a week, Paris to Minneapolis.

I got out a crock of Keiller's three fruits marmalade, knives and plates, butter, and a little wicker basket with a napkin to wrap the brioche. I was flattering her with my attention; my mind was empty of other things and the more people told me about this story, the more I wanted to hear. It was like killing time by stopping in at a movie you'd never heard of and getting hooked. Blankenship was the one who was dead but the one I was hearing about was Kim, the woman in the case.

Mrs. Dierker was admiring my shaded tuberous begonias and my two tomato plants, which stood a trifle hesitantly in the sun. But, after licking butter from a finger and a morsel of crumb from her lower lip, she wanted to get back to the story.

Ole Kronstrom and Tim Dierker had been partners for a long time, as their fathers had been in the twenties, and it was natural for Helga and Harriet to have become best friends. Their husbands had always gotten on well and on business trips the two women had come to be more than friends. They were intimates; they had no secrets from each other. And it was natural for Helga to turn to Harriet with her suspicions about Ole's chasing.

That was the summer Billy Whitefoot finally ran off and Kim Roderick (nobody had ever really known her as Kim Whitefoot) showed she had a real talent for tennis, among other things. That summer Ole Kronstrom took up tennis himself, fifty-two years old, married for thirty years to Helga, and maybe beginning to wonder if he'd had all he was going to get.

Harriet Dierker didn't go into any details about Ole's fall into depravity, though she must surely have savored them at the time.

"I knew Ole like a brother, he and Pa were that close," she said, her little jaw clamped hard on her beliefs, "and I saw him make a fool of himself over that wanton girl who'd already ruined one man and abandoned one child. . . . Oh, yes, it was Kim who ruined Billy Whitefoot, the rumors of what she was doing, the way she treated him—I mean it all fit, Paul —and she acted as if he didn't even exist, as if he were a mistake she could erase. Well, she erased Billy all right, and he went to pieces. That's the way it must have been. If you'd known them, you'd have seen it happen. Everyone knew it——"

"I don't think Hubbard saw it that way," I said. "She stayed on at Norway Creek, didn't she? They wouldn't have let her stay if it had been so blatant, would they?"

"The ones who understood things," she said coldly, "they could see what was going on. It wasn't our fault if the others—the men—were blind to the kind of woman she was. Is!"

"I see." She wasn't about to be trifled with and I didn't want to antagonize her. I wanted to see where the story went.

"Ole had no sense about her, of course. For a while he pretended that they were just taking tennis lessons together from McGill, that it was natural for them to sit on the porch and have a lemonade together when they were finished playing. There they'd sit, giggling over their lemonade, and then she'd have to go put on her uniform to serve dinner." She made a face, eyes flickering behind her oval glasses. "It was disgusting and Helga saw it all . . . but she wouldn't admit the full truth of it. It was my unhappy job to help her see it and give her my strong shoulder to cry on. Of course Helga eventually confronted him with it and he denied any wrongdoing, as I knew he would.

"But I was right. In the end he was taking her to lunch at Harry's and Charlie's out in the open, and he even—God forgive him—talked about adopting her . . . because she'd had such a hard time, he said, with her husband running off that way, and because she was such a fine girl. I tell you, Paul, there was just no end to his misbehavior. . . . Helga stood it through that summer and she thought maybe it was over when winter came but I knew it wasn't. One day in December, just before Christmas, I was having my hair done at Churchill-Anderson, I was under the dryer and I heard her voice, Kim's voice, behind me, she couldn't see me, and she was telling the stylist to hurry because her father was picking her up for lunch. It just sent a chill through me, Paul, a positive chill

—I can feel it now. And I watched in the mirror; I saw this *father* she was talking about come into the waiting room. It was Ole. It made me sick, seeing her hug him. . . ."

"Did you tell Helga?"

"What else could I do? She was my best friend."

It was like something from an old Joan Crawford movie; I felt myself being anesthetized by Harriet Dierker's voice, which grew increasingly short of breath as her plot thickened. But she held my attention. The story had momentum of its own and it just kept going on and on. Ole Kronstrom had refused to give up seeing young Kim, had funneled a good deal of his capital into clothes for Kim, a car for Kim, trips which Kim sometimes took by herself and occasionally with Ole. Eventually his money began to run low —it seemed incredible, but there it was—and of course Helga had left him, divorced him, and managed to come away with a handsome settlement.

What Helga got, Harriet noted, she deserved for all those years of fidelity; what Kim Roderick did was, of course, reprehensible, typical, and utterly bloodthirsty, and who was I to argue?

With Ole presumably on the ropes, Kim had then turned her sex ray on Larry Blankenship, who was still working for Pa (and for Ole, for that matter) but had moved from sales, through a company-financed accounting program, and into the public relations and advertising end of things. He'd had some "personality problems" and had consulted a psychiatrist but, even so, he was "a nice young man, very earnest," and making a good salary. The sex ray did him in, however: Kim nailed him where he stood, married him, and Harriet wondered why. Love was out of the question; perhaps it was Kim's misplaced striving for respectability.

Pa had done everything he could to talk Larry out of it; he'd gone off his feed, spent night after night worrying about what the marriage would do to Larry. Harriet had never seen Pa take anything quite so hard, as if Larry were a son. It was about then that his health had seriously begun to fail. She could almost pinpoint it, the night he'd come upstairs to bed gray-faced, shaking; Larry was decided, he said; there was nothing left for him to say. The girl had him and Pa had fidgeted all night; a week later he'd had his first coronary. As far as Harriet was concerned, Pa was another of Kim's victims. I wondered why Pa had taken it so hard; she offered no substantive explanation.

So Larry and Kim were married. Pa's health failed through a long winter, and what of Ole Kronstrom? Another peculiar facet glittered in the darkness of the story: Ole had given the bride away . . . and his wedding present to the happy couple was a honeymoon trip to Europe. He didn't seem to resent her marriage, which left Harriet Dierker with only one rational conclusion. His relationship with Kim was stable, enduring, continuing.

My head swam with the Byzantine complexity of it all. I had never looked upon myself as an innocent, but my God.

"But Larry was blind to all that, Paul," she said. The coffee was cold and the brioche were gone. "Self-deception. Was he happy? They were never happy, not really, I'm sure, certainly not after that first year. They had a child, who didn't turn out right at all—not long after that, Larry left Dierker and Company. Pa tried to keep tabs on him and he moved through several jobs, never seemed able to find himself. They —Larry and Kim—stopped by one Christmas to see us; we gave them some eggnog. I just sat there—I didn't know what to say to them—but Pa wanted to talk. . . . But there wasn't much to say. I don't know to this day why they came to see us. She said almost nothing; Larry seemed tired, drained. Not much after that we heard that they were living apart, then nothing. Pa had another coronary, then a third one, and we got rid of the house and moved in here. I don't suppose I thought about Larry or Kim for quite a long time. Until a month ago, when Larry moved into this building. Pa acted so funny about it when I told him I'd seen Larry in the lobby. . . . Larry dropped by to see Pa two or three times during this past month but Pa's been so sick, you know. And now"—she caught her breath—"and now Larry's dead. . . .

"Pa thinks I'm crazy; he wouldn't even talk to me this morning . . . but I want to know why Larry Blankenship killed himself. I really want to know, Paul. What did she do to him? I know she killed him, as surely as if she'd pulled the trigger.

"Why don't you find out for me?"

When I thought about it later, it didn't surprise me that Harriet Dierker would ask me to do such a nebulous, largely fractured sort of thing. It was precisely the sort of thing she would ask, unhesitatingly, without giving the question's implications any serious consideration. Her mind worked that way; she wanted to know and she asked me to find out.

But looking back on it, tweezing through the effects which the search for her wretched answer had on my life, yes, I do wonder at my ever having gotten involved. Like a pulsing swamp, it sucked me in and set me wondering if I were in some way defective in my resistance. So many things have seeped up around me while I wasn't paying attention. There is a kind of stickiness that overcomes you eventually when you realize that things have taken a peculiar turn. By then it has always been too late. Once, in an echoing, damp night I killed an elderly man in another country. . . . Once I married Anne. And just once I really paid attention to Harriet Dierker.

It would be unjust to blame her, though. If there had been no more to it than our balcony-and-brioche conversation, I'd have to let it go. Larry Blankenship's death would have given me pause and I would have doubtless remembered the story of Kim Roderick, but nothing more. I had other things to think about. I could have spent the summer reviewing the new movies, seeing what the Guthrie was doing, striking up hopeful acquaintances with moody actresses who would be there for a season and go conveniently away at the proper time. I had done most of that, as a matter of fact, and I'd interviewed the television personalities coming through and I played tennis and looked with dismay at my Porsche and lunched by the pool in the sunshine at the Sheraton Ritz. I pretended I was only thirty. I experienced the peculiar sensation of someone you recognize through a shifting curtain of people and realize with a flicker in your chest that it's you you're seeing, you when you were ten years younger, moving through time like a ghost. Not better, not happier, but more hopeful. Hope had been all around you then and more often than not it had looked like a woman.

Which brings back the dying end of summer and the Kim Roderick thing. As I say, it grabbed me before I really knew what was happening and it wasn't just Harriet. Pa got into the act, too. He called me later the same day when I was staring at a legal pad, pen poised, trying to think of something new and rotten to say about the Lou Reed album I was supposed to be reviewing. Lou Reed brings out the worst in me and I feel better for it.

If you can imagine a hearty groan, you know what Pa Dierker sounded like. I could believe he was dying but I couldn't quite take it seriously.

"Paul, this is Tim Dierker. Ma said she was talking to you today about Blankenship's mess. That right?"

"She was," I said, admiring the way Pa got right to the point.

"Well, she's just gone out and I want to disabuse you of whatever crap she was . . . telling you. Ma's so full of crap most of the time. Get over here. I'll set you straight and you can make us each a gin and tonic."

Until they moved into the building I hadn't seen Tim in five or six years. He'd once been a big, loosely put-together man with freckles and reddish hair. With illness he'd collapsed inward as such men do, as if the plug had been pulled and his gusto had all run out. The red hair was a yellowed white and sparse on a long oval face with cheeks sinking against the hollows of his elongated skull and the freckles had coagulated into brown disks which rested like coins on the parchment face. Red veins had exploded outward from his bony hawk's nose. He looked as if he'd been hurled forward from within his body and shattered the windshield of his face. He was wearing a cowboy shirt with one of those awful string ties held in place by something that looked like a turquoise napkin ring. Baggy old corduroys and furry slippers of indeterminate age completed the ensemble and his hand, weakly shaking mine, felt dusty.

"There." He gestured vaguely toward the kitchen counter, where the Tanqueray and Schweppes stood like soldiers beside the limes, the ice trays, the old paring knife. "Make 'em. I gotta sit down."

I built them quick, listening to the sound of the television in the other room. Hogan was suggesting to Captain Klink for the two millionth time that he just might be ticketed for the Eastern Front if word got back to Berlin. It was a funny show. I could hear the laughter but Pa Dierker was sitting in the dark corner of the room, scowling, wheezing. Expensive, very bad paintings hung in odd, conflicting areas of wall and made the room look empty. He sat in a Naugahyde tilt lounger, a rich old man who wasn't enjoying the sunset years. Somehow he made his corner of the room look like a documentary film about abuses in the nursing-home industry. "Siddown, Paul, and give me the drink. Did you put gin in mine?"

I nodded.

"I forgot to tell you I'm not supposed to drink. Ah, well, I'll tough it out." He took a deep swallow. He'd been a hard drinker once and at least you never lost the knack.

"Forget what Ma told you." He clicked a handset and the sound of *Hogan's Heroes* died. No more applause.

"How do you know what she told me?"

"I know. Poor Larry. Pa looked on him like the son we never had, that witch of a wife drove him to kill himself, their marriage broke Pa's health. . . ." He made a sour face. "Direct hit?"

"Yeah."

"Well, she runs off at the mouth and I learn it by heart. God hasn't blessed me with deafness, the one affliction I could make use of. But no, she talks and

I listen and I know she'll just keep saying the same thing until there's nobody . . . left to hear it." He took another deep drink and coughed wetly, turning gray beneath the exploded blood vessels. "It's all bullshit."

"You mean she made it up?"

"I didn't say that, Paul. But she gets it all out of focus. The facts are . . . old. They deserve to die. Larry killed himself; he's dead." He stared at the silent television picture. "Who cares why anymore?"

"Do you know why?"

"Me? How should I know, Paul?" He was grinning, overtly wily, possibly gaga, for all I knew. He looked suddenly as if he were playing a game I hadn't been told about.

"She said Larry'd stopped in to see you a few times. What did he want? Did he act like a man who was going to kill himself?"

"How should I know? What do I know about suicides?"

"Did he talk about his wife?"

"Yes." He grinned. "He rambled on about his wife. Shit!" he snorted. "Why can't we just leave women out of it? He was through with Kim; that was all over." The craftiness of the rodent gleamed behind his dull eyes. "Why would he care about Kim anymore? Women! Ma and her goddamned imagination. . . ."

"Your wife doesn't agree with you, Tim. She was upset about this whole thing. She said you were disturbed when Blankenship came to see you. Somebody's confused. She asked me to find out why he killed himself—she thought his wife was behind it." It seemed like a pointless conversation but Tim's face grew sly again.

"Maybe Kim did kill him." He chuckled bleakly. "How should I know?" He coughed and sipped. "You're not going to do anything about it, are you? You're a goddamn writer, not a detective . . . or a psychiatrist. . . ." His pale remote eyes left the television set. He was squinting at me from a past he was hinting at and simultaneously concealing and his breath was short. Watching a sick man who seemed to be nuzzling into senility was making me nervous; being watched by a sick man apparently getting sicker by the minute was worse. I looked away, came face to face with a coppery goldfish in an old-fashioned bowl. I looked back at the old man.

"I wouldn't know what to do," I said. "I wouldn't know where to begin."

"Good." He sighed. "You're a hell of a lot better off out of it." He pressed the button and Captain Klink was back explaining to the Gestapo why the priceless secret rocket had blown up. Laughter. "Much better off, believe me. . . ."

"What is this Kim like?" I said.

"A woman. What else is there to know?"

"Did she love him?"

"Larry . . . God, yes, she loved him. I'd bet on that."

"But you didn't want him to marry her?"

"It was a long time ago. Maybe I was just . . . giving him the benefit of my experience with marriage." His breathing was becoming increasingly labored.

"Did Larry solicit your advice?"

"Once too often." He wheezed.

"What the hell is that supposed to mean?"

"Listen, you . . . beat it! Just beat it and forget all about it. I mean that, you." He seemed to have forgotten my name.

"Well, I guess that's that, then."

Pa Dierker didn't say any more. The goldfish had lost interest in us and was peering at a little piece of green stuff floating around in his bowl. I got up and left Pa with his canned laughter. There were pathetic little bits of gray fluff from his slippers on the carpet; it reminded me of a doll losing its stuffing. Watergate had increased my vocabulary: Pa was stonewalling it. Why?

I was taking the hook. It was drifting down my gullet like an X-ray probe, something scary, and I was beginning to realize it. I was sitting at my typewriter, staring past it at the setting sun reflecting in the IDS tower, which brooded over Minneapolis like

a derisive gesture. Twenty-four hours had passed since
Hubbard Anthony and I had sat on my balcony,
twenty-four hours—the sum total of my experience of
Larry Blankenship and Kim Roderick. I hadn't
known them; suddenly I knew too much about them.
Thinking about it tired me out. I decided to go for a
walk.

There was a light on in the manager's office, very
peculiar for the evening. Bill Oliver was sitting at his
desk puffing on a cigar and staring into space. He
waved and I went in.

"You're working long hours," I said.

"Nervous as a cat," he said, peering at the ash,
leaning back in his leather chair. "This goddamn
Blankenship thing."

"What about it?"

"People asking questions all day, wanting to hear
all about it. People with theories. Mrs. Dierker bent
my ear for an hour this afternoon. I just couldn't get
rid of her. Jesus, what a nut case she is. . . ."

I laughed. "She spent breakfast with me telling me
the guy's life story. And his ex-wife."

He looked up sharply. "Me, too. I don't know what
she expected me to do about it."

"Did you ever meet his wife?"

"Well, at least I saw her. Not to meet. I think it
was about the only times I saw him with anybody—
he was usually just alone, he'd always smile, say hi,
friendly fella, always by himself." He got up restlessly,
stood staring out of the window with his hands jammed
down in his hip pockets.

"What was she like?"

"Good-looking," he said to the window. I could see
the reflection of his cigar in the window; the ash had
fallen off and it glowed like a pulsing flare. "Dark hair,
real tan, trim. Like an athlete, like she was in real
good shape. . . .

"But I didn't pay as much attention to her as I
might have because the second time she was here,
hell, just a few days ago, it was him I was watching.
Blankenship, the poor bastard. He was crying, or
damned near to it, face all red and going up and

down like you do if you're trying not to cry. I mean, a *man* doing that—I guess I was embarrassed for him. He was sort of following her; he had his hand on her arm and he was all messed up—his tie was loose and he looked all rumpled—his face was red, and she was so calm, looking straight ahead, not hurrying, not trying to get away from him. She wasn't mad, you know? Just sort of businesslike, perfectly dressed. . . ." He looked back at me, his head wreathed in smoke. "Some women are like that, never a hair out of place; that's the way she was."

"What did she have on, shorts or slacks—"

"No, a dress, with a belt, linenlike, dark blue, no sleeves, just long tan arms. . . ." He stopped, remembering.

"I'd say she made quite an impression on you." I could hear what Hub Anthony had said.

"Yeah, by God, I guess she did." He nodded. "More than I figured she did, I guess."

"So what happened? She's striding deliberately on and he's about to cry. What next?"

"Well, he followed her out into the parking lot and they stood talking beside her car. She seemed to have a calming effect because he stopped talking and sort of pulled himself together."

"Did they touch?"

He gave me a funny look, like I was talking dirty.

"Well, I told you he sorta grabbed her arm, like he wanted her to stop and talk. She didn't touch him." He paused and frowned. "I thought at the time, what was she saying to him? Y'know, first I thought she was his girlfriend—anyway, the first time she was here."

"Logical," I said. I wondered where my mind was poking.

"Sure, but that second time, that was different. I mean, that was no lovers' quarrel. She wasn't showing her feelings—she didn't look like she had feelings. God, she didn't even seem to be embarrassed by the way he was acting. Then I thought they might even be brother and sister—hell, I didn't know. Today Mrs. Dierker tells me the story. Ex-wife. It figures, I said to myself. Now why didn't that occur to me? The building's full of ex-husbands and ex-wives. . . ."

"Like me," I said.

"Well, sure, like you. And when she told me that, sure as hell, I knew she was right. Perfect."

He looked at his watch, put his huge hands on the desk, and pushed himself upright, all six four of him.

"Ten o'clock," he said. "Let's go topside, get everybody out of the pool. Lock up. Come on."

It was cool and breezy on the roof and you could see the stars like a planetarium diagram. The water glowed turquoise from the pool lights and if you watched it lapping at the sides, you began to think the building was tipping. A couple of guys in thick terrycloth robes were talking in one corner, plastic tumblers and an ice bucket between them on the cement and a telephone plugged into an outlet for the convenience of big-time executives. They saw us, waved their hands all weighted down with University of Minnesota class rings, started to pick up their party gear.

Bill got a pole with a hook on the end of it and began to fish for the lifesavers bobbing on the water. While he attended to his housekeeping duties, I leaned on the waist-high wall and looked southward out over the freeways and the quivering, jittery lights of the suburbs stretching away past Metropolitan Stadium and the Minnesota River. None of what I could see had any meaning to me; it had to mean something to somebody but I couldn't imagine what to whom.

I was surprised at Bill Oliver's ability to put me in that scene in the parking lot. He'd hit on the keys, the points which made me recognize what he'd been describing. I'd known women like that, tremendously controlled because the only alternative was to come utterly apart. And Larry, the sap with no hint of how you kept yourself protected, at arm's length from the disagreeable things. The scene in the parking lot made Harriet Dierker's estimate of the situation look reasonably acute. It made me wonder why old Larry was crying. It made me wonder what the hell Kim had done to him.

She was out there somewhere in the night.

In the elevator, when it stopped at my floor, I held the door and said, "What kind of car was she driving?"

"A gold Mark IV."

I decided not to go for a walk. I went to bed, opened *The Baseball Encyclopedia,* and began to read about Peanuts Lowery, another old Cub.

3

I AWOKE at four o'clock in the morning, the wind swirling the curtains. It's windy where I live, up so high, even when the night is calm. I couldn't sleep. *The Baseball Encyclopedia* lay beside me. I got up, took a quick shower while listening to Franklin Hobbs on WCCO, drank some of last night's coffee, and ate a huge breadlike doughnut from a restaurant called Sammy D's. At four forty I was pushing the Porsche through the cool gray of early morning, when the streetlights blink a little disinterestedly and the lonely people are having bacon and eggs at places like The Hungry Eye and the bleary old drunks just give it the hell up and die down on Nicollet Island. The perverts are falling asleep in Loring Park; even perverts have to sleep sometimes: Bothering little boys and girls is no picnic, not even in Loring Park.

My office is down a corridor out of sight of the city room. It's almost always quiet in my office because I don't work against rigid deadlines. I write my stuff and when it's done I feed it to the arts and entertainment editor, who frowns because he envies me my freedom, and then it runs in the paper. I have a contract that says nobody gets to cut my copy, which only goes to show you what a joke a contract can be. A good deal of what I write cannot possibly make any sense to my readers; sometimes it just stops in the middle of a sentence because a salesman brought in an ad at the last minute and changed the space allotments. In the beginning I used to read my stuff in the paper, at least until I knew what was going to happen to it—and then I stopped. The alternative was an early apoplectic's grave. My editor was and is a gruff man built a good deal like a Mayflower van. I used to complain about things to him and he laughed, slapped me on the back in an ill-concealed attempt to dislocate my shoulder, and said, "Ah, fuck it, nobody reads this kinda shit anyway."

Nobody was moving about in my part of the building. I unlocked the door to my treasure cabinet, where the new books and records are inevitably the subject of stealthy thieves who come by night to improve their minds. The books stood staring at me, daring me to read them. Every other one seemed to be a biography of a Nazi. I shut the door, sat down, and typed twenty-three pages of reviews from my notes. Very fast, lots of mistakes. It was eight o'clock when I finished and the building was throbbing with noise and movement. Nobody paid any attention to me. I am the invisible man, I am not their comrade. In their eyes, what I do is not to be confused with work. They know I am not a newspaperman but they do not quite know what I actually am.

I went out into the newsroom, dropped the copy into a wire basket on Mayflower van's desk. He looked up, squinted down his punched-out nose, bit through the plastic end of his Tiparillo. He said, "Shit," but he was looking at my copy. "Choking to death on a plastic-tip thing," he said, scowling. "A fitting end, God knows." I went away.

Later I stood by Lake of the Isles in the sunshine staring at the green mounds rising sweetly in the water, enough to stir the poet's pen. It was a beautiful day and I sat for a while on a bench. When I got up to leave, it occurred to me that I'd made love to a woman on that bench one summer night several years before. I looked hard at the bench but it looked like all the other benches. Mosquitoes had tended our pleasures that night.

I walked back across the grass, across the street toward the Kenwood tennis courts, where I'd left the car. A kid with a bike was looking at the car. "Is that yours?" he said. I admitted it. "Boy, it's really a mess." He rode away.

I got in behind the wheel. Tight fit, got to lose a quick twenty. I was nervous.

Why the hell did Larry Blankenship kill himself?

Events were conspiring against me, like Caesar's pals.

I yanked the Porsche into the fire lane by the lobby entrance and there was Mark Bernstein looking like something from a British sex scandal: His image makers were getting him used to dark pinstripes with suppressed waists, paisley foulard ties, and off-white shirts with spread collars. There was still something of the squad room about him but he was beginning to catch on. He didn't look comfortable yet but he wore his new getup with a confidence which suited a mayoral candidate.

"You can't park there," he said.

"I know, its a blight on the building. Should be one of your typical Mark IV's."

"You miss the point. It's a fire lane."

"I don't think I'm going to vote for you, Mark. You're ahead of your time. Fascism is still out."

We walked into the lobby. I followed him into Bill Oliver's office. Then the three of us took the elevator to the fourteenth floor. Bernstein told me I shouldn't be there but then he dropped it; we'd known each other too long. Maybe I would vote for him in the end.

Oliver unlocked the door and we went inside.

Blankenship hadn't gone in much for decorating. The place looked as if he'd been passing through, like the inside of a cardboard box. There was a new pasteboard card table that sagged in the middle, a plain wooden chair, a rather large cactus which struck me as balding and obscene. That was the dining room. There was a leather club chair with a rip in the seat cushion, a telephone on the floor beside it, a desk, a stack of unopened newspapers, a poster from the

Guthrie taped to the white wall, a small black-and-white Sony, some copies of the *New Yorker,* a well-thumbed *Playboy,* a pack of Old Golds, one of those awful yellow beanbag chairs, a large candlestick with a bayberry's remains hunkering about an inch above the rim, a puddle of wax on the floor around its base. That was the living room. It looked as if a man had been slowly dying in it, a minute at a time.

Bernstein looked at it for a surprisingly long time, considering the sparse furnishings. He took a Vicks inhaler out of his pocket and sniffed it. "No punch left," he said. "I always forget to get a new one. Just like ball-point pens." He turned and went into the kitchen. "Mine never write. Never."

Toaster with crumbs all over the top, an expensive frying pan with a crust of egg fried against the sides, a loaf of bread which appeared to have turned to stone after giving birth to enough penicillin to stop an epidemic of clap, a mug with a cream culture growing on top of a coffee slick. Plastic dishes in the cupboard. "Jeez, Bill. Smells bad," Bernstein said.

"Probably food in the disposal," Oliver said. "Put his garbage in and forgot to run it."

The bedroom had been done by the same fine hand. An unmade bed, a chest of drawers, a bottle of Old Mr. Boston brandy with an orange-juice glass beside it, a stack of books on another cheap, unpainted desk, a pocket-size transistor radio, two suits in the closet, several striped shirts, a couple of ties draped over the doorknob, a pair of black shoes with plastic trees squeezed into them. The bathroom: a can of Gillette Foamy, a straight razor, a bottle of Aqua Velva. Bernstein was staring into the bathtub.

"Scuff marks," he said.

"What?" Oliver looked up.

"The man was in the bathtub with his shoes on," Bernstein said. "That's all."

Oliver looked at me. I shrugged. Bernstein was detecting.

I said, "If I'd lived here, I'd have killed myself, too."

Bernstein pursed his lips, unbuttoned his suit coat,

and put his hands on his hips. He looked at the scuff marks awhile longer and walked back into the living room. "Me, too," he said. He looked at the desk, picked up a piece of scratch paper from beside the telephone near the club chair. He brushed off some gray stuff which lay in lumps here and there on the floor; some kind of dust or fluff.

"Somebody has been here," he said to the piece of paper. "Somebody has cleaned this place out. The drawers of the desk, both desks, are open and empty. Nobody has just *nothing*. Not like this. Everybody has something. Letters, bills, address book, just some damn thing." He bent down and picked up a gob of the gray stuff, peered at it, and put it carefully on the card table.

"Why are we here?" I said. "It's not murder. It's suicide, a guy killing himself. So why are you looking for clues?"

Bernstein opened the sliding doors onto the balcony. The sun was bright and cheery, the trees green, the air clean.

"Why?" I said.

He lit a cigarette, cupping his hands as Peter Gunn would have done, and exhaled. "Do you know a Mrs. Timothy Dierker?"

Bill Oliver laughed, shook his head. The rooms had made him pale, the feel of death. But he couldn't help laughing.

"Yes," I said.

"She asked me if I'd look around. So I am looking around. She tells quite a story."

"Yes, she does," I said. "To me. To Bill. To you. Very persistent lady."

"She said there was something funny about Blankenship's death. She was certainly upset. . . . Since I had to get hold of his wife, or ex-wife, anyway, I thought I'd just come and take a look. We've got a will he'd made out a couple of weeks ago, left with his attorney, and he leaves everything to his ex-wife. . . ."

"Lucky lady," I said.

"Well, he didn't have much."

"Did you talk to her?"

"By phone. I told her what happened."

"What did she say?" I was having a funny little biological reaction, a nervous flutter behind my ribs which I couldn't explain.

"She said she was sorry. She said she wasn't surprised. He'd been depressed lately."

"Was she calm?"

"Very." He looked at his watch. There was an American flag on its face and it didn't go with the suit. "Let's go downstairs. She said she'd meet me here at eleven." In the elevator he said, "She said she wanted to make an inventory of what was in the apartment. She'll have to sign for the stuff."

Kim Blankenship had not arrived by eleven forty-five and Bernstein stood up. "I've got to speak at a VFW luncheon." He turned to me. "Not a word, Cavanaugh, not one word." I walked outside with him. It was hot and dry with the kind of wind that can make you sick to your stomach.

"You've been stiffed, Mark," I said.

"Well, it happens. Funeral preparations maybe." He walked to his car and I strolled along with him.

"This strong silent number," I said. "Are you sure it's the real you? I'd have thought something a bit warmer, chummier—"

"I wish I hadn't come," he said, ignoring me.

"Why's that?"

"Because then I wouldn't know that somebody had been emptying out Blankenship's apartment. . . ."

"Is that a crime?"

"Yes, Paul. It's called theft. Often involves unlawful entry."

"Nobody forced that door."

"All right. So somebody has a key."

"Or the door was unlocked."

"But why? What did they take? I just wish I hadn't come." He looked into the sky, looked at his watch, and got into the car. "Paul, would you get your car out of the goddamn fire lane?"

My father, Archie Cavanaugh, is seventy-one years old and he never gets bored, never casts a backward, wistful glance at the past. His mind simply doesn't work that way, and while I envy him, being with him is still a tonic. Maybe, I wonder, when I'm seventy-one I'll be like him—wishful thinking if ever I indulged in it. The past clings to me like a starving, hollow-eyed waif, and I'm used to it by now.

I headed west on the Highway 12 tangle between the Guthrie and Loring Park and the Basilica, out past the nasty gore of the auto dealers and franchise fish shops and Shakey's Pizza and the General Mills complex where Betty Crocker keeps on keepin' on year after year, cake after cake, past a restaurant built at considerable expense to look like a mine shaft where I once survived the most wretched lunch of all time, past Ridgedale, where Dayton's has established its latest beachhead in the battle for my dollar, on toward Wayzata, where the Republicans pretend that Minnesota is not a bastion of the Democratic machine and Robert Taft and Harold Stassen slumber like Siegfried waiting for the call.

Archie lives on a knoll which provides a sweep of green down to the shores of Lake Minnetonka on one side and a rolling meadow on another, the white frame house snuggled in among maples and oaks with an air of quiet calm, the kind of place where Ozzie and Harriet could live happily ever after with little David and little Ricky, and Ozzie would never have to go to work. There's a frog pond with lily pads in back and a large flower garden. Inside, Archie has some good paintings, an army of panic buttons in case of burglars or worse, a leather pig to rest his feet before the library fireplace. He's got all the things he's ever wanted; he's got it about as good as things can be at seventy-one.

I plopped the car into a puddle of shade and went in the front door. It was a hot day but cool in the house, not the cool of whirring machines but the work of country shade and breezes. Archie was working in the library with the French doors open wide onto a flagstone patio. He was writing furiously on a legal pad—looked up and winked—and I stood gazing out across the emerald lawn with the sprinkler laying down plush wet arcs. Archie hadn't always had money and what he'd wound up with he'd made himself. During the thirties he'd worked at the *Star-Journal* in Minneapolis and taught at the University of Minnesota, where he'd met my mother when they were undergraduates. Shortly before the outbreak of war in Europe he'd gone to Illinois and then on to Washington to do intelligence work during our part of the war. While he was spending some time in London, my mother fell in love with a naval officer at the Great Lakes training station near Chicago and went off with him, taking me, of course. Archie had not been unduly distressed since he'd become fascinated with his new line of work; he amiably kept in touch with us throughout the war years and from 1946 on I spent summers with him in Chicago, where he'd gone back to being a journalism professor and I went to Cub games.

In 1950 he published a textbook in reporting which made him independent and very well off, indeed. It is frequently said that reporting today, for better or worse, owes its nature to my father, who of late had been insisting that he really got people headed toward the New Journalism decades ago but forgot to give it a name. Which may be true; I certainly don't know. He came back to the University of Minnesota in the fifties and quit the academic world in 1960, when he was fifty-seven, because he wanted to write mystery novels, which he'd been doing ever since— with a newspaper reporter as his continuing hero, which with television and film and paperback rights made him a millionaire more than once. He was working on a critical volume surveying and analyzing the genre since the debut of Raymond Chandler; that's how he was spending the summer. He was doing a chapter on the Englishman Michael Gilbert that day, the lawyer who writes them on the commuter train. Copies of *Smallbone Deceased, Close Quarters,* and *Overdrive* made an orderly stack on his desk. Galleys of a brand new one, *Flash Point,* were less tidy.

He finished his thought, capped his old art deco fountain pen, and leaned back, smiling beneath his white mustache.

"Gilbert knows very well what he is about," he said, "an exceedingly orderly mind." I nodded. He wanted me to stay to lunch and we went out and sat by a wrought-iron table near the frog pond. A haze rested lighly across the fields and I could hear the hum of insect life all around. White sails danced like knife blades on the flat, blinding bright lake.

Julia, my father's secretary and dear friend, brought us salads and a bottle of cold Blue Nun and sat down to join us, cool and calm in a blue denim shirtwaist. Everything was so quiet and gentle and my father talked about Michael Gilbert and Julian Symons for a while as we ate. There were large white-and-orange shrimps in garlic and oil among the lettuce. Julia said she was sorry, but she preferred Dorothy Sayers, and my father said it was because Ian Carmichael was doing so well as Wimsey on the tube. He added that there was no need for an apology, she shouldn't try to hide her intellectual pretensions, and we all chuckled rather dottily. Matey, we were all matey.

Finally I got down to cases: "What do you know about Tim Dierker?"

"Why, Tim's all right, isn't he?" My father's blue eyes flickered up.

"Well, nothing has happened to him," I said, "but it's hard to say he's all right."

He picked his tooth with a pick, made a face. "Hmmm, I've stabbed myself. Ah, well . . . Tim Dierker. I met him forty or so years ago, known him ever since. Your mother's family, as you know, had a good deal more money than was good for them, and I was sort of drawn into things like the Norway Creek Club because of it. That's where I met Tim and Harriet.

"Tim didn't have any phoniness about him; he was what we used to call a regular guy, which meant he took a dim view of bullshit, which you found a lot of at Norway Creek in those days. There were several of us out there in the long ago—we sort of hung around together."

"Was this the beginning of your hunting and fishing

club? I've seen pictures of you up north with Hub Anthony. Was he in this group?"

"Sure. We liked the chance of getting away from town—"

"And your wives, I'll bet," Julia said. She was ironic and wore very well. She and my father had met during the war and had taken up together fifteen years ago. She was his secretary, but she was a good deal more. Some of the time she stayed at the house, but she'd always maintained an apartment in town. She'd had a couple of husbands and that had cured her; she didn't want a third.

"Of course. My wife in particular, I assure you." He looked shyly at me, aware he'd insulted my mother, and I nodded. "What is behind this curiosity, if I may ask?"

I told them about the suicide of Larry Blankenship and the conversations with both Dierkers which ensued. My father is not the sort of man to become needlessly shaken by events occurring so far into the shadows, so far from his own concern. He nodded when I finished.

"Harriet is obviously as irretrievably nosy as ever and Tim is as irritated by bullshit. I've often thought of putting them into a book, what an absurdly mismatched pair—no wonder they never produced a child, it'd be like mating a Saint Bernard and a shrike. . . ." He sipped at the goblet of Blue Nun Julia had freshened and took a cheroot from his shirt pocket. Julia handed him a box of matches from the cart beside the table. Wind rustled gently in the trees.

"I never *knew* Blankenship. I have met him, the name is familiar, probably because of his relationship with Kim Roderick, whom I did know somewhat." He played with his cigar for a time and finally got it lit to his satisfaction. Julia slid an ashtray across the table toward him. A frog leaped onto a lily pad, the movement graceful, and sat squatting, staring at us. "It's peculiar, she was the sort of person who gets talked about by others, even those who may not know her. I've met women like that from time to time in my life, not very often, when I think about it, but Kim was one of them. Star quality, maybe? Who knows. Maybe it's genetic, just something in the blood."

"Did everybody feel that way about her? Did they notice her?"

"I don't know, but perhaps they did. It seemed that they kept talking about her. . . . You should ask your former wife, my boy. Anne knew her when they were girls—Anne was being terribly democratic, as you know she sometimes is, and befriended this disconnected girl—"

"Disconnected?" Julia said. "What does that mean, for heaven's sake?"

"Why, no connections, no family. . . ."

"You mean she just appeared? The existential being?" Julia's eyebrows arched.

"Yes, as a matter of fact, that's exactly what she did, as I understand the story. Just appeared one day, applying for a job. But then, I'm only recalling what I've heard. . . . But it's a cinch she wasn't one of the usual girls, wherever the hell she came from."

"That's about what Judge Anthony said," I said.

"Well, he may have had an eye for her, you know. She was capable of that effect." Archie drew on the cheroot, crossing his legs. Julia was pulling on her cotton gardening gloves. It was her flower garden and I could smell it, sweet, airy, like Julia.

"Was she liked? Did they like her?"

"Who? The men or the women?"

"You mean it was that obvious?"

"That's what my friends used to say, they talked about her when we were alone. Not dirty, just appreciative, as I recall." He sighed. "Julia would understand—Kim wasn't the sort of woman you'd talk about in front of other women."

"I do understand," she said, standing up. "I met this girl, too, Archie, one year at the Christmas dance at the club. She was there with her husband, this Larry fellow. We were introduced, and I know what you mean about her—I may not have talked about her, but I caught myself thinking about her afterward. She was beautiful but somehow preoccupied. She seemed to be somewhere else. She had a . . . quality. Now, I must get my trowel and play with my flowers."

Archie got to talking about his group of friends of almost forty years ago. It was very unlike him and maybe that was why he seemed to enjoy going back over it; he wasn't indulging himself, he was answering my questions, so maybe he didn't look on it as a sign of age.

"What did your friends think of her? Your gang, I mean."

"They liked her—admired her looks and her attitudes, I'd say."

"Even Tim Dierker?"

"Sure. Hell, he was the one who put the stamp of approval on her for a job. He told Lenhardt, the guy who was managing the kitchen then—manages the whole damn place now, by the way—Dierker told him she was the kind of girl who'd cheer the place up." He emptied the Blue Nun. The bottle was sweating. Julia had brought a bag of gardening tools and was kneeling by the border of lavender and yellow flowers circling the frog pond.

"I wonder what turned him against her?" I said.

"What are you talking about?" The breeze was blowing the cigar smoke away from us and the flowers smelled good. The lake glistened below, past the trees black and green with the sun's rays filtering golden through them.

"Well, Harriet said Tim's health broke when he was unable to convince Larry Blankenship not to marry her. She said Tim was very protective about Larry, like a son, and that he was desperately trying to talk him out of marrying her. And never got over having failed."

Archie shook his head with its slicked-back white hair, so carefully barbered, and shifted his weight. The blue eyes blinked and looked out toward the lake as if an answer might be hidden on the distant shore.

"I can't imagine what happened. He always seemed to like her. We all thought she was fine."

"Tell me about the group," I said. "Who all was in it?"

It was a varied collection.

In addition to Archie Cavanaugh, Timothy Dierker, Ole Kronstrom, and Hubbard Anthony, there were three others, all of whom had gone on to success and ease.

Jonathan Goode, four years younger than my father, was a career army man, retired now as a three-star general, but then a young captain stationed in Minneapolis at Fort Snelling. World War II had done some very good things for Jon Goode and the Korean War had done some more. He'd become involved in strategic planning at Pentagon levels, moving around with considerable familiarity in parts of our bureaucratic system which we taxpayers know nothing about. He wasn't a spy, but he knew what spies know, was in the intelligence gathering and analyzing end of things, and had in fact been the man who'd contacted me for a simple mission. I'd ended up having to kill a man on a train; I wasn't likely to forget General Goode, though I'd downed a good deal of scotch giving it a try. Although he lived in Minneapolis, retired and sitting on several boards, he didn't move in precisely my social set; Archie still saw him fairly regularly. I hadn't seen him in years.

Father Martin Boyle had been a youngish Irish priest in the thirties; now he was an oldish Irish priest, overweight and red-nosed and much loved at the University of Minnesota, where he'd been the force behind the flourishing Newman Center. At sixty-eight he was still connected with the center, as its "patron saint," some said, garrulous, full of gout, still playing golf with Jon Goode at Norway Creek. He lived still in a large turn-of-the-century house in Prospect Park, not far from the university, a house he shared with Father Conrad Patulski. They also shared a midnight-blue Cadillac limousine, which didn't say much for the poverty of the priesthood, but then this was the twentieth century. Archie said that Boyle was a priest you could trust: He ate too much, drank too much, and liked women. He was never self-righteous, a very fine quality in a man of the cloth.

James Crocker, seventy, had been a football star at

the university in the mid-twenties (Nagurski's time? How the hell should I know? But Crocker had had his greatest day against Grange and the Illini; it was a legend), very nearly an all-American. His heart was wearing out, the plague of ex-jocks. He'd played professionally with George Halas' Chicago Bears when Grange had made pro football happen. And by the mid-thirties he'd established contracting and land-development operations in the Twin Cities. As the years, then the decades, passed, he became a figure to be reckoned with in politics and gave his name to housing projects, then to a suburb. He'd given a good deal of money to Richard Nixon's Campaign to Re-Elect, realized too late that it had been laundered in Mexico, and been very irritable ever since. He preferred to remember his greatest game as a Minnesota Golden Gopher when Memorial Stadium was dedicated and he helped beat the great Red Grange; he wouldn't mention Nixon and Grange in the same breath.

"And everybody liked young Kim?" I said when he had run through the list.

"So far as I ever knew.'" He stifled a yawn behind a wrinkled, pale hand. It was that kind of afternoon.

"But she was a slut, a monster who made her husband kill himself. Drove him to it with her infidelities." I shook my head. "Inconsistencies, Dad."

"Life's full of them." He smiled lopsidedly. "Anyway, all you've got for evidence is the raving of Harriet Dierker, not precisely an ideal witness."

"But she *was* raving," I said, remembering. "That's the point. She wasn't gossiping, not really. She was worked up." I yawned, too. "And if Tim Dierker thought she was so wonderful, what bothered him so much about Larry marrying her? Pieces missing in there."

"Long time ago. Half of what happened people forget entirely, the other half they get wrong in trying to tell it. It all gets distorted. Faulty memories are right in the middle of writing mystery novels—the characters have them, the reader sure as hell has one, frequently the writer does, too." He yawned again. "Memories, on the whole, are for shit, Paul."

"Ole Kronstrom fell in love with her, for God's sake," I said. "Now I ask you, would he fall in love with a monster?"

"Hardly. Ole was a simple man. Or a fool, or maybe just lucky. I mean, after all, Ole is not necessarily the fellow you'd pick for Kim, not on the nice shiny surface of things, anyway."

"Did you know about them?"

"Tough not to." Archie stood up and kicked off his sneakers, wriggled his toes in the grass. Newly mowed grass mottled his white feet. We walked up to the house together. A motorboat whined into life down on the lake and the sound floated up the hill, a part of summer indistinguishable from all the other parts, the smells of the flowers and the Coppertone and the sounds of the insects. I followed him back across the stones into the cool library.

"Enough history," he said. "You want to know about the girl, not my old cronies." He sank down into a flowered-print chair, the slipcover casually off-center, and crossed his bare feet.

"I really wanted to know why Blankenship killed himself." I heard myself say it; it didn't seem strange. I did want to know; the curiosity had just sort of infected me, like a siege of walking pneumonia I'd once had.

"That's what I say, Paul—the girl." He stroked his white mustache with a bony knuckle. "The girl, I'm trying to remember what, what it is I know, or knew, about her. . . ." He sucked the knuckle for a minute and I could see Julia kneeling by the flower border. She was troweling moist, dark earth and looked as if she were enjoying herself immensely. The sprinkler caught the sun through the trees, held it for a moment, then sprayed along on its way.

"She came to Norway Creek not long after I came back to the university. I didn't pay any particular attention to her, though I couldn't help noticing her. The way she looked, that trim, neat figger, sort of a solemn face, dark eyebrows, dark shiny hair—stupid thing to remember, hair, but what can I tell you?" He shrugged. "It made you wonder if she had a line of that dark hair going up her belly. Well, hell, let's be candid, Paul. That's they way she made me think. . . ."

"You should be ashamed of yourself," I said.

"Harriet told you more about her love life than I ever knew. I can't vouch for the facts but it sounded more or less right to me. But she always impressed me as competent, the kind of person who'd get done whatever she set out to do. She always acted like a person right there in the present, very down to earth, not silly." He sighed and pursed his lips. "Now, you can call that sort of attitude calculating or mature, dangerous or determined, depending on your point of view.

"It seems to me that somebody—Dierker, I think—told me she was an orphan from up north, maybe from the town near where we had the lodge. That must be how Tim knew about her, sounds possible. She was a charity case, anyway, and the guys in our group sort of felt sorry for her—seems she was the niece of somebody. Christ, I'm hazy on this, Paul. . . .

"You really should ask Anne about her if you're sufficiently curious. Girls do talk to one another, don't they? They played a lot of tennis. Anne was taking lessons from her, I suppose. Anyway, that's about all I know. . . ."

We sat for a while, sleepy. Archie picked up one of the Michael Gilbert novels. I felt my eyelids getting heavy from the luncheon wine and the fact that I'd gotten up way too early. Something made me jerk and I looked at Archie. He'd gotten out of the flowered chair and was peering into one of the floor-to-ceiling bookcases built into the wall. They were glossy white. He finally reached up and withdrew a large brown leather photograph album.

"You awake?" He cleared his writing gear to one side of the old oak desk and placed the photograph album in the center. I nodded. "Thought you might like to see this," he said. He opened the album, which was held together by heavy brown twine threaded through each page. I went over to the desk. I looked

at my watch. An hour had passed since we'd come
back to the library.

"Sure," I said. "What is it?"

He spread the pages flat; black-and-white snapshots, some slightly yellowed, held in place by little
black pasted-down corner pieces. I'd seen the album
before, as a child, and later checking on pictures of
my mother. Archie was not the dramatic type: He'd
left her pictures where they'd always been, bearing her
no grudges but merely glad to be rid of her.

"Pictures we took up at the lodge. All these fellows you see as old men now, me and the rest of
them, this is the way we looked back in '33, '34. You
were just getting yourself born, Paul." He pointed to
the first picture, upper left, left-hand page, and began
telling me about them, identifying the men and what
they were amusing themselves with on those long-ago
summer days when they went up north to get away
from it all.

I wasn't really listening but I was getting enough,
like background music, and I was thinking about the
men. There was the picture of Hub with the slicked-
back hair, the shadows on his face, the bony shoulders
square and taut. Archie was smiling remotely, squinting from behind round, silver-rimmed spectacles, looking up from a book as he lay in a striped canvas chair.

Ole Kronstrom and Jonathan Goode bulked large
and white in swimming suits which clung tightly to
their wet bodies. They stood in the sand near the
water, fishing poles in their hands, shadows black on
the beach.

Martin Boyle in a sweater and a white shirt stood
beside a four-door Pontiac sedan, his foot on the running board, a hand raised in salute to the photographer. A dog of no discernible known breed stood
at his feet, staring up at him. Timothy Dierker sat
behind the wheel, framed in the window, his face in
motion, mouth open, saying something. James Crocker,
the football star overflowing his trousers ten years later,
looked down into the camera from atop a ladder where
he was painting a wall of the lodge. He waved his

paintbrush, carelessly letting white paint drip down the handle of the brush.

They appeared to be men from another age, another century; I didn't know anyone who went off that way anymore, hunting and fishing and away from their wives. I didn't know men who gathered in groups of any kind; a night out with the boys, it seemed an anachronism, the way nobody wrote like Robert Benchley anymore. It seemed unbelievable that those men could still be alive. They looked out from an innocent, pre-World War II past, sealed away like relics in a tomb. They didn't look curious or amused or even very intelligent. But they did look privileged, almost without care, in a way that was unheard of anymore. Arrogance of a subtle sort; the arrogance of innocence.

"Why are you laughing, Paul?"

"I'm not. It just makes me smile, that's all. Long time ago. People looked different then. Not just their clothing. The people themselves. Do you see it?"

He shook his head. "How can I? I'm one of them."

He slipped a finger under the next page and slowly turned it over. More pictures: the lodge, the boys.

"Do you still go up there?"

"Hell, no," he scoffed. "My God, I outgrew that a long time ago. . . ."

"Lost interest in hunting and fishing?"

"I never was much for that stuff. Did you ever go fishing, Paul? Sitting in a boat in the middle of a lake? It's like *An American Tragedy*. You begin to understand why Montgomery Clift wanted to push Shelley Winters out of the boat. He was bored." He sat down in the captain's chair by the typewriter table. "I used to take books up there, read all the stuff there was never time to read at home. Sinclair Lewis, John Galsworthy, Willa Cather, got hooked on S. S. Van Dine and Agatha Christie. . . ." He sighed, reaching for the cigar humidor on the corner of the desk. "It was really quite a civilized group at the beginning, surprisingly so, I suppose." He gave in and withdrew a cigar, stared at it appreciatively.

"It stopped being civilized?"

"Rowdy. Predictably, the jolly boys decided that what the hell was the point of getting away from it all if you behaved yourself? So a good deal of drinking was getting done and that was terribly boring and then the stag films with the naked guys in the black socks and Lone Ranger mask and the inevitable horsing around with ladies of the night . . . also boring. I was trying to get away from women and now, all of a sudden, they were talking about importing them." He lit a cigar. "And that was when I bowed out. Later we moved to Chicago and that was that." He beckoned for the album and I handed it to him. "I'm not a sentimental man," he said, "but I get a little twinge when I see these pictures. No point in denying your humanity, is there? We were a lot younger then and time has had a go at us since. . . . I can remember the days up there, cold beer and a good book and lying in the sun. Well, you can't get 'em back once they're gone. As I suspect you're discovering, my boy." He looked down at the album. "It was a nice lodge, big fireplace, lots of wicker furniture, big old oscillating fans on tops of bookcases, nice screened-in porch, rocking chairs. . . . Kept it nice and clean. That's what she did." He put his finger on a group picture, a brunette standing on the porch with the men grouped somewhat formally by her side. She looked as if she'd been taken by surprise, hustled out of the kitchen in her apron and snapped abruptly before she'd slid her public face into position. Archie was at the far left, looking away from the happy scene. Tim Dierker was smiling stiffly next to the woman, looking as if he were afraid he might touch her accidentally. The men all looked a bit self-conscious but the woman had a reserved, boys-will-be-boys expression of tolerance. She had an oval face and a widow's peak pointing at a straight, handsome nose.

"Who was she?"

"I can't remember her name. She came to the lodge from the town and kept house while we were there, did the dishes, got rid of the empties, generally tidied up." He closed his eyes and leaned back. "Nope, I can't remember her name. But it was a long time ago,

Paul. Almost as long as you've been alive. So why should I remember?"

"Who took the picture?"

He looked at it. "Must have been Ole. He's the only one of us not in the picture."

I decided to quit fighting it and go lie down in a lawn chair. But I stopped at the French window. Archie was putting the album back on the shelf.

"I understand you saw her last week."

"Who?"

"Kim. Blankenship's wife."

"Yes, I did. Playing tennis with what's-his-name, the pro at the club. She was giving him a run for his money."

"Has she changed much?"

"From when?"

"I don't know——from when you first saw her?"

"Who knows? I saw her often enough so that any change was a gradual one. But she's not the kind of woman who lets herself go. Minimal change, I'd say."

When I woke up, the sun had slid well below the treetop level and the long shadows had a furry purple color, like giant caterpillars stretched out across the lawn. I was stiff and had a headache. There was a green light hanging in the evening down by a boathouse. The days were getting shorter as August pressed on. I went inside. Julia was drinking iced tea in the long living room, curled at one end of a pale-gray modern sofa. The only light came from the see-through glass ginger jar beside her. Dusk had settled across the room and crickets made the only sound. She looked up and smiled faintly.

"Feel better?" she asked. She put her book down; it dealt with the peculiarly successful marriage between Harold Nicolson and Vita Sackville-West.

"Just a little worse, actually."

"Iced tea in the pitcher on the cart."

I poured a tall glass and added lemon and sugar, slid into a chrome-and-leather director's chair. My mouth tasted like an army had used it for a latrine all evening.

"Archie's gone. His Sherlock Holmes meeting."

"Right." I drank some iced tea. "What about Kim? What do you think? Was she a monster?" I was too tired to chat.

"Well, yes and no, Paul."

"Come on, Julia, what the hell does that mean?"

"Everybody's a monster to someone. Don't you think? And everybody has his own monster. So, yes and no."

"Why did he kill himself, then?"

"Love or money, those are the usual reasons, aren't they?"

"But which?"

Julia shrugged. "Why not ask Kim?"

After I popped three Excedrin I kissed her forehead and flung myself recklessly into the hot night.

4

DARWIN MCGILL was a handsome man but something had gone wrong in the vastness behind his large brown eyes. His skin looked like a very expensive piece of luggage, dark brown from the sun and unnaturally smooth, but puffed out from too much time spent in the bar at Norway Creek, which was where I found him. The room was dim and almost empty with the big *Casablanca* ceiling fans slowly rotating above us and the doors thrown open to the patio, pool, and putting green beyond. A few members sipped at tall ones in frosted glasses outside and a couple of teenagers splashed in the pool, the underwater lights casting ominous shadows across their faces and flinging rippling shadows against the thick oaks bordering the golf course. McGill looked up as I sat down on the

stool beside him, nodded, crooked a finger at the bar-
tender.

"Jack," he said, "another gimlet for me and. . . ."
He glanced at me.

"Gin and tonic," I said, and Jack went away. It
was cool in the bar and the sweat on my neck was
drying. "How's it going, Darwin?"

"The way it always goes," he said grimly, a slight
slur in his speech. "Spend all day in the sun chasing
whitey, get too damn tired and dehydrated for a man
my age, and take all night replacing the sweat with
gin."

"You're just down," I said. "You're in fantastic
shape."

"Bullshit." He frowned, rattled the remains of ice
cubes in his glass while waiting for the fresh one. "Bad
news today, I've got good reason to be down. . . . Liver's gone bad, Paulie, and you know what that means.
Doctor tried to break it gently. Botched it, of course."
He sighed and waited while Jack put our drinks down
on club coasters. "I cried for thirty-five minutes and
then gave a lesson at eleven o'clock. He said I didn't
have to cut out the booze—it wouldn't make much
difference one way or the other—but a bit of modera-
tion might be in order." He gave me a sour little grin.
"How can men be doctors, having to give people the
bad news?"

"Well, they get to give them the good news, too," I
said.

But he was in a mood and not to be cheered; was
it as bad as he seemed to think? I'd always found him
a jock, utterly outside of my sphere of caring, but it
was disheartening to hear the dribs and drabs of his
story while my mind was full of Blankenship and Kim.
My mind wandered, with my eyes, across the room
with its glossy tables and padded, leather-backed
chairs, the potted palms, the dusty Moroccan archi-
tecture, all arches and whatnot. Anne and I had finished more evenings in the room than was good for us,
a fact which put us well into the company of so many
of our friends whose marriages had come undone.

"My wife has left me, y'know. Called me a chaser,

called me a cradle robber. Said I'd be hanging about school yards and offering them candy soon. I couldn't believe my ears, the stupid woman." He yawned. "I'll never forgive her for leaving me, for beating me to it. She was a mistake from the beginning. . . . You're not married anymore, are you?"

"Nope."

"This place is turning into a goddamn singles bar," he reflected. "The only married people are the old ones." An eye gleamed at me. "Do you figure there's a lot of wife swapping or ex-wife-swapping going on here?"

"My God, I don't know. I sure as hell don't want a wife, my own or anyone else's."

He clasped my arm. "You tell 'em, Paulie." He sipped his drink and added sorrowfully, "I spend most of my time in the pro shop now, nothing to go home to, not even an argumentative bitch. Funny how you can miss even a bitch. . . ."

McGill's relationship with his wife had been stormy for as long as I could remember, something the members sometimes chuckled over. She was always accusing him, not only in private, of messing about with the women and girls he coached. She may well have had grounds, too, but no one ever made a scandal and Darwin inevitably rode out any marginal squalls. If he hadn't been such a fine player and teacher, he would probably have been fired; he was good, though, and personally well liked, so he survived the years. He must have been fifty-five.

"What do you know about Kim Roderick?" I asked. "You taught her the game, didn't you?"

He nodded, glass to his lips. "She picked it up quick and kept getting better. If she were fifteen years old today, what with all the indoor courts and improved competition, she might have made the tour, the Slims or something. TV would have picked up on her because she's so pretty and she's got the personality to win, kind of a Rosemary Casals game, short but strong, good musculature, hits a big overhead, death on lobs." He was talking like a pro now and I could see his mind recalling her making the shots. "Not too

fast but she gets into good position, goes for the win-
ners, very fast reflexes. And on top of that she's a
fucking killer. She's in her mid-thirties now but she's
still got that nasty quality . . . a lousy loser, let me tell
you."

"You still play with her?"

"Yeah, matter of fact, I do. She beat me last week,
ran me back and forth all day, wore me out, and then
just beat hell out of me. I know exactly what Riggs
felt like in the Astrodome. . . . The expression on her
face never changed, it was like she was doing an exercise. I've known women who screwed that way, mechanically, never show the slightest emotion."

We were on our next drink and the mood was right.
"Did you ever sleep with her?"

"Oh, hell, no—not for want of trying, though. Hell,
Paul, you know how it is, she worked for me, I saw a
lot of her every day, I couldn't help putting a little
move on her every now and then. You really can't
blame me, can you? That's one of the best things about
a job like this. Then, before you know it, it's your life,
not just your job, and there's nothing you can do about
it and your liver gives out. . . ."

"What was she like then back when you were making your moves?"

Darwin McGill's hair was dark and wavy, flecked
with gray, and he slid strong dark fingers through it
like an old movie star. He grinned, remembering, and
shook his handsome head, flashed the white teeth.

"It depends when you're talking about. She changed,
y'see." He scooped up a handful of Spanish peanuts
and suggested we go outside. He was still lean but
there was a little thickening about his waist. I was
sorry about his poor damn liver. Maybe it wasn't as
bad as he seemed to think. The breeze was cool, the
sky bright and spattered with blinking stars which had
actually burned away and died a million years ago.
He smiled at some of the patio sitters who spoke his
name and then we were on the grass, which was moist
in the night. The last purple fingers had lost their grip
on the western sky. He was heading instinctively for
the shadowy bulk of the tennis courts, the high fences.

"When she first showed up here, she was just kitchen help, then she did some waiting on tables, then she came to me in her spare time wanting me to teach her the game. She was very serious and very quiet and determined, very pretty. So I figured, what the hell, I'll spend a little time on her—I admit it, I liked to watch her move around and work up a sweat. I figured she was safer game than a member—you start messing around with members, wives and daughters, which I've done, God knows, you're running a real risk. You could get fired if you got caught at it. . . . Well, she picked up the game, really showed me something, and she began to loosen up a bit, get a little friendlier, than a lot friendlier—hell, the thing was she wanted to be my assistant.

"She was doing nothing more or less than a little cockteasing and I sure as hell went for it. She seemed to have some real supporters among the members and when I suggested that she'd be a real help to me running the shop, working with some of the members when I was booked solid—when I went to them with the idea, they said fine, she'd be a help, all right. She really impressed them, I think, industrious as hell."

We'd reached the courts and he hooked his fingers into the fencing and leaned against it as if he were counting the six courts. It was quiet; nothing moved but the wind in the willows.

"Once she was working in the pro shop I sort of waited for a chance and one night it came. I tried a little straight-ahead stuff with her, she yanked away from me and the buttons came off her blouse like machine-gun fire. She wasn't saying anything and I'd had a few drinks and didn't know when to quit. I kept at her and pulled her brassiere off and there were these tiny round tits, smooth, with big stiff nipples. . . ." He sighed and turned around to look at me. "I don't know why I stopped. Maybe it was because she didn't look flustered, maybe it was because she'd always seemed so distant and seeing her naked was so . . . unnatural, I guess. Anyway, I was really shocked at what I'd done." He shook his head as if he were reliving the confusions of that moment years before.

"She just looked at me, watched me looking at her chest, and told me that I was just one step from losing my job and facing a criminal action. She was so composed, Paulie, I just felt like I wanted to hide. She said she had friends among the members who would have me dismissed and give her all the legal advice she wanted. She didn't seem angry or out of breath or anything. I've never felt such a chill—I thought my dick was gonna just drop on the floor.

"I apologized and she said never to mention it again, to forget it. She just stared at me for a while, then she put her brassiere back on right in front of me, took a brand-new tennis shirt out of the cabinet, pulled it on over her head, threw the ripped blouse into a wastebasket, and left. I was absolutely terrified, for my job mainly. But she never did anything about it, nothing more was ever said . . . but she was a true-blue bitch, I've never seen anything to match it. She didn't have a pot to piss in but she was right at the head of the class and I've had to deal with a lot of rich, nasty people in this job. She just threw me the hell away, looked right through me from then on. . . . She doesn't forget, not ever. Billy Whitefoot really got the full curse, poor son of a bitch. The job she did on him was goddamn incredible. Then when he was all used up, she moved on to Ole Kronstrom and that poor asshole she married, Larry what's-his-name."

We eventually walked back toward the clubhouse.

"What brought her up, anyway?"

"Her husband killed himself the other day. Nobody seems to know why. I was just curious."

"Women. She probably drove him to it."

"That's a popular view."

"Yeah, I can see how she'd make a guy do something like that. Well, she's one of a kind."

On the driveway he put his hand on my arm.

"Look, you're not going to tell this stuff to anybody, are you? I mean, not your father or his cronies? They're the ones she meant when she said she had friends. . . ."

"No, Darwin, I'm not going to tell anybody."

"I'd appreciate it." He chuckled in the dark. "I've

got enough problems, Paulie. It's all catching up with me." Before he went back into the bar, he said something funny: "Women, if they didn't have cunts, they'd be hunted."

I left him alone with his liver and another gimlet and called Anne. I asked her if I could stop by for a minute on the way home. She said it was okay with her; she was just putting a steak on the grill. I asked her to make it two.

The house sat on a hill behind a vine-covered stone wall with a sharp drop of brambles collapsing downward steeply to Lake of the Isles. I pulled up the narrow driveway with the shrubberies' claws reaching hungrily for my face, clattering at the sides of the car. The house, which had had a peculiarly crumbly look about it for years, was dark but when I went in I saw the dim glow from Anne's workroom. The place smelled of airplane glue and there was a Moody Blues record playing. She was bent over a trestle worktable with a complicated lamp jutting out over the fuselage of a large Messerschmitt ME 109 she was repairing. The table was covered with spines of balsa wood, pliers and tweezers and little pots of paint and tubes of glue and wires and Exacto knives and dirty hand rags. A dead joint had burned away in an ashtray, leaving the faint memory of her homegrown grass hanging in the air. She looked up and for a moment I didn't quite recognize her: She had had her black hair cropped very short and it had been years since I'd seen her without a wig of one kind or another.

"Hi," she said. "I put the steaks on. Hand me that beer, will you, please?" She put down the needle-nosed pliers and looked at the dismantled airplane the way someone else might sadly inspect a bird with a broken wing.

"Have a crash?"

"A beaut," she said. "Sheared off a wing and took the undercarriage out. Shit." She sighed and swigged at the Coors she always brought back from her trips to Aspen, where her parents had a million-dollar retreat. "Well, it's time to be philosophical—it's the tinkering that's fun, right? And how's that antique carburetor system of yours working?"

"The car runs," I said. "What can I say?"

"You really should let me look at that for you. The timing is probably all shot to hell, too."

"I suppose." She handed me the beer and I remembered too late that it would be sickly warm. She'd probably been pulling at the same can since noon.

"God, how can you live in a world where you don't know how anything works? You don't know how your car works, or your television set, or the presses at the paper, or anything. . . . Doesn't it make you nervous, Cav?"

"Lots of other things make me nervous." We'd had this conversation before. Many times. Several hundred times. "Knowing would make me nervous."

She shook her head. Above us a red Focke-Wulf hung by piano wires swayed in the breeze. The night moved stealthily in the brambles outside.

"Let's go check the steaks," she said, wiping crud off her hands. "You want to split a joint? Homegrown organic shit," she offered as a final inducement.

"No thanks."

"Me neither," she said. "I'm beginning to believe all the brain-damage stuff." She was wearing a T-shirt with the big red Rolling Stones tongue dangling obscenely between her breasts; tight Levi's across her broad, firm hips. Barefoot she was within an inch of six feet. As she passed me, she brushed her lips across my mouth and I could taste the warm beer on her.

The huge kitchen was all ancient butcher block, dirty dishes everywhere, a collander with a wilted clump of lettuce that was probably a week old. She took another Coors out of a case on the counter; impossibly, she always just forgot to put it in the refrigerator; it wasn't that she even liked warm beer. She asked me if I wanted one and I made a face. She shrugged—"It's your funeral"—and we went out the back door. The steaks sizzled over reddish coals, there was a glass bowl full of lettuce and tomatoes and green peppers and bits of cheese and pepperoni, and a Dansk bucket with ice and a bottle of something in it, all proving that she could still get it together if inclined to do so.

She ate like a starved lion, demolished her salad. "Come on, eat," she said. "I made this for you. . . ." She smiled while I ate, finished before me, and lit a normal Winston and leaned back, legs crossed. The small lawn seemed isolated, dark, quiet, nestled between the bramble cliff and the moldering three-story mansion. Something ran across the back, near the thicket, something small and furry.

"Did you just want a free meal?" she asked, relaxed, her voice mellow. "Or is there something on your mind?"

"Something on my mind, something I'm getting into with no particular reason. Just things people have been saying. . . ." I didn't quite know where to begin.

"So?"

"Larry Blankenship—do you know the name?"

"Of course," she said patiently. "He was married to a friend of mine."

"Well, he killed himself a couple of days ago."

She froze the cigarette on the way to her mouth and stared at me, her face a mask of surprise and paling shock. "What?"

"He shot himself in the lobby of my building."

"Well, for God's sake . . . Larry. He was such a simple guy, so worried about everything."

"I wanted to ask you about your friend Kim Roderick."

"What about her? Do you know her?"

"No, I don't know her, but somebody mentioned that you knew her. People have been telling me that she may have driven Blankenship to kill himself. . . ."

She shook her head and dragged on the cigarette. "No, I don't think so. I'm not saying Kim wouldn't be capable of doing that to a guy—but not to Larry." She shook her head more vehemently, stubbed out her cigarette. "If you'd said that poor Indian kid, Whitefoot, had killed himself or drunk himself to death, that I could have attributed to Kim, at sort of second or third hand, you know. But not poor Larry . . . he was a Kigmy—"

"A what?"

"A Kigmy. Remember Al Capp? He had the Schmoos and the Kigmies. The Schmoos were just too good to be true—they laid bottled Grade A milk and when you broiled them they tasted like sirloin; fried, they tasted like chicken. The Kigmies were the perfect masochists—they wanted only to be kicked, that was their mission, they were there for the world to take out aggressions on, just waiting to be kicked. He made people nervous. And Kim usually treated him pretty benevolently—sort of like brother and sister. It was hard for me to imagine them in bed, he was so passive. But, then, she was always terrified of sex— or, anyway, I'd have bet on it. She seemed frigid to me, she always seemed so tightly controlled. . . ." She cocked an eye at me. "You'd have liked her, maybe. She was—is—very neat, determined, but there were signals every so often that something pretty spooky was going on underneath. That would appeal to you." Her eyes gleamed with the happy malice of people who knew each other overly well.

"Some people think she was a slut, a temptress, and I quote."

"Well, live and let live. I'm just telling you what I think." She paused. "Poor Larry. I never told you but when he was going through one of his depressions and you and I were on the verge of murder, I met him at Norway Creek, it was around Christmas, when your emotions are all shot to hell, and we were both lonely and kind of drunk and I felt this big surge of pity for him, the earth mother in me, and I brought him back here and plied him with hot buttered rum before the fireplace. I told him I had a special Christmas present for him, and I took off my clothes —pretty neat scene, actually—and I was going to do a couple of things he wouldn't soon forget. But he started to cry and talk about Kim and couldn't get a twitch out of his little thing." She picked some cheese and lettuce out of the salad bowl and licked the dressing off her fingers. The last piece of steak disappeared. "Now he's dead and never knew what he missed."

"Does Kim know that?"

"Sure, he told her, part of the Kigmy thing. He was that type, rubber mouth. But you know what Kim did? She came over very formally and told me that she appreciated what I'd done for Larry. We weren't seeing each other at all in those days, our friendship was from our teenage years . . . but she thanked me. Now, in the last few years since you and I split up, we've sort of renewed our friendship, carefully but for real. Of course I'm always optimistic about things like that."

"Is she one of your trophies?" I said. "Noblesse oblige and all that, befriending the friendless and whatnot?"

"Not really," she said without anger at my cheap shot. "I think I've passed through that phase. She started out that way but not anymore."

"Doesn't her relationship with Kronstrom bother you?"

"My God, you have been doing your homework, little man. But no, why on earth should it bother me? From what I can tell you, whatever they have works pretty well for them. I'm just in no position to judge her, or anyone else, on moral grounds. People just do what they do. . . ." She smiled sadly. "But I'm terribly sorry about Larry. As for blaming her, though, you'll have to ask somebody else."

We went back inside and stopped in the darkened front hall.

"I wish I hadn't started all this," I said quietly. "It just keeps me going round and round. It doesn't seem to lead anywhere. I keep hearing all these conflicting attitudes about this woman and she's a ghost, I've never seen her, I don't even know what she looks like. . . ."

"You can always just stop worrying about it. You don't have to do this, Cav." She was talking to me now as she'd done in the old days, when we'd been in love.

"I know. Maybe I'll just say the hell with it."

At the door she said, "Say, I don't mean to drag you back into it, but I just remembered that I do have a picture of her. A snapshot, taken about a year ago.

We were playing tennis and Sam Proctor had his new Leica and he took our picture. . . . Do you want to see?"

I thought about it and said I guessed I did. It was just another step into the swamp. But I wanted to see what she looked like. I waited outside wondering about the carburetor, debating if I could leave it to Anne's tender ministrations. It was almost midnight.

She came back with a white photograph envelope.

"There are more than I thought," she said. "Just take the whole bunch."

"Okay, Anne. I appreciate it. And it was a wonderful dinner."

"Umm, look—do you want to come back in and mess around? You know. I'm sort of in the mood." She looked demurely at the ground. "Or should I go back to my Messerschmitt?"

"Well, you'd better go back to World War Two."

"It was just a thought." She grinned.

I started the Porsche and moved around the circle to leave. She waved and stood in the doorway until I was gone. I'd once told Anne that she was my life and she'd looked across the breakfast table, pulling her robe tight at the neck—it was her Peck & Peck period —and said, "What a life, you poor bastard. . . ."

It was a black-and-white picture and the high winds outside were shaking the antenna, making the screen flicker, but I could hear Tony Martin singing "I Hear a Rhapsody" while the lower classes danced in the beachfront bar and Robert Ryan was being nasty to Paul Douglas. Barbara Stanwyck was married to big, bluff, kindly Paul but she had the hots for lean, hungry psycho Robert, who ran the projector at the little movie house. It was *Clash by Night* from a lot of years ago but I'd enjoyed it when it was new and I was enjoying it now that it was old. I was drinking a cold Grain Belt and Barbara Stanwyck was looking sexy and cynical, saying tough things to Robert to show him she cared: "If I ever loved a man again . . . he could have my teeth for watch fobs!"

Watch fobs, indeed.

"You impress me as a man who needs a new suit of clothes or a new love affair," she said, giving Robert the old one-two. "But he doesn't know which." That really made him mad and I sat there enjoying his seething. Then I put down the beer and picked up the stack of snapshots, which indicated quite clearly why Sam Proctor had bought the Leica. There were twelve pictures, two of Anne by herself, six of the two women together from different angles, and four of Kim, two standing by the net and two in action, stroking the ball.

I peered at her, trying to see into the third dimension.

Hitting a forehand: arm straight, eyes watching the blur of white coming off the racket, a tip of tongue clenched between her teeth, pigtails flying. Backhand: almost on tiptoes, slicing a shot coming too close to her body, face a mask of concentration, her one-piece two-tone tennis dress molded back against her strong thighs and slender torso. By the net, in close-up as Sam found out what his camera could do, she gave him a faint smile in one shot, sweat running down her face, eyes boring into the camera. Again, off guard, she looked away, long fingers brushing perspiration from an eyebrow, a pigtail tied with a ribbon hanging forward over a shoulder. Her dark hair was pulled tight, her skin dark and smooth and youthful; I'd have called her twenty-five at the most, yet I knew I was a decade off. For some reason my stomach clenched up as I stared at the pictures. She frightened me and I had no idea why; she was just a woman, of course, but she'd been a different woman for everyone I'd questioned.

Her dark eyes returned my stare.

Hubbard Anthony had called her the sort of person who made a strong impression on you, always busy, always working, being helpful, always bettering herself.

Harriet Dierker had said she was as good as a murderer, a hellion, a witch, lovely to look at, the sort of woman the word "bitch" was invented for, a tempt-

ress, always bending over and stretching and showing
her legs. . . .

But Tim Dierker had refused to say anything at all.

Bill Oliver had noticed a good deal more than he
thought he had: businesslike, never a hair out of place,
clothes just perfect, the way a certain kind of woman
always was.

For my father she was the sort of female who gets
talked about, with a trim figure, a solemn face, dark
eyebrows, shining hair. She had seemed a sexual creature to him: He'd said it made you wonder if she had
a line of that dark hair going up her belly; that was the
way she made him think. . . .

For Darwin McGill she was a cockteaser. "I
pulled her brassiere off," he'd said, "and there were
these tiny round tits . . . with big stiff nipples. . . .
She told me that I was just one step from losing my
job and facing a criminal action. She was so composed, Paulie, I just felt like I wanted to hide. . . ."

But Anne had had another view altogether, finding
her terrified of sex, frigid, so competent and organized and neat and determined. She thought I'd have
liked Kim, and what the hell was that supposed to
mean?

It didn't hang together; it was a patchwork of con-
tradictions and I couldn't piece it together. I couldn't
help but wonder if what I was really getting was a
series of impressions revealing more about the speakers than about the subject. I sat staring at the television picture for a long time. Tony Martin was
singing "I Hear a Rhapsody."

I finally padded on down the hallway to go to bed.
Someone had slipped a small envelope under my door.
Sighing aloud from weariness, I picked it up. It was
a note from Harriet Dierker on paper with a Raggedy
Ann doll smiling in one corner. Larry Blankenship
was being buried in the morning and she thought I
might want to attend the graveside service. She gave
me the details. She was a presumptuous little woman.
But I went to bed, eschewing my baseball researches,
and before I slept I decided I'd better attend.

Larry Blankenship's funeral was a peculiarly tearless affair and had something about it of an old fraternity meeting, something musty like the feel of Pa Dierker's handshake. It took me awhile to catch the falsity of it; it was a breezy, cool morning with the treetops rustling in the characteristic solemn hush of the cemetery. Past the various gray marble gravestones, past the trees and the iron fence, cars sped along a parkway but they were soundless, gliding.

I had gotten to the cemetery early while the other mourners were at the church. Standing on top of a gentle knoll, with a huge elm rustling overhead, I leaned on a very old, cracked marker and watched the hearse lead the small parade through the high gate, around the reflecting pool, and along the path of finely crushed pinkish gravel. There weren't many cars following the black Cadillac hearse but they were all top of the line: Mark IV's, Cadillacs, Mercedes. For a guy who never quite made it, who was such a persistent loser, Blankenship had very tony friends.,

I'm not sure who I thought would be there. But it didn't take a genius to identify them, particularly having had access to my father's photograph albums. One at a time they emerged from their automobiles, stood blinking in the sunshine before moving off across the green.

Father Martin Boyle arrived in the midnight-blue Cadillac limousine driven by another priest, doubtless Father Patulski, his housemate. Boyle was round, rolled when he walked, stumping a bit with the aid of a blackthorn stick, knobbed and lethal-looking. His gout must have been bothering him. His thin hair, red still glittering through the gray, blew silky in the wind and wraparound dark glasses hid his eyes. He plodded toward the open grave with its mound of moist dark earth.

The Dierkers came next in their Mercedes sedan. Pa shambled on the grass and Ma, birdlike, held his arm, steadying him. He looked pale, a sick man with his sickness accentuated by the string tie which seemed to be part of the uniform the gravebound habitually affected. His suit hung obscenely, like loose flesh, a skin about to be shucked. His wife looked like his keeper.

James Crocker, still giving off the illusion of fitness regardless of his heart troubles, drove himself in a gunmetal-gray Mark IV. He was wearing a dark-blue suit, carefully shaped, the vanity of an old athlete. His hair was silvery, wavey, thick; his glasses were heavy black plastic. He spoke briefly to Pa Dierker, then fell in beside the two priests. He looked fit enough to climb up and man a bulldozer himself; I'd have bet he spent a good deal of his time in a hard hat where the buildings were coming down and the buildings were going up.

General Goode looked very little changed from the old days when he'd learned I was going to Scandinavia and had asked me to deliver a package in a village not far from Helsinki. For a long time I'd thought him an evil, perverse man, and then I'd undergone some slippage. Perhaps he'd been as much a victim as I. But it had taken a great many nights with the baseball-record books to get rid of the picture of the old man dying.

Now Jon Goode was walking toward the gravesite looking almost unchanged; medium height but looking taller because of the formality of his carriage, the leanness, the gray hair cropped down close to his small, squared skull. He was wearing a navy blazer, dark-gray slacks, a white shirt, and a rep tie. His face and hands were deeply tanned and my father was with him looking rumpled in a blue cord suit.

I didn't move from my observation point as the casket was carried to the grave and placed across the heavy tapes which would lower it into the earth. Though I couldn't hear what was being said, I could see that the minister, a young fellow with a bookish, white face, had begun to speak when another car wheeled up the path: a bronze Mark IV gleaming in the sun like a lump of gold. Another older man got out quickly from behind the wheel and opened the passenger door.

She looked exactly as I expected.

Ole Kronstrom walked beside her to the group of

mourners as heads turned, sensing the new arrival. Since the ceremony of burial had begun without them, I assumed Kim Roderick and Ole Kronstrom had not attended the church services. They stood somewhat apart from the others and while he looked steadfastly at the minister and then bowed his head for the prayer; she peered into the grave, slowly moved her head to watch the others. She wasn't paying any attention to the minister; she was too curious. Her appearance was as advertised: sleeveless dark-blue dress, blue shoes, very darkly tanned arms and legs, dark hair curling under at her shoulders and held in place by a wide headband. It startled me when her gaze carefully moved upward and found me, as if she expected me to be there. I felt myself shrinking inwardly, knowing that I was reacting illogically, but unable to stop. Her gaze held me for a long time, as if to say, *I'll remember you and you'll be sorry,* and finally, as the minister concluded his remarks and the casket was lowered, she broke away and went to shake his hand.

Watching from the hillside gave me a sort of second-balcony perspective. I could see the choreography as one by one the men came toward her, each one taking her hand in his, a few words being spoke, then passing her on to the next member of the dance. She did almost nothing, acknowledging them with a nod, waiting for them to finish. The Dierkers stood near the grave, which was flanked by several arrays of yellow flowers. Harriet finally jerked her arm away from her husband's and strode off to their car, leaving him alone and old and weak. He took a tentative step forward, arms stiff and a few inches from his sides, seeking the proper balance. Then he gathered steam and walked slowly toward her. He was the last one and she was alone, waiting for him; at my distance it was impossible to know whether she was being patient or imperious, making him come the whole way by himself.

He was still huge in comparison to her and he leaned forward slightly to address her, using his grip on her hands for support. She listened at length, nodded, then spoke briefly, looked over toward where Harriet sat in the car. Then he made his way tortoise-

like across the rich greenery and she was alone. Ole
Kronstrom walked back to the car with Dierker, the
two old partners approaching the end so differently.

I watched Kim go to the grave again, saw her sigh,
with her shoulders giving a little heave as she said
good-bye to the loser who had been her husband. She
was quick and determined going back to the car. Ole
broke away and went with her and the cars slowly
peeled away. There were big white clouds jamming
up over the city by then and just a touch of moisture
was in the air.

General Goode and my father were the last to leave
and I went down the hill to join them. Goode smiled
ambiguously and said it was nice to see me again. I
wondered if he even remembered what he'd gotten me
into in Finland.

"Well, you got to see her," Archie said, squinting
at me with a malicious little grin. "I wasn't sure she
was going to show up at all."

"Was she the only family he had?"

"So far as I know," Goode said quickly. "Orphan,
I guess." He wore a thin gray mustache and his ice-
water eyes gave me a chill, like a cloud across the sun.
"She was holding up quite well," he said.

"Why not? It was all over between them." My father was a realist. "When it's over, it's over." He
shrugged. There was no more to the conversation and
after they'd gone I walked back across the lawn,
watched the workmen filling the grave. The clouds
really were beginning to nip at the edges of the sunshine. Did old men go to a funeral and wonder how
much time they had left? Dierker and Father Boyle
did not seem to be in very robust health. Did they dwell
on how short their futures might be?

There had been something wrong about the funeral
and I couldn't quite name it. I walked back up the
knoll, across another stretch of lawn, where a sprinkler was keeping things green and healthy. Mark
Bernstein, a shadowy presence I'd not seen before,
slid into a police cruiser and glided away. The bedraggled Porsche sat under a tree, ugly but comfortable with its rusty body and balding tires. As I drove

back to my office to deliver some stray book reviews which I'd completed a couple of weeks before and forgotten, I realized what had been wrong.

. It had looked like a family funeral. But it wasn't. Only the hunting and fishing club had been there, with the exception of Hub Anthony, who had a heavy work load. Had they been there as friends of Larry Blankenship? Or of his wife? It bothered me because it didn't seem quite real. There was something stagy about it, almost as if attendance had been required. But why?

There were other questions in my mind as I sat in the cluttered office, watching the afternoon turn gray. Who had been emptying Larry's apartment of the little personal bits and pieces? What had been going on between Kim and Larry in the parking lot the day Bill Oliver had seen them?

And why the hell did I care?

It was raining hard when I finally got home. The windshield wipers on the Porsche didn't work, which made getting home a treat. I fixed eggs and tomatoes and sausage and toast and sat on my balcony eating and getting damp, washing it down with a Bloody Mary. No good movies on the tube, no ball game; I put an opera on the record player and cleaned my plate and poured another Bloody Mary. I watched the rain, heard the girl laughing in another apartment—same girl as always. Her life must have been excruciatingly funny. I felt as if I were waiting for something.

It happened about ten o'clock. I was half asleep and the rain was still falling steadily, almost quietly. But I saw it go by my balcony, plummeting soundlessly through the rain. A bundle of somebody's dirty clothes, a joke. But it had arms and legs. I was terribly slow on the uptake, wondering if I'd seen it in my sleep.

I got wet looking over the railing. Whatever it was, it was lying in the street far below and it wasn't moving. It was just lying there in the rain.

I called the office in the lobby, realized it was

closed, put on my raincoat, and went down to Oliver's
apartment on the other side of the building. He swore
when I told him what I'd seen and together we ran
through the first level of indoor parking and out onto
the sidewalk.

The body had made a huge dent in the hood of a
new white Pontiac Grand Prix, glanced off, and
landed face down in the street. It was soaked and the
head was split open and the mouth was a dark wound,
blood-covered, as if the force of the impact had exploded outward like vomit. Water was damming up
against the body, drumming on the white car, soaking
us. Oliver looked at me, looked up at the building, rain
washing down his face. He was pale.

We didn't touch the body. Oliver picked up a soggy
slipper of gray fur which had been jolted off on the
other side of the car. It looked like a wet, dead animal. I remembered where I'd seen the gray stuff.

Pa Dierker was dead now and very messy with one
naked foot flung out like a bit of bone.

5

IT WAS a pearl-gray morning with mist hanging like
netting from the trees in Loring Park. I had an early
appointment with Bernstein at the courthouse, where
he worked in a tight little office just off the squad room,
a floor beneath the slammer itself. The traffic was sorting itself out more slowly than usual and I listened to
WCCO, the ubiquitous radio station, which was indulging itself in an orgy of self-congratulation on its
fiftieth birthday. They were working on my kind of
music, the kind you don't hear anymore. Somebody
with a mean sax was playing "At Last" and I remembered the words from a long time ago. I'd romanced
Anne to old stuff like that and we'd made love to

Claude Thornhill recordings, which probably made her think I was insane. "At Last" carried me down Memory Lane, Third Avenue, and into Court Park.

Bernstein was sort of white-on-white, nubby silk suit in gray with too much padding in the shoulders, Sulka tie: he looked like Francis Ford Coppola's idea of a fifties Mafia baron. I didn't know to whom this image was designed to appeal but it wasn't going to get him elected mayor, which was probably for the best, so I didn't say anything. He made a sour face, looking as if he'd been at work too long already, and we went to the coffee machine in the hall. He also got a sweet roll wrapped in a plastic diaper. The nutlike protuberances on top looked as if they'd have been at home with an archaeologist. We went outside and leaned against the wall of the building, where cops kept bustling past us in both directions.

"Murder," he said, crackling the wrapper, probing the roll with his finger. "Skin on his hands and feet all scraped to hell, little shreds of Pa Dierker stuck to the building. He didn't want to go over but he just didn't have the strength to keep it from happening. He probably didn't know what was happening until it was too late. So, you know the routine, he knew who did it, probably trusted whoever it was . . . that loose gravel on the roof near the railing, like a warning track on a ball field, it's all pushed around where they were standing and where they struggled. But beyond that, nothing—not the size of shoes, height and weight of the assailant, or the color of eyes." He bit into the roll and quickly washed it down with coffee. He was wearing heavy glasses and they were sliding down his broad, humped nose.

"Any motive? Have you talked to anybody yet?"

"Yeah, I talked to his wife and it's a good thing I did, right then, because once the shock set in she pretty well turned to stone. I talked to her nurse this morning and she hasn't said a word since I left her last night."

"Motive?"

"What motive, for Chrissakes? He's a harmless old man, Paul, he's already ticketed for a hole in the ground—the wife told me that, he had two or three months. . . . I mean, he wasn't gonna make it to Christmas, dead cert. So why kill him?"

"Maybe the killer didn't know that."

"All you had to do was look, he was a precorpse. Whoever wanted him dead wanted the personal satisfaction of killing him. That's my only theory." He flicked a nut off into the street and bit the soft part; being a detective was no snap.

"Is that it? That can't be all, Mark?"

"Before she went catatonic on us, all she'd talk about was this Kim Blankenship, or Roderick—let's call her Roderick. She said that Kim had something to do with her husband's death—said Kim had gone out of her way to talk to him at the cemetery, at Blankenship's funeral—"

"Vice versa, Tim took the initiative in the talking, but the point is they talked, I suppose."

"I know, I was there, but wait, there's more. He refused to talk to his wife the rest of the day, that's yesterday. She doesn't know what Kim said to him but she insists it made him act funny. Back in their apartment he had several drinks, which he wasn't supposed to do, and then he began to cry sitting in his chair. When she tried to comfort him he shoved her away, actually knocked her down. At that point she thought to hell with him, got dressed, and went to her bridge club with Helga Kronstrom. The last time she saw him he was sitting in his chair, the TV on, drinking, and she was just furious. She said she knew Kim had made him like that and he told her to shut up and get the hell out." He peered up at me over the rim of the bun. "Feisty old bastard, right? I think I'd of liked him. . . ." He finished the roll, stared at his sticky hands. "Anyway, let's see—ah, the scrapbook. He was sitting there with the old scrapbook or photo album they'd kept for years, looking at pictures of the vacation they'd taken back in '38 to Banff, a trip to New York, Hawaii after the war, stuff dating way back."

"Pictures from up north, too, I suppose," I said. "The club? The old days?"

"How should I know?"

"But he did have pictures from up north?"

"Paul," he said, losing patience, "how the hell should I know?"

"I guess we can just look in the scrapbook," I said primarily to myself.

"There's a little problem."

"You're kidding."

"Gone. Not in the apartment, not in the building's trash, not on the roof. Nowhere."

"Killer took it."

"Very good," he said, heading back inside the thick walls, into the sweating corridors. He ran a drinking bubbler stream over his hands and patted them dry with his monogrammed handkerchief.

"So what are you going to do?" His heels clicked on the marble floor. "You're a detective, Mark. You've got a dead guy."

"Check out his friends, but it's not easy. One, they're very snotty, powerful old farts who don't like Jews running for mayor in the first place, let alone involving them in murder investigations."

"You're too other-directed," I said.

"Two, who does he interact with? His doctor and his wife and his pacemaker. Very limited life at this point. So who's gonna kill him?"

"He talked to Larry Blankenship."

"Well, nobody heard them, Paul, and they're both dead, so you can drop that. His wife—she gonna kill him? Peck him to death? No way, she's airtight, right at the old bridge table and a dozen cronies in the same room. His old Norway Creek pals? My God, the idea is ludicrous. Kim? Okay, say Harriet's got something —I'm supposed to believe the lady throws him off the roof? What's she got to do with Tim Dierker?" We stopped at the door to the squad room and I didn't envy him his surrounding. "Dead end. So I'll poke a little bit and not try to get all het up. . . ."

Mark Bernstein's approach to the murder of Timothy Dierker wasn't very inspiring but I could see how unpromising the problem seemed. Where did you begin? So he assigned a couple of men to interview the building's inhabitants and check on anyone seen in the hallways who wasn't identifiable, to interview the staff and the Pinkerton night man and, presumably, the Pinkerton dog. It was a painstaking detail job and Mark didn't want to think about it. I couldn't really blame him. But I wasn't burdened with the search for details; I could look for the main chance, the long shot.

I had a late breakfast at The Hungry Eye. The guy in the next booth was listening to a transistor radio. It was another hideously depressing newscast about President Gerald Ford and Nixon, neither of whom had the charisma of Mark Bernstein, whose career might just be beginning. In a world with Ford and Nixon, with the smugness of a city like Minneapolis, where everything was so perfect and moral and came so easy, then everything might come to pass. Even Mark Bernstein. The fact that each day produced a new version of Mark Bernstein would logically work in his favor, would keep you from getting the other ones into proper focus.

I parked in the fire lane again and went upstairs to the Dierker apartment. I knocked and a small woman in starchy white opened the door and said Mrs. Dierker was indisposed. I was explaining who I was when a tall, angular woman came out of the darkened living room and took over. If Ma Dierker was a sparrow or even a shrike, this lady was an eagle.

"Mr. Cavanaugh? I'm Helga Kronstrom," she said, curling a wide mouth back past yellowing buck teeth. It was almost a nice smile. Her flowered dress, necklace, bracelet, earrings—everything matched the tobacco stains on her teeth. "Harriet has told me of her confidence in you, Mr. Cavanaugh. So it's almost as if we know each other, you know about me, I know at least a little something about you." She backed away with a formal gesture of entry, watching her, you know right away that she'd always looked the way she did just then and always would. She reminded me of a grade-school teacher I'd once had and I wondered if

Ole felt the same way. I thought of the snapshots I'd seen last night of Kim. It was an unfair world.

She ushered me into the living room, curtains drawn, Harriet Dierker lying on the couch with a washcloth folded across her eyes. She seemed to be asleep. Helga Kronstrom sat on a straight-backed chair and I found myself being motioned to Tim's chair. It felt like a sickroom.

"How is she?" I asked.

"As you'd expect," Helga Kronstrom said. "She knew Tim was dying, of course, but this is entirely different." She lit a cigarette and the cloud of smoke seemed to make the room tighter, hotter. "Murder," she said simply.

"Can you imagine why?" I said.

She stared at Mrs. Dierker for a long time and I waited her out.

"I understand that you know about Kim," she said at last, continuing to watch the inert form on the couch. "As you might imagine, I'm not one to be objective about Kim. And I won't bore you by dwelling on my grievances. But remember, Mr. Cavanaugh, that two men have died violently in the last few days and both of them . . . knew her." She sighed, eyes cold with what could have been sadness. "Her husband, of course. And Timothy, who had helped her, used his influence in her behalf at Norway Creek. You might say they had her in common." She finally turned back to me, her eyes half shut behind the smoke. Harriet Dierker snored lightly, turned on the couch, and brushed her hand across her face.

"That does seem to be stretching a point," I said gently. "I mean, a dislike—however justified—is no reason to suggest someone is a murderer." Both Harriet and Helga apparently were obsessed with the woman, and who the hell needed that? I wished I hadn't come.

"I'm not a fool, or I try not to be. And long ago I accepted my husband's frailty. But before you write me, and Harriet, for that matter, all the way off, you'd do well to learn something about this Kim. You've not met her, I take it?" I shook my head. "She is quite capable of anything, I assure you. She preys on men, her whole history is the same story."

"Has she preyed on your . . . on Ole?"

"Yes, I would call it that. On his weakness. His innocence."

"Which innocence is that?"

"Ole Kronstrom is a very simple man. I know that better than anyone else, Mr. Cavanaugh. A fundamentalist, an innocent, and she played on his misguided sense of—" She broke off and bit her thin bluish lip, the cigarette cocked short of her mouth. It seemed that she hadn't accepted Ole's departure as calmly as she'd thought. "I am not going to talk about it anymore. Not just now."

"His misguided sense of what?"

"Paul, don't badger her. Please." It was Harriet, lifting the cloth back from her face, speaking from the recesses of sedation. Nobody wanted to talk about it so I expressed my sorrow at what had happened the night before. I sounded ridiculous. Harriet croaked out the same story she'd told Bernstein: Pa refusing to talk to her, getting drunk, knocking her down and abusing her, going over the scrapbook and crying. She didn't know what it meant but Kim was part of it. The scrapbook was gone, she knew that for sure. She lapsed back into silence, the nurse came in to take her pulse, and Helga saw me to the door.

"Harriet tells me that you are looking into the reason for Larry Blankenship's suicide. Is that the case?"

"Yes, I guess it is," I said.

"Well, please listen to what I tell you." I felt as if she were giving me an assignment and I was ten years old. "The answer to one is part of the answer to the other." She shook her head, the grin struggling to return, rather ghastly, like an apparition. "Murder," she said softly. "When will she be done with us?"

Then I went away, leaving them with their obsession and sorrow.

The Twins were making up an earlier rainout so it was a twi-night doubleheader starting at six. I'd finished some work and had grilled knockwurst on my balcony, opened a Grain Belt, and settled down to listen to the game. The weather had cleared off but it was cool and I'd pulled a sweater on; maybe the summer was gone, snap, like a light going off. I turned to *The Baseball Encyclopedia* to check on Roy Smalley, the Cub shortstop of my youth. Ah, where was he now? And where was the boy I'd been? They didn't make shortstops like Smalley anymore but then what could you expect? The Golden Age was over, kid, hadn't you heard?

But the game wasn't working. I wondered briefly if I should tape the double-header. I had a library of taped baseball games, just regular everyday games; they helped to pass long winter nights when the movies on the tube were too new, no longer a part of the Golden Age. I didn't tape the double-header, though. Instead I thought about Timothy Dierker's scrapbook, wondering what it could have contained, why the murderer would take it away. What could it contain that the murderer wanted to keep or didn't want anyone else to find? Banff? Hawaii? New York? None of that made sense to me; all I could connect was the hunting and fishing club stuff, but that seemed almost equally farfetched. Just more familiar. I'd spent an afternoon going over Archie's pictures. Were Archie's pictures and Tim's the same? Had I seen what the murderer had taken away? Maybe, but I wouldn't have recognized it as a motive for murder, if indeed it was. Circles going nowhere. Who cleaned out Larry Blankenship's dreary little place? What had been taken? And did the same person take the scrapbook and Larry's bits and pieces? Talk about a headache. . . .

I didn't think about it for long. The Twins were batting in the bottom of the third when the telephone rang.

"Is this Paul Cavanaugh?" It was a woman, abrupt, quiet.

"Yes, speaking."

"My name is Kim Roderick, Mr. Cavanaugh. We haven't met but I'm beginning to feel as if I know you. And I must tell you that I'm not in the least enjoying it. I've been told by two people that you have been asking questions about my personal life. Whatever reasons you may have, I suspect they are insufficient. I want it stopped. You are making me very uncomfortable and very cross." There was a lot of silence while she let me think it over with the ball bouncing around in my court; I saw her in black and white, tensing, hair flying, about to hit her backhand. Her voice made me feel cold.

"Are you always this aggressive?"

"I am angry, Mr. Cavanaugh. And perplexed by what you are doing. Is that clear?"

"Abundantly. Look, I'm sorry if I've disturbed you. . . ."

"For disturbing me."

"Well, there are lots of disturbed people, Mrs. Roderick—"

"Miss Roderick."

"Lots of disturbed people everywhere I turn. Now, I don't want to be overly aggressive myself, you understand, but you're last in line at the moment. I've done nothing to invade your privacy. I have merely asked some innocent questions. Maybe I'm just working myself up to ask for a date. Have you considered that possibility?"

"It'll be a waste of time, Mr. Cavanaugh. You're not my type and I do consider it not only an invasion of my privacy but harassment as well. I don't want to argue about it. I want it stopped."

"Miss Roderick, you bring out the absolute worst in me. Why did Larry Blankenship kill himself?" I heard a little gasp which I found very satisfying and went resolutely on. "And who murdered Tim Dierker last night?" I began to whistle "Yes, Sir, That's My Baby" in the silence which followed, rather a nice touch.

"Who are you, Mr. Cavanaugh?"

"You answer my questions and I'll answer yours."

"I did not know Timothy Dierker was . . . dead. You took me by surprise."

"Your surprise is nothing compared to Tim's. As far as you're concerned, Miss Roderick, I'm simply trying to fill in the blanks. For a friend of mine. And I think I'm going to stay at it for a while."

"I think we'd better talk," she said. "We're off to a bad start." The words were vaguely conciliatory but her voice was coming from another planet. "Are you free tomorrow morning?"

"Yes. Where and when?"

"Here. Riverfront Towers. Eleven o'clock. Is that all right?"

"Sure. That's fine." She hung up before I finished.

She'd unnerved me, set my chest hopping about like something skittish and afraid. I spread the photographs of her out on my desk but looking at them made my mouth dry. I scooped them up, dropped them into a drawer, and made a list of the members of the club. I put Father Martin Boyle at the top by sheer chance, looked up his address in the telephone directory, and decided to drop by for a chat. Maybe he could remember something about those times up north, some reason why a murderer would steal an ancient scrapbook. A feast of memories.

Prospect Park is a slightly tacky high-rent district sequestered among trees and narrow curving streets, just off the bustle of University Avenue where Minneapolis and St. Paul converge in an array of warehouses, an Octopus Car Wash, some fast-food joints. The houses are large and canted against hillsides, the sidewalks are full of cracks and sprouts of grass, and you can walk to the University of Minnesota. Most of the park's residents are academics of one kind or another. Looking over their lives is a tower rising up from the crest of the hill at the park's center. When I left the Porsche sagging disconsolately beside the crumbling curb, the tower had lost its pointed top in fog coming up off the Mississippi across the East River Road.

Father Boyle's house was a large old frame affair that looked comfortable and needed paint. I climbed the two long steep flights of steps and was puffing when I rang the bell. It took some time but Boyle himself, leaning on a cane, finally answered it. He was wearing baggy tweed pants, a white shirt with the collar open to make room for heavy jowls, and a heavy cardigan. He had a stubble of white beard on his cheeks, a cigar clamped in the corner of his mouth, and in the light from the hallway his eyes had an unhealthy opacity which turned what had once been bright blue to a luminous gray.

I introduced myself as Archie Cavanaugh's son and he smiled broadly, the face of a garrulous man who loved to talk, motioned me inside, where the smell of cigar smoke had permeated everything, the walls, the draperies, the furniture. He had been the church's emissary to the university's student body for a long time. He was accustomed to visitors, practiced at making them feel at ease. He wheezed and mumbled as we went the length of the hallway, keeping a running conversation going all by himself; he waddled, spoke with a hint of brogue, and I wondered how he got around the golf course.

"Come on," he said, leading me into a large bookish room at the back of the main floor. "My study," he rumbled, "I hope you can stand the heat. It dries out the air on these foggy nights and my leg likes it hot and dry. Siddown, siddown. I'll get us a nip." He had a fire going in an oversize brickfront fireplace with his immense, bloated leather chair pulled up close. A small gout stool stood in front of the chair. While he got a tray of glasses and bottles I settled on a couch Freud might have used and checked the surroundings; threadbare Oriental rug, dark woodwork, leaded glass in the windows and bookcases, the remains of a pot-roast dinner on a heavy round table, an aged painting of an English countryside with a fox hunt in full cry. He came back and set the tray on an end table. "Irish whiskey, two fingers, it's my drink," he said. He put a recording of Chopin mazurkas on the Thorens turntable, flicked a couple of switches on the Pioneer receiver, and the sound began purring softly from speakers which bulked darkly in corners. With a deep, contented sigh he eased himself down into the overflowing chair and propped his slippered foot onto the stool. He toasted me with his glass, radiating the sensuality of a truly self-indulgent man, and asked what he could do for me. I told him that I was a friend of Tim Dierker's, that I'd had a talk with him just recently, that I was upset by his death. He frowned, nodding.

"It was the manner of his going, eh? We're all about to cross that bar, all of us elderly folks, and death doesn't hold quite the fears it once did . . . but to die the way Timothy did, now, there's an unpleasant death. Upsetting, yes, it is." He puffed at the wet-ended cigar, closed his eyes. "A Detective Bernstein, fella running for mayor, called me today, asked me what I made of it. . . What the devil could I say? What could I make of it?"

"I suppose he wanted a lead on a motive," I said.

"Violence—we live in an age of brute force, don't we? And since when has evil needed a motive? Crime, I'm thinking, is less involved with motive every day. We breed it here, in this time and this place, an incalculable evil. Don't you agree? My friend Father Patulski lives here with me, is fascinated by the existence of evil, acts as if it's something he's newly discovered—tonight where is he? Having a second look at *The Exorcist*. Can you beat it? Once wasn't enough for him. . . ." He shook his head at Patulski's innocence. "I can't remember a time when I didn't recognize evil, it's always been there, hasn't it? Now and again it rears up, spits at us, takes a life or corrupts a soul, submerges once again. Ah, I live with it. . . . Patulski believes in the power of goodness and faith, evil therefore attracts him. I believe in the power of evil, the banality of it, and I am almost bored by it. Evil sometimes wins, which is what Patulski cannot quite understand. Timothy Dierker, my old friend, is thrown off a high building—faith won't change that, will it? Dead as a doornail and we'd better hope his soul was in decent repair. . . ."

"Are you talking about some abstract evil?" I asked. "A *man,* someone he knew, took him up on that roof and pushed him off, someone with a reason. Bernstein is not impressed with philosophical evil, I'm afraid. He wants to know who wanted Tim Dierker dead—"

"I know who did it," Father Boyle said. I blinked. "A tormented soul, Mr. Cavanaugh, and does it matter just whose? Milton said it and it applies.

So farewell hope, and, with hope, farewell fear,
Farewell remorse; all good to me is lost.
Evil, be thou my good.

"Someone has said, 'Evil, be thou my good,' and killed Tim Dierker. Find that poor soul and for whatever good it does you, you'll have found a murderer." He drank his Irish whiskey and lapsed into silence, staring opaquely into the fire. "Patulski should be here. He could talk of the possessed, how evil infests a man. . . ."

"Did you ever read Conrad's *Under Western Eyes?*" I asked, dredging up an old quote.

"No, I never have. Though I expect Patulski has, a fellow countryman and all."

"Conrad had an idea about evil, too, Father. He said, 'The belief in a supernatural source of evil is not necessary. Men alone are quite capable of every wickedness.' Maybe I'm a subscriber to that one." The heat was making me sticky. A breeze wafted from an open window; I felt it shimmer along the back of my neck.

"Conrad believed in men," he said slowly. "I believe in the Devil. Among others. A personification of evil, the Devil. The problem is he has all the good times, or so I suspect. . . . He whispers behind the leaves, he rides outside and takes the hindmost, he is the author of confusion." He belched deep in his chest and looked at me. "Anyway, the man is dead and you want a reason why and you can't prosecute the Devil. I understand. I was merely indulging myself." He dribbled more whiskey into his tumbler.

"Do you have a scrapbook, a photo album? I was going through my father's the other day, looking at his old photographs of the bunch that used to go up north. . . I'm thinking of writing a piece on the north country and maybe using a photograph or two from those days to illustrate—" I wanted to get him on another track altogether. I didn't know what was going on in his mind or how much he had been drinking before I got there. I wanted to see his scrapbook, though, without alarming him.

"Somewhere," he rumbled again, almost sleepily. He brushed the white stubble; he seemed so much older than Archie. He seemed a man who had lived hard, unusual for a priest. He pushed himself out of the chair and, leaning on his cane, hobbled to a cabinet beneath a bookcase. After rummaging among stacks of papers, folders, journals, and magazines, he pulled a thick volume free of the litter. "Here," he said. He pushed the dinner dishes away and flopped the album down on the table. "I haven't looked in this book for twenty-five years, young man. . . ." I stood beside him as he slowly turned the pages past vestiges of a life which meant nothing to me. There were pictures of him with a series of young girls, invariably attractive across the years, then the young theological student in the company of others like himself. No more girls, at least not for picture taking. It must have been difficult for him: Why had he taken the turn he did? His faith was in the Devil, not man, but maybe that was whiskey talking, or maybe he'd meant merely that this trust was in the abstract, not the refuse of everyday life. How do you ever know what anybody else means anyway?

"There's Archie," I said. "This is the stuff I wanted to see."

His face was changing ever so slightly, as if the yellowing photographs were soaking up what life remained in him, as if the vigor of them drained away the strength of the old man he had become. "A long time ago, too damn long ago." He sighed, his breath whistling in his throat. I heard him muffle a belch, smelled his whiskey breath as he bent near me. The photographs were much the same as Archie's, the same scenes of camaraderie. Sociably I asked him to identify the various people; I wanted him to keep the album out so I could wander across the photographs in search of something which could strike me as anyway out of the ordinary—something a murderer would haul away with him. I knew it was almost pointless since I had no idea what I was looking for, but you never knew. He went through several rows of pictures, identifying people I knew. In one he gave the woman who kept house a name: "Rita," he said, just "Rita." And later, looking somewhat embarrassed by the attention, an ageless-looking Indian in a worn leather jacket and work pants; "Willie, he was our guide, hunting or fishing, he knew that country better than any map. Lived up there all his life. Absolutely at home, the deeper into the woods, the better. Willie. . . ." The memories were draining him off. I could feel him growing remote from me, as if he were slipping back into a lost and plainly preferable time.

"My God," he said softly, thinking aloud, "there's Carver Maxvill. Poor old Carver. I hadn't thought of him in years and years. . . ." He bent lower over the album, bringing the old days into better focus.

"Who was he?" I asked. "I hadn't heard of him before."

Father Boyle looked up sharply, accusingly. I'd become suddenly an unwelcome intrusion. "What?"

I pointed with my finger. "That one," I said, "who was he?"

"Maxvill, Carver Maxvill. He dropped out of the club long ago—that's all."

"My father never mentioned him."

"Not important. They probably didn't really know each other." He shrugged, rubbed his eyes. "Not important. I can't ever remember him." He straightened up. "I'm tired, young man. End of interview." He was gruff; he had undergone an abrupt change, startling me. He slammed the album shut, a mist of fine dust rising like faint specters. He shuffled across the skimpy carpet to the cabinet and shoved it roughly back in among the books and papers. "All this stuff depresses me," he muttered. "I'm old and unwell and that's that, Mr. Cavanaugh. No more prying into the past." He was a different man. He had even paled.

He stood staring at me, the friendliness gone from his face, his stance, his manner. He had become an almost ominous hulk, staring at me with the Chopin going on and on.

"Funny thing about the scrapbook," I said. "Tim Dierker had one, for instance. He was looking through it yesterday afternoon." I'd caught his attention. "The last time his wife saw him he was sitting in his chair looking at pictures just like yours . . . and crying. Now, doesn't that strike you as curious, Father? Why would he be crying?"

"Not so curious, no, not at all. I could have cried myself." He was moving me into the hallway. "I understand exactly why he was crying." His cigar had gone out, sticking out of the corner of his mouth like something held tight in a trap.

"Well, how about this one, then? Maybe you can help me out. . . . The album disappeared when Tim went off the roof. The murderer, you see, stole it. That's right, stole it, took it away with him. Now, the question is why. Why would the murderer want an old photograph album? What could there have been among those photographs? Now, that is curious, isn't it?"

Frighteningly, he began to quiver as if stricken with a palsy. He lurched at me, leaning heavily on his cane, passing a hand across his pale face where his nose shone like a hot coal.

"Are you all right, Father?"

He nodded, brushing me away.

Finally he said, "Go away, just go away. I'm overtired, worn out. Just leave me alone." He leaned on a small table before a mirror, swallowing dryly; there were two of him just then, like distorted figures in a fun house.

"One last thing," I said heartlessly, standing in the doorway. "Do you know Kim Roderick? What do you think of her?"

"Of course I know her . . . knew her. We all knew her at Norway Creek, Mr. Cavanaugh." He coughed and threw the cigar out onto the lawn. I was forced out the door onto the stoop. The screen door closed; he was still a shape behind it; I could hear his rasping breath.

"But what did you think of her? What kind of person was she?"

"I have nothing to say on the subject," he wheezed, his voice growing weaker. He was sick and Tim Dierker had been sick. I should have been a doctor but I wasn't. I seemed to make everybody feel worse. "Not now, not later, not ever. The past is dead. . . . And you have taken advantage of my hospitality. Archie would be . . . disappointed in you. Archie would never take advantage, never." He gasped.

"Are you all right, Father? Can I do anything for you?"

He made a spitting noise and slammed the heavy inner door.

I drove around the town for a while, listening to the Porsche's peculiar noises in the fog, hearing the old Sinatra recording of "Time After Time" on Franklin Hobbs' late-night mood-music show, vowing to dig out my own copy. The thing that stuck in my mind was Father Boyle's fear, the change in his attitude once we began thumbing through the photographs. Fear—that was what I called it on reflection, but it could have been something more acute. Panic. Or more generalized: shock. But, whatever the degree, it all belonged to the same family of reactions and it didn't fit with the priesthood, at least not in my innocence. What frightens a priest?

Father Boyle had been coping ably enough with Tim Dierker's death. It was later that he began to come unstuck. But I couldn't cut it much closer than that. Had he seen what I'd been looking for, the reason Tim's scrapbook had been stolen? And if he had, why hadn't he explained it to me?

I always had plenty of questions. It was the answers that gave me trouble. What had turned him around?

And who was the new guy, what's his name? Carver Maxvill?

I had the distinct feeling that I was the only person who was really interested. Boyle wanted the past to stay dead and Bernstein wanted to be mayor and I wanted to find out what was going on. I would have welcomed someone to talk it over with but I was tired and it was late so I finally went home, discovered that the Twins had dropped two, and took Roy Smalley to bed with me. No hit, no field, but he had been the shortstop of my youth. I should have been a White Sox fan. They had Luke Appling. Now, there was a shortstop. . . .

6

RIVERFRONT Towers is tall with lots of geometry in its appearance, its shadow falling across the no-man's-land of scrub brush and oily roads and debris which lies like a trench between Minneapolis and the Mississippi. Riverfront Towers is a self-sufficient environment rising out of a not particularly pleasant sea of concrete, railway stations, cheap bars, derelicts' dying grounds, and soot-coated warehouses. But Riverfront Towers denies it all: It gleams in the sunlight and offers cheery surcease from the gray day and the cold; its fountains catch the spins of colored lights in a million refractions and the sidewalk is made of tile like marble and its inhabitants pride themselves on living in the city, in the welter of the city. Riverfront Towers, with its endlessly peering security system and army of guards and high fences and rooftop gardens and maximum lockup underground garage, is absolutely as close to the real city as Jupiter or Wayzata or the IDS boardroom.

The doorman matched the building: tall, newly scrubbed, and businesslike. Once I had identified whom I wanted to see and he had checked his various lists, he personally let me into the lobby and told me that Miss Roderick was playing tennis on court number four. I should just go out and sit down by the courts, he said, she was expecting me.

Kafka would have recognized the lobby. There was

no sign of human habitation. Somehow the plants flourished against the glass and steel walls; even the ashtrays were clean. Strategically placed black leather couches looked as if they'd never been used. I went outside into the courtyard, where the scent of flowers dropped over you like a gladiator's net and the sun fed the trees and shrubbery and beds of random color. I could hear a fountain splashing and the sound of tennis balls being whacked to and fro.

There were eight courts but only two were in use. Kim was playing on a corner court and I moved along the shadowy platform where ice cream tables stood beneath a long striped awning. A sign said that lunch would be served from eleven thirty. I sat down at a table near a large potted tree and watched. She had her back to me and she played intensely without noticing my arrival; her opponent wore a white floppy hat, moved his feet while giving his body a rest, and looked a lot like the Riverfront Towers pro. She moved gracefully, her thoughts anticipating the flow of the game and her body swinging along with it, nothing jerky. Her strokes were strong but he was beating her badly; he carried her through a rally of eight or ten strokes on each point, then put her away with a little cross-court backhand or a lob she'd return into the net or a passing shot as she decided to come to the net. Then, shaking her head, pigtails tied with yellow yarn, she'd go back to the service. She was serving every point and I had a perfect view of her; she got the ball very high over her head, bent back, and swept the racket through, came into position on the balls of her feet, bouncing lightly, moving quickly to the return. She was very slender from the waist up with long arms which helped her get to the ball; from the waist down she was strong and long-muscled and you could see the flex in her thighs and buttocks as she got her weight into the shot. She wore a one-piece A-line dress, pale cream with yellow trim, a white terry-cloth sweatband on her wrist, and a flowered bandanna wrapped around her forehead. She came to play.

Watching her, I remembered what Anne had said:

She was my type—and frigid, whatever that was supposed to imply. I wondered if Anne were right. On either count.

I'd been watching for about half an hour, wondering how this woman had come to affect so many lives in such a variety of ways, when I saw her charge the net and be caught flat-footed, ready to volley, as another passing shot whistled beyond the reach of her racket. "Shit!" she hissed, and the word sizzled in the silence for a moment, then she was laughing soundlessly with the man at the net. He slapped her on the back and they walked the length of the net, picked their gear off the slatted bench. "Tomorrow, Kim," I heard him say, "same time, same place, and I serve. . . ." He was already calling to a Mrs. Watson on the first court, moving away across the green carpet in the sunshine.

Kim was coming toward me, dark-blue eyes level, mouth a straight line, slipping a blue Slazenger cover over her Wilson T-2000. I got up, glad I'd put on a blazer and gray slacks; she made me feel messy because she'd just finished playing tennis with a pro and everything was in perfect order.

"I'm Paul Cavanaugh," I said. She shook my hand firmly and fell in beside me, going back along the path I'd come.

"You're the man at the funeral," she said, looking ahead of her, smelling of sweat and perfume. But it might have been the flowers again. There were streaks of sweat on her smooth, tan cheek and working their way down the back of her neck. "The man on the hill watching us. I saw you." She opened the door into the cool lobby. "You certainly have been busy, haven't you?"

"Moderately," I said. I couldn't tell if she was being hostile or not. Maybe just curt. Maybe she was just lousy at human relationships. Every syllable, every step, every tense swing of the racket, every breath made me feel like an intruder. A messy intruder. The doorman was holding the door for someone as we swept past and he respectfully pronounced her name, she nodded, on up two stairs, along the glassed hallway to the elevators with their black doors gleaming wetly, like live things opening to swallow us up.

We were alone in the little ascending room. It was perfume. The sweat was drying on her face. She untied the bandanna, kept her eyes on the floor indicator. Nobody said anything. I looked at her legs. Her socks were rolled down over the tops of her tennis shoes. She reached down impatiently and wiped a trickle of sweat on the inside of her dark thigh.

Her apartment was on the twenty-fourth floor and it was dark, cool, quiet. She led me into the living room and said, "I'm going to take a quick shower. Make yourself at home. Then we can get all this taken care of."

I said that was fine, she should take her time, and she said she had lots to do today, she'd be only a minute. The draperies were pulled across floor-to-ceiling windows which faced east and got the full morning sun. The room was large, spare, linear, modern with lots of three-quarter-inch glass and chrome and steel and mirrorlike cylindrical floor pots with greenery of several varieties poking upward, spreading out, overflowing, turning toward the sunlight. A huge glass bowl of fruit stood on a rolling glass cart. I heard water running in the shower, a door closing. Boston ferns, dieffenbachia, split-leaf philodendrons, spider plants. There was a single very large graphic on one wall: a print of a Klimt poster, lots of gold in it. On a white fluted pedestal in one corner: a large copy of Houdon's remarkable bust of George Washington. Several Simulations Publications war games were stacked on a glass shelf: Borodino, World War II, War in the East, Kampfpanzer. No ashtrays. On a blue-and-white-flowered couch—the only item in the room that wasn't severe, straight, sharp or cool and distant—a copy of the *Tribune* was open to a story headlined INDUSTRIALIST'S DEATH A MYSTERY: MURDER OR SUICIDE? There was a picture of Tim Dierker taken a good ten years ago, smiling, confident, red hair combed back on the high forehead. I heard the shower go off. I didn't know what to do; any movement was bound to louse up the room.

She appeared suddenly in faded blue jeans and dark-blue Lacoste tennis shirt, moving silently on bare feet that caught my eye, white below the line of tan. She had a pair of loafers in her hand. The pigtails were gone and a wide blue headband held her hair back.

"Open the drapes," she said. "Pull the cord on the side. Would you like some breakfast?"

"No thanks."

"Coffee?"

"Sure."

"Sit down, I'm just going to throw my breakfast together out here." I heard her clattering about, then she was pulling the glass cart out from the wall into the bright sunshine on the blue-and-white couch and after several sections of grapefruit, she broke off a corner of toast and said, "Okay, let's get this thing straightened out, Mr. Cavanaugh. Darwin McGill and your former wife both mentioned that you'd been asking questions about me, about my past life. I am a very private person. I value my anonymity. I don't want people digging into my life. . . ." She chewed the toast and sipped the black coffee. "Now, what are you after?" She finally acknowledged me, looking into my eyes.

"All right, right off the top, Miss Roderick. I'm curious as to what you may be able to tell me about Larry Blankenship's suicide and Timothy Dierker's murder—"

"By what conceivable authority? You're a drama critic, a writer." She turned back to her breakfast, a woman uneasy with people. She wasn't laughing, not even with outrage.

"I have no authority whatsoever," I said.

"I've already talked with the police, that Bernstein who's running for mayor. He called me as a formality, he said, wanted to know if I had any thoughts as to why Mr. Dierker"—she glanced down at the newspaper —"either might have killed himself or why someone would have wanted to murder him. Mr. Bernstein and

I had talked before, about Larry's death. In any case, I told him I was at a class the night Mr. Dierker died, at the university, and had a dinner engagement after class ended. What more could you want to know, even if you had the authority, and why? We don't know each other." She broke off another bite-sized morsel of toast and began chewing. "So why?"

"It's Harriet Dierker," I said. She was wearing rust-colored nail polish, like ten pieces of exotic candy. "She was distraught by Larry Blankenship's suicide, she asked me to look into why he might have done it."

She nodded. "I can believe that, yes. Mrs. Dierker is an unstable woman. Poor thing."

"She believes that you caused Larry's suicide, that you in some way drove him to it. She told me a long, desperately involved story about your relationship with Larry. . . ." I shrugged. "I don't know what's true. Or if any of it's true. Which is why I was asking questions." It was a beautiful room in the sunlight and the coffee smelled freshly ground. I never drink coffee black but this stuff was all right.

"*I* didn't cause Larry to kill himself," she said calmly, only marginally involved. "He was born with the need to kill himself, Mr. Cavanaugh. Did you ever hear the story about the scorpion and the frog?" I shook my head. "Well, the scorpion and the frog both arrived at the riverbank at the same time. They both wanted to get across but the scorpion couldn't swim. So he asked the frog to carry him across on his back. The frog, carefully keeping his distance, said that he'd like to help out but he couldn't because if he let the scorpion get on his back the scorpion would sting him and kill him. Well, the scorpion argued that what the frog was saying made no sense because if he killed the frog he, too, would drown. Now this made perfect sense to the frog, who listened a while longer and finally said okay, he'd carry the scorpion across. So the scorpion climbed on the frog's back and they set out across the river. Way out in the middle of the river the scorpion stung the frog and as they were both dying, about to drown, the frog croaked out his last words, 'Why did you sting me? You're going to drown as a result,' and the scorpion looked at him sadly and said, 'I couldn't help it. It's my nature.'" She licked crumbs from her fingers and looked away, into the sunshine. "It was Larry's nature, that's all. He had to kill himself." Her voice was remarkably even.

"Harriet Dierker believes you are also involved in her husband's murder. She says that you said something to him at Larry's funeral that he went home and sat down and cried over his scrapbook and hit her and went up on the roof and somebody threw him over the edge. . . . She says you're involved in a murder." I got up from the couch. The river looked clean from the twenty-fourth floor.

"All I can say is that I haven't the vaguest idea of what she's talking about." She spooned out a chunk of grapefruit. "Mr. Dierker told me how sorry he was about Larry, that's all. I thanked him and he left. He and some of his friends were very good to me when I was a frightened teenager who'd never been to the big city before. But that was almost twenty years ago. Do you realize that? I am thirty-five years old, Mr. Cavanaugh. . . ." She leaned back and crossed one ankle over a knee and slipped her foot into a tattered loafer. "Some of the wives were very hateful toward me. . . ."

"With some reason, I understand. I mean, you do have a record of going through men pretty damned quick." I felt a twinge of perversity: I wanted to break through the wall of composure. I didn't have a reason. It was a purely destructive impulse, maybe because she made me feel like such a slob. "First Billy Whitefoot, then Larry, now Ole Kronstrom."

She just sat there putting on the other loafer, forcing it over her heel. She pushed the cart away.

"Since you don't know me," she said very quietly, "I wonder why you would say such things, why you would accept them so readily. I wouldn't if I were in your place. I wouldn't want to run the risk of making such a mistake, you know? Why not jump to the conclusion that I'm the injured party, that men go through me? I've had two children, you must be aware of that since your researches have been so thorough. . . . It all depends on your point of view. Everything in life seems to depend on your point of view. Objective truth is an illusion. History teaches us that."

"Does it?"

"Yes, it does. Look, I'm perfectly willing to help you. Your concern is something which is absolutely none of your business—it intrigues me, it really does." For the first time she wore a faint smile. I was beginning to think she was rather beautiful in a tight, inhibited way. "But I don't quite know how. Do I know why Larry killed himself? No, I don't, beyond the fact that he was a doomed man, a man whose unhappiness was as much a part of him as his unfailing hope. Of course, yes, our marriage breaking up hit him hard but, good heavens, it was never going to get any better. He was a waiter, a maybe man, a hoper, a passive man with no sense of his own worth, no dignity. I am a doer, I am aggressive when I'm required to be, I'm a person with a very good idea of my own worth and dignity. I care what I think of me." She pursed her lips, thinking. "Larry. Do you know what he was doing there in your apartment building? Do you want to know?"

"Did you ever visit him?" I remembered what Bill Oliver had said. I remembered the scene in the parking lot which had stuck so firmly in his mind, remembered it as if I'd seen it myself.

"Yes, I came by to see him a few times, mainly in my role of psychological counselor. He was fully aware of the difference between us, at least eventually, but he thought he could prove himself to me by pulling himself back together. He insisted on believing that I might come back to him, no matter what I said, no matter how carefully I reasoned with him." Her face was composed, serious, as if she had resigned herself to reasoning with me. There was a tiny round smallpox scar between her thick, dark eyebrows. She was massaging her knee absentmindedly with her right hand, the rust-colored nails moving across the faded denim. "But I figured that if I befriended him enough to make him confident, to help him feel secure again after our breakup, then he could make it on his own without me. He needed some success. . . . Then he'd be all right." She sighed, recalling past agonies. "Well, Larry got a good job, an account man working in a middle-sized advertising agency. I really believed he was catching on there. . . ." She smiled. "He started wearing their double-knit suits, the white belt, and the shiny white shoes—I know, I know, don't make faces. It sounds pathetic and in a way it was, but it meant that he was fitting in. He grew long sideburns. He was becoming happy in spite of himself. But it never got that far. The recession hit, advertising budgets were cut, and the agencies had to begin laying people off. He was the newest man with the newest sideburns and the newest Thunderbird, so they let him go and told him not to worry, it was only temporary, they'd be asking him to come back as soon as business picked up." She stood up and went to the window, where we both stood looking out into space in the middle of a sad story.

"So there he was with his new unpaid-for Thunderbird," she went on quietly, "gas was up to sixty cents a gallon, he didn't have a paycheck, and he just went to bed, acted out his own self-fulfilling prophecy. He was convinced he was a failure and he kept making it come true." She turned to look at me, underlining her dismay. "Can you imagine, Mr. Cavanaugh? Here was a man in some degree of difficulty and instead of going out to find another job, he stayed up in that nasty little apartment sitting by the telephone, watching his silly game shows in the morning and adding up what he'd have won if he'd been playing for real, and in the afternoon he watched the soap operas, all the time waiting for the phone to ring. . . ." She paced the circumference of the room, pacing off the steps, picking an apple out of the bowl and taking a neat little bite. She shook her head. "He really thought the agency was going to call him back, that it would just be a matter of weeks and he'd be back on the job . . . so innocent." She'd circled all the way back and was standing beside me now; she held out the apple and I took a bite. It didn't strike me as the kind of gesture she'd normally make; it reminded me of a peace offering.

"I'm talking way too much. You're like an analyst I used to have, very nondirective. You don't say anything and I just keep talking. I must be nervous, mustn't I? I'm not usually very communicative about this sort of thing. Ask me about the commando raid on the heavy-water plant in Norway and I'll talk your head off. . . ."

"Is that what you're studying?"

"World War Two's my specialty." There was a peculiar lavender cast to her eye, speckles, maybe it was the sunlight. "I'm doing my dissertation on resistance movements in the Scandinavian countries. And I'm warning you. I hate people who say it isn't a very ladylike subject. I'm not very ladylike, not in that sense."

"Why history in particular?"

"The past, I guess. I'm fascinated by the way the past changes shape and coloration and significance as the years go by. How the past affects the present, that kind of thing." She turned away self-consciously, took another bite of apple, and didn't offer me any this time. "Anyway, Larry just began to disappear as a human being and it was very painful for me, a terrible thing to watch, and what could I do?"

"Well," I said, venturing another needle, "you could have gone back to him—"

"Don't be ridiculous," she said sharply. "Don't you see, haven't you been listening to me at all? I'm not going to disappear, Mr. Cavanaugh. I started out pretty far back in the race but I've worked hard, I've held up through tough times, and I've learned I can make my life what I want it to be. It hasn't been particularly easy and maybe it never will be. But I'm a bright, capable person—I'm not very warm, I'm not overgiving, but I'm not scared to be thirty-five and I'm not going to disappear either. My God, going back to Larry would have started my own disappearing act, it was obvious. I won't contribute to that—I've come too close twice, with Billy and then with Larry. . . . In any case, I visited him, I tried to cheer him up, and I failed miserably. Yes, it occurred to me that he might kill himself but I misjudged him, I didn't think he'd do it because that would have been the final failure, it would rob him of all the enjoyment another forty years of failing would give him. . . ." Another woman might have shed a tear at this point but not Kim.

"That's harsh," I said.

"Just realistic, that's all." She knew I was judging her; I could see it in her face. There was a battle going on inside her head and I figured it was between her own inclinations and the desire to disarm me and get me out of her hair. And yet there was something about her that made me feel calm. The morning was drifting away and I liked being there with the bust of Washington and Klimt's gold-leaf lovers. She went back and sat down on the couch. I watched her, not wanting to notice her as a woman, not wanting to notice the way her hips swelled to pull the Levi's tight and the rich dark hair and the tan ankles and the sexy old loafers. "What else?" she said.

"What about Tim Dierker? Why would Harriet say that it was something you said that sent him off the deep end when he got home?"

"Really, you'll have to ask her, won't you? Tim expressed his sympathy"—I could see the slow, agonizing walk across the green grass with the smell of clover and the clouds moving across the sun, as if the old man were walking toward his death—"and I asked about his health, the usual things. We just talked for a moment. Meaningless funeral talk."

"Can you imagine why he was killed, then?"

"You said you knew him. How can you ask? Mr. Dierker just wasn't the kind of man who made enemies. He was a booster, a joiner, the kind of man who works hard each year on something like the Aquatennial. . . . Who could want to kill such a man? He just wasn't the type."

"Look, I found the body, Miss Roderick."

"I'm sorry. I realize that somebody must have

killed him—I didn't mean to be insensitive. But he just always *seemed* to be such a good man—"

"But he didn't want you and Larry to get married, did he? His wife said the marriage sent him into a decline. From which he never quite recovered, she says. Why did he oppose the marriage? You were two of his favorite people, by all accounts."

"I never discussed it with him. I'm not at all sure that what you say was true." She was staring at me, coolly, remote.

"Maybe this is an easier one. Why did Tim and his friends take such good care of you?"

"They weren't taking care of me, Mr. Cavanaugh," she said, an understandable edginess chewing at the corners of her voice and slowly invading her eyes. "They were helping me. They helped Billy. Did they need any particular reason? Why not just look on us as borderline charity cases? And anyway, I worked very hard. I made a good impression, I've never thought it was any more than that. What can I say? I applied myself to what I was supposed to do . . . why not settle for the plain, obvious truth? Too simple for you?"

"Not at all. It's just that the simple truth so often turns into something else. It's like history, remember? It changes with time, becomes something altogether different the more you look at it."

"Well," she said, looking at the Cartier tank watch on her strong left wrist, "I've got to get over to the university. Any more questions?" She was smiling. The interview was almost over.

"Only one," I said. "I'd like to hear your life story."

She laughed aloud, shook her head. "Oh, no, not that. Never, much too boring. Anyway, I don't even know you, Mr. Cavanaugh."

"You said I'm not your type. Maybe we never will know each other." I gave my boyish, rueful grin a try and deeply regretted it. "But I enjoyed this morning. And I appreciate your giving me so much of your time. You didn't have to. Anne said I'd like you. . . ."

"I am fond of Anne," she said, moving toward the door. "She's living her own life, too. We have that in common." In the doorway she smiled a little mechanically. "Good-bye. And forgive my telephone call. Please." She was still smiling when the door clicked shut.

I moved the Porsche over to the Sheraton-Ritz driveway, gave the keys to the doorman, and went down the outside stairway to the pool. The tables were almost deserted at the tail end of summer. The lifeguard gave me a surprised glance, tugged at the seat of her swimming suit, and went back to her book. I sat in the sunshine and ordered a gin and tonic and a well-done hamburger. The lifeguard, whose name was Sheila, had long tapered legs and broad shoulders and a mahogany tan. She had spent the entire summer reading Graham Greene thrillers and was working on *The Confidential Agent*. I'd suggested the reading program. She came over finally and scraped her chair across the cement. "Poor D," she said hoarsely, "he's having a hell of a time." She bent down the corner of a page and put the book on the metal table. "What are you doing?" she asked.

"Waiting for my drink," I said, "and thinking about a woman."

"Me?" She was stroking her arm, touching herself without realizing it, the way athletes habitually do.

"No, someone else."

"Is she pretty?"

"My God, you're such a chauvinist," I said. "Can't you think about a woman in any other terms than how pretty she is?"

"I suppose I can, sure. Just curious." She coughed; she had had a cold all summer long. She hated the water but what she did, she contended, beat working. "Is she?"

"Very pretty, in a sort of funny way. Not obvious."

"Is she nice?"

"I don't know. Some people think she's a monster. Other people think she's okay. I don't know what to think. . . ."

"You can't trust your feeling," she said. "You think too much. You should follow your gut reactions—but you're too inhibited. You're always trying to validate your experiences, that's your problem." My drink arrived and she took a sip, sucked the lime slice out of it, and kept it.

"That doesn't mean anything, Sheila. Validate my experiences? Jargon, kiddo. I may be inhibited but you're a prisoner of your jargon." My hamburger came in a little wicker basket. She took the first bite and went back to her book, as if I weren't there. A siren swept past up above us, on street level. The hamburger was rare and I pushed the basket back to her. I closed my eyes and leaned back, feeling the warmth of the sun. I could hear her chewing, turning pages, breathing.

I thought about the way Kim had handled our chat, how she'd sat so primly on the couch—no, not prim, but so carefully, physically guarded as well as mentally. I heard her voice, the careful pronunciation, the little pauses, the solemn cadence. She occasionally pursed her thin lips between words and frowned at the corners of her mouth and her eyebrows grew so gracefully, like the perfect grooming of an animal who had nothing better to do than be perfect. I kept seeing her face, the straight nose, the lavender in her eyes, the crescent of smallpox.

I opened my eyes. Sheila was gone. I remembered what Helga Kronstrom had said in the doorway of Dierker's apartment. Did they know the woman I'd spent the morning with? How many Kim Rodericks were there?

I called Ole Kronstrom's office from a pay phone in the hotel's lower lobby. He said he had a free hour and he'd be glad to talk. There was warmth in his voice, a comforting quality after a morning of playing peculiar games with Kim Roderick, games quite possibly without rules.

His office was high up in the First National Bank building so I walked. It didn't occur to me that I was still prying into Kim Roderick's life; I didn't yet know how her mind worked. As far as I was concerned, she had satisfied my curiosity and was slipping out of the equation. Her role had been created by Harriet Dierker and life had revealed it as a figment of her imagination. But my subconscious was whirring away on its own. There was one question which did matter at the back of my mind. Why had she stood still for all my snooping when it had obviously irritated her the night before?

Mainly I wanted to know who killed Tim Dierker. And there was always the chance I could validate an experience or two along the way.

The name on the door said OLE KRONSTROM: BUSINESS CONSULTANT, nothing else. The secretary was a perky white-haired woman in a tailored suit which bespoke a life-long charge account at Harold's. I gave her my name, she smiled and told me to go right on in, Mr. Kronstrom was expecting me. If Kim Roderick had ruined him financially, then ruination was a very relative matter.

He was sitting in an Eames chair with his feet cocked up on the leather footrest, facing the glass wall with its view of the IDS building and the top of the rest of Minneapolis. He turned quickly and got up smiling, engulfed my hand in his, which was about the size of a catcher's mitt, and pointed to a chair. The *Wall Street Journal* was open on his desk top but the *Tribune* lay across it, open like Kim's to the old photograph of his late partner. Ole Kronstrom had a lot of stiff white hair, the pale large-featured face of so many Scandinavians, and an aura of good health. On his desk there was a black-and-white photograph in a gold frame: He and Kim stood side by side in ski togs on the balcony of a chateau with something which looked suspiciously like an Alp in the distance behind them.

"I'd gotten the impression you were retired," I said after I'd told him how sorry I was about Tim Dierker. "But this. . . ." There were manila file folders stacked on a long cabinet, file cabinets, piles of mail in the in/out trays.

"Oh, my, no," he said in a high, hearty voice. "Once I left Tim I'd intended to do a great deal of traveling, catch up on all the things I'd wanted to read for thirty or forty years, and generally find out if I was still alive." He chuckled deep in his broad chest.

"So I traveled and read and proved to myself that I wasn't quite dead yet. Then I got the itch. Clipping my coupons—pardon the cliché, but you know what I mean—wasn't very satisfying after a lifetime on the job. I looked around, checked out a thing or two, and came up with this little enterprise. I wanted to work at something where I could do some good and this was perfect. I'm a business adviser, but only to our senior citizens, those who have found themselves forcibly re-tired before they were ready for the home—if you see my point. My clients want advice about setting up their own companies, all sorts of undertakings, lots of interesting problems. One elderly couple—just to give you an example and then I'll stop boring you with my own little passions—this one elderly couple decided to go into the jewelry-making business. Gorgeous stuff, all made from Swedish horseshoe nails. By jiminy, that one caught my eye. They were going about it in a small way, selling at little art fairs and the like . . . well, that was a couple of years ago. Now we've got them doing in excess of one hundred thousand dollars a year, supplying shops all over the Midwest, investing in some very nice bonds, building up quite an estate for their grandchildren, wintering in the Bahamas . . . and still working the little art fairs they enjoy so much." He paused and rubbed his nose energetically. "You get an idea of the kick this kind of thing gives me. I'm an enthusiast, Mr. Cavanaugh, always have been. Hell of a salesman, I was. And still am. Clients pay me a few percent, not enough to hurt me taxwise, and it beats a vacation any day. Fun, that's what it is." He sat back down in the Eames chair and turned to-ward me. "You look surprised?"

"Well, I am," I said. "You're not quite what I'd ex-pected."

"How's that, pray?" He leaned forward with his el-bows on the desk blotter and his hands kneading each other, his big mouth smiling slightly, the sun behind him blacking him out. He wore glasses like Nelson Rockefeller's, black plastic and just off center.

"I'm going on what Harriet Dierker had to say," I began, and his big laugh boomed off the walls like cannon fire and he shook his head.

"Well, you're starting off in the hole, young man, I'm sorry to tell you. Harriet's quite a gal but she never has known what the heck she's talking about!" He brushed his huge hand across his mouth, lessening the smile, shook his head. "This must be a terrible time for her and I don't mean to poke fun . . . but she does have some flaws that used to drive Timothy crazy, I mean more than most wives. Never stopped talking, for one thing, and had a positive ache—you know what I mean by ache?—well, she had one for gossip. Thing was, she never got it quite right, always misunderstood what she heard. About three-quarters of the time Harriet was out there in left field getting hit on the head with fly balls. . . ."

"She depicted you as a broken, ruined man," I said.

"Well," he sighed, reality intruding on his heartiness, "that's wishful thinking and I'm sorry she feels that way. I suppose you've noticed that some people have a way of making the world fit their ideas about it. Harriet's that way. My wife, Helga, she's not that way so much—more of a down-the-line martyr, you know? These women, they're all so wronged, so determined to be the wronged party. . . ." He took off his glasses and rubbed his eyes with his knuckles like a little boy and leaned back in his chair. "Some women seem to feel, and stop me if I'm boring you, but they seem to feel that putting in their time is enough. They marry, put in their time, and never mind the quality of the time, and then they seem to think you owe them something. It's a peculiarly feminine trait, maybe we men have made them that way because we've treated them like employees . . . I don't know. Awfully well-paid employees, with permanent access to the company funds—then, when the thirty years have been put in, the husband conveniently dies and the women go to Palm Springs to do some serious bridge playing at long last." He was nibbling on his glasses. "Well, it's the way of life, isn't it? I'm not complaining and I'm not angry. But I'm relieved that I didn't keel over in harness. I'm glad I lived long enough to figure out the game and get out of it." He came back to the present. "So what can I do for you, Mr. Cavanaugh? And may I congratulate you on your taste in fathers, by the way?"

"Actually, Harriet Dierker was one of the subjects I had in mind. She asked me to look into the death of Larry Blankenship, that's how it began, and then Tim was killed and she told me, or your wife did—they were together—that the deaths were connected. . . ."

"And what's your interest?"

"Curiosity, not enough to keep me busy. . . . I'm a writer, maybe I can smell something. I don't know. But the murder of Tim has sort of locked me into it, for the time being. I had a talk with him the other day . . . and now somebody's killed him. I'm curious."

"All right. You're an interested observer and your father writes mystery novels, a perfect team." He smiled perfunctorily and got to business. "Harriet Dierker isn't a liar, Mr. Cavanaugh, she simply has an untidy, imprecise mind. Most of the time she doesn't know what she's talking about. Add to that her innate malice, her feigned concern for others' misfortune, and you've got her to a T."

"Nothing she says seems to be quite true," I said.

"That's right." He poured two glasses of water from a pitcher on his desk. I heard ice cubes rattle. He wet his lips.

"Can you imagine why anyone would want to kill Tim?"

"No. He was a kind man. If he made a mistake or treated anyone badly, he made it right. If he had a code, that was it. Personal accountability. He was human but he was a man of honor. That simple. Wanting to kill him? It's hard to imagine."

"You've known him for a long time?"

"Oh, yes, socially and in business. We go back a long way, our wives and ourselves."

"The hunting and fishing club, you were one of them, too?"

He paused and looked at me head-on, thoughtfully. "I was never much involved with the club, now that you mention it. My memories of Timothy have nothing to do with the club. My attitude about it was a good deal like your father's. Adolescent hijinks going sour when you grow up. I was never comfortable with the club. Oh, hell, at first it was good, fun to get away from our jobs and our wives. . . . Funny thing, Harriet was one of the primary reasons there ever was a club! Timothy just had to get away from her. So he pushed the club idea. . . . It was fun, yes, at the beginning, an adventure, we felt like kids off on our own for the first time. Then, well, it changed and I figured it was a pain in the ass. . . ."

"How did it change? What went wrong?"

"Men in groups are to be avoided," he said as if he were stating a physical law. "The men changed after the beginning. The club, the lodge began to represent something I didn't care for—a release from normal behavior, a place they could go and be themselves, that's what some of them said, that we could go up to the lodge and be ourselves. Well, hell, I finally told them one night that if this was what they really were, they could all go to hell. . . . I'd had a drop to drink, of course, but still, I was right. They were getting into some cutthroat card games, they visited a whorehouse up on the Range. . . . It all just got a little raw for my blood. It's my nature, I didn't take to it. What they did was their nature, I guess." He opened a drawer and took out a blackened old pipe and stuffed it with Prince Albert, packing it down with his forefinger.

"Did you ever hear the one about the scorpion and the frog?" I asked. He just went on packing but a grin spread quietly across his face, deepening the wrinkles, softening the Scandinavian toughness.

"Do you know that one, too, or have you been talking to Kim? I told her that one. It's a favorite of mine. I believe it, too, you can't change your nature. Behavior yes, but nature no." He lit the pipe, drew noisily, and wreathed his head in curls of smoke. Air ducts began pulling at the smoke immediately. "That was the problem with the club, anyway. Their nature got the best of them, I guess, and the night I got mad at them they got pretty sore at me." He shrugged and I heard his teeth click on the pipestem. "So I left my gear right there, went out, and got in my car and came home. It seemed the best way to handle it. . . . I only went up a few times after that, nobody ever said anything about it to me, but the group kind of tightened the circle with me on the outside. As I say, your father wasn't really one of them either and of course he moved away. Once your father was gone the fun was completely out of it for me. I'm not a worldly man, I suppose, and whoring and such is not my idea of a rip of a time. . . ."

"What about Father Boyle?" I asked. "Surely, he took an equally dim view of what was going on."

Ole Kronstrom was shaking his head slowly.

"I've known Marty Boyle for a long time, like the others, and I've never really understood what made him tick. Of course, I'm not a Catholic and that may have something to do with my inability to understand him. I'm a fundamentalist Lutheran, as you might guess, and Catholics are far too sophisticated for my blood. But even for a Catholic, Marty's too worldly to fit into my view of churchmen generally." He puffed thoughtfully.

"You mean he did what the rest of them did?"

"I'm not saying that. And I'm not judging anyone. I've always figured that every man is alone with his own conscience in the end. Beyond that I'm not much of an expert on Marty Boyle."

"I talked with him last night, at his home. He didn't seem at all well. . . ."

"Gout, I understand. Funny illness for a priest."

"I made him sicker, I'm afraid."

"Why, for heaven's sake? Or how?"

"I got him talking about the club. The thing is, Tim Dierker was looking through his scrapbook the night he was killed. And he was crying. Harriet saw him. But when they went over the apartment after his death the scrapbook was gone. The murderer apparently took it. Stole it. Must've had a reason."

He tamped the ashes down into the bowl and applied another match, sucking dryly.

"I wonder why," he said.

"That would seem to be the question. I told Father Boyle and asked him if he had a scrapbook, one which might contain pictures taken up at the lodge. He did, he got it out, and we looked at it, and then he went all funny and threw me out. . . ."

"Strange. But, ah, let me ask you, what would the connection be? Between Timothy's death and the lodge?"

"Just that the scrapbook had his pictures. Along with other stuff from various vacations he and Harriet had taken years ago. I couldn't see any point in connecting their trip to Banff, for instance, with all this."

"All this?"

"Right, all this. You see, I'm working on an assumption which could be all wrong. But what if there's some thread between Larry Blankenship's suicide and Tim Dierker's murder? Then it would all seem to somehow draw closer—Larry, Tim, the club."

"Quite an assumption, though." He was watching me through the blue smoke.

"Another little oddity. Boyle mentioned a man named Carver Maxvill, a new character. Do you know anything about him."

"My gosh, Carver Maxvill. Now, that is a name out of the past. Sure, he was the fellow who up and disappeared one day. Just went off, I suppose. He was an original member of our group, a lawyer, quiet fellow. I knew him least well, I think. I've forgotten who was closest to him . . . Hubbard Anthony maybe, they were both lawyers."

"He disappeared? What does that mean?"

"Just that. Caused a commotion when it happened, about thirty years ago, Judge Crater kind of thing. One day he was there, the next he wasn't. Gone without a trace. But I'm no authority. I hadn't run across him in years, not since I'd stopped going on club outings. You could look it up in the papers, though. But he couldn't figure in this thing, he's not your connecting thread, he hasn't been heard from, quite literally, in decades." He smiled a trifle wearily, as if all the memories were just this side of boring him.

"As far as Marty's scrapbook goes, it may have been a case of guilt which gave him a turn. Haunted by the past. It's possible is all I'm saying."

"Well, anyway, Carver Maxvill isn't the thread. I'm thinking that Kim Roderick may be the common denominator." He didn't react, just puffed calmly, watching me. "Oh, I'm reaching, I realize. But she was a part of their lives, you might say. Larry's wife. And Tim took an interest in her, took her under his wing."

"I see," he said. "Kim. Which is why you're here."

"One reason. And you were right. I did hear the one about the frog and the scorpion from her. I talked with her this morning."

"And what did you think of her? You're so close to her age, I'm genuinely curious." He waited. Very patient fellow, Ole Kronstrom.

"She was a bit of a surprise, actually. I'd been led to expect something else—"

"By Harriet?" he said, a chuckle just being born.

"Yes, by Harriet."

"Her batting average isn't so hot, is it? First Kim, then me."

"No, it's not. I liked her. She's distant, I don't think she much enjoyed talking to me. But why should she have, for that matter? Harriet had told me that you'd been preyed on and destroyed by Kim, financially and morally ruined. . . ." I let it lie there for a moment and then he picked it up.

"You know, I'm not a man to deal in confidences. I've always kept to myself, refused to gossip or to listen to gossip, never talked much about myself to others. Stoic Swede, Helga used to call me. She could never make me angry, she said I always kept everything to myself. And she was right enough about that —I'm not an open man, not candid about my innermost thoughts and feelings. Naturally, I've never had anyone I could talk about Kim to. . . . I've wanted someone, at times, but there wasn't anyone. Now"— he looked over the tops of his glasses, rather shyly— "if I want to, I can talk to you, can't I?"

"I wish you would," I said. Describing himself, he

might just as well have been describing Kim Roderick. "If you can spare me the time."

"For a chance like this?" He chuckled and peered inquisitively into the gray ashes, pressed them down, and lit a third match, got the dregs going again, and waved the match in the air.

"Quite naturally, given the state of human nature," he said, settling back in the embracing chair, "people assume that I'm an old fool having a final fling with a very young woman, though Kim is at least a decade older than she looks. People assume that we have made a trade, her body for my money. It happens often enough, so why not to Ole Kronstrom, the sanctimonious old fart of a Swede? The joke is that they are wrong. Ours is not a father/daughter relationship by any means but neither are we lovers, you see? Friends. Never lovers. I've never slept with her. I've never seen her naked body . . . and I don't care. I have had no use for sex for many years. My needs died early. Quirk of fate and, contrary to what you may think, a blessing. People always say some fellow is a poor devil, can't get it up anymore, you've heard them. Let me tell you, when desire itself ends, by definition you don't miss it. There's no sense of longing—you've lost interest. Literally.

"So Kim and I are very quiet together, very relaxed, we read together or she tells me about a new movie we should see or she talks to me about her courses at the university. Kim doesn't want a close physical relationship any more than I do. We enjoy each other, we go to Europe, we have a fine time. I love Kim, she loves me, but it's not what Harriet thinks. . . . It's been my good fortune to know Kim, to be at peace with her. Do you grasp what I'm saying? Am I making myself clear?"

"Helga and Harriet believe that Kim killed Larry Blankenship and Tim Dierker. One way or another. . . ."

"Well, that doesn't surprise me at all, Mr. Cavanaugh. Not at all. Harriet is a gossip, neurotically so, maybe psychotically so, for all I know. Helga has been hurt. She won't get over it now and she'd enjoy my feeling guilty. I don't, however, and I won't. Harriet and Helga mean nothing to me. . . ." There was a pinkness rising in his cheeks and his eyes were narrowing as he talked. "I'm profoundly grateful for Kim, for what she has meant to me. I'm an old-fashioned religious man, from a farm in North Dakota, direct line from Sweden, and I have my share of faith, a strong belief in God." He sighed, short of breath. "You cannot pay attention to people like Harriet and Helga. You've got to take control of your own life, make your own destiny as best you can . . . that's what Kim is to me, she's what's going to see me through to the end. . . ."

"What about what she did to Billy Whitefoot? Think of the shape Blankenship was in at the end."

"Have you been listening to me, Mr. Cavanaugh?"

"Yes, I have."

"Well, then, think about what I've said. Purge yourself of some of your preconceived ideas. She's not the woman you've been told she is. . . . Talk to Billy Whitefoot. He went back up north somewhere. . . . And think, for heaven's sake. . . ."

It was time for me to go. The sun was gone behind the IDS tower.

"Did you keep a scrapbook?"

"Good Lord, no. What a thought."

"Look, you've been very patient," I said, "and I appreciate it. Just one last question: Where is she from? What's her background? Do you know?"

"The north country is a maze, Mr. Cavanaugh, at least to me. You'll have to ask her, I'm afraid."

"Oh, I don't suppose it'll come to that. Just my curiosity." We shook hands and he gave my hand an extra little squeeze. He was a nice man. I thanked him again and went away, the funny man who kept asking questions. I was exhausted.

7

IT WAS a relief to sit down at my desk at the end of
the day, in the quiet, away from all the voices. I was
exhausted from the talk. There was no point in even
trying to assimilate all the data, speculation, and
hearsay. An article waited to be written, a free-lance
piece I was working my way through on the summer's
smash film, *Chinatown*. For once the nostalgia had
really worked: Suffused with it, the film hadn't seemed
phony. There had been a quality of heightened reality
to the past that *Chinatown* portrayed and at just that
moment I got to thinking about Nicholson standing on
the bridge with his binoculars watching the soon-to-
be-murdered water commissioner poking around in
the dry, dusty gulch. It was an astonishingly real
moment, but the question I was trying to answer was
"Why?" It was a relief to think about somebody else's
murders. . . .

Which was when Julia called to ask me out to the
house for dinner. Archie wondered if I was still on
the "case," as he called it, she said, and he was dying
to know what was happening. I told her that was a
regrettable choice of words.

Driving through the early evening purple with little
patches of fog lifting up from the marshland, I let
the Porsche glide a little and listened to Bobby
Hackett's trumpet recording of "Time on My Hands,"
humming the words I remembered, phrasing them to
Hackett's blowing.

Over lamb chops, mint sauce, and a corn soufflé
I told Archie and Julia of the day's interviewing. As I
droned on, I wondered if Kim was still wearing her
jeans and the Lacoste shirt, or if she changed to a

117

dress for dinner with Ole, or if she had to study. Summer school must be over; she had to be between summer school and the fall term. Maybe she was working on her dissertation.

"Well, I've been giving it some small thought," Archie said, lighting a cheroot and staring for a moment at the Dufy over the sideboard with its chafing dishes, bowls, darkly gleaming candlesticks, pewter odds and ends. "I've been trying to treat it as a plot, as if it were a book I was writing, trying to create a little order and make the pieces fit." He stood up and patted his tummy. "Very nice chops, Julia. No meat, of course, but that's a lamb chop for you, isn't it? Come on, let's go into the study and think through this out loud."

We followed him, carrying our coffee cups, and sat down in big flowered chairs. The student's lamp on the library table glowed yellow and there was a bitter little breeze from the open doors. The wind off the lake was spending its nights chewing away at the end of summer. Archie turned on a couple of table lamps and prepared for a demonstration. He used a large schoolroom-size blackboard on wheels when he was planning a book and he was rolling it out now from the wall so we could see it. He got his boxes of colored chalk from a desk drawer and banged a couple of erasers together. I could smell puffs of chalk dust, remembered coming to see Archie and knowing his work was going well by the smudges of chalk all over his clothing.

As we watched him, like a crowd drawn to a magician, he wrote the word SCRAPBOOK on the black surface. "This seems crucial to me," he said, smoke billowing around his head, "the scrapbook. It sticks out of the general mess. Why does a killer steal a scrapbook? Now, that's a hell of a question." He slashed two thick yellow underlinings beneath a yellow word and dropped his chalk back into the proper box. Next came a blue piece of chalk. TIMOTHY in blue. KIM in red. LARRY in green.

"Timothy was linked to both Larry and Kim, Kim to both Timothy and Larry, Larry to both Timothy and Kim. Now, the first thing a mystery novelist sees is the classic, basic triangularity of it, the strongest possible structure. The triangle forms the most widely used basis of all for the mystery novelist, and the novels should reflect life, at least on such an elementary level. The triangle is usually sexual, yes, and that is obviously unlikely in this instance. But there are other kinds of triangles: money, jealousy, revenge—those are also basic plot motivations and I'd be willing to bet they play a part in the murder of Tim Dierker." He drew connecting lines between the names, forming a triangle.

"But does any of it connect with Blankenship's suicide?" Julia was quietly doing her nails with a Kleenex dipped in Cutex and a bottle of polish. "Can you devise a plot which links the murder and the suicide? That's the point Helga and Harriet make, that they're related. They say by Kim but we can probably all agree that they're a little wacky on the subject of Kim." She wadded up a Kleenex and dropped it into an ashtray, plucked another, and dried the nails. "But is there another link?"

"Right," Archie said, staring at the names on the blackboard. "Does Larry's motive for killing himself in any way connect with the murderer's motive for killing Timothy? That"—he sighed—"would be perfect . . . but devilishly hard to pin down. Revenge?" He wrote the word. "Jealousy?" He wrote the word. "Money?" He wrote the word, shaking his head. "One driven to suicide, the other murdered . . . but what's the link, mmm? A fertile field for investigation but they are, unfortunately, both dead."

"At least I don't have to go talk to them," I said. "That's something."

"Why, Paul," Julia said disapprovingly.

"Honest to God, I'm talked out," I said.

"Nonsense!" Archie said, finally turning away from the blackboard.

"You can't possibly be talked out yet, you're just beginning—you've got ninety percent of your talking ahead of you. Read my novels, you silly fellow! It's talk, talk, talk. You're the interrogator, the man on the track, you're the man who is trying to make sense of events which on the surface resist having sense made of them. Read me. Read Ross Macdonald. Read Raymond Chandler." He brushed away my exhaustion with a quick, impatient gesture. "Talking to people— that's the way it's done, in fiction or in real life. What do you think Mark Bernstein and his chaps do all day? They interview people until their faces are blue. . . ."

"Archie," Julia warned, "for heaven's sake, he merely said he was tired."

She chuckled, applying the tiny paintbrush to her pointy nails.

"Well, he's got to pull his socks up and get on with it," Archie trailed off, muttering. He looked back to his block-letter printing, wiped his hands across his seersucker slacks, leaving a faint, dusty rainbow. "How many times in your life do you get a chance like this? I haven't been this close to a murder in thirty-five years, not a civilian murder anyway. Makes my teeth ache, I wish I could get into it. . . . Ah, hell, I don't know what I wish. My fictional murders"—he waved at the bookshelves—"they're satisfying, too. I always know what's going on in them." He undertook serious cheroot smoking and we lapsed into silence, staring at the blackboard. Archie sneezed in the chalk dust.

"We've forgotten another factor, a particularly curious one," Archie ventured slowly. "Maybe the link. . . . Somebody cleaned out the personal effects— whatever they were—from Larry's apartment. The same somebody who stole Tim Dierker's scrapbook? Does that tie it together, Paul? Something was stolen from each of those apartments. . . ."

"Hurray for Archie," Julia said as Archie beamed.

"Fenton Carey would be proud of you," I said. Fenton Carey is Archie's fictional reporter/detective, hero of what seems a thousand bizarre adventures, all dealing with murder.

"Indeed, I expect he would," Archie said. "I'll fetch some fresh coffee," he said happily, and headed jauntily from the room.

"What do you think?" I said to Julia.

"I think that Archie Cavanaugh never stops thinking, theorizing, wondering. Here, would you screw this cap back on? My nails are wet." She wafted her hands through the air. "And, Paul, could you close the doors? And light the fire?" I got up and went about it. "He's just beginning, you know," she went on. "He's determined to treat this like one of his plots. I wouldn't be surprised if he eventually figured it out. Deep down, he's still the indomitable Fenton Carey. The difference is only that Fenton Carey will always be forty. Archie's awfully good when he gets to the blackboard. And he's got a perverse mind. He just might figure it out, one way or another. His theory about the possible line—I hadn't thought of it. But it makes sense. Maybe."

I lit the crumpled newspapers under the birch logs and watched while the curling bark popped, caught fire. Archie came back with the Chemex coffee beaker and poured.

"Of course," he said as he passed out the cream and sugar, "there's Carver Maxvill. I'd actually forgotten about him. But I've heard the story, even though we weren't living hereabouts anymore. And in those days people dropped out of my life fairly frequently—hell, it was wartime, I was working with people like Jon Goode in Washington and London, running agents into France and Norway and Germany and Greece and Yugoslavia, and some of those men died. . . . So the fact that a man I'd known briefly years before had just opted out wasn't so terribly thought provoking. . . .

"But in retrospect, in terms of the hunting and fishing club and the fact that the stolen scrapbook points to the club, Carver Maxvill takes on a large aspect." He put the coffee gear on his desk and placed a disc on the Panasonic Technics turntable with the little rubber feet. Quietly the Debussy thing for the saxophone began; Archie had the knack of making me completely relaxed. Julia had sugared and creamed my coffee and handed it to me.

"Now, if I were plotting this thing," he went on, choosing a piece of lavender chalk, "I would be very drawn to Carver Maxvill." He lettered the name quickly, decisively, dotting the *i* with a bang that broke the tip off the chalk. "I get most of my plots from the newspapers, anyway. A body turns up in a lake, no identification available, and I read the papers or call a friend on the force and watch what develops, who the guy turns out to be, and it almost always turns into something that could be made into a novel right on the spot. People lead the most extraordinarily complex lives, more often than not because what happens to them in the present began somewhere in the past, mired in interrelationships which twist and turn through the years, back and back and back to events which are almost forgotten. The past . . . Paul, it's a good lesson to learn. The past is loath to relinquish its hold on people's lives. It's always a question of something coiled and hissing under the smooth surface . . . always something that somebody doesn't want revealed." He chuckled over the rim of his coffee cup. "Even in Minneapolis, believe it or not.

"So I find myself drawn to Carver Maxvill—just as a colorful possibility, a supposition. But he was a member of the club, and the scrapbooks, Timothy's and Martin Boyle's, tie the club into it." He got up and brought out the old scrapbook we'd gone through the other day. "Now, let's see, I must have a picture of Carver in here. . . ." He flipped the heavy black pages, stopped. "There he is, that's him. I didn't even register on him when we were looking before." His finger rested on a blond man, long-haired, in baggy pants with a tight belt, a white T-shirt, and dark glasses. His face was rectangular, even, and without the severe shadows in the sun he might well have been handsome. He appeared in a few other snapshots, approximately the same man. "Doesn't tell us a hell of a lot, does it? Well, a picture is only a picture." Archie watched the blackboard for a while, either thinking or expecting the blackboard to make a run for it.

"Now, it stands to reason that he'd be in Timothy's photo collection, as well. He begins to show some signs of taking his place in the dance. Juicy prospect, indeed, if we let our imaginations go a bit. Suppose he's still alive and out there, a different man after all these years. Suppose he's come back. Suppose he went to see Larry Blankenship and after he left, Larry killed himself—suppose he got back into the apartment and took something that connected him to Larry . . . and what if he then went to see Timothy Dierker?" He was smiling, happy, knee-deep in his own element. "Ah, well, it's a line of inquiry, you'll surely grant me that."

When I staggered sleepily to the door, my moth-eaten old Rolex told me it was two minutes to midnight. There were certain things in my life I trusted: my *Baseball Encyclopedia;* my old Rolex, which knew nothing of watches that told the date or drew their power from quartz chips; the Porsche, which refused to say the hell with it and die.

"Let me think about it some more, Paul. And don't give up on your little chats with the interested parties. When in doubt, remember Fenton Carey and push on. As my English cronies used to say during the war, it's early days. Be patient." He slapped my back and sent me into the night. On the way back to town I listened to the music from *A Man and a Woman,* wished I looked like Jean-Louis Trintignant doing Bogart, and let my mind drift back to Peanuts Lowrey running down fly balls in the vines at Wrigley Field. Very peaceful.

There had been dry snow blowing on the platform, swirling in the lights and stinging my face and sifting down inside my coat collar the night I killed the old man in Finland. He had worn a black overcoat flapping around his ankles and the fur collar was dusted with snow; he'd believed he was safe at last, had come carefully through the snow-packed, squeaking streets of the village. I'd watched him from an alleyway, shaking with fear and sick to my stomach, tanked up on vodka, my toes nearly frozen. He'd walked as quickly as he could, clutching a worn briefcase to his chest, looking behind him and expecting the worst. By the time he got to the station he'd begun to believe he was going to make it and I'd puked the vodka into the snow. It made my head clearer and clammy sweat soaked through my clothing. My joints ached; it was hard to walk.

We were the only passengers. A wood-burning stove glowed, spit when the old man brushed snow off his coat. He caught my eye, his round spectacles flat and shining in the light. He sniffled into an old gray handkerchief and sat on an uncomfortable hardwood bench. Together, in the hot stillness, we waited. Just the two of us. My Rolex, old even then, said eight minutes to eleven when he scuttled over to the counter and bought his ticket. I stood behind him, mutely bought my own ticket. At four minutes to eleven he went onto the platform, holding the briefcase like an infant, protectively, determined. He went cautiously toward the tracks, peered down the darkness. I moved close to him, as if I, too, wanted the first glimpse of our way back to Helsinki. There was a powerful light mounted on the front of the engine and at two minutes to eleven we saw it, poking through the blowing snow, making a halo of whiteness in the darkness. . . .

I was remembering it all because I was going to see General Jon Goode. It was early and bright with the morning sun slanting on Lake Harriet, turning it into the beginnings of flat silver that replaces summery gold. It was funny, the way that worked. I've never figured it out. Maybe it was me; my stomach felt just the way it had all those years ago and I had Jon Goode to thank for the memory.

What I'd done that night to save my own life had been something less than a success: Part of me, part of my humanity, had died with the old man. When it was over I was remote from life, cool to the passions of happiness. Maybe that was what I sensed in Kim Roderick, what drew me to her. Maybe that was what Anne had meant.

General Jon Goode met me at the door of the lofty brick home where he lived alone. The paint on the columns and window ledges was pristine, the walk straight, and the lawn neatly, precisely trimmed. A man in a vest and work pants was at work on a hedge with old-fashioned manual shears, beside him a wheelbarrow full of sacks of fertilizer and potting soil and tools. Goode smiled grimly, frigid lines chipped out of the rock of his face, and wished me a good morning. In his gray sweat shirt and sweat pants and striped Addidas running shoes, he had the quality of a miniature cut from a book of paper soldiers, square shoulders, small square head with its thick gray, close-cropped hair. His nose bisected his rectangular face vertically, with gray eyebrows and narrow mustache trisecting it horizontally. His ears were small and fine, shell-like, and even the tips of his tanned fingers were delicately squared off. He positively reeked of self-control, a viceless, taut, distant man.

"Good timing, Paul," he said as I followed him back to his sun porch, which throbbed with plants and hung heavy with the output of a pair of whirring humidifiers. "I've just finished my morning's run around the lake, like clockwork. The shape I'm in"—he chuckled dryly, settling into a wicker chair and waiting for me to sit opposite him—"the shape I'm in, I'm likely to live forever. Never felt better. I'd offer you coffee but, like smoking, I've gone off the stuff. The less you put in your stomach, the better off you are. I fast one day a week and. . . ." He considered me appraisingly and frowned. "You'd do well to fast yourself, Paul. Two days a week, that would be my advice. You've really got to get a grip on yourself or it'll be too late." He gave his excuse for a grin and rubbed his hands together. "Well, what can I do for you, Paul?" The son of a bitch had just spent an hour running and he wasn't even breathing hard. I gave him the folderol about writing the nostalgia story; it was beginning to sound so false to me that I cringed at repeating it.

"So I'm just gathering recollections about the club," I said. "Dad got me onto it, then I talked to Tim Dierker, just before he took the big fall. . . ."

"Awful thing," he said brusquely, pouring orange juice from a glass pitcher into a cut-glass goblet on a wicker table beside his chair. A Swedish ivy drooped over the tabletop from a basket above. He gestured to me with the goblet and sipped the juice.

"But death doesn't bother you quite so much, as it does other people, I mean. Not with the life you've led." There was an edge in my voice and the way I felt about General Goode was working its way toward the surface of the morning. Goode ignored it, if he noticed it at all.

"Death is waiting for us all," he said philosophically, arrogantly, as if he were wise in the ways of dying, as I suppose he was. "Death is the winner in the end and the sooner we stop fidgeting about it, the better off we are. I've seen a death or two in my time, men cut off in their prime and that's a bad business, but Tim . . . Tim had a long and prosperous run for it. It's not his death that upsets me, but the manner of it, yes, that's upsetting. Result of a permissive society, some people say, and they may be right—hoodlums pushing old men off rooftops, violence in the streets, it's everywhere. Neighbor of mine was out walking around the lake one evening a month or so ago. Our lake, *my* lake, goddamn it! And he was beaten, robbed, left out in the rain to die . . . car after car went by him as he crawled toward the street, nobody helped. I found him in the fog the next morning, unconscious, fractured skull and pneumonia, but alive." He sipped some more juice and crossed his slender, gray-clad legs. "Hoodlums ought to be dealt with the way we did it in the army, in combat, or on a mission. I've seen bullies, criminals, psychotics—shot to death by their fellows and I shut my eyes to it. . . . Simple justice, I'd say." He leveled his pale eyes at me. "You're right, I don't look at death like most people. Death had been a part of my job. But that doesn't lessen my sorrow at Tim's death. Don't confuse my feelings, Paul, because you don't understand them."

"Is that an order, General?"

"A request, Paul."

I shrugged. I knew all about his requests. I asked him to tell me about the hunting and fishing club.

"I'm no fisherman. I'm a hunter, fulfilling the general destiny of man. . . ."

"Ah, bullshit, General," I said. "Don't be obscure."

"What's the matter, Paul? Get out of bed on the wrong side?" He summoned up the taut little smile and poured some more orange juice. From a milk-glass bowl he scooped out a handful of pills, shoveled them into his mouth, and downed them with two long drafts of orange juice.

"What do you mean, the destiny of man? That sounds suspiciously like crap—"

"Men are predators, it's our nature to hunt. We're only animals, after all. There's a predator lurking inside each of us and it's the wise man who deals with the impulse. That's one of war's most beneficial aspects, provides a runoff for our aggression. The need to hunt, to kill, to strike at the crucial moment decisively, irrevocably—that's to accept the nature of the human species. . . ."

"And you can't change your nature, is that it?"

"Now you're getting it, Paul." The gardener had made his way along the hedge and was working his shears rhythmically beneath the screens of the porch. "That killing instinct, it's the same damned instinct that leads a man to collect. To collect rare books or stamps or beautiful guns—it's a version of the old killing instinct, a sublimation of it."

"Behavior is changed, modified," I said. "But not nature."

"On the button, Paul."

"Did you ever kill anyone? Personally, I mean."

"I never talk about that kind of thing. Never."

"I don't blame you."

I poked around in club matters for a bit, getting nowhere. "Going over the club members," I said, "I ran across one I can't find. Fellow called Carver Maxvill. I'm told he disappeared, whatever that means."

General Goode pulled back fractionally, straightened in the chair, and set his goblet down.

"What the hell has that got to do with anything? How should I know what happened to him? He used to come up north with us, odd fellow. I wondered if he were a queer for a while, but I suppose that was uncharitable of me. . . . But I was in Washington most of the time then. I don't know anything about what happened to him. I don't really care."

"It's funny," I said. "No one wants to talk about the

poor bastard, old Carver Maxvill. Father Boyle gave me a couple of funny looks and asked me to leave."

"Well, I'm not asking you to leave, Paul, but I do have an institute board meeting on tap in about half an hour." He glanced at the round gold watch with a butter-colored strap that blended into his tan. "I've got to take a shower." He stood up, came up to my shoulder, but his presence was commanding.

"One last thing—"

"You sound like Columbo on the television, luring his guest star to death row. . . ." He laughed quietly, moving out of the plant room into the long dark hall. I heard a power mower fire up in the backyard.

"Why would the murderer—who was no hoodlum, by the way—why would he steal Tim Dierker's old scrapbook?"

"I haven't any idea."

"Well, I think it had something to do with the club, it fits, he kept all those old pictures from up north in it . . . and his wife told me that he was crying and looking at the scrapbook just before he was killed. . . ."

"Listen to me, Paul." He stopped, put his hands on his narrow hips. "You're on your way into a swamp, I'm afraid. You're wasting your time. Tim's murder didn't have anything to do with the club, which is what you seem to be implying. We were just an innocent bunch of friends, young men who enjoyed getting away from it all. . . . Nothing sinister at all."

I stopped again at the doorway. "Did you know Larry Blankenship? Or his wife?"

"I knew Larry through Tim Dierker. Not well."

"Well enough to attend his funeral."

"A favor for Tim. Wanted a turnout, the man had no family of his own, from what I understand."

"And his wife?"

"I knew who she was, from Norway Creek. Nice enough kid, hard worker, that's all."

"You didn't know where she came from?"

"My God, why should I? She's nothing special to me."

General Goode was growing impatient, which gave

me considerable pleasure. He was controlling himself, however, which wasn't.

"Well, when you can spare the time, I'd like to hear some of your memories of the north country, what it was like thirty, forty years ago. . . ."

"Pretty much like it is now, I'd think. It doesn't change much up there."

"You don't happen to have any snapshots, by chance? For the piece I'm writing."

"Oh, there's a box of them around somewhere, I suppose. In the attic. Or maybe they got thrown away —I don't live much in the past, Paul, I don't think about the past much."

"I wouldn't either, I'm sure, if I were you."

He'd had enough of me. Failing the opportunity to court-martial me, he began to close the door in my face.

"I don't think I can help you," he said, all smiles gone. "I'm sure of it."

The Crocker estate was only hinted at from the highway that circles through the village of Long Lake, curves back into the hills rising from the lake itself. There were fieldstone gateposts and a white fence which looped over the hills and disappeared in the middle distance among stands of trees; farther back still, glimpsed through the trees, was a green-tile roof, acres of green-tile roof with one chimney after another. The driveway clocked out to 1.4 miles, by which time I felt as if I'd passed at least one national border and was among another kind of people altogether. I was driving over crushed rock, watching horses wander across the white-fenced fields, two children in jodhpurs and boots strolling among them. A huge turnaround with a dry fountain in the middle fronted the house, which lay in a crescent of three wings. There were several automobiles lying carelessly about the grass and rock, as if sprinkled: Crocker's gunmetal Mark IV with the sun roof open, a red Cadillac El-dorado with the white top down, a Ford station wagon, a Mercedes 450 SL in gold, an old Thunderbird. . . .

I put the Porsche in the shade of a tree and hoped no one would be offended by it. It was one o'clock.

I was standing there like an idiot, staring at the vastness of the house, the multitude of long windows, wondering where to begin my search for Crocker, when my second gardener of the day came earnestly around the nearest corner. On the whole, it beat pounding the sidewalks of the inner city in search of a poverty-stricken killer who did his dirty work for money or out of habit or social pressures or indifference for his fellowman.

"Excuse me, sir," he said, this elderly gent with calluses on his hands and a stub of corncob pipe stuck in his mouth. "Are you Mr. Cavanaugh?" I 'fessed up. "Mr. Crocker said you'd be coming and I should tell you they're back by the pool. Just make your way around this corner and you'll see them. Just join right in." He sucked on his pipe and watched me around the corner.

The day was changing the way they do toward the end of summer, the sunshine of morning giving way to furling banks of white clouds rolling across the crystal-blue sky like surf. A breeze had sprung up and flickered in the trees, worried at the striped-canvas awnings along the back of the house, above the rattan and glass and fieldstones. The lake looked gray as a cloud blotted out the sun.

A large oblong swimming pool lay midway between the house and the lake, maybe a hundred yards from either, and there was a bathhouse with patio and screened-in porch, a tennis court past some poplar trees closer to the lake, a stone barbecue area with tables and chairs and more canvas umbrellas. Smoke was drifting up from the gas-fed black barbecues and I could smell it as I began trekking across the thick soft lawn. Maybe twenty people of various ages and sizes dappled the area, which was so large they looked vaguely lonely, as if there'd been a party and nobody came. It was a long-enough walk to try to figure out who they were. Crocker in white shorts and a Harry Truman Hawaiian shirt was tending the grills; his wife in a flowing drapery of terry cloth was sitting with a couple of women a generation younger, all obscured behind sunglasses; husbands threw a football around with teenage boys; a couple of beautiful rich teenage girls sauntered back from the tennis court with their tawny hair and bodies flowing like syrup, positively edible. Some other people were standing by a dock way down at the lake, heaving lengths of rope back and forth, tussling to either untie or make fast a sailboat. A couple of small children flailed away at croquet balls, swinging their mallets with malicious abandon. The royal family at their leisure. I wondered if they were having fun and decided it was a stupid, middle-class question if ever I'd heard one. In their place, I sure as hell would have been having fun.

Crocker was by himself and nobody seemed to have noticed me in my chino slacks and red checked shirt with the epaulets you couldn't see because I was wearing a beat-up denim sport coat. I hadn't done the beating up. It came that way from France and cost me more because somebody else had obviously spent a lot of time kicking it around an empty room. Radical chic. And I was disappointed in myself for being so smitten by it.

James Crocker, with wavy white hair, heavy features, black horn-rims, and a gold University of Minnesota ring with a red stone roughly the size of a horseshoe, ground my hand in his and returned it marked damaged goods. It was a bad beginning; a kick in the nuts was the only possible civilized response. But he seemed a gruff, kindly man who probably doted on John Wayne movies and loved hanging around his construction sites in hard hat and gear. There were ten chickens laid out on the grills, sizzling and turning reddish brown.

"My famous barbecue sauce," Crocker said, licking some of it from his stubby fingers. "Family tells me it's wonderful, but what the hell can they say, hunh? Got the recipe down on the Johnson spread during his Presidency, real Texas-style barbecue sauce. . . ." He grabbed a towel and wiped his hands, reached behind him and untied his smeared apron.

"I'd have thought you were a Republican," I said.

"I'm a winner," he said, rumbling some thunder in his deep chest. "I'm for whoever's in office. Basic principle of mine, since all politicians are alike in the end. They're no damned different than anybody else. Look, you want to talk, let's leave these goddamn chickens. . . ." He motioned to a ten-year-old. "Hey, Teddy, come here, do your grandpa a favor. Watch the chickens, okay?"

Teddy nodded. "How?"

Crocker gave him a dipper, pointed to the stainless caldron. "When they get to lookin' dry and crinkly, dribble some of this red stuff on them. Nothin' to it. Got it?" Teddy said he had it and Crocker led me off across the sloping lawn toward the lake.

"Love to have my family around me," he said reflectively, hands jammed in the back pockets of his shorts. "It's about the only kind of immortality you can have, I figure, through the generations you leave behind you when you go. At my age you get a new perspective, you see the end up there ahead of you. . . . Doesn't scare me the way I used to think it would. I've always been a realist and I know there's no escaping it. So I enjoy seeing the young ones who'll be carrying on for me. I want them to remember Jim Crocker with some pride." We stopped to watch an impromptu softball game that was just beginning. The two tawny girls were running sort of awkwardly around, showing off their bodies, and I felt a twinge of panic for their fathers. "Now, what was it you wanted to see me about, Paul?"

"Well, it started out as an article I wanted to do on the thirties, the hunting and fishing club you fellows had up north . . . but then I sort of stumbled into the Blankenship suicide and Tim Dierker murder."

"What's Blankenship got to do with it? I don't quite get the connection."

"I don't really know. Harriet Dierker thought it had something to do with Blankenship's wife. Sort of nebulous, but she asked me to find out a couple of things, snoop around a little. I was doing a half-hearted job and then Tim gets pushed off the roof. . . . The thing is, Tim was acting very strangely the day he died. You remember, it was the day Larry Blankenship was buried. Kim talked to Tim at the funeral, then Tim went into a funk for the rest of the day, got drunk against doctor's orders and the last time Harriet saw him he was going through his photograph album, sort of wallowing in the past, crying—"

"Damn shame," Crocker said quickly, a catch in his voice, a sentimental man. "Poor Tim's health was shot to hell. Who knows what was going on in his mind? The body and mind go together, one begins to fail and as likely as not the other starts to go, too." He shook his huge head. "But I still don't see what's so unusual. Tim was dying. He comes home from a funeral, he's depressed, his mind wandering around in the past, the old days when he was well and hearty, gets loaded and has a crying jag—seems pretty easily explained to me."

"The thing is, the murderer stole the scrapbook."

"Ah, who cares? Some nut, that's all."

"No, it won't wash, Mr. Crocker. Not some nut, not an act of random violence. Somebody lured Tim up onto the roof, gave him a push. Somebody Tim knew, or so it would seem, not someone he feared."

"Well, I sure as hell don't have any candidates."

We'd reached the shoreline and were pacing along the damp sand toward the dock. The sailboat was well out into the lake and the clouds were gaining on the sun. The breeze off the water had a snap to it. We walked the length of the dock and leaned on the railing. Shouts drifted from the water, from the other estates. If Gatsby had settled in Minnesota, where he belonged, he would have grown up and become James Crocker, contemplating eternity from the bosom of his dynasty. Crocker had made his money, building on his football fame. He'd worked his ass off so his descendants might have the opportunity, at least, to be wastrels. He waved to the lads on the boat, his sons, and they waved back, tacking or whatever you do against the wind. I'm no sailor. They could have been sinking, for all I knew.

"What do you think of Harriet Dierker?"

"Gabby. Sweet, though. Give her credit for that.

She never really got over not having any children. I think she liked to pretend that Blankenship was their child, at least at one time."

"She told me that Kim Roderick, his wife—"

"I know who she is," he said, grinning sourly. "Pack of trouble, that girl. Temptress. Anyway, so I'm told. . . ."

"Harriet told me that Kim had something to do with Blankenship's suicide and Tim's murder."

"Oh, Jesus," he exploded, his surprise going off like a bomb, "like what? She threw Tim off the building, I suppose? What an imagination! Oh, I can believe she drove that poor bastard of a husband to kill himself. I can believe that easily enough. From what I've heard and seen she's just that kind of woman. Makes good use of her sexiness, you know—"

"Some people tell me she's sexless."

"Some people think that's sexy, that act of hers. She uses her looks, that cool quality. . . . Let me tell you something. I'm a happy man, happy with my life, but she even tempted me. Thank God, I've got too much sense. She was much too close to home, thanks."

"How about Ole?"

"She's his problem. No business of mine."

When we began strolling back, I said, "Do you remember a guy named Maxvill?"

He stopped and looked at me, his face furrowing in peculiar ways.

"Carver? Carver Maxvill? Asshole! He couldn't take it, ran the hell away from it."

"It?"

"Life, man! Life. . . . I don't know." He swung back the way we were heading. "Poke around in that mess and you'll find a reason; he was in trouble somewhere, pulled some shady lawyer bullshit and took cover for good, never came back out . . . just crap." Teddy was playing with the chicken as we arrived back at the barbecue. "I never liked the guy. What the hell brought him up, anyway?"

"Martin Boyle mentioned him."

"You've talked with Marty, too?" He shrugged and grinned. "Well, I'll be damned. You should ask

Hubbard Anthony about Carver, he was his pal, brought him into the club—Jesus Christ, the chicken's on fire!" He made a grab for the tongs and picked up a flaming chicken, waved it in the air like an unusual banner. Teddy watched in amazement. The fire died. I smelled the burning barbecue sauce. Distracted, Crocker stared at the frazzled chicken for a moment, then placed it out of harm's way in a corner of the grill.

"Well, look, I'm busy, Paul, got all these hungry people to feed. And I sure as hell don't want to talk about Carver Maxvill." We shook hands again and I went away licking barbecue sauce off my fingers.

"Give me a call, though," he shouted, waving another chicken. "I'll tell you some hunting stories. That's what you're after, anyway."

I nodded and went on. The gardener looked up as I went around the corner.

"Find everything all right, sir?"

"Sure. I found everything."

I'd pulled off the highway to buy some fresh fruit at a roadside stand when the gunmetal Mark IV shot past at about eighty. I couldn't see the driver but the odds were good enough. I put the bags of apples, plums, peaches, grapefruit, and sweet corn on the passenger seat, offered up a frail prayer for the Porsche, and followed the silvery blur. I picked it up at the last stoplight in Wayzata, at Bushaway Road, and then stayed with it all the way into town, south on Hennepin, past the Walker/Guthrie complex, past the Lake Street intersection to Thirty-Fifth, right to Lake Calhoun, then left around the southern curve of the lake, through the parkway to Lake Harriet.

For the first time it was making sense to me; somebody was actually doing something that gave all my poking and puttering the semblance of a point. James Crocker, still wearing his shorts and his silly shirt, had run out on his dynastic picnic, driven all the way to town, and was running up the stairway to Jon Goode's front door.

I parked up above the house, in the shade beneath

some thick shrubbery. Five minutes later they came back down together, grim-faced, saying nothing, climbed into the Mark IV, and took off. I wasn't worried about following them. I knew where they were going.

I lost them at the Lake Street light but picked them up again on the freeway heading toward St. Paul. They slid off up the University of Minnesota ramp, wound around the back streets to University Avenue, and turned right beneath the tower in Prospect Park. From the corner I saw them going up to Father Boyle's place. I was what had set them in motion. I didn't bother to wait. I'd touched a nerve named Carver Maxvill and set them running. The thing was, I didn't know why. But they were all tied together.

8

MY BODY felt like a clenched fist and I hadn't been near the Y in a couple of weeks. I parked in LaSalle Court late in the afternoon and went upstairs to the smaller of the two running tracks, the one that's dished and threatens to pitch you over the railing into the basketball players below. Five minutes of running and any sane commander would have left me for dead. I went downstairs and shot some baskets, grunting with exertion out beyond the circle, sagged down in the dry sauna amid some gentlemen who were just possibly in worse shape than I was, and concluded by collapsing across the rubdown table for about ten minutes. When I left I felt a good deal worse than when I'd entered but I had rinsed Goode and Crocker and Dierker and the whole sad bunch out of my mind for at least an hour. By the time I got back to the Porsche I was thinking about them again.

I was too tired to eat a real meal so I cut some cheddar, sliced an apple, spread out a big slice of Dimpfelmeyer rye bread on a cutting board, put on a sweater, and went out on my balcony. The ball game hadn't started and WCCO was telling me what a hell of a year 1932 had been. They played Bing Crosby's recording of "Night and Day" and then told me that on March 1 the nineteen-month-old son of Colonel Charles Lindbergh and Anne Morrow Lindbergh was taken from his crib at the family home in Hopewell, New Jersey. On May 12 the boy's body, little more than a skeleton, was found in the bushes a few miles from the house. In the end, maybe, you never got far from home. Then Fred Astaire sang, "A Shine on Your Shoes" and I began to nibble my dinner.

There were so many pieces to try to fit together, to interlock, but all I could see or feel—anybody who had talked to the people I had was bound to have the same feeling—was that they all belonged to the same puzzle. It was like having pieces from each of the four corners of the puzzle; none of them seemed to touch. I suppose it was a good example of the untidiness of life as compared to the formal complexity of one of my father's novels or one of Agatha Christie's. I sat and munched on apple and damp rye bread and felt like a child crouched dumbly in the playpen with all my toys collapsed around me, not knowing which one to fiddle with next.

I kept thinking back to Archie's blackboard, wondering how the diverse elements might make a real, visible pattern rather than a felt pattern, the kind I was arriving at by intuition. I could picture the blackboard in my mind but whatever I felt we'd be closing in on was utterly gone. In school geometry class had affected me the same way. It always seemed so pure and logical as the teacher worked through the theorems on the board; I never had a question, never a doubt as I watched the clean little miracle unfold out of her chalky hand. But once I sat down in my room with my homework it never made sense. Somewhere between school and home the logic had gotten lost and I couldn't produce my own. All I really wanted to do was turn on the radio and listen to *My Friend Irma* and think rude thoughts about Marie Wilson's bosom.

What was the pattern? There was the *scrapbook.* And the dead people: *Larry* and *Tim.* Who both spoke with *Kim* shortly before they died. And the *club* had known Larry and Kim, if only peripherally. And *Carver Maxvill.* The mention of his name, a man nobody had seen in thirty years, frightened *Father Boyle, General Goode,* and *James Crocker.* I sorted through the stuff in my mind, made entries on filing cards of different colors (my father's son, yes)—a card for names, for things, for possible motives. . . . I almost forgot to make a name card for *Billy Whitefoot,* the all-but-forgotten man. "The Forgotten Man" . . . Franklin D. Roosevelt had made that popular during the 1932 Presidential campaign. The club was meeting up north, snapping their pictures and drinking too much and catching fish and raising hell, and Franklin D. was running for the White House in a wheelchair Had they cared? Had they really been a part of their times, or just a sprinkling of warts? It was so hard to tell. Forty-odd years ago, who had they been, really? Could they even cast a glance along the track of time and remember?

On the radio Barbra Streisand whacked out another hit from 1932, "Brother, Can You Spare a Dime?" pronouncing it "doime," and I remembered seeing her at the Blue Angel in the early sixties (or had it been the late fifties? So much for trying to remember how it had all looked in 1932). *Of Thee I Sing* won the Pulitzer Prize that year and to commemorate the event, just before the 1974 Minnesota Twins took the field against the Kansas City Royals, they played "Wintergreen for President" and I was tapping my feet and humming. I wondered if Archie had seen Charlie Chaplin in *City Lights* that year. Had he cheered on June 21 when Jack Sharkey decisioned Max Schmeling and brought the heavyweight championship back home? Had he seen Paul Muni in *Scarface?*

I sat in the dark for a long time listening to the ball

game and picking through my memories of everything
I'd seen and heard since Hubbard Anthony and I had
come back from playing tennis that first day. I tried to
remember it all and I came up with one peculiar scrap,
one connection between two people who had died: the
gray fluff from Timothy Dierker's slippers. . . . That
was what I'd seen sprinkled on the floor of Larry Blankenship's sad, hollow, echoing apartment. The dirty
gray fluff hadn't been kicked into the corners; it was
out in the center of the room. . . . Timothy Dierker had
been down to visit Larry Blankenship not long before
he died. Did he know what had driven Larry to
suicide? Or was it Pa Dierker who had cleaned out
Larry's apartment *after* the suicide? My problem was
that I kept coming up with more questions and whenever I had the glimmering of an answer it would split
apart à la Walt Disney and transform itself into several
new questions. I finished the apple and cheese,
chomped up the rye crust, and opened a can of Olympia. The Twins had just gone ahead on Carew's double up the middle. It felt as though autumn were
definitely in the air.

I decided I'd never get on top of the mess of detail
and fact and implication without applying a new discipline to it. A clear mind, a healthy body; God knows
what had gotten into me. A diet revision seemed a
good place to start and I was peering warily at a half
of pink grapefruit, my entire breakfast if you didn't
count the coffee with Weight Watchers sweetener, when
the phone on the desk beside me rattled like a snake.
It was Hubbard Anthony. He wanted me to meet
him for lunch at the Minneapolis Club and there was
a vaguely judicial, oddly insistent quality in his voice.
It wasn't a command but on the other hand it wasn't
a chance suggestion. Clearly, I wasn't supposed to
make my apologies.
The vines still clung to the brick in the sunshine and
the hush lay like the soft cloud of tradition on the dining room. Minneapolis is not an old city but it is a
wealthy one. The Minneapolis Club therefore pur-
chased its aura of age, turning new into old with a pe-

culiar kind of social alchemy. Money had done a good deal for Minneapolis but it was still a trick, the city was built on a trick; it was a thought which had subtly invaded my thinking years before but I held onto it with the strength born of conviction. I had the feeling that no matter how long Minneapolis lasted, it would still be new, wanting to be old.

Hubbard was tall and elegant in blue summer-weight pin-stripe, a gold collar pin tweezing the long points tight beneath his striped tie. He smelled good, too, as he led me up the stairway and into lunch. He was a perfect reflection of the typical Minneapolis power broker, though somewhat better dressed than the grain barons and the department store princes and computer tycoons. He moved through the room like a saber blade and I followed, a large fellow in need of a diet. It was quiet with the gentle clink of cutlery on china and ice in tall glasses of tea. Beyond, in the dark, polished lounges, there were occasional elderly gents reading the *Wall Street Journal* or writing odd little notes on the club stationery or sleeping it off in the little compartment tucked behind the library, out of range of families and impatient offices.

"Clear soup and the sole," Hubbard said thoughtfully, as if it were the day's big decision. Proudly I required two soft-boiled eggs and two slices of dry whole wheat toast. Hubbard raised his eyebrows, nodded, and sipped his perfect martini.

"Well, we're surely not here to arrange a tennis date," I said.

"Hardly." His eyes settled on a man two tables distant. Thin, sallow, worried in his glen plaid. "Andy Malcolm over there—have you heard of his problems? No? Well, you surely will. In the papers." Hubbard sighed, wistfully mocking. "He's about to be indicted —that's his lawyer he's about to weep on. Andy, as it happens, has been caught up in his enthusiasms for Mr. Nixon, running in and out of the country with satchels full of cash, 'laundering it' as we've been learning to say in recent months. At this point in time, Andy's rather afraid he's headed for the clink. After golf at Woodhill people will mention his name and chuckle behind their hands . . . which causes him much distress." He sipped at the martini and made a sour face. "Crooks of his class really do have a pathological fear of being revealed for what they are. Not overly bright. Can you imagine committing a crime for Richard Nixon? It's really rather astonishing."

"Will he go to jail?"

"Good lord, no. Did I give that impression? He belongs there, of course, but we must be realistic. He'll avert the final disaster."

Lunch arrived and I sliced open the eggs. A gasp of steam escaped from each one. They required salt and pepper. I could see Andy Malcolm and luckily the sight took away my appetite; he wasn't laughing or smiling. His face was yellowish and deeply lined, jaw clenched, and he looked as if he had to go to the bathroom. I hoped Mr. Nixon appreciated his sacrifice.

"I got a call from our aging football hero, Jim Crocker, last night, Paul. Threatening more or less to run you over with one of his bulldozers. He demanded a meeting. Have you ever confronted a hysterical fullback, or whatever he was? Even at his advanced age the prospect is alarming." He chewed a bit of sole and nodded happily. "So I met with him. And Martin Boyle. And Jon Goode. Talk about a cabal, it was remarkably offensive in almost every detail. Their hysteria differed only in degree. Crocker appeared in danger of an apoplectic fit and Boyle was, as is frequently the case, about two-thirds gone—on Irish whiskey, I assume. All"—he sighed—"because of your little social calls. . . . Really, Paul, we're going to have to get you straightened out and the old lads becalmed before they croak out of pure terror and indignation." More sole disappeared. An egg was gone and I was choking on the odd bite of whole wheat toast.

"Hub, I don't know what you're talking about. . . ."

"I shall explain." He patted his mouth with immaculate linen. "The crux of the matter is Carver Maxvill. You've exhumed old Carver and scared them half to death. Yes, I can understand your confusion, yes, and I agree that it is surprising in men of such substance. But they're not as young as they once were and they're not cool, as the younger generation would say. The mere mention of Carver Maxvill, as you can see, hardly renders me a basket case . . . but, by heaven, it bothers them." He shrugged impatiently. "Damned old ladies . . . but it's an exposed nerve and there you are."

"Well, why?" I asked. "What's their excuse for behaving so stupidly?" I rustled my own indignation, such as it was, reminiscent of creeping damp.

"All we know—all anybody knows, for that matter —is that Carver disappeared. I'd known him for some time, in law school at the university, and his father, since deceased, was an insurance man. Carver was a nice-enough fellow, no Norway Creek connection—the only one of us who didn't have—but he was an avid outdoorsman, brought up on *The Open Road for Boys* and the Scout manual, trustworthy, loyal, friendly, courteous, kind, on and on. He wanted to join us. . . . I convinced the others he was a straight lad, hail-fellow. Actually he was like an F. Scott Fitzgerald character, loved wearing tuxedos, had saucer eyes and a kind of flapperish innocence which appealed to a decidedly lower class of women." He smiled faintly, tolerantly. "His women ran to waitresses, maids, and the general category of easy girls, as we used to call them, but still and all a good fellow. Anyway, he went up north with us regularly, was a good sport, established himself in a top-drawer firm—Vosper and Reynolds—and was generally an enjoyable companion. Tendency to drink a bit heavily. . . ."

"Was there a lot of hell-raising done up at the lodge, Hub? Heavy stuff?"

"Ah, we were young, Paul. At moments our high spirits got the better of us—nothing of moment but a kind of naughtiness I associate with the twenties and thirties, killed off by the war. The spoiled, idle rich, rubbish like that."

We took our coffee in the dim library, deserted, smelling faintly of furniture polish and cigars. He went on about Carver Maxvill.

"There was nothing untoward or even noticeable about him. Oh, a spot of infatuation with a woman up north who did some cooking for us but nothing to make a fuss over. Then one day, during the war, he simply was gone, taking nothing with him. . . . Do I have an explanation? Only theories. After all, men do take flight, take cover, get swallowed up from time to time. Missing Persons is full of people who've never been found. My own feeling is that he's almost certainly dead. There's never been the slightest hint that he's alive. Hypothesis . . . he probably went slumming and tied one on, got mixed up with the wrong guy's girlfriend, and got himself killed. I've known of drunks who lost consciousness in Minneapolis and wound up dead in Chicago the next day and nobody knows how. He was the kind of irresponsible fellow that sort of thing happens to . . . fatal flaw and so on. Hell, Paul, he was probably dead within forty-eight hours of his disappearance."

It reminded me of the Lindbergh baby, in the bush a couple miles from home. Nobody ever gets very far. Hubbard Anthony was probably right. Thirty years of mystery was a waste of time and the man was dead, anyway.

"So why does this set the jolly boys atwitter? Boyle, Goode, Crocker . . . what's it got to do with them?"

"Well, it may sound peculiar to you, Paul, but the best excuse for their behavior I can find is just that Carver Maxvill is an irregularity . . . something that doesn't fit with the rest of their lives, doesn't square. Do you know what I mean, Paul?"

"Sounds weak to me," I said.

"People get old and less resilient, they can't adapt anymore—that's what's happened to these guys. Try to understand. The memory of Maxvill opens up an old sore, something they'd rather not have to think about anymore. . . ."

"Sounds a hell of a lot like guilt to me," I said.

"Come on, Paul"—he chuckled—"don't be ridiculous."

"My explanation makes more sense than yours, that's all."

"Perhaps, but mine has the advantage of being true." He fixed me with a somber stare. "So, please lay off the boys. As a favor to me. I've had enough of dealing with elderly hysterics." He stood up and checked his watch. "All right?"

"All right, Hub."

He slapped me on the shoulder and we went back outside together. I wasn't going to get any more of an explanation out of him. I sat alone for a while, squeezed uncomfortably in behind the Porsche's steering wheel, contemplating a growing rip in the fabric of the top. Ah, so much to do and so little time to do it in.

But Hub, an eminently logical man, hadn't made much sense. What the hell was he talking about, anyway? Nervous old men; it didn't stand up. Jon Goode and James Crocker—it was ridiculous. Father Boyle, maybe, but not the others.

I remembered what Kim had said and I tried to fit it into the pattern. It seemed to fit, if I could only jiggle it around, gently, linking it to the rest of what I knew. She said she was fascinated by the past, by the way it reached out and affected the present, how it changed as the years went by and became something new, a different reality from what it once had been. It made a good deal more sense than Hubbard's explanation.

But how?

What was it about Carver Maxvill, with the saucer eyes and the tuxedo? Had he ever gotten away? Or was he close to home, closer than the old men wanted him? Did Carver Maxvill have something on them? Did he know where the skeletons were buried?

The mention of his name had turned them decidedly green around the gills. And they had been the core of the club. And the club had been somehow entwined, I was increasingly convinced, like a choking vine, with the deaths of Larry Blankenship and Timothy Dierker.

I parked in the newspaper lot, stopped briefly by my desk to throw the jumble of press releases into the wastebasket, and went downstairs to the subbasement to see Orville Smart, head librarian and keeper of the morgue. There were a good many very up-to-date knicknacks throughout the great slablike building but none of them pertained to Smart's bailiwick, which changed only in the number of dark-green filing cabinets aligned in Kafkaesque rows. There had been talk of converting the entire morgue to microfilm and he never really argued against it; he didn't push for it, though, so the operations committee kept letting it slide as bright boys in aviator sunglasses and Italian suits yelped their way to bigger budgets. That was fine with Orville Smart. He liked things down in his vault the way they were.

He sat at a green metal desk, looking unhealthy beneath the fluorescent lighting. He was drinking coffee from a cardboard container. He'd made his way through most of a liver-sausage sandwich and looked up, running his tongue around inside his mouth. He wore a striped shirt with a starched collar, the cuffs rolled halfway up his forearms, a narrow black tie carefully knotted with a horseshoe tie clasp, and about a dozen gray hairs were combed across the top of his head. Grant Wood might have painted him.

"Well," he drawled, looking me over slowly, a visitor from topside. "Don't see you down here once a year. Nice day, is it?" He always asked about the weather. I'd been to the morgue half a dozen times and he always asked about the weather. I told him it was a nice day and he bit off a piece of sandwich. I sat down on a metal chair. Aside from a distant whirring sound, it was quiet. "So what is it you're after? Let me guess. Old movie reviews? Some old theater reviews?" He produced a toothpick and leaned back, staring at me through round rimless spectacles.

"Not this time, Mr. Smart. Something else altogether." He perked up. "I want to find whatever we've got on a disappearance about thirty years ago. Local lawyer named Carver Maxvill, just walked off one day and never turned up again. Slick as a whistle, gone. Mean anything to you?"

He put down his toothpick and belted down the coffee and stood up, about six and a half stooped feet. He looked like an ambulatory parenthesis.

"Mean anything to me?" He cackled, as if such a question were too absurd for serious comment. The past was where he lived. "That's good! Sure I remember Carver Maxvill, made quite a stir in its day—little pieces followed the lead for about a week, the war was pushing it out of the way. It was winter, the winter of '44–'45, the Germans broke through the Ardennes just when we figured we had 'em licked. . . ." He blew his nose into a gray handkerchief and shuffled to the first rank of file cabinets, then slowly down the aisle, took a left, and led me to the *M*'s. The cabinets were arranged alphabetically, the subject matter in manila reinforced folders which grew stained and dog-eared as the years passed.

"Ought to be right here," he said, toothpick jutting out from his thin, bloodless lips. He pulled the deep drawer out and we discovered a peculiar fact. The Maxvill file was gone.

Orville Smart jabbed quickly through the drawer's contents, fruitlessly, and stood back, cupping his bony chin in a heavily veined, bony hand. "Real strange," he mused. "It ain't there." He leaned forward, head down, a little vein pulsing high on his white forehead the only sign of concern. He slid out several nearby drawers, checking to see if the file had been misplaced. But I knew it wasn't going to be there and I felt little prickles of sweat on my neck. The file on Carver Maxvill was gone as surely as he was himself, as surely as Tim Dierker's scrapbook. . . .

It took awhile for Orville Smart to accept fully the disappearance of the folder. Then he straightened up and looked down at me, eyes quizzical and almost ashamed. "Damned thing's gone."

"Where might it be?"

He led me back to the green metal library-size tables, two of them with six chairs at each, said, "See for yourself, no place to hide 'em. No drawers in the tables, no hiding places, the damned thing's gone. Unless . . ." He turned back to the sea of cabinets and frowned. "Unless you figure that it could be anywhere, *anywhere,* from A to Z in the entire system.

Golly, that's too horrible to think about, ain't it? No, it couldn't be just stuck anyplace—"

"You're sure there was a Carver Maxvill file?"

"Oh, hell, yes, that's like being sure there was a file on Floyd B. Olson or Hubert Humphrey or Kid Cann. Sure there was a Maxvill file. Musta been ten, twelve clippings anyway, counting the morning and evening papers. . . . And we've been the only newspapers in town all this time. . . ."

"Would there be a file in St. Paul?"

He shook his head; no he didn't think so. Like a man treading carefully, away from familiar ground which had betrayed him, he trudged back to his desk. He folded up into the swivel chair and scrounged a Chesterfield from a flattened packet. His fingers were stained yellow with nicotine. He snapped a wooden match on his thumb and lit it, inhaling deeply, cocking his head philosophically. "Been twenty years since I missed a file and that one turned up on the garden editor's desk upstairs. Just walked out with it, contrary to every rule of man or beast . . . none of this stuff is ever supposed to leave this room. . . ."

"So where's your security?" I asked. The sweat on my neck was soaking my collar and my stomach felt funny. Somebody was stealing the remnants of Carver Maxvill.

"Security? What security? Who needs security? Everybody knows the rule—don't need security. Staffers can come down whenever they need something, they can depend on it to be here. It's a good rule." He was looking at the remains of his sandwich, which was growing a bit leathery at the edges of the liverwurst. "It's always been a good rule."

"Who can use the files, Mr. Smart?"

"Staff people, writers and researchers and editors—"

"Anybody from the outside?"

"Nope," he snapped, then backed off, "at least not the public, they're private files. We get college professors and fellas writing books, they can get permission—"

"From whom?"

"What, permission? From me, of course."

"How?"

"Well, they call me or they write a request. Sometimes they just come down and ask."

"Do you just take their word for it?"

"Now, look," he said edgily, "there's one file missing in twenty years—golly, in the forty years since I been here, one file—"

"Two," I said. "And you're not going to find this one upstairs, Mr. Smart." He scowled through the smoke. "Do visitors have to sign in? Write down the files they want to see?"

"Believe me, there ain't that many visitors, Mr. Cavanaugh. They just ask and I tell 'em where to go. Informal."

"Do you remember them? If there are so few?"

"Not that few." He pursed his lips, cigarette dangling, eyes squinting. "If you could give me a name, I could maybe remember it . . . but I don't remember every person. Nobody has asked for the Maxvill file in years. I can't remember anybody ever asking for it. . . ."

"If they were going to steal it," I said, "they probably wouldn't have asked for it."

There was nothing else to do. "Do you remember, or could you check the date of the man's disappearance?"

"I don't remember it," he said. "But I could check upstairs. Montgomery probably covered it, he might remember the dates."

"Good idea," I said. "Do it. I'll get back to you on it." Montgomery was now an editorial vice-president and I didn't want to run him to ground, more likely than not at the polo grounds in Hamel. Orville Smart scratched something on a piece of yellow foolscap and picked up a begrimed black telephone. I climbed back into the sunshine, worried, confused. Who was trying to erase Carver Maxvill's poor life from its meager resting places?

I went home and took a shower, changed clothes, and called Ole Kronstrom's office. He was gone for the day. He wasn't home either. On the off chance, I dialed

Kim Roderick's number. It rang several times and she was out of breath when she answered. I apologized for interrupting and I imagined her pursing her lips before she spoke.

"It's okay, I'd just come out of the shower and was drying off. I just finished a couple of hours of tennis, with Anne, as a matter of fact." She stopped for air.

"Did you beat her?"

"Oh, yes, but she's improving, she really is."

"Look, is Ole there? I couldn't get him at home or the office, so I thought maybe he dropped in on you."

"No, I haven't seen him today. I really don't suppose I will because this is his boating night. He goes out on the St. Croix on his cruiser one night a week, with some of his cronies—tonight's the night." She sniffed water in her nose and the towel muffled her voice. "What did you want to see him for?"

"Just some questions about the club, some people he knew in the old days. Loose ends—nothing important."

"I'll bet, nothing important. . . ." But she wasn't sounding unfriendly, just neutral.

"Look, Kim," I said, trying to ingratiate myself just enough, "maybe I could talk to you. You're right, it is important. Or it might be. You never can tell, you might remember something Ole said if I hit the right switch."

"You know," she said slowly, after a moment's hesitation, "you sound suspiciously like a man who hasn't stopped poking around in other people's lives. Ouch!"

"Ouch what?"

"I don't know, I lost my rhythm today, started hitting my forehand badly. I picked up a blister, first one since last January—I got into some bad habits then, too. It's like a golf swing getting out of square, damn it. Anyway, I just peeled it back. . . . Does sucking it help?"

"Beats me," I said. "Look, it's not your past I'm poking into, and I'd certainly rather talk to you than Father Boyle and the rest of the Wild Bunch . . . it's you or them. Have mercy."

She laughed, high, clear. "Do you remember, you threatened to ask me for a date the first time we talked. Is that what you're doing now?"

"Almost."

"Well, I must be interested," she said. "I read your book yesterday, the one about the Caldwell murder. It was hard to find, I finally got the paperback at Savran's on the West Bank. I also picked up six of your father's Fenton Carey stories at Shinder's, they must have a dozen different titles. You're quite a family. It's scribble, scribble, scribble, eh, Mr. C?" She didn't offer an opinion, holding that back in the reservoir of her remoteness.

"So I get another interview?"

"Sure, if you'll buy me a lemonade. I'll meet you in an hour at the Cheshire Cheese, in the Sheraton-Ritz. Bye."

I caught myself reflecting that I was making headway with her and that snapped me to. What the hell did I mean by headway? What made me think in those terms, that I was trying to get someplace with her? She was a difficult woman with a curiously undefined past, open to misinterpretation, and without known antecedents. It didn't make any sense. Except that the simple fact of her existence was a gauntlet, a challenge to break through her reserve.

At six o'clock we were sitting on white wrought-iron chairs at white wrought-iron tables on one of the little balconies dangling above the Sheraton-Ritz swimming pool. Sheila was down below with a long-handled squeegee pushing puddles of water toward the drains, then moving the featherweight lounge chairs back against the wall. The sun was angling into Kim's eyes; her sunglasses were conservative in shape but constructed of hundreds of layers of delicately shaded colored plastic. The shadows of the balcony supports were long, slicing across us like penciled streaks. She sipped her lemonade through a straw, a bright red cherry floating on top of the ice cubes.

"Watching her reminds me of the job I used to

have at Norway Creek," she said. "I can remember evenings just like this, putting a terry-cloth jacket over my swimming suit, cleaning up and rearranging once everybody was gone." She looked over at me, smiling thinly. I couldn't see her eyes. "It was such a long time ago, going on twenty years ago. There was a time, wasn't there, when the very idea of something happening twenty years ago was inconceivable. Now it's turning out to be pretty conceivable after all. I used to have a kind of net for fishing stuff out of the pool, leaves and tennis balls and sandwiches. . . . Labor Day weekend, that was always the last really busy time of summer, and then it wouldn't be long until we drained the pool for good. Long time ago."

"Billy," I said. "I suppose he'd be mowing the golf course."

"That's right. Another life, light-years away."

"But only a couple of miles from where we're sitting. Space and time, two entirely different stories. Sometimes I think people never get very far away from where they start after all." The lemonade was watery, not sweet enough. No taste, from some frozen concentrate; lemonade was like a lot of things they didn't make the same anymore.

She wasn't afraid of silences and she didn't seem to mind my watching her. She was wearing a gray linen dress with a camel-colored sweater around her shoulders. She wore a turquoise necklace and the gold tank watch with the sapphire on the winding stem caught the sunlight. Her arms and legs were tan and bare.

"The past really does interest you," I said.

"It's always changing," she said. "You're right, it intrigues me. History of any kind."

"But you won't discuss your own history."

"Not interesting at all." She pursued her lips as if to elaborate, then didn't, and sucked on her straw. She sat there, relaxed, but composed, drew her sweater about her as the sun ducked lower. Sheila lowered the umbrellas on the tables, scraped chairs along the cement. "What is it you wanted to talk to Ole about?"

"The man I mentioned before, Carver Maxvill. Did I mention him to you?"

"I don't recall."

"Well, has Ole ever said anything about him? Try to remember, Carver Maxvill. . . ."

"I don't have to try. He's the man who disappeared a long time ago." I nodded. "I've heard Ole mention him, not recently, but in a conversation. We talk a great deal and I suppose the disappearance of a man you know is the kind of thing you might bring up in one context or another. I can't remember when, it was casual, you know . . . just a reference."

"Did he ever suggest why? Or give a character description, maybe about drinking or chasing women? Anything that comes back to you. . . ."

"No, I'm sure not." She took off the sunglasses and focused her searching eyes on me. Her headband, holding every dark hair right where it was supposed to be, matched her turquoise necklace. She folded her long arms beneath her small breasts, which rose so slightly beneath the pale linen. "Look, Mr. Cavanaugh"—and she made a point of the formality— "what is it you're after now? Whenever I begin to trust you, think you're a nice, slightly nosy fellow, you start coming on again with all this picking around in the refuse." There was so little overt charm in her; in that respect she defied femininity, the wiles and strat- agems. It appealed to me but, as a product of my own times, I was pitched off balance by it. Which, when you thought about it, wouldn't have been such a bad stratagem.

"I'm leveling with you," I said. "I'm not digging around in your life, I've told you I'm not." I didn't know if that was true but I pretended. "But I am still kicking around in the ashes of the old hunting and fish- ing club. I am, I am, I am . . . I admit it. But I don't know why it should bother you . . . Kim." That last was a sort of tentative afterthought I immediately re- gretted; her sympathy was not to be won quite so easily and I knew it.

"But why, why, why?" she mimicked, without a smile.

"Because it's a mystery." I waited. "Because Tim Dierker is dead and Carver Maxvill's name scares hell out of everybody and scrapbooks and newspaper files are being swiped. I've waited for a pattern to form, the indication of another presence, a person on the other side . . . I've waited, I've talked the ears off people and I've listened hour after hour, I've tried to tie things together, get a feel for what's going on beneath the surface. Today, this afternoon, down in a room like Jack Benny's vault, I got convinced—"

"And how did that come about?" She liked substantive talk, not shy smiles. I got a glimpse of white teeth.

"Somebody has gone to the trouble of stealing a file from the newspaper morgue. First time in twenty years or so, according to the keeper of the files, that one has left the room at all, let alone been stolen. It fits into a pattern, it makes an assortment of facts and suppositions take a shape, because it was the file of clippings about Carver Maxvill. Why and who . . . it's a mystery, kid, and the sap is rising."

A laugh bubbled out and she winked. I swear she did. "Oh, he is, is he?" She touched my hand for an instant and quickly leaned back. "This fascination with mysteries, it runs in your family, I assume?"

"My father's the expert. I'm a critic who happened to write a book about a murder." It was perceptibly cooler; gooseflesh prickled on her long dark arms.

"But Fenton Carey is a newspaperman. Perhaps he's your ideal—are you trying to live up to your father's expectations?"

"No, I'm more in the tradition of Steve Wilson of the Illustrated Press."

"Never heard of him."

We drove the few blocks to the riverbank and ate dinner at the Fuji-Ya, where you sit on the floor and hope your socks don't have holes in them. We watched nighttime come to the river, hiding the junk piles and warehouses and drunks across the little dam and rapids. The food was fine, shreds of this and that steamed before your wondering eyes and shrimps that seemed mysteriously to have exploded. You weren't hungry an hour later either; you were hungry the moment you finished eating. But there was the plum wine, a good deal of it. We drank glass after glass, eyes meeting fretfully, talking in spurts separated by lengthy, calm silences.

"You said you didn't want to disappear," I said. "How's it coming?"

"Very well, thank you. Each day I'm more aware of my own existence."

"History. You're going to teach?"

"Law school," she said. "That's the scheme at present. I've got the right kind of mind for it, organized, analytical, daring when I think I can pull it off. Courtroom work, at least the idea of it appeals to me."

"To have gone so far, that appeals to you, too. I'm beginning to know you. You're proving all sorts of things. You're way beyond validating your own experience." I sighed into my plum wine and she held up her empty glass.

"I never, ever do things like this," she said. "You may not believe that, but it's true. I can't remember ever, in my entire life, going out to eat and drink with a stranger, on the spur of the moment. I'm a planner, a plotter, and besides that I've had almost no opportunities." Our wine was replenished. "It is fun, I really can't deny it. It's not me, but then behavior can change, even if your nature can't." She smiled openly for the first time, her nose crinkling and her large eyes squeezing together. She put her hand over her mouth, somewhat surprised at herself. I hoped she wasn't going to frighten herself and come to earth.

"How did you come to Norway Creek?" I said.

"I've told you, I don't like to talk about my past. . . ."

"Where are you from?"

"A little town up north—now that's it, no more, or you're going to become Mr. Cavanaugh again." She stared off through the glass wall into the night and I leaned back against the bamboo or whatever it was. Lights flickered on the far shore, past the black river. But she went on. "I'm a different person from the one I was born." She hiccuped quietly. "I don't want to sound like a fanatic, but I look on myself as reborn, dating from the moment I realized that I had better be the most important person in my own life, not in someone else's life. . . . I've truly changed the course of my life, more than most people, I've decided to get somewhere. I care what I think about me. I know what I was and what I am, I know what people have said about me . . . and I have made myself not care what they say." She took a long swallow of plum wine and I blinked. The wine was getting to my eyes and the base of my well-worn skull. I was hot; but I knew I should be paying attention to the recitation. "You've already talked to Darwin McGill and Anne, they must have given you a clue or two to some of the stages I've gone through, surely Darwin had a story to tell. . . ."

"Yes," I mumbled, "he told me about one incident. . . ."

"He ripped my blouse and brassiere off," she whispered, her eyes flat, the sparkle suddenly extinguished. "He stood there looking at my breasts, grunting like a pig, and it shocked him when I wouldn't be frightened by him, or ashamed, or try to cover my breasts. He grabbed me and I felt his erection against me and I just chilled him. . . . I was the sort of girl then, or in the position then, that men thought they could have, handle, use. . . . I had to work hard, I had no money, no status, I was nobody . . . but that's only the way it seemed to people like Darwin McGill. And he discovered he was badly mistaken. Did he tell you that?"

"Indeed he did. You taught him a lesson, no doubt of that. He tells me he's dying, by the way."

"I'm desolated," she said tonelessly, her glass newly full.

"Are your parents still living?"

"Absolutely none of your business. And I'm going to feel terrible in the morning."

We went outside and walked slowly toward the river. The cool breeze took the punch out of the night, the change that had been building. I put my arm around her shoulder.

"And Anne told you I'm frigid, didn't she?"

"She said she thought you might be. Or that you think you are."

She shrugged. "It doesn't matter."

"We're kindred spirits," I said lightly.

"What do you mean?"

I turned her around and we walked beneath the dimly glowing windows of the restaurant where the kimonos passed quietly.

"That's why you're willing to talk to me. You sense that we're alike. Somewhere, like an electronic probe plunged into our brains, we've been wounded. I know where it happened to me, when, how, and why. About you, that's something else again. . . ."

"Oh," she said as we were getting into the Porsche. She was wrapped up in her own life; she didn't care about mine and I didn't blame her for that. She was, or seemed to be, utterly egocentric, private. Her control; it wasn't necessarily a sham, but it was a calculation, a conscious effort. Envying it, I admired her. We drove in silence back to Riverfront Towers. I pulled into the curving drive. The doorman waited inside, secure.

"Are you up to giving me a tennis lesson?" I asked.

"Season's almost over. There's not much time left. I'm going away for a holiday. . . ."

"Yes, so am I."

"Well," she said, "we'll see. Maybe." She got out of the car, motioning me to stay put. She stopped on my side, a safe distance away. "Good-bye. And thank you for dinner." An almost smile glittered in the night and she clutched the sweater tight, making her shoulders seem narrow and her hips broader. "I enjoyed it. I think."

I nodded but she didn't see me. She'd turned and was gone. She didn't look back.

I fell asleep with *My Little Chickadee,* watching W. C. Fields fight off the redskins with a slingshot which kept bouncing back and striking his forehead. Turning away from an argumentative Margaret Hamilton, he muttered, "I hope she doesn't get any more violent . . . I haven't the strength to knock her down." I thought about Kim, sleepily, and chuckled happily, eyes lowering, feeling young again, a nipper once again. . . . As he bathed, he said, "Reminds me of the old swimming hole, when I was a nipper . . . that was where I caught malaria, what a foul summer that was . . . the summer the Jones boys murdered their mother . . . I remember her well, carrying the wash on her head. . . ."

I slept badly, just skirting the edges of consciousness all night, and woke early, yawning. There was a peculiar anticipation in the blood. After my grapefruit I trundled off in the Porsche, fancying I could smell her next to me. Romantic twaddle, I told myself.

The two cracked flights of stairs leading up to Father Boyle's home seemed to be getting longer and steeper. There was a thick morning fog sitting on Prospect Park, obliterating the neighboring houses and the tower. He stared at me through the screen door, taken by surprise, his face veering between fright and surprise. He'd known Hubbard would warn me off; he hadn't expected to see me again. His eyes squinted, the broken veins on his cheeks stretching.

"Good morning, Father," I said. "I just wanted to stop by and apologize for the other night. Have you got a cup of coffee?"

Trustingly, believing me, he swung the screen door wide and let it slam behind us. I followed him to the kitchen, marveling at what a friendly word can do and how badly people want to hear one from time to time. Takes the sting out. Useful for a liar, too.

He was still shuffling about in baggy tweeds, thumping the knobbed blackthorn stick, and his stubbly white whiskers seemed to have gotten stuck at half an inch. The kitchen reeked of bacon grease and a crusted frying pan sat on the gas stove. He motioned me to a booth in the breakfast nook and I squeezed in behind the oilcloth-covered table. He brought mugs of coffee. The warm cream from a jug on the table separated the instant it hit the hot coffee, forming nasty little gray clots floating in all directions. He lumbered back, muttering, and laboriously got himself opposite me, wheezing. A plate of eggs with mushrooms and onions had cooled and hardened before him; he chipped at the remains with a fork. He slurped coffee and picked his binoculars off the oilcloth and peered out the window beside us.

"There's a finch out there," he growled, "in the patch of fog just beyond the birdbath. Don't see him often, the wily finch." I saw a flicker of movement in a looming bush. On the table next to his plate were several soiled, oily-looking copies of *Penthouse* and *Playboy,* a ceramic Hamm's beer ashtray with a cigar ground out in the bear's grinning face. "Harmless enterprise, bird-watching," he said, "but I'm strictly the backyard variety. No field trips and hiking through brambles for this old specimen. . . ." He put the binoculars down on the *Penthouse* and rubbed his eyes. When he took his hands away his eyes stared dully at me, slightly glazed, and I wondered if he'd been at the booze already or if the night's painkillers were still working.

"I am sorry about the other night. I had no intention of upsetting you."

"Ah, yes," he remembered, "you're the young philosopher, the Conrad man. . . . Still chewing on the idea of evil, are you?"

"Not especially. I told you what I thought. What Conrad thought."

"So you did. I was blaming the Devil for mischief, aha, and you believed that . . . let me get it right, you believed that 'men alone are quite capable of every wickedness.' Is that it? Have I got that?"

"You have."

"Well," he mused, slyly poking at the mushrooms, "I've been thinking about it and it's quite possible that you're in the right and I was . . . copping out, as my young university friends say. After all, when you can blame the Devil, man's load is substantially lightened. And if I can blame the Devil for my sins, all the better. It all comes down to the old question we've been debating since the year one, free will. Are you responsible for your acts or can you say, along with Mr. Flip Wilson, the devil made me do it?" He wheezed, staring at me, sucking in air, face turning florid, hand gently patting the table. "Perhaps men can be driven to any evil act . . . to survive, to protect themselves. Perhaps."

"What happened with Goode and Crocker?" I asked. "I was called to account by Hubbard Anthony and it isn't that I can't take my medicine, but I wish I knew what it was that made everybody so angry." I was innocent; I'd come to my priest for counsel.

"Goode and Crocker, we're all old, time is running out. . . ." He blinked, trying to focus the empty, glazed eyes on me. "They came to see me, with the wind up, telling me you'd been to see them talking about Carver Maxvill, that I'd told you about him." He waved a white hand. "Yelled at me, told me to keep my mouth shut and not to talk to you anymore, I'd only make a mess of everything. . . . Can you credit that, *I'd* make a mess of everything? Hail Mary, what next? Told me not to rake up the past—" He broke off, chuckling, shaking his head. "I told them it was bound to happen sooner or later but I got to wheezing and they outyelled me. Farcical, those dumb bastards yelling at *me* . . . well, maybe they're right, maybe it will stir up a mess, but if it does, what difference does it make, what real difference? We're all gonna die, even the young ones, everybody dies, so what difference does it make? What is there to be afraid of here? It's afterward, then's the time to be afraid, and keeping it quiet here isn't gonna do any good afterward, anyway. . . . Oh, yes, they're fearful men, afraid of what's long gone, dead and buried." He swilled cold coffee and worked the binoculars again, sucking in breath. The fog was lifting very slowly and the finch was visible, considering a short flight to the birdbath.

"Am I fearful?" He grinned sourly, beneath the glasses. "What the hell would I be afraid of?"

"I don't know," I said, "and I wondered. You seemed frightened, not just upset, when I left the other night. What had I done?"

"I was tired. Looking at all those pictures from the old days, your father and Hub and all the rest, Carver and Rita, it made me remember the old days. Wait till you're old, young man, and you'll see, you'll feel the terrible loneliness that comes with snapshots from long ago. . . . The Dorian Gray effect, seeing yourself and your chums, young and alive, knowing full well that you're old and half dead now or just plain dead. . . ."

"Who's dead? You guys all still know each other—"

"Tim," he reminded me sourly, "Carver, Rita. . . ."

"Rita?"

"The cook, housekeeper—"

"She's dead? You know that?"

He looked startled for a moment, then the sluggishness returned, the malicious grin. I wondered if he were wholly sane; he seemed fine at first, then wandered off the road.

"What are you jumping on that for? She's as dead for me as Carver is—who knows if either one of them is dead? I don't see them, so as far as I'm concerned, they're dead as the birdbath, you get me?" He smirked, working his mouth, shaking his head at my stupidity. "Don't jump on me like that. You sound like General Goode at his most . . . military."

I leaned forward on the oilcloth.

"What went on up there at the lodge?" I asked quietly, driven by my own Devil, curiosity, whatever name it went by. The inability to leave well enough alone. "You must have seen it or been informed—did it get a little rough? Ole said it got a little raw."

He guffawed. "Ole. He knows nothing! He says it got a little raw. . . ." He shook peculiarly, rumbling, wetness seeping like rheum in the eyes of an old dog.

"Well, forget Ole, then," I pressed on. "But for you as a priest, wasn't it difficult for you to see what was going on?"

"Are you—you, of all people, not even a Catholic! Are you presuming to tell me my responsibilities as a priest? Should I have turned my back on them and their pursuits, left them to it? Or was my responsibility to remain at hand, to act as a reminder, a governor? No simpleminded questions, please!" He took the cigar butt from out of the bear's face and snapped a kitchen match on a ragged thumbnail, puffing until the flame burned through squashed ash to tobacco. It smelled like my worst fears.

"What was going on? Why did Carver's name scare everybody?"

"I don't know what you mean . . . what was *going on?*"

"The women, the gambling?"

"You lascivious fellow," he said reprovingly, as if the misbehavior were mine. He was slipping away from me, candor evaporating with the fog.

"But I keep wondering why Maxvill gets to you guys the way he does. . . . What could you feel so guilty about? You, a priest. . . ."

He got out of the booth and beckoned me to follow him, out the back door onto his narrow patio, where the old lawn furniture was rusting beneath paint blisters. The finch was perched on the chipped birdbath. Everything about Father Boyle's house and life seemed chipped, damaged, ready for the junk heap. He picked up a rake, poked at the long wet grass, a soggy brown paper bag.

"The priesthood," he rumbled, gravelly in his chest, "two views of that calling. Either a priest, familiar with sin as he is, should be particularly prey to guilt, on intimate terms with all of his own sins however small . . . or, leading a good and moral and helpful life, he should be, in his saintly wisdom, impervious to it. The problem," he wheezed, gasping, "the problem is that he this priest of ours, is human and vulnerable and frail. At best, not an easy position. In any case, what evidence do you have that I have a damn thing to be guilty about, anyway?" He stopped, puffing, and looked up the hill. "Fog's going. There's the Witches' Tower."

"What do you call it?"

"Witches' Tower, that's what everybody calls it. Please, don't ask me why, Mr. Cavanaugh. It's just what they call it."

"So you don't feel guilty."

"I don't think about guilt any more than I have to. But you have to realize that the boys in the club were just getting away from it all, a little misbehavior's no cause for lifelong guilt. They never got out of control. . . ."

"Your presence was a restraining influence, I suppose?"

"You might say so."

"Sort of the club chaplain, so to speak?"

"So to speak."

"Which brings us back to Carver Maxvill, doesn't it?"

"You, perhaps. Not me."

"But what was it about him? What did he do?"

Boyle, beyond my reach now, laughed chummily. "Now, talking about Maxvill was what got me into trouble in the first place, wasn't it?" He pushed the rake into a mat of grasses and trash along the bottom of the fence, pulled outward, fetching up a tin can. He wheezed with the effort.

"You mentioned Rita—your housekeeper. Was she the one Maxvill got entangled with? Maybe a little jealousy among the old lads?" My mind was overworked; for an instant it all seemed plausible.

"How should I remember? Really? Child's play." He poked with the rake and a bunny leaped from the mound of sweet, wet grass, ran across our path and under a bush. "How should I remember who might have made a pass at the cook, a thing like that? I think her morals were, perhaps, in question, but it was so long ago and what difference could it possibly make to anyone? It gives me a headache."

"So it was a long time ago," I said. "What's thirty, forty years, in the scheme of things? A wink in the eye of time, right? Could he still be alive? Maxvill?"

"Could? What a word. Of course, he could . . . he could also be the Christ of the Bottomless Pit, the Wrath of the Lamb, or the Paraclete of Kavourka. But I don't think so . . . I think he's probably dead."

"If he's dead," I said, "do you think he's in Heaven, Father?"

He stopped his pacing and leaned on the rake, a grin spreading across his Irish face. He didn't look as if he were absolutely all there: He wore the expression of a man who had opted out; he wore it like a new suit and he was getting used to the fit.

"No, I shouldn't think he is," he said calmly. "I sometimes wonder if anybody gets to Heaven, Mr. Cavanaugh."

I never saw Father Boyle again.

9

THE HAZE burned off by noon and it was a warm day with a white glowing sky. The Porsche behaved itself admirably and the new tape deck played some tapes I'd put together myself; the result was that I listened to movie sound tracks all the way—*A Man and a Woman, Picnic, The Quiller Memorandum*. Wonderful driving music, the green fields swishing past, memories of Kim Novak dancing toward William Holden on that long-ago picnic evening from my youth. I could still see her, body rhythmically twisting, hands clapping slowly, beating out the passing of the years.

The wind whipped at me, the music was loud, and moving fast made time stand still. My mind flickered in and out among the shadows of my past, nodding to my mother, to a young Archie, to Anne, and finally settling on Kim. I went over the previous evening as closely as I could, trying to see it all happening, remembering not so much what she said but exactly how she'd looked as she talked, the gestures and mannerisms and the sound of her voice. I felt a childish euphoria, as much the next day as when I'd been gone from her a matter of minutes; I knew it was childish. I'd always been one to rush in, taking more for granted then I ought, assuming incorrectly that others felt about me as I felt about them. I'd been hurt, of course, but like the Bourbon kings, I learned nothing from the wounds. I considered Kim on two levels, intuitively and rationally, and there was never the slightest doubt as to which would predominate. I tried to pretend there was. I tried to remember how convoluted her life had been, how others saw her; helplessly, I knew how I felt about her . . . or at least how I wanted to feel about her. I should have spent some time wondering how she felt about me. But that would have been out of character. One flaw among many was that I'd lived quite a long time and learned nothing about the bargains you strike with life. My dogged belief was that you could make it all turn out the way you wanted it.

North of Duluth, having dropped down to the lake's valley, the temperature fell off twenty degrees and you began to feel the wilderness around you instead of people. Off to your right, Lake Superior chopped itself to pieces, wicked and icy in the wind, and the woods and raw fields and taconite plants made something ominous of the landward side. The sun dimmed and the white glow blurred, grew murky and gray and plaintive. The little towns hung on the rock ledge that disappeared abruptly into the lake. The streets were potholed and the children in the playgrounds wore quilted jackets already and kicked at footballs. The cars at the chipped curbs were muddy and old and sagged on lifeless springs and roadside taverns looked like polished log cabins with red neon signs. A big mining town, with dreadful black pyramids crisscrossed by catwalks, looked prosperous for an instant but you whisked by too fast, saw the ramshackle quality behind the veneer of flashy motels and executives' homes. It wasn't deep woods and it wasn't city; it was that dirty, gnawed half thing that scuttled nervously in between, looting and despoiling the land at one end, spewing out jobs and salaries at the other end. Hobson's choice.

I pushed the Porsche on through the afternoon, burrowing deeper into the gray, like a man in a tunnel, feeling the north tightening around me, collapsing in on me. I'd never felt it quite so strongly before, never felt the intimidation. It could have been my imagination; it could have been the peculiar, muffled quality the day had taken on. It could have been my mission.

Matt Munro was singing the song from *The Quiller Memorandum,* a sorrowful song, and I'd heard it a thousand times. I joined him in a fervent duet as I swept past the black pyramids and out along the lake once again. I was following the long angling drive up the lake and my eyes kept being pulled toward the whitecaps, the sailboats thrashing recklessly among them, ignoring danger, because summer was almost over; time was running out.

I reached Grande Rouge about three o'clock and pulled over by a green strip of parkland which lay between the main street, which was the highway, and the rocky beach. The wind was cold and the only people in sight were wandering around the gas pumps at the Standard station. Two brokendown, wheelless cars from the late forties lay like ancient ruins beside the station and a mud-caked station wagon was being serviced at the pump.

Named for a towering outcropping of reddish rock just behind and a hundred feet above the town, Grande Rouge struck me as a lousy place to start a vacation but it was the weather. In the sunshine or decked out in shimmering snow, it would have a certain charm. Gray with a faint mist slipping quietly in off the lake didn't do it justice.

I left the car where it was and walked across the highway to the Chat and Chew Café, a white frame building with a picture window and the obligatory red neon sign. There was a counter along one wall, tables in the middle, and booths along the other wall, a series of coat hooks on the wall, an authentic Wurlitzer free-standing jukebox, a glassed-in case of pie, cake, and doughnuts, and crockery three-quarters of an inch thick. It smelled like hot coffee and fresh baking and maybe Grande Rouge wasn't so bad after all. I sat down on a stool and had coffee and a piece of apple pie with a moist, rich crust that crumbled and fell apart at the touch of a fork.

The counterwoman, who had the proprietary air of

an owner, leaned on the stainless-steel counter across from me and wiped her hands on a clean towel. She was about fifty and had a nice, tight hairdo from Ruth's next door and smelled of a little too much face powder. She looked at me and grinned out of the corner of her mouth. "Busy, busy, busy," she said.

"Well, you can't expect much from the middle of the afternoon," I said.

"Summer's gone, that's the reason," she said. "Just up and left about ten days ago, been cold ever since. Hasn't been above sixty. It'll be this way—slow and gettin' colder—all through the winter. Makes you want to hibernate. Or go south." She made a little clicking sound. "Am I right, Jack?"

A man of about her age, wearing a blue policeman's windbreaker, heavy dark-blue whipcord pants, and a revolver strapped into a holster on his hip, moved among the tables, coming toward us. He had sad eyes and a wrinkled, weatherbeaten face. He was carrying about forty pounds too much gut. "How's that, Dolly?"

"Summer's gone. We're in for a long winter."

We all looked out the picture window. There was nothing moving but the surface of the lake. A few drops of rain spattered hurriedly on the glass.

" 'Bout ten days ago," Jack said, rubbing his chin, "got colder'n a witch's tit. Summer just shut down."

"Just what I said," she said.

"Where you headed?" The policeman was looking down at me.

"Here," I said. "Right near here, anyway."

He sat down two stools away. "Might as well have a cup of coffee." He sighed and unzipped the windbreaker. "Sure ain't no crime wave to stop. And Dolly's coffee beats watchin' Leo pump gas over at the station. Quiet little town," he added, watching the steam rise off the coffee as she poured it. "Hell," he said conversationally, "there ain't nothing *near* Grande Rouge, not so far as I can tell anyways." He looked up expectantly, his eyes on me. "That apple pie pretty good, is it?" I nodded. "You sure you're in the right town?" He chuckled.

"Oh, I'm sure," I said. "But I've got to drive back

up into the hills a few miles. My dad and some friends used to have a cabin, a lodge actually, pretty good size, back up in the woods. They used to come up here and fish, hunt. . . . They tell me it's still there and it still belongs to them. I thought I'd like to see it."

"Sure, I remember those fellas, huntin' and fishin' fellas, used to come up from the Cities. Hell, back in the thirties and forties, when my dad was the police hereabouts—you say your dad was one of 'em, eh?"

"For a while anyway. Then he moved away."

"So now you're taking a little vacation in the old lodge." He shoveled some pie into his mouth, dribbling crumbs on the counter.

"Quite a bunch they were," Dolly said. "Used to come into town for bait, have some beers, raise a little hell. Pretty damn near tore up Helen Little Feather's . . . ah . . . house of ill repute one night, or so I heard. That's, oh, fifty miles north of here, but news travels fast, I always say."

"Well, Helen had to expect that from time to time, catering to these city boys out on the loose in the woods. That and the damned woodchoppers. . . ." Jack grinned at me. "Your daddy's bunch knew how to have a good time, that's something."

"I don't think he was in on that," I said.

"No offense, mister," Dolly said quickly. "Just remembering the old days and all. Long time ago, thirty, forty years anyways."

"I wasn't taking offense," I said while she filled my cup again. "As a matter of fact, I'd like to hear anything you can remember about that group of men. I'm a writer and I'd like to do a piece, a story, on what it was like up here in the old days. . . ."

"Nostalgia," Dolly said firmly. "It's what they call nostalgia, Jack, real big now, they say."

"Anything like neuralgia?" Jack said, guffawing suddenly. "My God, Dolly, you don't have to tell me what nostalgia is. I'm the town cop, not the town retard!"

"Do you remember much about it?" I asked. The coffee maker hissed. A Regulator wall clock ticked beneath the pressed-tin ceiling. It was very peaceful. I ate another forkful of apple pie. "Anything?"

"Well, I'd have to sit and recollect a bit," Dolly said, eyes far away, as if she'd already begun.

"Course, there was that business about the house-keeper, or whatever the devil she was—Rita, Rita Hook, that was her name. Old Ted Hook's wife." Jack peered into the bottom of his coffee cup, stirring the remains. "I was about eighteen, nineteen, maybe twenty, sort of helping out my dad, and there was this funny business out at the lodge." He rubbed his chin again. "I couldn't make head nor tail out of it, my dad couldn't neither, hell, nobody could." He lapsed into silence.

"Well, what was it? Don't leave me hanging. . . ." I was forcing a smile.

"Not real clear what did happen out there, y'see. But Ted Hook's wife, Rita, went out there one winter night and damned if she never came back! You remember that, Dolly?"

"She ran off with somebody," Dolly said matter-of-factly without bothering to look up from a huge stainless steel kettle. "Married to old Ted, him an invalid, she just got herself all excited and ran off with some fella. . . . Plain as day."

"Nobody from Grande Rouge, though," Jack said. "Nobody else showed up missing."

"But what's her running off got to do with the lodge?"

"I said what." Jack grinned. "She went out there one night, dead o'winter, to check the water pipes or something, some bit of maintenance, told old Ted she'd be home later or come back in the morning if she had to stay overnight. . . . You understand I'm just getting this off the top of my head, mister, and I may not have some of it quite right. . . ."

"The place was deserted, then? Nobody from the club, the men, none of them were there?"

"Not so far as I know. That spaghetti for supper, Dolly?"

"Yep, sure is." She leaned back and shifted the kettle onto an electric grid which glowed red. "She never came back. Ted Hook never heard another word from her. Never one word. Just left him."

"Left him pretty well fixed." Jack was lighting a cigar with a Zippo lighter which had a leaping-fish emblem stuck on the side. He exhaled an enormous cloud of smoke, engulfing his head. "Old Ted built a motel with a roadhouse, been living off it ever since—"

"He's still alive?" I asked.

"More or less," Dolly said. "He's been in a bad way ever since the war, the Great War, that is. Old Ted, he must be near eighty. But he could tell you about that night. If you really want to know. He could probably tell you as much about your dad's club as anybody left around here. Because of Rita working out there, I mean. You could go see him, he's a great one for going over old times. Real talker." She opened a huge commercial can of tomato sauce, pitched the lid into a waste can, and dumped the sauce into a kettle.

"I could just drop in on him?"

"Sure. It's just called Ted's, on the north side of town. He's usually at his table in the roadhouse."

"There was another guy, too. That old Indian guide—well, he wasn't so old then, I guess." Jack picked up his peaked policeman's hat from the counter and stood, zipping the windbreaker all the way up to his collar. "The men at the lodge, they had this Indian guide, Willy I think his name was, my dad knew him. . . . I just remember him riding a bicycle around town. He may still be around somewhere. . . ."

"He died," Dolly said. "A while back. He's dead."

"Well, I'd better go pound my beat," Jack said. "Nice to meet you, Mr. . . ."

"Cavanaugh," I said. "Paul Cavanaugh." We shook hands. "Thanks for the information. Very helpful."

"Enjoy your stay." He turned at the door. "Say, do you know how to get to the lodge? It's sort of twisty. You've got to know your way or you'll wind up nowhere."

"I don't really."

He told me in detail, went over it twice. "Maybe you should leave a trail of bread crumbs." He burst forth with a guffaw.

I went back to the counter and paid for the pie

and coffee, thirty-five cents. I left a quarter tip beside the coffee cup.

"No tipping," Dolly said, stirring the spaghetti sauce with a long wooden spoon. "Not for strangers who pass a quiet afternoon." She smiled and I hoped her husband, if there was a husband, appreciated her good heart. "Go talk to Ted. He'll bend your ear, bet on it. And if you feel like it come on back for spaghetti. It's not bad spaghetti for Grande Rouge, Minnesota."

It was still misting when I walked back across the highway. Dark clouds were piling up behind the red rock and the scraggly trees on its crown looked like dancers cavorting at the end of a Fellini movie. The lights were on at the gas station and a white lantern flickered through the mist, obscuring the lake. I got into the Porsche and sat staring at the warmth in the window of the Chat and Chew, behind the red neon. A block farther on, Jack was rocking on his heels, hands in hip pockets, talking with a white-coated pharmacist in the doorway of a Rexall drugstore. It was nearly five o'clock and night was slipping down like a hood over Grande Rouge.

TED, in huge neon lettering, hung in the darkness over the water and I swung down off the highway onto gravel, moving slowly toward the lake. The moist air was full of water smell, the chill blowing landward. It was a long, low timbered cabin with a few touches, like leaded glass windows above the shrubbery, uncommon to the north shore. Torches burned in wrought-iron hardware beside the front door. The motel, softly floodlit in blue, arched outward around a bay to the left. There were several late-model cars parked by the door but no signs of life.

The roadhouse was expensively rustic with just the beginning of the weekend crowd lapping at the bar. I smelled frying shrimp and beer. A center aisle divided the restaurant from the tavern and straight back there was a long open grill with a guy in a white hat moving huge slabs of steak around on the spokes over the glowing coals. At the rear of the building, on both restaurant and tavern sides, there were long glass bays looking out into the void where the lake was supposed to be. I went to the bar and asked the young man polishing glasses if Ted was around.

He nodded toward the bay window.

"He's always in the same place," he said with a touch of bitterness. "You can hear the wheezing. Just follow it and you'll be there." He made a sullen face and pointedly turned away. He looked too young to be so nasty.

The old man was sitting in a wheelchair facing the lake. He wore a flat golfer's hat and a heavy woolen overcoat with a scarf high on the back of his neck and covering the chin he'd tucked down into its folds. Round spectacles perched on the bony ridge of his nose and the kid was right: All I had to do was find the wheezing. It rasped, in his chest and in his throat, and I'd heard that kind of agony once before, escaping from an old professor I'd had who'd been gassed in France during the Great War. It was an unmistakable sound.

"Ted Hook?" I said.

"All my life," he said, his voice crackling, a peculiar whisper, his head down.

"My name is Paul Cavanaugh, Mr. Hook. I wondered if I could ask you a couple of questions?"

"Only if you sit the hell down," he said. "I can't bend my head, I'm slowly turning to stone or some damned thing. Makes me irritable. I can't recollect what it was like to be well, hell of a note, ain't it? Sit down, sit down. Hand me my spoon, it's on the floor. I dropped it. Can't reach it. I could starve to death before anybody would come to pick it up." He wheezed deeply and sniffed. I handed him the spoon and he took it in a gloved hand. A plate of mashed potatoes sat untouched before him, butter melting in yellow puddles. His hatchet-shaped face, the jawline the edge of the cleaver, was etched with pain, and around the eyes a hint of something more. He'd lived a long time, nearly sixty years, with the effects of a mustard gassing, and I supposed he knew his share about pain of any kind.

"Is this a family operation?" I sat in the captain's chair.

"Hate to call these little shitheads family," he said glumly, shoving the spoon into the potatoes, "but they are. Little prick at the bar is Artie, my brother's grandson—he oughta been drowned as an infant!" He guided the spoon mouthward and began to lick it with a darting, purple tongue, as if it were ice cream. He squinted at me, caught me watching. "If you don't like it, don't look. What the hell do you want, anyway? Do I know you?"

"No, not me, but you just might have known my father—Archie Cavanaugh? He used to come up here with some friends, they had that lodge back up in the hills. . . ."

"You mean my wife knew 'em, don't you? I never had much truck with 'em but Rita, she worked her ass off out there at that lodge." He chuckled to himself, dribbling a mist of potatoes down his chin. He lifted a beer stein to his ragged, concave mouth, sipped. "I can't remember their names—Archie or any of the rest of them. Why should I?"

"What kind of men were they? I mean, how did they behave themselves? Was there ever any trouble?" My mouth was dry.

"Trouble? Christ, I can't remember. I'm eighty years old, give or take a couple years. I can't remember my own name some days. I'm not jokin' you, youngster." His gloved fingers throbbed on the tabletop. "Only trouble I know about is the thing with Rita, that's Rita, my wife. Quite a girl, Rita was, but too much for me . . . I was all shot up and gassed, sick all the time, not a whole hell of a lot different than this poor old fart you see before you now. . . ." He shot me one of his crackling wheezes, blinked behind the thick round spectacles; one eye was grayish-white, opaque with cataract. "I never really held Rita's way of acting against her, our marriage was not one of passion, you get me? You follow? I ain't talkin' to myself, am I?"

"I follow," I said. "Tell me the story."

He looked out the bay window. The beach beneath his restaurant and his motel had a gray and rocky look, dimly lit by lamps at the back of the buildings. A red sand bucket stood out, glared against the sand. The waves thrust themselves on the shore and their fingers crept toward us.

"Pretty damned curious, I'd say," he said cagily. I shrugged.

"Well, why should I care? You're somebody to talk to." He held the beer to his lips, hands clutching the heavy stein like a baby's. "Rita was a hard worker, never idle, working at our old place, the café and the cabins we used to have north of here, cabins were the thing in the thirties. Before this new kind of motel, y'see. Then she went to work out at this lodge, for these young fellas from the Cities. They came up to hunt and fish and get drunk I guess, and they needed somebody to cook sometimes and keep the place tidy. I never knew what they paid her, Rita and I kept ourselves separate, but she paid her way with me. . . . She wasn't a bad wife, not a bad bargain, as things went. Hell, everybody's got some skeletons in the closet." He peered at me, one eye sharp and gleaming, like a watchful animal. "Ain't they, ain't everybody got things they don't talk about?"

"Sure," I said, "everybody. You're sure right about that, Ted."

He nodded, wise and sly in his antiquity.

"When she died, Rita left me one hundred and fifty thousand dollars! One hundred and fifty thousand dollars. . . . Can you believe it? It took awhile to get at it but the banker here in Grande Rouge, I known him for years, all my life, he knew the money was there and he let me borrow against it—"

"Rita died? I thought she . . . well, I didn't know she was dead."

He nodded again. "Yeah, I know what you mean. Whatever happened to Rita Hook? People used to gossip about that all the time, day up, day down. What became of Rita? Where is she now?" He sang it, like a child, or someone whose mind was nipping in and out of corners. "Well, the truth is I don't know any more than anyone else. But she either went so far away nobody could find her or she packed it in, died. Anyways, she never showed up again after that night she went out to the lodge for the last time. . . ."

"You say you don't remember any of the men in the club, but maybe you do. How about Jon Goode? Or Jim Crocker?" No answer. "Maybe . . . Carver Maxvill?"

"Nope. Just can't recollect at all."

"Funny," I said. "One of them disappeared, too. Long time ago, man named Maxvill, a Minneapolis lawyer. Like your wife, he just wasn't there one day. . . .'"

"That's how it was with Rita. Gone. She said she was going out to the lodge one night, dead of winter, cold as a bitch. I told her that. 'Rita,' I says, 'it's too cold, it can wait till tomorrow.' But no, she says, she wants to get it done that night, she said she had some picking up and straightening to do, pipes to check, one damn thing or another." He sucked air in, wheezed it out, clapped his gloved hands around the gleaming wheels of his rolling, invalid's chair. "It was a snowy night, blowing and cold, not long before Christmas, she had old Running Buck—what was his name?—Willy, it was Willy, the Indian guide, drive her out in his old pickup. Willy was the guide for them city boys, he was out there whenever they were, taking 'em hunting, fishing. . . . So he took her out that night and about midnight he shows up at our place, poker-faced as usual, tells me that Rita decided there was too much work to do out at the lodge, so she figured she'd stay overnight. . . . Didn't make any difference to me, she was a big girl. Running Buck bought a bottle of hooch from me that night, wanted to keep warm, I suppose, and drove off. . . ." He blinked, looked away from me again, toward the lake, remembering the night he'd last seen his wife. The memory didn't seem to hurt him but he was an old man and maybe none of it seemed so bad anymore. It all came to this anyway, he seemed to be saying, so what difference did it make? But there were the ridges in his face, a kind of glittering madness in his one good eye.

"Next day she didn't call me—those fellas always kept the lodge on the telephone line year round—so about noon or so I called the lodge. No answer. Well, I was worried. I called the law and the sheriff went out there in the snow, I was down sick all that winter, and there wasn't no trace of Rita out there. It was raining and sleeting and snowing, no tracks, car or otherwise, at the lodge, just a wet mess . . . and that was the last of Rita. Evaporated. Didn't take no money, no clothes, but I figure she musta gone off with some fella. . . ." He drained his beer and burrowed his chin down into his scarf. He muttered. I couldn't understand what he was saying. The tables had begun to fill and the noise level was rising. I hitched my chair closer to him.

"Son, niece, wife, all gone to hell. . . . Gone." He shook his head slowly. "Draft in here, I'm cold. Brrr." I was sweating. Logs were burning in the fireplace behind me. "Everybody's gone, all but these shitheels waiting for me to pack it in, can't be too soon for them." He sniffed, rubbed his nose. "Well, maybe I'm ready to go, maybe tonight's the night. I can feel the cold in my bones . . . what's your name again?"

He didn't look at me.

"Paul."

"I don't know you, do I?"

"No, not really."

"I suppose I'm boring you?" He had snapped back into focus. He was alert again, smiling slyly up at me.

"Not at all," I said.

"I'm alone, an old man, dying in slow motion," he wheezed, breath whistling in his throat. "My family gone—oh, yes, I had a family, a son and a niece and a wife, all of us living together for a time, but there were problems, things we didn't ever talk about. Skeletons in the closet," he repeated, chuckling into the wrinkled scarf. He shoved the plate of potatoes away. "We had a boy, lucky, that was. I wasn't up to much on the bedroom front, y'know? After the gassing? But we had a boy. Long gone, probably dead somewhere, too, like his poor mother. Then Rita went clear back to Chicago that time to be with her sister while her sister was having her baby, no husband, y'know, not that I'd hold that against her, poor wretch. . . . Died having the baby, she died in a place called Merrivale Hospital it was, same place Rita'd went to have our boy, with Rita by her side, holding her hand as she slipped away. The baby lived and Rita brought her home and. . . ." He coughed, sniffling, rubbing the drop hanging from the end of his pointed, bony nose. "She's gone, too. Once Rita left us I had the two kids and what was I to do? My poor health kept me from being the father they needed, y'see? And now they're gone and old Ted's by his lonesome. Sad, sad story. . . . Could you fetch me a beer, young man?"

I went to get him the beer and when I returned he was snoring, mouth hanging slack, asleep. I put the stein on the table in reach and went outside. It was like leaving a grave. TED shone like blood against the sky and the mist was thickening, turning to a cold rain.

I grabbed a hamburger and a root beer at the A&W, which was the only drive-in in town, passed the Chat and Chew, which looked crowded with its window steaming over, took a right through the sparse residential section, and found myself on a blacktop heading into the black night. I smelled the rain and the wet trees but beyond the penumbra of the headlamps the evening offered a void. There was no moon; it was like slipping quietly, unnoticed through infinite space. The night Rita Hook left Grande Rouge might have been dark like this, snow blustering before the pickup truck. Countless times on countless nights the members of the club had driven out from Grande Rouge toward the lodge on the same scraps of highway. Now it was my turn.

I wondered what I was learning, made sure I remembered how I'd been pulled into this whole thing in the first place; it seemed a long time ago, a thousand questions ago, the first ones buried beneath all that followed. The secrets of the past leaped up in my mind, like figures stepping from the roadside, from the deep blackness, into my headlamps. What was it Father Boyle said—something or other was bound to happen sooner or later? Bound to come out sooner or later? Something along those lines. Something. Carver Maxvill had disappeared in Minneapolis; no one wanted to talk about it anymore. But it was bound to come out sooner or later . . . What? The fact that a man kicked over the traces, let go, and was swallowed up, Jonah-like, in the whale? Surely there was more to it than a matter of public record; after all, he'd been stolen from the newspaper morgue. But what in God's name had the man done? What could have been so awful that the thought of his name sent the wild bunch scurrying, angry, fingers pointing like characters in a Daumier etching?

Ted Hook, living out the end among the shitheels, people he despised, heading for the grave not knowing whatever happened to Rita. . . . Where did she go? Was she still alive and did she remember the old man she'd married, who'd given her a son?

I turned off the blacktop onto a wet gravel road winding its one lane between a thick outcropping of shrubbery. Water dripped steadily onto the hood and windshield.

There were ridges in the roadway and sharp bends and I needed to concentrate. I felt alone, as if the state of solitude were pressing down, closing around me, as if it were my fate and nature, had always been. Born to be alone. . . . No point in kidding yourself. Anything else was an illusion: You were always alone and without a map, no matter what your analyst or your mother told you. You picked your way, carefully, as best you could. Men were capable of anything and you had only yourself to blame in the end.

Where had Rita gotten $150,000? Hadn't Ted wondered, just a little? $150,000! A housekeeper. Christ. Why hadn't she taken it with her? Maybe she never went anywhere. But, then, why couldn't they find her? Because sometimes people lose themselves. Carver Maxvill did it. Why not Rita Hook?

The lodge was a blur in the night, indistinct in the

darkness and the fog and the rain. I didn't stop to inspect it beyond recognizing it from the snapshots. The smell of pine needles and wet fir trees was over-powering. I yanked my suitcase out of the back and opened the door with the key Archie had given me. He hadn't been there in all those years but he assured me that he'd been told the key would work, that he was welcome to use the lodge anytime he wanted. Goode, Crocker, Hub, and Boyle still came up a time or two each year for the fishing and he was welcome; once a member, always a member.

The door opened easily and the lights clicked dimly on, yellow and warm with shadows everywhere. A moose head gazed benevolently from a place of some honor over the fireplace, which was high and expansive with wood stacked to dry beside it. A huge braided rug lay before the fire. Three couches, one of wicker, one of leather, one of loose cushions on a wooden frame, made a square on the rug with the fireplace the fourth side.

I twisted a sheet of newspaper, lit it, and thrust it up the chimney to see if the flue was clear. The smoke sucked quickly upward, drops of rain spattering my hand. I built a fire in the long charred grate and watched it roar. It was a comfortable, large room. A 1937 copy of *Esquire* lay on an end table. I opened some of the windows, heard the rain in the trees.

There was canned food in the kitchen, a set of plain dishes, assorted scotches, bourbons, gins, mixes, brandies. Dishes stood in a rubber rack where they'd been placed to drain. A copy of a Minneapolis newspaper from a month before lay on the oilcloth-covered kitchen table. Maybe that was why the place didn't seem echoing and cold and deserted. It was never left unattended for long.

The fire took the chill out of my bones and left me half hypnotized. I watched the flames lashing the dry logs for what seemed like a long time, my conscious mind utterly blacked out. When I snapped out of it thunder was rolling overhead and rain was drumming steadily in the gutters beneath the eaves. I got stiffly up, went back to the kitchen, opened a can of Folgers coffee, filled a glass percolator with water, put coffee in the basket, and set it on the gas stove. I went out on the front porch to wait for the coffee, stood listening to the rain and the wind and the thunder. It was so dark I couldn't see the trees. In Minneapolis the sky would be pink with the lights. It never got this dark in Minneapolis; the night both lured and frightened me.

I drank coffee and brandy by the fire, eyes closed, wondering what Kim was doing. Last night seemed a long time ago to me, but I summoned her up again, called her into my mind's eye. I was very tired and my mind wandered. Was Ma Dierker getting herself pulled back together? Did she realize what a mission she'd sent me on? Her hatred for Kim had started the whole thing. It was like falling down a mine shaft, waiting for the splash you were going to make at the bottom. Waiting. Waiting. It was too dark to see the bottom, you didn't know where you were, but the farther you fell, the more certain you were that it was down there, waiting for you.

10

I WOKE up to the earthy smell of a wet morning and the evocative aroma of freshly perking coffee. It took me a minute to square myself with my surrounding. I'd fallen asleep on a couch before the fireplace, where the coals had died, and I came to, groggy and stiff. Where the hell was the coffee smell coming from? I staggered up and rubbed my eyes, smoothed out some of the wrinkles.

"Good morning. Have I been making too much noise?"

It was Kim Roderick, standing in the front hallway,

wiping her hands on a dish towel, smiling cheerily. Her teeth shone white in an uncharacteristic smile.

"Ah, no, I smelled coffee—look, what the hell are you doing here?"

"Don't look so fierce. Are you angry? I hate people who drop in unexpectedly. . . . But I guess I thought you wouldn't mind, I thought you might be pleased. . . ." Her smile had turned quizzical, almost hurt, surprisingly vulnerable. She waited expectantly. A cold breeze flapped through the open windows.

"No, give me a second and I'll be pleased," I said. "I feel it coming on already, a definite sensation of pleasure. No other name for it." I yawned. "But you take me by surprise, madam. I did not expect to wake to find you in my kitchen. . . ." I followed her to the kitchen, where she had a plate of sweet rolls and coffee cups at hand.

"I told you I came from a little town up north—Grande Rouge happens to be it. I came up to visit my father. I told you I was going out of town for the weekend. . . ." She poured coffee and dripped cream into mine. "It just turns out we were going the same place." She was smiling again, making very precise little moves around the big kitchen. She wore faded Levi's, a checked blue-and-white shirt underneath a baggy old blue sweater. I excused myself and ducked into the bathroom. When I came back she was perched on a counter sipping coffee with a rim of confectioner's sugar on her lip.

"But how did you know I was here?" I said.

"He told me—my father. You talked to him yesterday."

"I did? The cop? The town cop. He's your father?"

"No."

"But that's all . . . there wasn't anyone else—"

"Ted Hook," she said, peering at me over the old green cup.

"Ted Hook!" I couldn't keep the shock out of my voice. "My God, he's eighty or so. . . ."

"Oh, please, don't look so startled," she said, her mouth making a tiny move, as if to say it would all be explained if I'd only give it time. "Look at it this way, you've been curious about my past, haven't you? Now events—and my own inclinations, which I haven't tried to explain to myself—are conspiring in your favor, you're going to find out where this peculiar woman has come from, what her secrets are."

I nodded a trifle dumbly.

"Maybe it's my fate, that you should find out about me. In any case, it's a small world, everyone knows that, and everyone has to come from somewhere. This place is where I come from, at least partly, this is one of the things I've spent my life trying to get away from—but here you are and I'm beginning to think there's no escaping you." She frowned at me. "Oh, you should have seen me when Ted told me you'd been here—my God, I was positively frothing. Not even up here could I get away from your poking and digging. But then I calmed down, he told me what you'd had to say, and my paranoia cooled somewhat —I decided you weren't out to get me, that you had no idea I'd come from Grande Rouge. So, I decided a surprise visit might be fun." She caught my eye for an instant, looked quickly away. "And I could prove to myself that I'm not afraid of you . . . that was a factor, too."

"I don't see myself as someone threatening you." I took a bite of cherry Danish. "It's all in your mind."

"Granted." She sighed, then straightened her shoulders, as if getting a grip on herself again. "So," she resumed, "Grande Rouge is a place I've tried to forget."

"Why? It's not such a bad place—"

"Memories, some bad memories. It represents what I don't want, lots of people feel that way about the place they come from. And it's a country of the mind, too, isn't it? Where we come from." She gave a small nervous laugh, self-deprecating.

"Well, it's one of those things, I guess. Subjective. But Ted said he had a son, not a daughter—"

"That's right, actually—just a bit of shorthand on my part. I think of Ted as my father, simply because I didn't have one. Ted's my uncle, my aunt's husband." She nodded at my expression of curiosity.

"Right, Rita Hook was my aunt. Whoever my father was, he was only a biological entity, not a human being—I suppose my mother knew who he was. But she couldn't have told me anyway. She died when she gave birth to me." She was getting it out quickly, precisely, making it absolutely clear so she wouldn't have to go over it all again. "This was all in Chicago, of course, and my mother's sister, Rita, took me back home, here, to Grande Rouge. It all sounds complex in the telling, but it's not, not really."

"So Rita brought you up. . . . Funny, all the connections. Coincidence," I mused, my mind slowing down to cope.

"Coincidence is another name for fate, isn't it? But, no, Rita didn't bring me up. I hardly knew her . . . I was four years old when she went off." She went on evenly, controlled, retaining her good temper in the face of what had to be a painful subject. "It's peculiar, the way everybody kept sort of leaving me—my mother dying, my aunt going away, no father at all . . . then there was poor old Ted, so sick, just an invalid, and he seemed so remote from me, like a great-grandfather of some kind, he didn't know what to make of us children . . . my brother and me." She shook her head, shaking off the inaccuracy. "No, not my brother. He was my cousin . . . my God, I get so confused when I talk about all this, on those very rare occasions when I do talk about it." She smiled, transparently seeking understanding, and I was having my own problems relating this Kim to the Kim I'd seen previously.

"I can understand your problem," I said. "It is confusing. But why didn't you just tell me straight out when I wanted to know? It was inevitable that I'd finally discover your connection—God knows it's slight enough—your connection to the hunting and fishing club. Hell, I'm determined about things like that and once I got on to Rita I'd have come to you—"

"Oh, come on, Paul! That's not true at all . . . there was surely no certainty that you'd lead back to me, none at all. . . ."

"But what do you have to hide?"

"Hide? Nothing to hide." She sniffed and rubbed her nose, wiped crumbs from her mouth. Her dark eyebrows pulled together, almost meeting at the small-pox medallion. "But it's not my favorite topic of conversation, as I've told you. Don't be so dense! And, anyway, how could I possibly know that you'd turn out to be a maniac? That you'd just keep digging at it?"

I laughed, warming to her. She wasn't remote. Her face knit together and she glared at me. "Bullshit!" she shouted at my laughter.

"Bullshit nothing. . . . You're right. How could you have known? I'd forgotten I'm a maniac. Out to get you." I stood up without giving it a thought, compelled by the chauvinistic realization that she was awfully pretty when she was mad. One look from her, knowing what I had in mind, that I was going to touch her, stopped me short.

"I don't know what it is," she murmured, "but you do worm it out of me, don't you?" She paused and put her hands flat on the width of her thighs, her feet drumming on the cabinet door beneath her. Her ankles flashed tan. "Nobody, not a soul I know now, except Ole, of course, knows all this old stuff about me, the archaeology, the prehistory of my life. And, really, why should they? It's my life, my business . . . I'm a different person now." She slid down off the counter and went to stand by the kitchen's screen door. Rain pattered softly on leaves.

"But why isn't your name Hook, Kim Hook? Where does Roderick come into it?"

"Foster home," she said, back to me, voice monotonic, getting it over with; but she must have known this would happen when she made the choice to come to the lodge—she must have. "We went into an orphanage in Duluth after my mother—after Rita, I mean Rita, my aunt—went away and Ted didn't know how he'd be able to take care of us. Then I went into a foster home. I took their name." She hugged herself in the doorway, standing straight, legs apart as if to brace herself.

"And your cousin, the boy—Ted's son—what happened to him?" I poured some fresh coffee and bit into another Danish.

"He was older. He went to a different home, I never saw him again . . . I wouldn't have known him anyway, would I? I don't think Ted ever saw him again either. He was older, Ted's told me the boy resented being taken away from his home . . . he lost his mother, his father, his home. He never came back to visit Ted, held it all against Ted. . . ."

Later we went back into the front room and I threw fresh logs on the last night's ashes, lit some newspapers beneath them. We sat down close to the fresh, snapping warmth, me on the couch, Kim on the floor, clasping her knees, staring into the flames. The cold dampness in the air penetrated to the bone. I wondered if she were sorry she'd come. I hoped not but that didn't keep me from pursuing my own hares across the long fields of her past.

"But you didn't hold it against Ted? You came back, you stayed in touch even though you were hellbent on escaping from the past. . . ."

"Sure, why not? I never felt Ted had been unfair to us. He was a sick man. I was too young to hold it against him and when I was older I realized it hadn't been Ted's fault . . . it wasn't anybody's fault. Then, when I was older, in my teens, I began to come back to visit Ted on my own, came back to live in the summer, work in the restaurant. . . . He's not a bad man. Life has played some nasty jokes on Ted, sometimes he's confused, but he's not bad."

"When did you drive up?"

"Late last night. I wasn't sure I was going to stop and see him so I didn't tell him I was coming. . . . I might have just driven on through and gone up to Thunder Bay, sometimes I don't want to see anyone. . . . I need to be alone at times." She shifted her weight and glanced at me over her shoulder, smiled quickly, nervously. "As it turned out, I decided to see Ted—"

"Are you sorry you stopped?"

She looked back again, more tentative than she'd been the other times I'd seen her. Maybe it was the effect of the place, the memories. She shook her head, no.

"I had breakfast with him this morning. He gets up at five thirty or six, says he doesn't need sleep anymore. He told me you'd been there last night. . . ." She turned to face me, dark-blue eyes shining, searching my face. "I'm not impulsive, you know, but coming out here was an impulse. . . . I wanted to see the place." She swallowed, sighed. "I thought you might be here. I was sure you'd be here, wasn't I?"

The fire crackled. I looked down at her in the quiet. My heart fluttered nervously. I felt very young. Her thick dark hair was pulled tightly back in pigtails, the tanned skin stretched tight across her bone structure. Her head was small and delicate and the lines of age etched only faintly, the merest hint of what the distant future might hold.

"Did you know the club members then, when you were a kid? Did you know who they were when you went to Norway Creek . . . or was that a coincidence? Fate?"

"No, not a coincidence. I knew who they were, vaguely. I'd met them when they came to have a drink or dinner at Ted's. They would come in once in a while, visit with Ted, because of Rita, the fact that she'd worked for them before she went away, and they were nice, well-behaved men . . . they'd say hello to me, ask me how school was coming, whatever middle-aged men say to young girls. . . . So, when I finally made the break and went to Minneapolis, I went to the Norway Creek Club—after all, it was the only angle I had, the only connection I had. I called Mr. Dierker and he helped me out. With a word or two to the right people. . . ."

"Did you meet Ole back then?"

"No," she said, "he wasn't in the group by then. . . . I met him later, at Norway Creek."

"I'd have thought by the time you were a teenager you'd have had plenty of financial backing from Ted. I mean, he was in pretty good shape once Rita disappeared, leaving all that money. You could have done anything you wanted, gone to school. . . ."

She shook her head, lips pursed. "You don't know me, or didn't know me then. I never let Ted give me any money. It wasn't mine and I think I always had the funny feeling that Rita might turn up one day and want her money. . . . It was hers, Paul, however she got it. And since no one ever knew where she went, why mightn't she come back? Seemed quite possible to me."

"Do you still think she's coming back?"

"I suppose not," she sighed, "but then, you never know. She might. Stranger things have happened."

"Yes," I said, "they have, indeed. Coming back from the dead is nothing anymore."

"And who says she's dead? Nobody knows. It's a mystery." A smile twinkled up at me. She'd gotten through the interrogation. I could feel her relief. "It was a matter of pride, Paul. I didn't want the money. Even then I was beginning to realize that it was important for me to make it on my own, do things my own way." She stood up. "Th-th-that's all, folks," she said.

Together we explored the lodge, an unremarkable but intensely comfortable place, and went outside, where the rain had slackened to a fine mist. The trees dripped and the grass was fat, spongy underfoot. The water beaded up on the oily sweater I wore; she had on a beat-up old khaki windbreaker that was threadbare and bleached clean. We followed a path cut back through the beginning of forest, angling upward past slick rocks and mossy, damp tree trunks. Ahead, a hundred yards from the lodge, a cave yawned like a moist, toothless mouth. The path was almost overgrown, hadn't been walked on in a long time. Standing at the opening, you could feel a stark chill, like the blast of winter from inside the earth's hollow.

"It's the ice cave," I said. "I've heard my father mention it. Sometimes when the ice wasn't delivered in the old days, they'd keep beer up here. It's a natural ice cave, year round—look, you can see your breath. Even out here—"

"I don't like it," she said, a shiver jostling her voice. "I have claustrophobia, it's terrible. And the

cold . . . come on, let's go back. . . . I didn't know it
was up here, let's go, Paul." There was a fabric of
panic in her voice, irrational, skirting terror. She was
pulling at my arm.

"Okay," I said. "It's okay. We'll go back."

She looked away quickly but I saw her eyes, wide,
frightened. I put my arm around her shoulders, instinctively pulled her toward me, a protective gesture,
and felt her take a deep breath. Then she pulled
away and shook her head with a faint smile. "I'm all
right. Really. Just a phobia, everyone has one." Her
hand brushed my arm, but her mouth was tense; her
hand fluttered, moved away. "Don't worry," she said,
brightly forcing it. "I've brought a picnic lunch . . . I
know a good place. I bet you'll like it." She was fine
again but something had happened back there; I was
seeing all sorts of things she'd not shown me before.
The view of her past with all its attendant vulnera-
bility acted like a relaxant on me, made me drop my
own mask a bit, something I hadn't done in a very
long time. I wondered which one of us had more to
fear, more to hide, back there in the corners of our
minds.

She drove the Mark IV, a brown bag of groceries
in the backseat. We wound all the way back to town,
then swept north along the lakeshore for a few miles,
past Ted's, past a scattering of isolated cabins, then
down a rutted gravel road toward the lake. Light rain,
almost like surf spray, glazed the windshield, and I
could smell the water and the wet sand. She pulled
off between clumps of gorse rooted in the sand and
rock and I followed her down a narrow, natural stairway of rock slab. Driftwood, worm-eaten and smooth
as marble, lay everywhere and I was winded when
she stopped, gestured at a point of rock and land
ahead of us.

"My favorite place on the whole shore," she panted,
excited by the sight of it. "You can just see it, past
the brush at the very edge. It's a miniature castle, a
one-room castle. . . . God only knows who built it but
I found it years ago and I've never seen anyone else
here. I've never heard anyone even mention it." She

moved on, over the flat edges, across the treacherous loose stones, and I followed her with the brown bag. It wasn't my element but she seemed at home, an altogether different person from the one at Riverfront Towers; she knew what she was doing; it was as if she'd truly come home.

She'd gotten several yards ahead of me and when she called something back over her shoulder the rumble of the surf washed it away. I smiled and followed, watching her stretch and flex as she climbed up from the stones to the ledge of earth with the slippery grass. I handed up the brown bag and took her hand, pulling myself against her weight. She had color in her cheeks and a big smile across her face; she was the picture of health and security and independence, reminded me of a bitchy, too-blessed girl I'd known in college, a girl who'd seemed unapproachable to all of us who were not ourselves exactly godlike. Instead of making me feel an antique, beset by entropy and creeping damp, Kim pushed me to feel young, to make me want to lose weight and take to regular exercise and recycle myself into the time of my life when I could still fall in love.

"Come on," she said, tugging my sleeve. "There it is."

She pushed through some head-high shrubbery, led me into a sandy clearing, circular with a carefully built tower erected in its center. The stones were native, from the large chips of boulder studding the shoreline, and the largest ones at the base could easily have weighed a thousand pounds or more. They had been meticulously placed, mortared, and fit against adjacent stones; a fireplace had necessitated a chimney up one side. There was a single entrance opposite the hearth. At eye level above a wide stone bench was an opening which provided a view of the lake.

We stood inside, out of the lashing rain, which had intensified in the past minutes, and she hugged herself gleefully, happy to be there. I set the bag on the bench and looked at her, at the glittering eyes, the controlled energy as she surveyed the simple interior of her castle.

"It's always just the way I left it, whenever I come back. See, my logs stacked beside the fireplace, a pile of newspapers, box of matches in an oilskin." She widened her eyes at the wonder of it all. "Never any evidence of anyone else. . . ." Her pigtails hung forward over her shoulders.

"Whose land is this?"

"No idea. Somebody went to the trouble of building it and just went away. I come here every time I come north . . . sleep on the bench in the summer. It gets cold at night but the fire is enough to keep you warm." She started unpacking the groceries. "Lake air makes me hungry."

"Me, too," I said.

"You get the fire going," she said.

The heat radiated from the stones, filling the castle with aromatic, woodsy warmth. When I was done she was uncorking a bottle of wine, pouring it into an old-fashioned blue metal coffeepot she took from under the bench. She dropped in pieces of apple, raisins, orange sections, and cinnamon sticks and put it on the grill above the snapping logs.

While the wind blew an occasional spray of rain through the window, we sat on the earth floor before the fire and ate slabs of crumbling cheddar on fresh bread we tore from the loaf with our fingers. She sliced thick chunks of summer sausage and we washed the garlic away with the spiced hot wine.

"Cozy, isn't it?" she said, wiping her mouth on the back of her hand. "It's like a nest . . . when I was a child I always tried to make a nest out of my pillows and blankets. I pretended I was a squirrel. I always thought a squirrel must have it pretty good in his tree. Walt Disney effect, I suppose." She sighed, munched on cheese. "My analyst never pursued it, much to my surprise. He kept nudging me toward my sex life and I kept telling him that what I most liked to do in bed was build nests and pretend I was a squirrel. Poor man."

"I like it," I said. "It's a long way from real life."

"Well, maybe this is what's real. All the rest of it is pretend."

"Maybe," I said.

We bundled up again and went for an hour's walk along the beach, our faces tingling in the rain and wind, leaving a long trail of double tracks. The wind dug at us and we didn't talk much; it was hard even to think. The enjoyment came from the physical effort and it was the first quiet time I'd had in a long time. Up the curve of shoreline, well beyond any last sight of the castle, she nodded to go back and we turned, went back climbing along the flat ledges of rock that lay wet and black like gigantic shingles.

Anxiously we sucked the hot wine, battling the bone chill. She sat opposite me, the fire between us, our backs propped against heavy stones. She smiled softly, her hands locked round the hot metal cup.

"I've never brought anyone else here," she said solemnly.

"Why me?"

"I honestly don't know. The fatalist in me surfaces when it comes to you, I don't know why. I can't quite seem to get rid of you—I don't mean that unkindly, Paul. We just keep coming together. It wouldn't be unusual for most people. But it is very unusual for me." Her mouth tightened characteristically.

"Without meaning to sound rhetorical, pretentious, or overly windy," I said, "I don't know you, who you are, Kim. The more I'm with you, the more I learn about you, the less I know . . . the less it seems to me I know, the more of a mystery you are." I heard myself laughing nervously; she watched me levelly.

"You learned a good deal about me this morning," she said. "I've never known anyone who wanted to find out so badly . . . maybe now you know enough." It had become a game between us: I seek, I find a bit here, a trinket there, fragments of who and what she was. Sometimes I wasn't even sure why I wanted to know. It had begun with a suicide and moved on to a murder. Now it had become something within me, something I didn't want to name.

"Well, there's something funny going on with us, isn't there?"

"No point in asking me," she said. "You're the one—"

"But there is. You know there is. You can feel it." I wanted her to admit it.

"Look, I only hope you're satisfied now. You can't say I've avoided you, that I've closed myself to you. I came to you this morning. I wouldn't have had to, would I?" She shifted against the stone, bent her knees up, looked at me from between them. "Be satisfied with the present, the way I am now . . . the way you know me now."

We listened to all the muttering sounds. I threw another piece of driftwood onto the fire. Through the window the sky was darkening.

"Has it occurred to you how much alike we are?" I asked.

"How could it? You're the one who's been finding out about me. I know nothing about you."

"Well, you and I are insulated from life, I think, we're afraid to let ourselves get caught up in it. We've been betrayed, hurt . . . this morning you told me the story of a child who was batted around like a handball." I sipped my wine and she sniffed, her chin resting in a bridge of her hands. "If you're frigid, *if,* it all fits, in my mind. . . ." I watched her; she remained expressionless, eyes impersonal, listening. "And I'm the same, too far from people to make contact easily. Sometimes I feel like an icy disk skimming through the dark, never touching anything."

"You're very poetic," she said tonelessly.

"You've told me some secrets," I said. "You've brought me here, where you've always come alone. . . ." I took a deep breath. "Now I'll take you somewhere . . . where I've never taken anyone else. I'll tell you a true story."

I'd been thinking for several days about what happened to me in Finland, when I'd killed a man. I'd never told anyone. General Goode knew the story, its bare facts, but I'd never told him what actually happened. How it felt and what it did to me. He may have known that I hated him, more than hated him, but he didn't really know why. No one knew but me. I'd never wanted to tell anyone before, not even Anne.

I followed the old man onto the train, up wooden steps into a machine that was very old and drafty and threadbare. My first plan had been to kill him by "accident," by shoving him onto the track in the path of the locomotive. It was the way they did it in the movies but two men alone on a platform in the middle of Finland, with a stationmaster watching from about twenty paces away and a locomotive that was rolling very slowly to a stop—that was real life and it did not lend itself to murder.

I sat across from him in the uncomfortable, rocking compartment, watched him doze intermittently between spells of staring out into the utter darkness. It was something over an hour to Helsinki and it was a peculiar necessity I faced: If the old man reached Helsinki with his tattered briefcase, both he and I would be killed. He by the Finnish Communist *apparat*, I almost surely by the CIA. If I, on the other hand, managed to terminate the old man and deliver his briefcase to a Mr. Appleton at the arrival dock in Helsinki, then Mr. Appleton would not kill me and I'd be in London by noon of the next day.

As the train bumped along, the old man's noggin bouncing in his half sleep, I considered my situation with unalloyed dismay. Terror is a relative thing—relative to what you are in danger of losing, in this case my life—and what I felt had surely oozed into a netherland on the far side of terror. I had become, through my own innocence and the calculations of General Jon Goode, a man with a mission, without the slightest hint of what I was actually doing, only that it had to be done. Once in, never out, Goode told me a safe time later in the course of apologizing for having landed me in such a "pickle"—his word, not mine.

I did not know then, nor do I know now, what it was I delivered to Mr. Appleton's office in Helsinki (he dealt in bicycles, his office cluttered with instruction manuals, spare chains, bicycles in various states

of assembly as if they'd been abandoned in haste).
He accepted it, a thick manila envelope, and asked
me to return the next day. He hoped I would enjoy
myself and urged me to take in the world's largest book-
store and wasn't I surprised to find it in Helsinki? Mr.
Appleton had thinning hair, a Ben Turpin mustache,
and when he stood up he looked quite miraculously
like a human bridge piling.

The next day he told me that "my friend in London"
—that would be Goode, who had prevailed on me to
do this dirty work over a dinner he was buying me
at Claridge's because I was the son of an old friend
—had another small errand for me to undertake. I
asked too many questions, because Mr. Appleton
became cross with me and concluded a most per-
suasive oration by smashing one of those snowfall
paperweights against his office wall. He told me that
I had to do what he asked, that there was no reason
for me to know what the errand involved—only that my
life depended on it. The discussion took several hours
but that was the thrust of it; it was unfortunate but
I would have to make contact with an elderly doctor
in a village not too far from Helsinki and pick up a
package. The village was not safe for Mr. Appleton and
his friends; I would be perfect, in Mr. Appleton's
view, and he told me that the doctor had been alerted
to have ready for me what I was to take out.

Nothing went quite the way it was supposed to,
of course, and when I got to the village the doctor
had decided not to cooperate. We left notes for each
other in the best tradition of pulp fiction; under no
circumstances were we to be seen together. For three
days, while I nervously pretended to be a tourist
(not the easiest thing to do in a village of only a few
hundred souls in Finland, during the restrictive, windblown, snowy winter), we argued in our pathetic written notes. I spied on him, saw who he was, kept to
myself. Finally, confused, I saw him steal out that
night and, like an animal scurrying for its life, make
for the railway station.

Mr. Appleton had given me instructions for several
possible eventualities. In case the doctor took flight,

in whatever direction, I had only one task: kill him.
He told me several ways to do it. If he had the briefcase, take it. Give it to him, Appleton, in Helsinki.
He explained with great care the crucial advantage
I had in this unlikely, obscene situation; the other
side (I have no idea who they were) had no way of
knowing me or what I was up to. By the time they
discovered it, it would be much too late to do anything
about it. Thus, I was the man my country needed. It
was insane.

But Mr. Appleton was, I was absolutely certain,
capable of killing me. And all I could think of was
how best to save my own skin. Watching the night
whisk by in spotty bits of moonlight, listening to
the heavy breathing of the doctor across the way, I
fought it out of my mind.

Who was less likely to kill me—Appleton or the lads
who were going gunning for the doctor? If I killed
the old man, Appleton had told me I was safe, out of
it, on my way. If I failed to kill the old man, Appleton
had assured me that he himself would kill me. But
would he? Would he really kill me? Would I die without ever knowing what I'd stumbled into?

I killed the old man with the .38-caliber pistol Mr.
Appleton had given me. I did it in the compartment
while he slept, pressing the barrel where I thought his
heart would be. I couldn't risk a head shot; I didn't
want anyone to know he was dead until, at least, the
train reached Helsinki. I got off the train in a suburb,
took a taxi to the railroad terminal, and surprised
Mr. Appleton, who was waiting to greet me and take
my briefcase or kill me.

I felt as if I'd turned into a dark hallway where I
would walk forever. I heard Appleton chuckling underneath the absurd brushlike mustache, felt his huge
hand on my back. He told me he was sorry I'd gotten
involved and had to do what I did, but I should remember that it was a war and we all had to be ever
vigilant.

I didn't see Goode in London; I was afraid I'd
try to kill him with my bare hands. For months, then
years, I dreamed about the old man, the white stubble

on his chin, the deep lines scooped out of the pink white cheeks, the smell of cologne and age. I would wake up in the night, nauseated, hearing the rush of breath, the rustling of dry lips, the soft grunt from the unconscious sleeping man as he took the impact of the bullet. . . .

My life was never the same. I became a different, less human being and I mourned the loss of myself. I split apart, as if cleaved by an ax, and half died. Half a man remained and that half knew a terrible thing: It had killed a whole man to save only half of itself. There was a built-in error. How could the thing that remained ever prove that the price paid for continued existence was worth it? And how could it ever reach out to another human, a fellow, and make the connection? There was something missing. Something necessary.

It was dark when I finished the story. I felt as if I'd undergone some extremely punishing physical activity. I was out of breath and my memory had been beaten to jelly. Self-consciously I tried to laugh and produced a groan, tried to muffle it by clearing my throat. Confession was good for the soul, and I'd never quite located mine.

The shape that was Kim, a shadow in the faint glow from the embers, leaned toward me, her face pink in the memory of the flames and her cheeks wet. I heard her sniffle, saw her hand swipe across her face. She rested her hand on my arm, consoling.

"I know," I said. "I've cried, too. I've cried for that poor old man . . . but he's still there, there's no getting free of him. He's there, he'll always be there. He'll die when I die, only then." I took her hand in mine, felt the wetness of her tears.

"No," she whispered, "no, for you, I'm crying for you, not the old man." She swallowed hard. "Killing someone to save yourself. . . . We're programmed to survive. It's not unnatural to kill, particularly not for survival. Jesus. . . ." She pulled her hand away and threw a pebble into the embers, sparks showering upward, a bright fountain. "He was right, your Mr.

Appleton. It's a war, it *was* a war, and war rules are different. You got caught in it, you had to kill someone. It was the only way out. Sometimes you have to do things. . . ."

"It's the living with it," I said. "The killing was easy. Knowing what you did, the choice you made . . . that's hard."

She let herself lean against me as we walked back across the ledges to the car. I had my arm around her shoulder. We drove in silence, sat quietly in the turnaround before the lodge. Rain came and went, mist clinging and ground fog building up in pockets.

"Thank you for the picnic," I said. "The whole day. It's been a nice surprise. Better than nice."

She smiled and nodded. I leaned across the car, touched her face, turning her toward me. I kissed her tentatively and she kissed me back, without passion, but comfortably, without resistance. It didn't last long.

"I'm going back to spend the evening with Ted. Go to bed early. Days outside in weather like this can wear you out."

I nodded.

"Yes," she said. "I enjoyed the day, too."

I got out and looked back through the window. I could taste her faintly on my mouth. She pulled the huge car in a slow, deliberate arc and moved serenely off into the night, snatched from my sight by an abrupt turning in the narrow roadway.

I stood on the porch for a while watching the clouds of fog gather around the lodge like the mists of Brigadoon. My father and all the rest of them, the good and the bad, had stood where I stood, watching identical nighttimes softly closing around them. I was aware of them, the fact that they had been there once, frail and human and foolish, but the woman was pushing them into the perspective they deserved. She was in the here and now, and I had told her my most awesome secret. And I had kissed her, which may not have been much of a seventies accomplishment but then I wasn't much of a seventies man.

I sat on a living-room couch, half reading a beat-up paperback copy of C. P. Snow's *The Masters* which had been left in a pocket of my suitcase from a trip long ago. But the image in my mind was Dana Andrews in *Laura,* sitting in the empty apartment with rain streaming down the windowpanes, falling in love with a painting. He was a forties man and I knew how his mind worked. And I wondered what the day had meant to Kim, the day and the kiss. It seemed so large to me. Could it possibly have meant anything comparable to her?

Unfortunately just enough of my mind was still functioning to make me realize that though she'd now revealed with a flourish the mystery of her parentage, she was still mostly a puzzlement. She had said nothing about Billy Whitefoot, where he'd come to play his part in her life. She'd ignored the story of Larry Blankenship. Yet they were there, gentlemen of indistinct proportions, mute in the past. I could see them, I kept signaling to them, but I couldn't make them hear.

I was back to the facts of what I knew. Rita had been employed by the club members and Rita had been Kim's surrogate mother. And Rita had gone to the lodge one winter night and never been heard from again. And the members of the hunting and fishing club had taken care of the little girl when she'd come to the city. She owed something to those men who had reached out to a frightened, north country girl with no place to go. . . . But did she really? Did she ever owe anybody anything? It didn't seem to be in her makeup. She kept even, she never fell behind when it came to her debts.

Later, in bed with *The Baseball Encyclopedia* and the career of Hank Sauer, who had become the Cubs' big home-run hitter after Bill Nicholson had been shipped to Philly, I got to thinking about the disconnected, random selection of people and events which make up the grid of one's life. All those Cubs I'd watched as a kid, they'd come from all over the country, from dozens of Depression backgrounds, and entertained me at Wrigley Field, where you could smell the greenery of the vines on the walls in the outfield.

What had happened that day in the lobby was much the same thing. A man I'd never known commits suicide and the event develops a hungry life of its own, reaching out ravenously to consume whomever it touched. Harriet, Tim, the club members . . . Rita and Carver and old Ted. And Kim. If Larry Blankenship hadn't pulled the trigger, I'd never have met Kim. It was a bond, like a muscle, flexing, pulling us together. I felt close to her and, through her, to all the points at which she was bound to the pattern. . . .

To Larry by marriage; to Harriet by hate; to Tim through his sense of responsibility; to Rita by her mother's blood; to Ted by chance; to Billy by marriage; to Darwin by lust; to Anne by friendship; to Ole by love and caring; to the members of the club by fate.

To me . . . by what?

It made a hell of a list. Great for an old-timers' game. Maybe I could throw out the first ball. Finally I went to sleep.

I woke up lonely and cold, badly in need of some human companionship. I resisted the faint desire to call Kim. She needed plenty of room. I hoped that she had some thinking to do about her own life, about Ole; but in the morning light I was unsure of her. There was the nagging fear that she didn't take me so seriously, that we were on different wave-lengths like Chekhovian characters rattling on to each other in our own private worlds, neither hearing the other.

I packed my suitcase and went outside to find a brisk, clear morning with heavy dew lingering in the grass. The Chat and Chew Café was steaming with eggs and bacon, several locals fueling up for the day, glad to see the sun hanging in a pale-blue sky above the lake. Dolly smiled at me when I came through the door and I sat down next to my friend Jack, the cop.

"You must figure I do nothin' but eat," he growled. "And you wouldn't be too damn far wrong. Har, har, siddown, siddown, you find your daddy's place all right?"

I nodded, ordered the ranch breakfast, which included a steak and hashbrowns as well as eggs, the works. Hot coffee perked me up.

"Y'know, ever since I was talking to you the other day, I been thinking about what I said, about Ted and Rita, the two kids—"

"What about the kids?"

"Well, there was the boy, he was older, course, and he was their natural child, or so everybody said." He mopped up some egg with a corner of toast, leaving a yellow stain on his lower lip. "Well, I shouldn't say that because a lot of people figured that maybe it was someone else who put that particular bun in Rita's oven, not old Ted . . . but, what the hell, Rita and old Ted said it was their own, and what harm was there in that? Officially the boy was theirs. Robert, Robert Hook, that was the boy's name. Real fat kid, eyes just like raisins in a rice pudding, always looked like he was peeking outa that fat face. Real quiet kid, always had his head down, looking at the sidewalk. Funny, the dumb stuff you remember, ain't it?

"And then there was the girl. I reckon Rita was real close to that sister of hers, down there in the Windy City, Chicago. She musta been gone, aw hell, six months taking care of her down there . . . you know how sisters are sometimes. I had a pair of sisters, kinda unhealthy, they was so close. Anyway, she came home with the little baby girl, Shirley . . . just a tiny baby. Then once Rita took off and Ted was in bad shape, he sent 'em out to the orphanage. . . .

"Wait a minute," I said. "What is this Shirley thing? I thought the girl's name was Kim?"

He looked at me, surprised. "Oh, you know the family, then?"

"No, I just happen to know the girl . . . Kim."

"Well, you're right about that, but they didn't name girls Kim back in those days, see. Little Shirley decided she'd become Kim once she was gone. When she came back to town, years later, hell, she was all growed up, one of them damned teenagers, and she was Kim by then . . . made sure we all got it right, too. So we called her Kim Hook, but she'd taken another last name—I forget." He looked at my plate. "Eat up, for God's sake, your steak's gettin' cold. She still visits Ted, I hear, little Shirley." He watched me go to work on the steak and eggs. "Look, though, here's my point. I got to thinking about our little chat with Dolly the other day and I was reminiscing with a couple of the boys, havin' a beer the way you do, y'know, and somebody remembered something about the Indian guide I told you 'bout . . . Running Buck?"

Dolly stopped to listen, sweat beaded on her brow, still smelling of powder. Two girls were bearing the brunt of the serving and she rested a fat arm on the pie cabinet, blew on a hot cup of coffee. She listened attentively, eyes flickering away at her clientele.

I said, "The man who took Rita out to the lodge that last night."

"Well, this guide had a kid with him most of the time, kid was 'bout the only person he ever hung around with or said more 'n two words to. Me and my memory, I can't recollect the kid's name—"

"I remember the boy," Dolly interrupted, eyebrows knit as if on the verge of a discovery. "But I can't get his name either. Anyway, he must of been Running Buck's son, wouldn't you expect?"

"Funny thing is," Jack said, pausing for emphasis, chins quivering over his open-necked blue policeman's shirt, "the kid's still in these parts, that's what I remembered whilst we was having a beer! Hell, he come back after going down to the Cities for a spell but he didn't stay long, went off to college somewhere, Mankato or St. Cloud, anyway now he's running the Indian Affairs Center up in Jasper, up on the Range. . . ."

"Running Buck's boy," Dolly said. "Sure is funny the way people turn out, ain't it? Who'd a thought it?"

"I figured I oughta tell you, seein' as how you turned up here for breakfast." Jack scowled in thought. "If you're interested in the club, the boy might be able to fill you in on some details, your father and his friends. He used to help Running Buck, I'm sure he worked out there at the lodge from time to time . . . doing errands, odd jobs." He drained his coffee cup and covered it with his hand.

"Where's Jasper?" I asked.

"North and west of here, not too far from the border. Ely, Coleraine, Hibbing, Virginia, Jasper, they're all up there together." He gave me directions and I finished my breakfast, listening to him ramble on. "Once you get there, go to the center and just ask for the director, name just on the tip of my tongue—anyway, he must be So-and-So Running Buck, don't you see? I don't know."

The highway branched off to the left north of town and I had to pass Ted's on the way. The bronze Mark IV was sitting in the sun. The morning felt like fall, clean and fresh and pure, as I headed inland toward the Canadian border, toward Jasper.

11

JASPER waited quietly at the foot of a two-mile-long slope laid between open mining abscesses where a forest had once stood. The town's dust was reddish in the wide streets but the lawns were green and the air smelled clean. Holiday Monday and there wasn't much moving. The swings in the school yard hung straight and above them purple clouds hulked like treacherous strangers. Tomorrow it would rain and the kids would go back to school in their slickers and boots and pee in bathrooms made of marble dating from the days when the Iron Range was throbbing, booming with vitality, money, power. The trees in the park reminded me of blackish-green inverted ice cream cones.

There was one main street, one key four-stop corner with high curbs, a Red Owl supermarket, a couple of gas stations with plastic pennants hanging limp and tattered. I kept on until I came to the Indian Affairs Center. It was a small one-story brick building that had once been a tiny post office, dating from the WPA. A picture window had been cut across the front, drawn curtains blocked the view, and there were three steps leading up to the front door.

I went in and stood at the counter where they'd once sold stamps. A beige-colored Indian girl with long shiny black hair held back by a beaded headband was banging away erratically at a typewriter. She nodded, smiling to acknowledge my presence, and finished typing with a flourish like a concert pianist's. She got up, shapely in jeans, a triangular face with high, wide cheekbones, the kind that might wind up on the cover of Paris *Vogue*. She looked to be seventeen or eighteen.

"I'm no typist," she said. "But I'm André Watts when I finish a letter. So, what can the Indians do for you today?"

"I just came up on the chance the director might be in," I said. "If he's not too busy. . . ."

"You must be a Gemini," she said. "It's your lucky day."

"I am," I said. "There are two of me, two personalities."

"And they come and go, right?" She held open the gate for me. "I know all about it. I'm one, too. Come on, back into that cloud of smoke." She pointed to the office at the rear.

"Well, you're a much newer model," I said.

"I suppose—they just don't make Geminis like they used to." She was laughing to herself, a happy girl, as she went back to her desk. She reminded me of Kim, her eyes and her figure, but she was sure as hell happier. Carefree.

The director was in his late thirties, wiry, athletic-looking, in a faded madras shirt, faded blue jeans, horn-rimmed glasses, flecks of gray over his ears, and a huge turquoise ring set in worked silver. He was putting papers in a filing cabinet, puffing on a pipe which was putting out enough smoke to fill the room. There was a can of Brush Creek on his desk.

"Hi," he said, "what can I do for you?"

"My name's Paul Cavanaugh—I've got a couple of questions I'd like to ask you. If you've got a minute?"

"Sure, why not? Got all day. Have a pew." He went and sat down behind the desk, stuck a pipe cleaner up the shaft of the pipe. "My name's Whitefoot. Bill Whitefoot. Shoot."

It was the sort of moment you have dreams about, the elevator beginning to fall free, the parachute failing to open, water closing over your head. *Billy Whitefoot.* I saw his framed diplomas on the wall, a BA from Mankato State, an MA and PhD from the University of Minnesota, awards and commendations from Kiwanis, Boy scouts, Lions. . . . I thought of the boy driving the lawn mower tractor at Norway Creek, getting drunk because his beautiful young wife was over at the pool putting on a show for the rich men and wouldn't pay attention to him anymore. Somehow he hadn't turned out to be a deadbeat, drunken Indian after all. . . . Wrong again, Harriet.

"Well, ah, bear with me a minute," I said, trying to compose myself. "This probably won't make much sense to you at the beginning. I understand that your father was a guide in the old days? In Grande Rouge?"

"Well, yes and no," he said a trifle quizzically. "The guide, Running Buck, wasn't my father. He was a friend of my father's, or maybe he was a distant cousin from back in the reservation days. It's a little hazy." There was no particular bitterness in his voice, but the friendly shoot-the-breeze warmth had vanished. There was a depth behind the gleaming surface of his black obsidian eyes.

"Can you tell me?" I pried, hesitantly.

"My father was a warrior by nature, quixotic I'd call him, one of those doomed Indians who went into the white man's world with a chip on his shoulder, blood in his eye. . . . He went down to the Cities, Minneapolis, and broke his spear pretty damn quick. One winter did it, died an old drunk on Nicollet Island, age about twenty-four. . . . For some reason the scavengers who picked over the corpse left his identification. Running Buck went down to claim the body, didn't have the money to get it back, didn't understand the red tape, finally had to come home, left my father for the city to bury." He flexed his muscles, clasped his hands behind his head, and propped his feet against the edge of the desk. "My mother died in a tar-paper shack the same winter, half frozen, half starved, poisoned by antifreeze someone told her to drink to stay warm. Just a little Indian nostalgia, Mr. Cavanaugh, the good old days." He sighed. "Shitty way to end the morning. . . . Running Buck took me to Grande Rouge, which was quite an improvement on the reservation. Running Buck was a survivor, he coped, didn't think about the way life was treating him any more than he had to. . . . The State of Minnesota, America's vacationland, even used him as a model of the trusty guide in a tourism brochure. He coped. God only knows what all this has got to do with you. . . ."

"I was curious about a club my father belonged to in the old days," I said. "They had a lodge near Grande Rouge, they went up from the Cities to hunt and fish."

"Your father?" He sat quiet, waiting, eyes like wet pebbles on the beach.

"Yes, a man named Archie Cavanaugh. I knew Running Buck was their guide and I went up to find him, but I found out he'd died a few years ago. . . . I wanted to hear what he remembered about the club, for a story I'm writing about the old days. I'm a newspaper man."

"But how did you find me? I haven't set foot in Grande Rouge in almost three years. . . ."

"The cop there, Jack. I met him at the café, we got to talking, he remembered who you were, where you were, what you were doing . . . but he remembered you as Running Buck's son."

"Not surprising. One little Indian kid is pretty much like another and who cared whose son I was?" There was a dark shading to his voice but he was only stating a fact, not looking for an argument.

"Well, why would he have known all that?" I said.

He popped out of the chair like a spring, ran his hand through the black hair, went to a hot plate, and poured water into a teapot. I could smell the lemony aroma and the smoke. The typewriter clacked irregularly in the other room.

"I guess you never escape the past—you can kind

of forget it, but you can't get away from it. It's like
being an Indian or having a beard, looking out at the
world, you may forget your color or the fact that
you've got hair all over your face, you may think
for a moment you're like the people you see . . . but
you're not. You can't escape being an Indian and
you've still got your beard. And you can never
change your past, your history . . . no matter how far
you go. Something happens, there's a Wounded Knee
in your heart or your head or in the newspapers, and
you're socked in the guts with reality." He wiped a
mug with a towel and held it up to me. I shook my
head.

"I just wondered if you ever spent much time out
at the lodge, if you remember much about it?"

"The lodge," he sighed, as if he were trying to remember, but a muscle jumped in his cheek and he
looked away from me. "Well, I was born in '39, I
don't believe I was ever out there until '49 or '50 . . .
I did a few odd jobs, helped change from screens to
storm windows and back, cleaned up the yard. I
don't remember anyone named Cavanaugh, though."

"No, he was gone by then." I watched him pour
hot tea into his cup, add cream and sugar. "Do you
remember much about the rest of them?"

"No, I don't, I didn't pay any attention to them.
You've wasted your time, I don't know anything
about those men. It was a long time ago. Frankly, I've
had better things to think about." He regarded me
coolly; he was not the same man who had welcomed
me. The transformation was complete and I was
wasting Billy Whitefoot's time.

"But, of course, you got to know them later," I
said. He was going to get a surprise and I enjoyed the
prospect, shattering the pipe-smoking, tea-drinking
calm.

"What? What do you mean?" His eyes focused as
if they had tiny laser beams at the center.

"Well," I went on innocently, "at Norway Creek,
when you worked for the Norway Creek Club. You
must have known them then. . . . They helped you
get the job, didn't they?"

He sipped his hot tea, deciding how to handle this unknown son of a bitch who'd loused up his lovely, quiet morning.

"Look," he said quietly, "I don't see what business this is of yours. You come out of nowhere throwing this stuff at me. What am I supposed to think?"

"Nobody made you trot out your autobiography," I said. "I just asked a couple of questions. Don't blame me for your neuroses. . . . . But what's the point in lying to me?"

"What's the point in even talking to you?"

"You don't have to. Unless you're curious as to who the hell I am and what's on my mind." I grinned at him, smiled into the scowl. "I can leave. Should I leave?"

He went to the window and stared out at the vacant lot behind his office. There was a vegetable garden in it and everything had taken on the darkness of the clouds.

"I was an Indian kid," he said at last, returning to it like a comforting theme, "and they were doing a good deed. There's no story in that and I wasn't lying to you. If I ever lie to you, Mr. Cavanaugh, I guarantee you'll never know it."

I nodded. He was standing with his back to the window, everything under control again.

"Did you ever hear the story about the Truthful Whitefeet and the Lying Blackfeet?"

"No," I said. "Anything like the frog and the scorpion?"

"There were two tribes of Indians," he said, ignoring me, "the Truthful Whitefeet, who always told the truth, and the Lying Blackfeet, who always lied. Say you're walking through the forest and you come upon a fierce-looking brave, you're terrified, and he beckons you to come closer. . . . Is he gonna skin you alive? Or is he going to lead you out of the forest? You don't know what to do. And then this fierce-looking brave says, 'You can trust me. I'm a Truthful Whitefoot. . . .' So, what do you do? Which is he, a Truthful Whitefoot or a Lying Blackfoot?"

"I don't know," I said. "You can't tell."

"That's right. All you can do is take your chances and go with him."

"Which are you?"

"Oh, don't worry." He laughed. "You can trust me, I'm a Truthful Whitefoot. Billy Whitefoot."

"So did you know the Norway Creek connection?" I almost liked him, just for being a smartass like me.

"I knew who they were, they remembered me. They helped me out. Nothing too amazing about that."

"They wonder what happened to you, Mr. Whitefoot. They've told me so. . . . You disappeared and they wonder."

"They do, do they? It's been quite awhile. As I recall, they weren't too terribly concerned at the time—"

"What do you mean?" I asked. "Did they mistreat you? That's not what I heard. . . ."

"I don't give a good god damn what you heard. Got it?"

"Good grief, don't be so hostile—I'm only interested in the club, the history of the club. And they still speak fondly of you. . . . But, look, let it go. I didn't mean to pry." I smiled at him. His was an adversary personality, life had made him that way; at the same time it was teaching him he could take care of himself in any company.

"I'm sensitive about those years," he said, staring at his dead pipe. "I was a kid, very conscious of being an Indian, very aware of charity but needing it, too. The story wasn't quite the way I told it to you. . . . My dad did die drunk on Nicollet Island, froze to death in a snowbank holding onto a bottle of muscatel, the Minnesota Indian stereotype, living up to what was expected of him." He began to scrape the ash methodically into the wastebasket. "He came back from the South Pacific, found his wife shacked up in Ely with a miner, took me and kicked her around pretty badly . . . she died that winter and the beating he gave her didn't do her any good. He tried to make a living on construction crews, road gangs, finally saw he wasn't going to make it, the booze kept getting to him, he'd go down and disappear in the Cities for

several days at a time . . . one time he went down
and didn't come back, Running Buck went down and
found he'd just died one night. . . ." He was packing
Brush Creek into the pipe, keeping his hands busy. "I
grew up with Running Buck, went down to the Cities
—they're like a magnet, y'know, it's where you go from
up here, you've gotta go to the Cities, try to crack
it down there in the white man's world. Well, the only
connection I had was those men at Norway Creek,
those men from the Grande Rouge lodge, and I
asked them for a job. They were real nice about it,
thought it was a good idea. . . . I liked it, then I married a girl I'd known a little up in Grande Rouge. . . .
I was too young, we were too young to get married,
but we were both scared by life in general, it was
easy to hang onto each other. It didn't work out. Lots
of things got to me, I didn't amount to much, full
of frustrations and anger. I started drinking, missing
work, my wife left me. . . ."

"Women!" I said, thinking of how odd Kim, the
Kim I knew, would seem with this man, but leaving
him the opening to go on about her. "Where are they
when you need them? No loyalty. . . ."

"No, no," he said, "you're wrong about her. She
was a fine girl." Memories brushed across his face;
he put a match to his pipe and drew. I waited. "No,
we were just wrong in getting married. Common error."

I stood up.

"Well, I've taken up a lot of your time—and I'm
sorry, Mr. Whitefoot, I didn't mean to upset you."

"Maybe it's fate," he said. "I haven't talked about
all this in a long time. I suppose it can be argued that
it's good for me to get it out, cleans the system." He'd
returned to an academic cool which irritated me, the
way the mask changed from time to time. It made the
next bit easier.

"There was one other question."

"Yes?" He puffed calmly.

"Do you remember anything about the night Rita
Hook disappeared?"

It was better than I could possibly have hoped. He

looked as if I'd driven a nail into his forehead; he blinked, his teeth drove down on the pipe stem spraying a bouquet of gray ashes onto his shirt, his dark eyes summoned up storm winds. "I mean, it's such a bizarre story, isn't it? People don't just disappear that often, do they? It kind of sticks in your mind—it's sort of an adjunct to the history of my father's hunting and fishing club." He just sat still, watching me, something behind the mask I couldn't identify. Fear? Hatred? Betrayal? "I don't know, I thought maybe Running Buck might have said something to you about that."

"Nope. Nothing. I don't know anything about it." He was ushering me toward the door. He slipped a dark-blue windbreaker across his wide, square shoulders. "You're back to wasting your time."

"Did you hear about one of your old benefactors, Tim Dierker? Somebody murdered him."

He closed the door to his office. "Yes, I read about that in the papers. It's a shame. Life's a lottery." He was cold now, businesslike, sorry he'd talked to me at all. He was a blank wall. I was used to it. He might as well have been a member of the club, just stonewalling it in the best tradition of the day.

He followed me out to the counter, where I'd confessed to being a Gemini. The pretty girl came up to us and spoke. "We going home, Daddy?" She flashed a toothy, dazzling smile at me.

"In a little while, honey. We'll stop at the Burger Shack. You go ahead and finish what you're doing."

He followed me out to the front door, onto the top step.

I went down to the sidewalk. There was no handshake. I looked back up at him.

"Nice-looking girl you've got there," I said. "Your daughter?"

"She's a good kid. Very bright."

I nodded. "She looks like her mother."

"I beg your pardon?"

"She looks like her mother. She looks like Kim."

His eyes narrowed. He watched me get into the car, restraining his curiosity. I had an enemy and I wasn't quite sure why. I drove back to Minneapolis, got there in the early evening. I wondered why Kim hadn't told me that Billy was up in Jasper, but then what business was it of mine? And I kept seeing her and her daughter, the similarities I'd seen at once, another connection between past and present.

When I got back to my apartment the telephone was ringing.

There had been another murder.

12

"WE'VE got another stiff. Brand-new one . . . well, I take that back. I don't know how new this one is. You want a viewing?" Bernstein sounded weary and hoarse, as if he were coming down with a cold. Too much campaigning. He coughed.

"Who is it?" It was still dark in my apartment. I'd heard the ringing as I got off the elevator.

"I want it to be a surprise, Paul. Fifteen minutes." He slammed the telephone down and I threw my suitcase on the bed, brushed my teeth, drank half a can of beer, and went downstairs to wait. It took him eleven minutes. He was alone in an unmarked green Ford.

"Have a nice holiday?"

He looked at me grimly, dug a Sucret out of the wrapper, and popped it into his cheek.

"People who want to be mayor don't have nice holidays," he said. "They make speeches. They stand in the rain and eat beans and hot dogs. They get sore throats and wish they were dead. Where were you?"

"Up north."

"Can you prove it?" He was only half joking.

"Yes. Kim was with me." I liked that, the intimate implication. He looked at me, snorted.

I shut up. Bernstein was wearing a bright-red nubby sports coat, a pink shirt, pinkish plaid slacks, red-and-white shoes with a shiny gold buckle. He needed a new *costumier*. We hit the freeway at a gallop, took the University Avenue exit, and squirmed into the labyrinth of the crescents curling beneath the Witches' Tower in Prospect Park.

There was a police car and a police ambulance pulled up at the bottom of the long stairway to the brooding, dark house, windows black and sightless.

Father Martin Boyle was sitting on his back patio, grass poking up through the cracked cement. A half-eaten sandwich had turned to stone on a plastic plate, a glass of flat beer looked like an enormous urine sample, a thick cigar had burned down to a bulging stub, leaving an ash collapsed behind it like a slug. His flesh looked like gray putty, his head draped forward on his chest like a scraggly, white-haired albatross. The front of his white shirt had blossomed like a blackish-red flower, petals of dried blood opening outward from a hole burned in the left side.

A police photographer was taking pictures in the light of bright, glaring portable lamps on stands. The coroner puffed on a cigarette and belched softly as I watched him. A couple of cops told me to keep my distance, presumably not to demolish clues and such. Bernstein leaned against the back of the house, blowing his nose. He pointed to a rusty, chipped lawn chair which was drawn up to the metal table, facing the corpse of Father Boyle.

"Somebody sat down in the chair," Bernstein said softly, "and probably chatted with Father Boyle for a bit, then took out a gun and shot him through the pump. Bang. Father Boyle goes to Heaven."

On a rickety tray table a few feet away a small black-and-white Sony flickered in the night. The Twins were playing baseball on Channel 11.

"TV's been on ever since he died. But nobody in the neighborhood noticed. What a world. . . ." He went off to have a word with the coroner and came back. "Looks like he died a few days ago, two, three days, maybe more. He'll have to take him apart to get closer than that. Christ, what a job!"

Father Conrad Patulski was somewhat younger than Boyle, a small, delicately constructed man with thin red hair, freckles, and large pink ears. He seemed emotionally uninvolved, smelled of root beer, a bottle of Hires clutched in his tiny hand. He kept scratching his head and wiping foam off his upper lip. He'd come home from a holiday visit to this family, found the body—he called it "carnage," as if the fact of it made him shrink inside himself—and called the police.

Bernstein asked him questions. I watched the technicians with their busywork, my mind centered on memories of Father Martin Boyle. I had enjoyed him because he went his own way, indulged his weaknesses, and looked at life slightly askew. I enjoyed him because I'd talked of evil with few men and Father Boyle I'd won over to my way of thinking, or to Conrad's, at least partially. I remembered the way he'd reacted to the visit from the jolly boys in their flap over the mention of Carver Maxvill. . . . Father Boyle hadn't really given a god damn and there was something else he'd said. . . . But it had slipped my mind.

It struck me as a scene from another planet, as if the accompanying baseball game on television were part of a mysterious ritual for the dead. In the end they unfolded Father Boyle, as best they could, plopped him awkwardly onto a stretcher, and struggled away with him. A man dusted for fingerprints, someone else peered at the earth around the patio for footprints, another was depositing everything from the sandwich's remains to dust from the second lawn chair in a variety of envelopes. It looked a lot like something on television with everyone waiting for Peter Falk or Telly Savalas to come upon the scene.

Bernstein finally beckoned to me. The night had begun thundering and a breeze had risen in the treetops.

"Look, I'm going to have to get hold of the members of this goddamn club. Just to be on the safe side. Two of them are murder victims." He looked into my eyes and behind the weariness I could see the seedling of panic putting out its feelers. "Paul, the only reason you're here is because I like you in spite of my better judgment, because you've been sort of involved in this mess from day one—sort of, Christ—and because you're not on the police beat.

"You're a private citizen, not a newspaperman. Because we're gonna have to go easy on this one." He coughed and cleared his throat. *"Homicidim seriatim* —that mean anything to you?"

"Serial murders," I said.

"Right. In this case, members of this ridiculous hunting and fishing club who are getting killed. Throw out the suicide, forget that. We've got two murders, men in a small group. . . . Once this gets out, the membership part of it, the media can make a real dog-and-pony show of it. Who will be next? That sort of crap. It'll become better than the comic strips. Now, I don't want that to happen, Paul . . . but I'm going to have to warn all these old farts. Will you tell your daddy?"

"Of course," I said.

"He'll understand, of all of them, he'll be the one who understands it. . . ." He sighed. "Good, I feel awful . . . he probably wrote a novel just like it." He waved me away with his hand. "He probably knows who did it already. Go ahead, use the phone, call him, get outa here. Go to bed, you shouldn't catch what I got. . . ." He went away into the mob of waiting cops and I called my father.

"Archie," I said. "Siddown. I've got some bad news."

"Your mother's in town," he said sourly. Archie wasn't an alarmist. "It cannot be worse than that, sonny."

"Well, depends on your point of view."

"So what is it? You've got cancer? I've got cancer? What?"

"Somebody murdered Father Boyle."

There was a long pause.

"Ah . . . how? Wait, don't tell me. He was pushed from his pulpit and plummeted to his death three feet below?"

"I'm not kidding," I said. "Somebody shot him on his patio. Just found him . . . he's been dead for days. Just sitting out there watching television."

"Marty . . . well, you'd better come out. How was your trip? You been talking to people, as suggested?"

"Look, I'll tell you when I get there."

"Put on your thinking cap, Paul."

Julia was doing needlepoint, curled in one corner of the airy flowered cough in Archie's study. Her presence was acting as a calming influence on Archie, who was bubbling over with enthusiasm. It was that sense of excitement which surprised me, but I should have known Archie better than that. He was standing in the doorway watching lightning crackle and pop across the lake. He turned to face me as I went in, his pink face split with a grin, white brush of mustache dancing on his upper lip, hands jammed in the hip pockets of his seersucker slacks, rocking on his heels.

I slumped in a soft chair, stretched my legs, yawned impolitely, and told Archie I thought he wasn't showing much respect for the dead.

"Balderdash!" he said succinctly. "You're a sentimentalist. At my age you're an idiot to whimper about things like this. Marty could just as easily have wheezed himself to death, or choked on one of his endless eating orgies, or fallen dead drunk down his front steps. . . . He'd given up on life years ago, he was a shadow man. He's gone. Good-bye, Marty. See you soon." Julia smiled into her needlepoint, a startlingly beautiful representation of a 1920 *Vogue* magazine cover, all peacock feathers and a daring lady who appeared to be ten feet taller than her Bugatti roadster. Archie had begun to pace, Patton addressing his troops.

"I know. . . ." He watched us, setting us up, and I imagined Fenton Carey doing his number in *The Dog*

It Was That Died, one of Archie's best. "I know . . . there will be more murders."

Julia said, "I knew it," and didn't miss a stroke.

"God, that's a relief, Arch," I said.

"There will be more murders," he repeated weightily liking the sound of it. "You must see that we're on to something, the kind of thing that almost never comes along in the banality of . . . real life. Sequential murders are very, very rare outside the underworld. And I'd wager almost anything—my reputation if it came to that—that there will be more murders. Possibly several murders if the killer is working his way through the entire club. . . . That has occurred to you, hasn't it, Paul?"

I nodded. "Thinking cap," I said, tapping my forehead.

"Well, it is precisely this kind of occurrence which is irresistible for the amateur, that's us. By applying my experience as a writer and reporter, Julia's good sense, and Paul's . . . er . . . stout back and willingness to do the legwork, there's no telling—"

"My God, you're making us sound like an Ellery Queen novel," I said.

"You scoff but you will stay to wonder at it all," he said. His mind was racing, as if he were overdosing on an actual murder case after creating so many in his mind and on paper. "I can tell you for certain that the police are absolutely lost. They have none of the special knowledge we have of the club, the relationships which exist between the victims and the victims-to-be." He blew a stiletto-thin blade of smoke before him and pointed in our general direction with the cheroot. "The police are not particularly good on cases like this, exotic cases. They have so little experience of them, they are untrained to deal with what you might call the esthetic brand of murder. . . . It is extremely unlikely that an informant will come forward in this case unless, of course, the killings of Tim and Marty were hired murders by professionals—then, for whatever reason, one of the police sources may come up with something and lead the cops to the hit man. But, good gracious, these seem very unlike the work of professionals—"

Julia interrupted. "Why not let Paul give us the details, Archie?"

"In a minute," he said, pushing on. "I'm trying to convince you two that I'm not being foolish, grinning and babbling my way into senility over this. Be patient, Paul. I'm in mid-point. . . ."

"Right," I said.

"Without a tip, then, the police investigation almost assuredly will run into heavy going. When they are driven to fall back on deductive reasoning—rather than prints, MO's, clues, names on file, and so on— then the poor devils begin to come undone. They're not trained to be psychologists or historians, both of which are required here, and they *are* trained to weed out whatever imagination they have. . . . I've known only one cop in my entire life who had imagination, real creativity, a man named Olaf Peterson, used to work here in Minneapolis but he married rich and cleared out to a little place called Cooper's Falls, but that's another story—anyway, the police are just trained away from using their imagination, from indulging in luxuriant hypotheses, because technology has tyrannized them, they're slaves to all their machines and to their stool pigeons . . . not much romance in it anymore. But still, once in a while there comes a case like this one, which I believe will prove to be impenetrable, a thicket of complexity and brambles which will drive the machines back in confusion and will not yield to science!" He stumped over to his desk in search of a match.

"You should be taping all this," Julia said reasonably, "it surely belongs in a book. I'm not so sure about real life, but a book, definitely."

"I don't think they're going to have any luck," Archie said, lighting up again, pouring himself a cup of coffee from a pot on the bookcase, "because they're going to be looking for a killer. That's what they're trained for, find a fingerprint, check an alibi, do ballistics, find a gun, hit the street and shake down the hoods, rattle the underworld until something falls

out. . . . We are not, however, dealing with the underworld, the criminal element. There's something very
personal in these killings and the only way we're going
to find out who's doing them, barring an unforgivable
lapse by the killer, the only way is to pinpoint the motive. . . . Going from motive toward the act of murder
is not scientific, it's intuitional, hunch playing, and
cops seldom indulge themselves in guessing—which
is why I've never written a police procedural novel.
They tend to leave out the fun, if you see my point."

Julia put aside her needlepoint. "End of lecture.
Paul, let me get you some coffee. I'm dying to hear
what *you* have to say. Archie, stop pacing, sit down,
relax . . . you'll have a fit, imminently, if you're not
careful." She poured coffee for me and got Archie settled behind the cluttered desk. Lightning popped like
flashbulbs and the trees and the lawn furniture materialized for a moment like stealthy figures caught in
the act, then were gone. "So, what about Boyle? How
did you find out? Give us a report." She settled back
on the couch but didn't resume the needlepoint. Archie
sipped his coffee, watched me, his pen ready to jot
down notes on the recital. And I began, giving them
the full treatment, everything since I'd last seen them;
the interviews, a brief once-over of my relationship
with Kim, the trip north, Ted and Billy and Kim and
the Chat and Chew Café. It took me nearly two hours
to get it all in and there were almost no interruptions;
they paid attention, Archie's pen scratching steadily.
When I finished it was past midnight and rain was
beginning to patter in the trees. But we were all wide
awake, recipients of a kind of adrenaline rush, the
excitement that comes when you know you're breaking
a code, or solving the *Times* crossword, or creating
something that just may be remembered next season.

Finally Archie got up and came around the desk,
sat on the corner, looked at his pad of notes, looked up
at us.

"The problem is," he said, "as it always is, the problem is to decide on which of the facts and observations
is important, which offal. Solve that, solve the case.
But here are some aspects, some components, which

strike me as possibly crucial." He ticked them off on his fingers.

"The behavior of Crocker and Goode when you set Maxvill loose among them. They clam up, quick run bitching to poor Marty, who had himself not wanted to discuss Maxvill, then they go tattling to Hub Anthony with the request that he get you to lay off . . . and instead of telling them to go to hell, as you'd think he'd do, he quick takes you to lunch at the Minneapolis Club and tells you to drop Maxvill . . . without giving you any rational explanation. You don't have to be Ellery Queen to see that there's something about Carver Maxvill that scares hell out of them. Now, that's interesting to me . . . and Mark Bernstein and his flatfoots aren't going to get anywhere near the truth of it.

"Second, you, Paul, true to your father's genes, go immediately from lunch to the newspaper's morgue to find out what more you can about Carver Maxvill and his strange disappearance. And what happens? Nothing could be more extraordinary than what you found—absolutely nothing. The file has been stolen, a unique occurrence, according to their keeper . . . but it is gone. Obviously someone else is tremendously interested in Carver Maxvill. It fits. The man himself disappears and incredibly enough thirty years later his file is also gone. Someone is trying to erase him. Very strange.

"Which leads us to a third point. The stealing of the file marks the third instance of bizarre theft in this case. First Larry Blankenship's apartment is cleaned of personal matters. Then Tim Dierker's scrapbook is stolen by his murderer. Now Maxvill's file. . . ." He beamed at us. "I'll be interested to know if Father Boyle's picture collection is gone, as well. It would seem a likely bet, wouldn't it? Why? Why is all this stuff being snatched up? The answer would tell us the name of the murderer. Absolutely."

Julia said, "There's another point which fascinates me. How many people have you ever known, or known of, who actually disappeared? Just *phffft,* were gone? Not a great many. In my life no one until I became aware of Carver Maxvill. Now, within the same general grouping there's another utterly inexplicable, untraced disappearance—Rita Hook's. One day she's there, the next day she's gone. Duplicate of Maxvill. Coincidence? Possibly . . . but think of the possibility of their disappearances being somehow linked. Then it would count as only one disappearance on a statistical frequency table . . . and it wouldn't be quite so astonishing. But to have to swallow two stories like that? I have a hard time doing it. Think I'm crazy if you like, but I say there's a connection between the two disappearances, Carver's and Rita's. . . ."

Archie had been jotting more notes, looked up. "Excellent!" he exclaimed, face pink with joy. "Now we're thinking, we're trying out conclusions."

"Way to go, Julia," I said. She smiled. "As a matter of fact," I went on, "I keep going back to something Father Boyle said. . . . Let me see if I get it right now. . . . It was something to the effect that Rita was somehow the woman that Maxvill had gotten entangled with up at the lodge. It wasn't that he said it, I think he said something in the I-can't-remember line, as if it weren't important—he said she was a loose woman, morals in question, but there was a look on his face, a look that made me think he was implying that Maxvill was in fact screwing around with Rita. . . . It's just a feeling on my part but Boyle put it there, made me feel it."

"So they both evaporate without a trace," Julia said, "and Father Boyle implies they were sexually involved. . . . Now, that's what I call food for thought. Which reminds me that I'm hungry—anybody for chicken sandwiches?"

We trooped to the kitchen and sat around a butcher-block table eating sliced chicken, fresh bread, sweet pickles, potato salad, and cold baked beans, a feast, fueling us for the night. It was raining harder, splattering on the open windows' screens. A cool breeze ruffled the kitchen curtains; coffee perked.

"All right," Archie said, munching steadily. "We'll add that into our formula. Rita and Maxvill disappear, may have been lovers. Very nice, that, I like it. Opens

up all sorts of avenues. As does the Running Buck–
Billy Whitefoot connection. I mean, the connections
are exquisite. Running Buck joined Rita the night she
vanishes, Billy marries Rita's niece . . . and Billy clams
up on the subject of the disappearance. Hell, he must
know something—he wasn't deaf and Running Buck
wasn't mute. Chances are they talked about it. They
must have. So why does Billy play dumb?

"Now, Paul, we've discussed the idea of the web of
apparently unconnected human beings, with Miss
Roderick or Mrs. Blankenship or whatever the devil
she calls herself at the center. And it's true, in a peculiar way, I admit, that everyone seems to have one
kind of connection or another with her. But that
seems to be stretching a point, the links are not strong,
not emotionally compelling. . . . And I rather doubt
that this young woman is dashing about in the dark of
night pushing people off skyscrapers and shooting old
men at dinner! I doubt it."

"Well, obviously so do I," I said. "But I was trying
to describe a pattern. And she does seem to tie them
all together . . . the only person who does. . . ."

"No," Archie said, "There is someone else in the
web, at another center or moving deliberately around
the edge, stepping softly and carefully so as not to be
trapped. And that person, whoever it is, has a motive
for wanting Tim, Marty, and the victims-to-come dead.
And that person is a murderer. . . . And tonight, I
daresay, we're closer to the solution than we can
possibly imagine.

"And I would remind you of another triangle we
must consider. The triangle of classical motivation.
Money, jealousy, revenge. One of these, at least, I in-
sist, comes into play. Think on't."

We concluded the evening back in the study, where
Archie rolled his schoolteacher's blackboard into the
space between his desk and the couch where Julia and
I sat.

The words went up on the blackboard, staccato,
exact, like nails being whacked into a casket.

A square with four sides: TIM, LARRY, KIM, BOYLE,

but a question mark following Kim's name and WHY? scrawled to the side.

Then a web radiating out from Kim's name in another diagram: LARRY, HARRIET DIERKER, TIM, RITA, TED, BILLY, OLE, HELGA, CROCKER, GOODE, BOYLE, DARWIN MCGILL, ANNE, PAUL, ARCHIE, MAXVILL . . . all caught in the web. I didn't like that diagram. It was Kim's web and that made no sense. She wasn't controlling anyone.

And a similar web but a nameless spider in the center. In this web: LARRY, TIM, BOYLE, OLE, GOODE, CROCKER, ARCHIE, RITA, and MAXVILL. They were all either dead, candidates for murder in Archie's mind, or gone, lost, vanished. It was his general projection of what might be.

Finally he wrote:

> STOLEN: LARRY'S EFFECTS, TIM'S SCRAP-
> BOOK, CARVER'S NEWSPAPER FILE.
> ANYTHING OF BOYLE'S?
> DISAPPEARED: RITA AND CARVER
> WHY DOES MAXVILL SCARE THE LADS?
> AN AFFAIR: RITA AND CARVER?

Covered in a rainbow of chalk dust, Archie stood away and stared at the list.

"What do you think?" I asked.

"Somewhere in there, there ought to be an answer. *The* answer." He grinned wryly and stroked his mustache, babying it, sneezed on the dust. "But it doesn't just jump out at you, does it?"

13

I WOKE up thinking about Kim and methodically tried to put her out of my mind with the morning paper, breakfast, and a lukewarm shower. It didn't work. So I reached past the orange juice, picked up the phone, and called the Chat and Chew Café in Grande Rouge. Jack was right on time; in my mind I could smell the bacon frying and see Jack wiping egg off his face.

"Sure, sure," he said, surprised, "hell, yes, I remember you. Was only a couple days ago . . . my memory ain't gone yet, y'know."

"Well, Jack, your memory is what interests me."

"How's that?" I could hear the burble of conversation in the background, Grande Rouge blinking its eyes, looking out at the timeless gray plane of the lake, getting it into gear for another day. I could almost smell the beginnings of autumn, the way it comes early to the north country. "What do you mean, my memory?"

"I want to know when Rita Hook went away."

"I told you what I remember, Mr. Cavanaugh."

"No, that's not enough. I need the date . . . the actual date she went out to the lodge with Running Buck."

"Well, jeez. . . ."

"You said your dad was the law up there then. Well, there's got to be a record of it somewhere, in the police files or in the newspaper—a clipping, something. Or, hell, ask Ted, maybe he can remember. You can do it, Jack, and it's important."

"Well, I'll try," he said, considering the challenge. "Okay? I'll do what I can. You're right, there's got to be a record of it somewhere." He paused and I heard

222

him slurp coffee. "Say, did you go see Running Buck's boy? Up to Jasper?"

"Yes. Billy Whitefoot. It was a real help, Jack, that's what made me think of you on this thing. I know you can do it."

"How soon you need to know?"

"Today. Soon as you can. I'll give you a buzz at lunchtime. Will you be at the café?"

"You better believe it," he said. "Hot roast beef sandwich, potatoes, and gravy today. I'll be here. You call me. And keep your fingers crossed. I'm gettin' on it right away."

My next call was to Mark Bernstein, who was sniffling and coughing.

"What, what, what?" he snapped. He sneezed for emphasis, like Victor Borge's old phonetic-pronunciation routine.

"Two things," I said.

"Look, I'm busy, Paul," he said wearily. "Really busy." He put his hand over the mouthpiece and yelled at somebody, came sniffling back to me. "What do you want?"

"First, check on Martin Boyle's photo album—"

"His what?"

"Photo album, snapshots—he showed it to me one night, it was in a bookcase or a sideboard, we looked at it on his dining table. He kept it in that room. See if it's still there or if it was stolen—"

"Like Dierker's," he said, a niggling tot of admiration in his voice. "Okay. Good idea. What's number two?"

"You had a disappearance here in Minneapolis about thirty years ago. Carver Maxvill, the incredible vanishing attorney. I want the date. Exact date . . . or when he was last seen. He was a member of the club—"

"Yes, yes, I know. I've got Missing Persons digging it out now. Look, why the hell do you want it? What are you doing?"

"Ah, Archie wants it. I told him you'd know."

"You're not getting into my area, are you, Paulie?"

"Are you kidding? What do I know?"

"Yeah, what do you know?" He let that one lie there for a moment, then his cold got to him. "Look, give me an hour on this, I'm going to get some antibiotics shoved up my ass and they should have it all sorted out by the time I get back. I'll call you." He hung up, coughing, worried.

There was a difference between Bernstein's way and mine. He had the resources to dig out the primary level of facts but he was limited by procedures. I was free to shuffle through the people, looking at each one for the crucial giveaway, the key to the next door. I knew that I'd have to sift through the jolly boys again and I wasn't overly excited at the prospect, but I was warming to it. I wanted to know what was happening. I was intrigued by the puzzle aspect of it, which was typical of my bloodless nature, and Kim had given me a personal involvement. How did she finally fit into it? Where did it touch her . . . if it touched her at all?

The morning was darkening, another ominous, oppressive day with clouds and the smell of rain. I gave in and called Kim's apartment. She answered sleepily and I told her I had some bad news. She groaned. I pictured her in bed, rubbing her eyes, stretching her athlete's body.

"Father Boyle—another member of the club—they found him shot to death last night. At his home." I explained the circumstances briefly.

"Do they know why? I mean, was it something simple like robbery?" There wasn't much hope in her voice.

"No, they don't know anything."

"Does Ole know yet?"

"Bernstein said he'd be talking to all of them, in the way of a warning, I suppose. He'll probably question them all again. Pretty closely, I imagine."

"My God," she sighed. "When did it happen? Last night?"

"No, they think a day or two before. He just sat there dead on his patio for a while. Nobody noticed."

"Well, I'd better get hold of Ole. He may want to talk about it." She paused. "But I don't see why it has to be connected with the club, do you? I mean, there may be some other rationale behind it . . . maybe Boyle and Tim Dierker were involved in something else that led to this. I don't know."

We chatted aimlessly for a few minutes, then I asked her something personal.

"Why didn't you tell me that Billy was up in Jasper?"

For a moment I thought the line had gone dead.

"What business is that of yours?" She'd hit the switch again; life and warmth had ebbed out of her voice in seconds.

"I don't know. I just thought you might have mentioned it. I got a tip that he was up in Jasper and I went up to see him——"

"About me?" She was controlling her anger again, rigid. I knew her mouth was tightening.

"No, not at all." I wished I hadn't brought it up; her reaction made me realize how much I wanted her liking and approval. Affection, that too. "But, you see, his . . . guardian, I guess you'd call him—Running Buck—took Billy out there, to the lodge, to do odd jobs and whatnot, he'd met those people, I thought he might be able to remember something about them. . . . About either Maxvill or your aunt's disappearance. You'd have saved me from relying on pure chance if you'd just told me what you knew about him, where he was——"

"I've told you I want you to stop this," she snapped. "I've taken you into my confidence, I've told you more about myself than . . . well, it doesn't matter. I don't want to discuss it with you anymore."

"Kim, listen to me. I care about you. I've shared things with you, it hasn't been a one-way deal. I'm not investigating your life, not anymore, even if that's how I started out. . . . I'm trying to find out who's murdering these people, how it's tied to the club and my father and the rest of them." I heard her breathing. I had to convince her. I couldn't lose her now and I knew how she was, that she could for whatever reasons inside her psyche be gone in an instant, irrevocably gone. "Try to understand me, what I'm after. It's not you I'm digging at. . . . I want you in my life, Kim. I want to be in yours. Trust me."

"You infuriate me," she said.

"I don't mean to. I don't want to. . . ."

"Well, I don't know what to say. Was Billy of any help?"

"No, not really. I think he knows something, it was there behind his eyes, but he wasn't telling me. He thought I tricked him, by not telling him I knew you. We finished up in the red, on the hostile side. It just worked out that way. I think he's got something on his mind and it's bothering him."

"He's hard to understand," she said. "He's an Indian, he doesn't open up easily. And there's bitterness, too. I gave him some of that, I suppose."

"He spoke very highly of you. Very highly."

"I thought you didn't—"

"It came up, that's all. And . . . well, I saw your daughter."

"Sally." She pronounced the name clearly, without inflection.

"She's a charming girl, a Gemini—she and I are both Geminis."

"She's got to get out of there," Kim said. "She can't be a professional Indian. Like her father."

"She's very beautiful," I said. "She looks like you."

"Yes."

"Are you still angry with me?"

"I don't know—it isn't anger, Paul, it's a kind of fear. I feel terribly threatened by you. Your ceaseless, pushing determination. You make me feel as if I'm not making myself clear. I feel drawn to you— I would certainly never, ever have gone to anyone else the way I went to you at the lodge . . . but I didn't think twice about it, I didn't worry about being rejected, I wasn't afraid that you'd have a girl with you, I just flung myself into it, went to call on you. So I admit that, that I'm drawn to you . . . which by itself I find frightening. I wonder, what will I do if our relationship becomes sexual, if you expect me to respond sexually? Will I be able to do it? I can feel myself start to sweat just thinking about it. . . . And there's my fear, I don't know what else to call it, my fear of my old life, the old times, and the way you keep picking at it. That frightens me, angers me, my life is my own—and you are invading it. I don't know what to do, that's all. If I don't see you again, will my problems be solved? I don't know . . . but I want to see you. Every time we talk, more of my life seems to get peeled back, more of my privacy torn away. . . ."

I sat watching the fog mass over the park, dropping down like spray through the treetops. Her voice quivered at the end and when I tried to speak my mouth was dry.

"Look, come to the Guthrie with me tonight. They're opening something or other, I've got to review it. Will you? Can you? I don't know about Ole."

"I've told you, Ole is my friend. He has nothing to say about what I do, where I go, he's my friend. Yes. I will go to the Guthrie with you tonight. I'll come for you, we can have a drink at your place."

"You don't mind coming here, to this building?"

"Come on, Paul, don't be absurd. Seven o'clock?"

"Fine."

"You see, I'm from the old school," she said, a smile in her voice for the first time. "I believe in facing up to things, doing what you have to do, doing the things that frighten you."

"So you're going to do me?"

"We'll have to see. But I'm no chicken. So, I'll see you at seven and you can reveal the latest murder bulletins."

I'd wanted to ask her about Blankenship, where the hell he fit into the story, but, talking about fright, she'd pretty well conditioned me. I was afraid of her, afraid of upsetting her and losing her for good. I wasn't at all confident about how many more run-ins she'd be willing to put up with—maybe none. That scared me. Which made us two frightened people. I had all sorts of questions about Larry Blankenship but if he stood between me and the woman, the hell with him.

The adrenaline rush I'd gotten from going through Kim's morning therapy got me on the street again. I felt like a tiger and tackled the tough one first. I flicked on WCCO to hear Ella Fitzgerald singing "I'll Be Seeing You" and that got me around Lake of the Isles and Lake Calhoun, moving the Porsche like a burrowing ferret through the fog, past the mushy glow of stoplights, across the flow of traffic on Lake Street to the sudden hush of the lake itself, gray and choppy beneath the blur of fog, a man and his dog at the end of a jetty watching the droop of a bamboo pole. Peaceful. Quiet. Only the clunking of the Porsche's guts loused up the morning and I vowed to turn Anne loose on the damn thing.

General Goode's gardener looked up from a pile of fertilizer and told me it wouldn't do any good to ring the doorbell because the general wasn't home. I looked at my watch.

"He's doing his roadwork," I said. "Right on schedule."

"Sure is," he said. His eyes were sunk deep in his lined face, a permanently dirty face, as if he wore his occupation at all times. "Been down there about half an hour."

I left him to his fertilizer and rolled the Porsche down to the cupped old bandshell and slid it to a stop by the shuttered popcorn stand, full of life one day and nothing but peeling paint and padlocks the next. The green benches stood before the stage and I walked through them, along the pier, listening to the water slap the pilings. It was hushed, as if everything had died at the end of summer. From across the water a bell rang and sailboats bobbed in and out of fog banks, sails furled, masts thrusting up like toothpicks in leftover canapés at a leftover party. I walked out into the fog, to the end of the wooden planks, and when I looked back the popcorn stand had disappeared. I was alone in the fog and I wasn't absolutely sure I liked it. Wonderful place for a murder.

I walked back to land and sat down on one of the green metal benches. Quiet, lap, lap, lap. . . .

I could hear him coming long before I could see him, the sound of the Addidas running shoes pounding the walkway. He was hitting a pretty good pace, muttering cadence under his breath, and when he saw me his internal discipline kept him from showing surprise. He jogged on over and stood looking down at me, gut sucked tight, breath beautifully controlled. A violent boot in the groin would have done wonders for him.

"Rather inclement," he said, "and no concert scheduled. Do you just like to sit in the fog? Or are you waiting to see me?" He released a humorless grin from his dwindling store; at his age they were running out, and he gave them grudgingly, coldly.

"Yes, I am, General," I said. "Hoping to continue our wonderful talk from the other day. I figure each time one of the club gets murdered, I'll drop by and see if you've remembered any more about the old days." He grimaced at the heavy irony. "Father Boyle seemed harmless enough, didn't he?"

"He was harmless. We're dealing with a psychopath —and if you're assuming there's a connection between Tim's death and Marty's, you're reaching. Really reaching, Paul." He stood with his hands on his hips, fine perspiration on his flat forehead. "You'll find it was a disgruntled Catholic student who decided there was no God and Father Boyle a fraud, something in that line. People sometimes get killed."

"Bullshit," I said. "Has Bernstein been out to see you this morning?"

"He's coming after lunch. To no avail, I'm sure."

"Boyle wasn't harmless, General. You can pull that with Bernstein, not with me. I know all about you and Crocker. You got hysterical after I talked to you and went tear-assing over to Prospect Park to give him hell, to get him to shut up about Maxvill—"

"You actually followed us?" He drew his flat, regular eyebrows together. "Incredible, simply incredible. What do you think you're doing, Paul?"

"And after you got through yelling at Boyle, I talked to him. And the poor old bastard told me all about you two blowhards and how Carver Maxvill scares hell out of you. . . . Then, with all the subtlety of our famous Finland adventure, General, you had Hub Anthony soft-soap me at the Minneapolis Club. Jesus, talk about obvious! Do you get that from being a general?"

"I suppose you've told Bernstein all about this?" Sometimes I couldn't help admiring him; he controlled his anger because he wanted to know where I was, what I was thinking. But there was an animal wariness in the normally expressionless eyes.

"What if I had? He doesn't give a damn about somebody who disappeared thirty years ago. Carver Maxvill's buried so deep in the past, Bernstein will never find him. And what would he do if he did find him—a guy who's been gone for thirty years? What I'm curious about is this: Why do you guys worry about him so much?"

The sound of the bell drifted out of the fog. General Goode put a foot up on the bench, draped an arm casually across his thigh, and leaned toward me.

"I don't like the past being dragged up again," he said. "Nothing more than that, Paul, an unpleasant incident, a man vanishes, and now you are apparently obsessed with making some connection between the club and their deaths, between *us* and the deaths." He took a deep breath. "Perhaps we overreacted, Paul, perhaps we should have just let it go. . . . I'm sure we should have. But we did what we did. What can I say? My God, I was in Washington when the man disappeared."

"Well, it's gone too far," I said flatly. "You're not the only people interested in Carver Maxvill."

"What's that supposed to mean?"

"Brace yourself. Somebody stole the file on Mr. Maxvill from the newspaper's library. Stole it." That one got to him. "Now, I wonder who could have done that. A murderer, maybe?"

General Goode had paled beneath his tan, face tightening like the fellows on horses in public places, heroes made of bronze. One more turn of the screw enjoyed. He turned abruptly and went to the edge of the water, arms folded, staring out across the lake, waiting for reinforcements. He believed that men are predators, that it is their nature to hunt and kill. If he'd looked inside my head, he'd have been terrified. He'd have believed he was right. I went and stood beside him.

"Why don't you explain about Maxvill?"

"There is nothing more to explain. We should never have made such a big thing out of it. . . ."

"You know, you're going to stonewall yourself right into the grave, Jon."

"You're mad. Disturbed. Are you threatening me, Paul?" He wouldn't look at me; his eyes searched the fog.

"A prediction, not a threat."

"You are mad."

"I don't send men to kill other men. I may be mad but you, Jon, are something very like a monster. If you would tell me the truth, whatever it is, you might save your life . . . but they're gonna get you. The monster destroys himself."

He finally turned toward me, half smiling, and put his arm on my shoulder. I looked at him in surprise.

"If there is a secret," he said, "if there is, I feel quite sure you'd never understand. Only old men would understand." He squeezed my shoulder. "Now, I must finish my run, Paul. One last word on the subject—I don't fear death. When you're old and almost finished there are worse things than death. All that's left is what your life has meant, your reputation, what it's added up to. You know, you see, that you're going to die. The one thing that you leave behind is the memory of you. You want to leave it . . . intact."

He chuckled and began to jog away into the fog. Suddenly I was alone again.

I got back to my place at noon and called Grande Rouge. Jack came to the telephone with the hubbub of lunchtime at the Chat and Chew behind, his voice gravelly. He was excited and just a little smug.

"Well, I checked it out," he said, "spent the whole damned morning going through my daddy's logbooks. I knew the war was still on when it happened. Y'know how you associate things with things? Anyways, I was looking at '42 and '43 and gettin' eyestrain when I remembered it was right around the time of the Battle of the Bulge, just popped into my mind. . . ."

"1944?" I asked.

"Right, December of 1944. And it all began to come back to me, the Christmas decorations up, hanging over the street, my sister visiting . . . she was a Wac, see. . . . Anyways, I went through the log and sure as hell, there it was. The night of December 16, 1944, that was the night Running Buck said he took her out there. Daddy's log shows that he talked to the Indian, talked to Ted, the weather was just terrible, snow on the fifteenth and sixteenth, then it warmed up and rained like billy hell on the seventeenth, eighteenth, nineteenth. . . . The police car got stuck in the mud out at the lodge when he went out there, he's even got that in the log. . . ."

"Well, I'm in your debt, Jack," I said. "You've been a real help."

"Y'know," he said, "it's mighty funny looking at them logs. My daddy's been dead here, what, fifteen years now, and he actually wrote them logs, he was about fifty then, and now I'm fifty and he's gone and I'm reading what he wrote. . . . Sorta makes you think. Know what I mean?"

"I know what you mean," I said.

"It's like he wrote that stuff down and put it away . . . and it's been waitin' there all these years for somebody to get hold of it. And when the time came, it was me—his boy. Funny. Well, my roast beef sandwich is gettin' cold. You come visit us again, young fella. We ain't goin' nowhere." He chuckled, apparently at his own inertia.

I hung up, then called Bernstein.

"How's your ass?" I said.

"Got more holes in it than God ever intended, I'll tell you." He was eating lunch at his desk and his mouth was full. He finished chewing and slurped some coffee.

"So what's the word on Maxvill?"

"I got the report right here—let's see. Ah, right,

Carver Maxvill, attorney. Oliver Avenue South—nice neighborhood—was last seen by his secretary, one Miss Anita Kellerman, leaving his office at four forty-five on the afternoon of 16 December 1944. *Finis.* No more Mr. Maxvill—"

"Jesus Christ," I blurted.

"What's so amazing about that?" His voice was suddenly edged. "Jesus Christ what?"

"Well, nothing," I lied. "It was a long time ago. . . . That's all."

"I hope you're not fucking me over, Paul," he said with exaggerated gravity. "I'm a very busy fellow and I don't have time to play silly games. If you know something about all this, do yourself a favor and don't get me pissed at you. . . ." I didn't know what to say. "What do you know about Maxvill?"

"Nothing. Just that he was a member of the hunting and fishing club, that's all. He disappeared."

"I *know* that. Are you connecting him with Dierker and Boyle?"

"Not beyond that."

"You think Maxvill was the first to go? Dierker and Boyle the second and third?" He chewed on some more sandwich.

"Look, I'm a drama critic, a patron of the arts. I don't know nothin' about nothin'."

"Paul, fuck yourself."

In the months since this business came to an end, I've often counted up the turning points, and there were a great many of them. It was all so terribly complex. Every little aspect seemed to have a fulcrum of its own, on which it slowly went out of balance. December 16, 1944. That was certainly one of them, as important as any. It hung before me in neon during the few moments after Bernstein hung up on me, like the TED's in Grande Rouge. Then I called Archie to meet me for lunch.

Norway Creek slows to a crawl at the end of summer. The kids are all back in school, many of the golfers are sufficiently golfed out, and the club returns to the employees, the people who make it run. The dining room was thinned out by one thirty, when Archie arrived, and I'd finished my second old-fashioned. Darwin McGill wandered through, clutching a couple of tennis rackets, eyes bloodshot; he nodded and went on his way, forlorn, nursing himself toward the end. He was brown as a penny, all the damage done inside.

We ordered sliced chicken sandwiches and I told Archie about my chat with Goode and the information from Grande Rouge and Bernstein. He listened quietly, raising his eyebrows at the proper moments.

"December 16, 1944," he mused. "Well, that's a break, a real break." He shook his head, smiling faintly beneath the white fringe. "You just never know, do you? Truth being stranger than fiction and all. The possibilities just radiate out from a thing like this. Exponential growth."

"It looks like it's pretty well tied together, Dad," I said. "Coincidence carries you only so far."

"I agree. We have to assume there's a connection." He peeled back the bread and salted, then peppered the sliced chicken, scraped mayonnaise off the bread, put the bread back on, and then with his knife and fork cut a piece of sandwich. Archie had a method for everything. "The point is, what's the connection?"

"They went off together?" I ventured. "I mean, it fits with what Boyle was hinting at about Maxvill and Rita . . . that he had a yen for women generally and, just maybe, for Rita Hook in particular. It fits what we know, Archie."

He did it to the sandwich again. "But it's awfully convenient, don't you think? I know, I know, just because it's easy doesn't mean it can't be true . . . but everything about this mess has been so obscured, so deep, it's hard for me to take the easy way out.

"For instance, Paul, if they were going away together, as lovers, why would they leave all that money —one hundred and fifty thousand dollars of hers, according to Ted, and who knows how much of his? On principle? Because they were turning their backs on their previous lives? Very romantic but utterly senseless. . . . No one would do that, surely. Unless they had some other source of income, a cache we know nothing about. . . . Still, I think the money left behind casts doubt on their just pulling up stakes."

"But why else would they be tied together like this? Why else do they disappear on the same day if they aren't going away together?"

He made a bridge with his fingertips and pursed his lips behind it. "We must cogitate on that, I expect." He squinted at me, looking into the past. "And how in the world did Rita Hook, not a particularly prepossessing person, ever amass a fortune of one hundred and fifty thousand dollars? That seems to me as big a question as any. As well as the matter of Blankenship. *Who* was this dreary fellow? We still don't know why he did himself in, do we? He's so terribly easy to forget, in death as in life, apparently. Yet he began this whole thing. I suggest you do a bit of work on Blankenship. And don't look like that, Paul. It's important."

We walked back along the path past the swimming pool. It had been drained, lay like the fossil of something very large. Fog wafted across the golf course and as we watched, a ball dropped out of the grayness, plopped on the green. A muffled cry of "Fore!" came from the fairway. "Nice shot," Archie said. "But such a stupid game."

McGill trudged across a tennis court behind a wide broom, swishing puddles away. The more he pushed, the more the water drifted back into the same slight depressions.

"Where were you in December of '44?" I asked.

"Washington," Archie said.

"That's where General Goode says he was."

"I know."

"Well, I've been thinking about why Maxvill bothers them so much. Just suppose, somehow, they—Goode and Crocker and Boyle, at least—know where he went. What if Maxvill was in trouble . . . what if he had done something criminal, maybe embezzled some money? Now, that would explain his decision to hotfoot it and it would explain why they didn't have to take their other money with them. And say the lads felt his deeds would reflect on them, maybe they were even unwittingly involved. Now, that would frighten them, wouldn't it? And it might explain Goode's concern about his goddamn reputation."

"Very creative, Paul," Archie said. Our shoes crunched on the gravel driveway. "Not bad at all."

"And, carrying it a bit further, what if the lads were instrumental in arranging Maxvill's disappearance? What if they talked him into it?" Archie was nodding at me to go on. "What if he'd done something naughty that didn't succeed, didn't make him rich . . . then what if they went so far as to pay him off just to get him out of the picture? Then he took Rita and with a promise never to come back, poof—they're gone. . . ."

"Ah, there's hope for you yet, my son."

"Could you possibly find out if Goode was in Washington on December 16, 1944? Is there any way to check?"

"Maybe. I could try."

"Why don't you? Hell, maybe he was in Minneapolis giving old Carver a send-off. . . ."

Archie just smiled at me and slapped me on the back.

14

"AT THE risk of life and limb, I'm going to bring up your prehistory once again. Need I duck?"

She leaned against the balcony, profile pointed, eyes scanning the western horizon, where a pinkish blur lay above the Walker Art Center and the Guthrie. It was typical of the time of year; the only memory of what we'd called the sun came at bluish nightfall, like a bloody wound, and then slipped away when you weren't looking.

"You make it so hard for me to like you—"

"Wrong. You like me okay. I make it hard for you to love me, sugar." I curled my lip wolfishly like Bogart but she wasn't looking. Humor was not her long suit; she thought I was serious.

"I've told you," she said deliberately. "The kind of love you talk about is quite beyond me. At the moment."

"I was joking."

"I wasn't." The breeze was moist, a faint chill lowering around us. "What about my prehistory?" There was a vague resignation in her voice, not a promising hope for the evening. Our first date.

"Well, your aunt and Carver Maxvill disappeared from the face of the earth on the same day. December 16, 1944. Interesting, don't you think? Surely not a coincidence."

"I was four. What difference could it possibly make to me?"

"Difference? I don't know. I thought you might like to know. . . ."

"Well, think again." She finally turned to face me. She struck a characteristic pose, arms folded beneath her tiny breasts. She was wearing a chocolate-brown velvet pantsuit, a paisley scarf, her hair pulled back so tight you'd think her eyes wouldn't close. I focused on the smallpox scar between the dark, thick eyebrows. "You're the one who's obsessed by my past. And your assorted murders and disappearances. Not me."

"Let's have a drink," I said. "Salvage the evening. Okay?"

"By all means," she said softly, touching my arm as she went past me into the living room. "Scotch on ice." She watched me while I poured the drinks, clinked the ice. "Look, don't pout. It's the way I am. You want to tell me about Father Boyle. Go ahead, tell me. I'll pay close attention." I handed her the fat little glass and she batted a faint smile my way. She was trying. She was doing her best; she was the sort of woman I couldn't turn away from and dear old Anne knew it better than I ever would.

So I told her about Father Boyle, the old man sitting on his patio with a slug blasting his heart to pieces. She winced at the overly graphic description. She crossed her legs and stared down at her elegant little tan shoes with the dark-brown stitching. I ran out of story at some point and just sat staring at her, the tilt of her head, the slender tanned fingers curling around the glass, the long thigh, the cuff of her belled slacks hanging loose, a glimpse of ankle, the Italian shoes. . . . She looked up finally, saw me watching her, said nothing, sat like a statue, neither happy nor sad, just there. Just breathing. Then I heard her ice rattle in her glass; her hand was shaking. But nobody was saying anything. It was dark in my apartment.

The telephone rang. She jumped, a trace of watered scotch landing on her leg. I reached for the phone on my desk, watching her smooth the spot away.

"Paul, Bernstein here. You old son of a bitch!"

"I'm busy," I said.

"You sound doped up—"

"Not really. Bust not called for."

"Look, kiddo," he said with curious exuberance for a man who worked the hours Bernstein did. "Get this. Turned Boyle's place upside down, not just where you were but the whole damned house. No pictures, no photo albums, nothing. The man with no past. You were right on the button, baby." I could see him leaning back in his chair, puffing a cigar, loosening his Sulka tie, waiting. "So, give. What do you think?"

"I think that whoever killed him took the stuff. Now, you're the hotshot cop—wouldn't you call that an MO? Whoever kills these people steals their pathetic little pasts. . . ."

Kim was watching me, expressionless, listening.

"Confirms the pattern, I guess." Bernstein said. "Club members, stolen pictures. But where does the goddamn suicide fit—Blankenship?"

"Mark, you've got to do a few things in this life for yourself. That's one of them." He told me to fuck myself and hung up.

I finished my drink and said, "Funny thing, everybody who dies gets robbed. . . . Blankenship's odds and ends, Dierker's scrapbook, Boyle's pictures from the old days. Whole thing is tied to the past, funny—"

"I don't want to hear about it," she said, standing up. "Let's go, shall we? The Guthrie awaits."

The first act of *The School for Scandal* went all right; slow, overly broad, rather too close to a De-Millean model, but all right. Kim laughed moderately —more than I did, if it came to that—and we went to the lobby for the intermission with the storm clouds almost out of sight. We were having a Coke in the front foyer, wedged between the glass wall overlooking Vineland Place and a white wall. Happily we discussed Lady Teazle's headdress and the very real possibility that it might collapse into the second row, doing someone bodily harm. Kim was enjoying herself more as the evening progressed, coming quietly to life, and I was standing close to her, possessively touching innocent planes and curves of her body with mine. It was all coming right—I felt it inside me—and then I looked up from her face and saw them, birds of prey, watching us. Harriet Dierker and Helga Kronstrom.

They wore long gowns, Ma Dierker's blue gown matching her hair. Helga, in pink, looked horsey enough to win at Santa Anita; she smiled at us and those awful stained teeth took on a nightmare quality.

Helga was leaning down toward Harriet, straining to whisper in her ear, trying to talk her out of something. Harriet, gray-faced, didn't seem to hear, her eyes darting from me to Kim and back. She advanced.

"I see you've found her, Paul," she said, high-pitched, quavering. "Aren't you afraid? You must be so brave. . . ."

"Mrs. Dierker," I said, "please. . . ."

Kim was suddenly standing apart from me, bracing herself, feet apart as if preparing to ward off a physical attack.

Harriet's head pecked forward, eyes sparkling behind her blue plastic frames. Helga's hands fluttered, a hapless magician trying to make it all go away.

"I asked you if you weren't afraid, Paul."

"I don't know what you mean," I said.

Harriet let out a piercing, derisive laugh and a bearded man in a maroon tuxedo turned to look conspicuously. I felt my chest constricting; we were cornered and the two women blocked our escape.

"I told you, Paul, she's the kiss of death, you know that. . . ." Her smile was deeply ridged, fixed in place like something a thousand years old, long devoid of its original meaning. She hadn't yet looked at Kim, who stood and waited, eyes straight ahead.

"Please, Mrs. Dierker—"

"Why, she drove poor Larry to put a bullet in his head . . . and *he* was her husband. At least until she took up with Ole. Isn't that true? Aren't those the facts? Helga, who knows better than you?"

As she raved, a spray of spittle settled before her and I smelled liquor.

"Come with me, Harriet," Helga said, trying to stay calm, "you don't want to do this." Helga looked at me pleadingly. "This is the first time she's been out since Tim . . . she's overwrought, seeing *her* like this. . . ."

"I may be overwrought," Harriet said distinctly, her voice progressively higher, shriller, "but I am not a murderer!" A girl in a Mickey Mouse T-shirt, with deep, heavy breasts, nudged her boyfriend, tugged the fringe on his leather jacket, nodded toward us. "And I am not a paid slut! A whore!"

Kim's head, small and dark, shook in a spasm of fright or anger. She clamped her teeth, her jaw flexed.

"That's enough," I said. "Excuse us, please," and I began to push past but she wouldn't move, jabbed my chest with a clawed, blue-veined hand. She was disfigured by her hate and grief. Helga looked away.

"No, I will not excuse you. This woman—" At last she glared at Kim, who was backed against the white wall, the tan draining from her fine, delicate face. "This woman killed my husband . . . and now she comes out in public, among decent people, and expects to go about freely. . . . A murderer. . . ."

The Guthrie house manager was pushing past the crowd, some of whom snickered at the scene, smiled at their good luck to be so close. "Typical Guthrie opening," someone said, "all the nuts come out." The man in the maroon tuxedo curled his lip, a wit.

"Harriet! Leave them alone." Helga verged on tears.

"Is she *your* whore now, Paul? Is that the way you behave? I send you to learn how she killed her husband, you pretend to be my friend . . . and then you make her your whore? Can you afford it?" She moved to the side, took aim at Kim, who stared impassively at her. "Did you kill the priest, too? Did you? First Larry, then Tim, then the priest?"

"For God's sake," I shouted at her, raising my hand to frighten her into silence. I took Kim's hand. She shook it loose.

Helga reached for Harriet's arm but she slapped at her hand. Helga began to cry, eyeliner coursing down her cheeks like black rust on a very old building.

"Don't touch me," she cried at me, "don't you dare raise your hand to me. . . ." Harriet had turned the corner, her mind coming unstuck. "You bitch," she screamed at Kim, "you whore, slut. . . ." Spittle flecked her thin lips but she was past caring.

The Guthrie man had reached us, red-faced in a too-tight crested blazer, looking both frightened and horrified. "Now just what the hell's going on here?"

"Better than the show inside," someone said. Others were drifting away in embarrassment; some were closing in on us.

Harriet made a sudden move, lurching past me toward Kim, and before I even began a reaction, Kim's open palm flashed up and slapped Harriet's face, the flat sound of a cleaver's side on a piece of meat. The blue glasses floated past me, bounced on the floor while Harriet sagged backward, screaming, a line of blood trickling across the bridge of her nose. She reached for Helga, missed, and toppled over, sitting down heavily at the feet of the Mickey Mouse girl, who jumped back to make room for the falling body. Harriet's head smacked down hard on the girl's sneaker, thus averting a fractured skull. Suddenly it was quiet in the lobby, the only sound Helga's sobbing as she leaned over her prostrate friend.

"Get a stretcher," the Guthrie man yelled to a thunder-struck usher.

Harriet was leaning on an elbow, struggling to right herself with Helga's aid. "I'm all right, I'm all right," she moaned.

Kim fixed me with a blank look. "Too bad," she murmured.

"What?" I didn't know where to look.

"I'm leaving." Kim pushed past me, very nearly stepping on Harriet's hand. I picked up Harriet's blue glasses and handed them to Helga. She dropped them again.

I caught up with Kim on the steps outside. She was standing quietly, taking a deep breath, arms folded. Through the glass windows I could see the glowing lobby, white like a surgery room, the two old women being attended to by more Guthrie ushers. We were forgotten, the observers filing back inside for the second act.

"Just not our night," I said lamely. "Are you all right?"

"Of course," she said, moving off along the sidewalk, toward the steep hill with the parking lot at the top. "There's very little I can't handle at this point in my life. But, my God, what a deranged woman. . . . I can understand her, though, I know what she's thinking."

"She's gone off the edge—"

"Not really, not so far as you'd think. She's acting on the evidence of her eyes. She's misled, but to herself she makes sense. . . . She's a little obvious, I'm afraid." She stopped and looked at her right hand, holding it open before her. "It stings but I suppose it's all right. Nothing broken."

"I suppose Harriet's okay," I said. "I'm sorry it had to happen."

"Sometimes things happen to me. You'll get used—"

"What?"

"Nothing." She unlocked the Mark IV and we sat for a moment smelling the leather. "I'd better go home and take a bath and get rid of this feeling. What will you do about your review of the play?"

"Frankly, my dear, I don't give a damn. Let's get a drink or something. I don't want you going home, being alone right now—it's better to unwind with somebody after a shock like that."

She nodded and slid the Lincoln down the hill, past the theater with its empty lobby, across Hennepin, alongside Loring Park, which I look down on from my tower. She braked abruptly at the curb. She took a deep breath and passed the back of her hand across her forehead.

"I feel a little strange," she said softly. "Disoriented." She looked at the globes glowing dimly in the park. "Maybe we could walk for a moment."

The little lake was flat, a mirrored reflecting pool, and there was no one in sight. I took her hand, said, "It's not really a good idea to walk here at night, freaks and creeps wandering around."

She shook her head; her hand was limp, she was breathing deeply, regularly, getting her equilibrium reinstated. I wasn't surprised. I didn't feel right myself, adrenaline overloading my system. We walked across the damp, thick grass, past a bench, to a path at the lake. We walked slowly, quietly, and didn't see the man on the bike until it was too late to escape. He came whirring out of the dark like a phantom, one moment indistinguishable from the faint breeze, on top of us the next, skidding to a stop in front of us. I yanked Kim back, out of the way, and the voice, high and clear, like a choirboy's, cut across the quiet darkness.

"Why don't you get her out of the park, buddy? I know why guys like you bring them down here at night. . . . I know, I've seen you in the bushes. . . . Why don't you do it at home and keep it out of the park?" He remained on the bike, not more than an arm's reach away, in Levi's and a windbreaker, his voice high and expressionless as if he weren't involved with what he was saying, like a guide in a museum which bored him. Kim's hand tightened on my arm and she moved against me.

"What in the world are you talking about?" I asked, my anger blurred by surprise.

"You and your whore, who else? Did you pay her yet? Ten bucks? Twenty-five? Look, I don't give a shit what you do with her—just get it out of the park, okay? My job is keeping the park clean, keeping creeps like you and your goddamn whores out of it—"

"You're insane. She's a friend of mine." Anger was welling up in me. The boy wasn't threatening us, and he was obviously insane, riding around in the park insulting people, one of the freaks and creeps.

"Don't bullshit me, okay? You paid her, she'll do whatever you make her do." He was grinning behind the monotone and I could hear a bat squeaking in trees. It was the grin that did it. I pulled away from Kim toward him and he dropped his bike, took a step back, and braced himself, fists clenched. "You want to make something out of it? It's okay with me . . . just remember you started it. I didn't do a damn thing to you." There was an edge of taunting laughter in his voice and I felt as if I'd stepped into a dream sprung directly from ptomaine poisoning.

Whether I'm cowardly or rational I don't know, but my little orgasm of anger passed and I felt foolish, staring into his eyes. He was a real person, grin fixed, a little quaver in his voice, raspberry jello for a brain.

"Let's just leave," Kim said tightly, eyes fixed on him. "He might have a knife, Paul. Come on." She was pulling me away.

He laughed nastily. "Remember, this is my job, keeping guys like you and cunts like her out of the park. Keep the park clean for the rest of us."

"You're insane," I yelled. "Sick, nuts. . . ."

"Sure"—he laughed—"just get her out of here."

I was panting by the time we reached the car. Kim hadn't said a word. I looked back; he was sitting under one of the lamps, staring at us. When she pulled away from the curb I looked again and he was gone.

"Do you still want a drink?" I said. My heart was pounding and my head felt as if tiny men were pounding my eyeballs with ball peen hammers.

"Sure," she said. She swung around the edge of the

park and was cruising along its eastern perimeter when the boy materialized across the street on her side, straddling his bike, watching us. There was an absolutely fearless kind of insolence in his stance, as if he thrived on confrontation and wasn't satisfied with our encounter.

Before I could point him out, I heard Kim suck her breath in, felt the Mark IV swerve across the deserted street. The boy grinned malevolently, his face clown-white beneath a streetlamp, teeth bared, and he pushed off into the street, dared her. It was instantaneous and I felt dumbstruck, a spectator. He went too far. It was too late: She spun the steering wheel at the last millisecond; the heavy car sunk sideways and shimmied back across the street. The left front fender caught the bike's front tire, exploded it sideways and upward, knocking the boy like a doll against a parking meter, bouncing him off the streetlamp, dropping him in the gutter. She mashed the power brakes and I braced myself against the dashboard. The engine died. Kim draped herself forward across the steering wheel, shaking.

I got out and went over to the boy. He had pulled himself into a sitting position, hunkered over, head down.

"Are you all right?" I asked.

He looked up at me, half grinning, lip split, glassy-eyed. He waved me away, croaked something short and indecipherable. I backed off. He shook his head and slowly, gripping the parking meter for support, pulled himself upright. He sagged, turned away from me. His bicycle was twisted beyond repair, like a dead animal. He moved off into the darkness of the park.

Kim was leaning back, tears on her cheeks. I closed the door and leaned back, wishing my heart would calm down.

"You know," I said, "we could have killed that kid."

"You had nothing to do with it. . . . Oh, God, this whole evening has been too much for me." She wiped at the tears and sniffed. "He just kept on coming. . . . I couldn't turn back in time. . . ." She sighed heavily and started the car. "I don't know what to say, Paul. I'm terribly sorry, but this isn't one of my usual evenings. . . . I really do want to go home." She tried a tentative smile. "Don't worry."

"I guess I am worried . . . about you, I mean," I said. "It comes down to that. What a god-awful evening—"

"Memorable, though." I could hear the irony in her voice; she was totally composed now. "The terrible irony of it," she said, "is the slurs being cast on my moral character. Everyone—the crazies, I guess—seems to think I'm some sort of whore, *your* whore, specifically." She laughed softly. "And you know how true that is. Only you, Paul. And Ole."

"Well," I said, "it just goes to show you, doesn't it?"

"Good night, Paul." She leaned across and gave me a dry, sisterly little peck, then a softer one and my tongue hit a wall of her teeth.

It took awhile to get to sleep. A second-rater named Jack Brohammer, who played second for Cleveland, was tattooing the Twins' ace, Bert Blyleven, when I finally drifted off, troubled, turning.

15

THE morning's telephone calls began early. Don Magruder from the Guthrie called to ask me what the hell I knew about the rumble in the lobby the night before. I blamed it on a couple of drunken elderly ladies who had insulted a friend of mine—presumably a case of mistaken identity—and tried to grapple with her and had been slapped. I said that my friend was not going to sue the little old ladies or the Guthrie for harboring offensive tipplers and that had him thinking for a moment. I told him he needn't worry, then asked him what the little old ladies had to say and he said not much, that one of them had somehow fallen down and spent the night in a hospital under observation but was being released this morning. "From what I hear," he added, "your friend's got a pretty good right hand."

"Well, Donny"—I chuckled knowingly—"she won't take any shit. But, then, she's not suing anybody either. So have a nice day." Then I called the office and told them to have somebody else see the show and write the review because I'd come down with something. He didn't believe me and said so and I hung up. Bad telephone manners.

I was in the shower trying to figure out Kim's behavior the night before, half in awe at her violent reactions and half frightened, when Archie called. I stood dripping in the hallway, looking out at what seemed to be a summer sun. The wind was whistling and shaking my geraniums.

"It was easier than I thought," Archie said. "They've got all sorts of old files in Washington and one of my old comrades-in-arms detailed some poor bastard to check on Goode's 1944 Christmas." He paused and sipped at his morning coffee. "Where do you think he was?"

"Archie," I said threateningly.

"He was in Minneapolis. Departed Washington on the tenth of December for Minneapolis, leaving a telephone number where he could be reached, and didn't return to Washington until the night of December 26. All there in black and white. Nice, wouldn't you say?"

"Very. So why did he lie?"

"Why, indeed? Lovely plot we're building."

"But what does it mean?"

"Doesn't matter. We're just collecting tidbits of information. Finding out what it means comes later. For now, be satisfied that we know Jonnie lied and that he was on the scene when Maxvill disappeared. And Rita. Why is she always an afterthought? Well, anyway, keep it all in mind."

"My mind's in danger of shorting out, Dad."

"One other thing. Have you found out anything about Blankenship? Where he came from? Who he is . . . was?"

"No."

"Well, I'm going to have a go at that. I've got a source or two. . . . Paul?"

"Yes?"

"Fun, ain't it?"

"I don't know. Is it?"

"If you don't get personally involved," he said. "What are your plans for the day?" He couldn't imagine my doing anything but working on our case.

"Crocker," I said.

The wind and heat hit me in the face like a wrecking ball. Bill Oliver was standing in the parking lot peering at the fountain, which had ceased working altogether. A bird sat on the fountain nozzle and stared back at Oliver. Neither one of them looked at me as I went past and climbed into the oven I used for a car.

A heat haze hung in the air about six feet over my head and the wind shook the car before I started it. It wasn't summer and it wasn't fall; it was worse. WCCO informed me that it was ten o'clock and the temperature was already eighty-six with wind hitting gusts to forty-five. Crocker's office had told me he was at the North Side site, which meant he was hard-hatting it on a huge plot of earth a block off Lyndale North, where a new high-rise complex of office buildings, retail outlets, and apartments was going up. Turning into the Hennepin/Lyndale bottleneck, everything—the purple mass of the Walker, the rich green of the park where our marauder had appeared last night, the gray spires of the Basilica—was blurred behind the heat, like a world packed in cotton wadding. I curled around the Highway 12 exit and continued on up Lyndale past the Farmers' Market and the Munsingwear plant, past the low-income housing that already seemed to be coming unstuck right there in the middle of the best of all possible worlds. Behind me the cancerous black roofing factory, long an eyesore and a source of constant civic hysteria, squatted, malignant, mocking.

The huge maroon-and-gold sign, exact duplicates of the University of Minnesota colors, loomed two stories high above a flat, scrubby vacant square block—three block capital C's, in gold outlined in maroon, with CROCKER CONSTRUCTION COMPANY beneath it and THE GLORY HILL PROJECT beneath that, followed by rows of specifics as to cost, funding, a sketch of the final *megillah* as it would look in a couple of years, all spanking new. No sketch of it being torn down twenty years later for the rapid transit system or the domed soccer stadium.

I cruised the length of the three blocks facing west, then hung a right for the two-block depth of it, then back along its eastern three blocks, around and around, listening to Dick Haymes sing Cole Porter's "In the Still of the Night," which had been very big in 1937, according to Roger and Charlie on WCCO. The park which was being demolished was crowned by a huge green hummock laced with tall shade trees, oak and maple and elm, and latticed with walkways, a perfect spot for sledding in the white winter months. Progress was having its day, however, and another neighborhood was being bombed out, leveled, and department stores and sleazy plastic steak houses and car washes and fragile cheap-jack apartments were going to make life better for everyone. 1937. . . . I circled the area again, looking for any signs of a headquarters trailer among the dozens of maroon-and-gold vans, trucks, trailers, cars, pickups. 1937, the radio lads told me, found the Duke of Windsor marrying Mrs. Simpson on June 3, Amelia Earhart vanishing in July in the middle of the Pacific, and the *Hindenburg* exploding on May 6—a very big year. Of special interest thirty-seven years later, in the summer that Richard Nixon finally got caught, was the note that on December 20 the Supreme Court had ruled that tapped telephone conversations could not be made public. Then Fred Astaire sang "A Foggy Day" and when it was over, my daily history lesson complete, I put the Porsche in the shadow of a likely-looking trailer and went in search of James Crocker, the footballer who made good.

Dust was blowing and the wind bore the groan of the earthmovers working on the green hill. A tree went down while I stood there, feeling dirt mixing with sweat on my forehead, and my old blue blazer was sticking to my back and turning a funny color. Crocker came out of the trailer, slipping his maroon hard hat onto his head; he wore dark aviator glasses, khaki work clothes, and boots. His sleeves were rolled up on dark tanned arms covered with curly gray hair like steel wool. He was frowning and seeing me didn't help. But he was alone and couldn't avoid me.

"What the hell are you doing here? Writing a review?" He was very different from the family man barbecuing chicken for his grandchildren. He was larger, harder, and the deep lines in his face gave him a cruel aspect. He was carrying a walkie-talkie handset in a gigantic reddish paw.

"No," I said. "Just wanted to apologize for getting everybody so upset the other day. Hub told me I'd struck a nerve somewhere."

He grunted, put the walkie-talkie down on a trestle table covered with elevation charts, and lit a Lucky Strike.

"And I'm sorry you took it out on Boyle. He meant no harm, I'm sure. Now he's dead. . . . Too late for you to apologize for yelling at him." I watched him for a reaction but it wasn't easy with the wind and the dust. His glasses were crusted with a fine layer of it. He stared at me and finally flung the match away. He didn't seem inclined to speak so I went on trying to think of myself as Humphrey Bogart needling Ward Bond, trying to force the issue.

"Now that two of the old gang have been murdered," I said, "I wondered if maybe you've remembered anything more about the dear dead days beyond recall, like about Maxvill. . . . Really"—I forced a snicker—"it's amazing the way his name gives you guys the shakes."

"Are you going to keep talking to me, Mr. Cavanaugh?"

"I thought I would," I said.

"Well, then, you're going to have to follow along. Fellow on the dozer, up there on the hill, says something funny's happening and wants me to take a look. So, let's go."

We set off up Glory Hill, just the two of us, other workmen and drivers busy with their own duties, and soon we were out of the dust, on the green grass, in the pools of shade, beginning the slow climb.

"Are you keeping it a secret, too?" I asked. "Whatever it is about Maxvill—?"

"I'm afraid you've been misled and while we're talking about apologies, I figure I owe you one on this Maxvill deal. The general and I obviously were off the track on that, but try to look at it our way. We're both hardheaded men, working in the real world, where things like reputations, old scandals and irregularities— they can crop up and get people talking, and we had enough of that when Carver went off in '44. For instance, I had Carver doing a little legal work for Crocker Construction in the thirties, a lot of people thought of him as one of the firm . . . then he ups and disappears, and that combined with his reputation—"

"What reputation?"

"Well, hell, half the people who knew him figured him for a goddamn homo and the other half knew damn well he was a chaser, always after some silly-ass waitress or bar girl, so his reputation wasn't so hot. But what the hell, I used to say, he wasn't a bad guy— hell of a shot, really a crack shot with a pistol or rifle or shotgun, and that always impressed me . . . and he wasn't a bad lawyer, either, come to think of it. Funny, he wasn't an outdoorsman, but when he felt like it, he was the best flycaster and the best shot of the bunch. . . . Anyway, Father Boyle wouldn't give two hoots about stuff like business reputations, probably didn't occur to him that people like Jonnie and me would want to keep his name out of things—"

"What did he do, embezzle money from Crocker Construction?"

He stopped and thrust a thick finger with a broken nail at me, but he was smiling. "See, that's what I mean! First damn thing you think of is embezzlement, old Carver took the money and ran, is that it? Hell, no, he didn't take any money . . . but rumors like that spread all over town. Which is exactly what I want to keep quiet now. Got it?" He sat down heavily on a cement bench just off the path. "Rest a minute. I got me one of those pacemaker things stuck under my collarbone here, but there's no use in climbing so fast it blows out. . . ."

"Do you think he's dead?" I asked.

"By now? He might be. I don't think he was dead then, hell, no . . . he ran off. . . ."

"With Rita Hook?"

"What?"

"Do you think he ran off with Rita Hook?"

"Well, for Chrissakes! Rita Hook!" He was pale underneath the tan and in another age, before Medtronic developed the pacemaker, he might have been dead. Now he was just resting. "A name from the past, that one is. Carver and Rita, what an idea! It never occurred to me—"

"Why not? They disappeared the same day, December 16, 1944. Seems that it might have crossed your mind."

Crocker's face clouded and he took a last hit from the Lucky.

"Same day," he mused. "I guess that's right, never really stuck in my mind, I guess, because by the time the Grande Rouge law questioned us it was the next week, almost Christmas, and we were all wondering where the hell Carver was and not worrying much about Rita. . . . I mean, what the hell was Rita to us? Cook and housekeeper. . . ."

"Just Carver's type, wouldn't you say?"

He squinted at me and took off his sunglasses, wiping the dust from them with a red bandanna.

"You sound like you're building up to something," he said.

"Nope, just collecting bits and pieces." I stood up. "You see, I think everybody's lying to me about Maxvill."

"Why the hell would I lie about him? What is there to lie about?" He shook his head, looking up at me, hooking his glasses behind his ears, hiding his eyes.

"I sure don't know. Maybe Carver's alive . . . maybe Carver's the one who stole his file from the newspaper morgue—"

"Jon told me about that," he said. "Funny thing."

"Not too funny, actually. What if Carver were alive and what if he stole the file? Do you see what I mean?"

"No, I don't." Up ahead of us, toward the top of the hill, the sky seemed to be fluttering like a tattered awning. It was the birds skittering out of the treetops, frightened of something. I heard their cries.

"Well, if Carver stole that file, then he probably stole the snapshots from Tim and Father Boyle . . . which means that he killed them." I watched the birds swarming above, as if their minds or communicative sense were one, each interlocking with the other. "Can you imagine why Carver Maxvill would be coming back to kill his old buddies? One at a time? Is that the secret, what you all did to him?" We were trudging uphill again and sweat was running down inside my pants leg.

"Aw, hell, you're way out in left field," he growled. "That's plain nuts—anything happened to Carver, he brought it on himself—"

"What did he bring on himself?"

"Look," he puffed, "and god damn it, let this be an end to it, I don't know what happened to Maxvill and there's no point in bringing it all up again. . . ." His face had regained its color and was flushed now.

"But Rita was his type, you admit that. . . ."

"Jesus, yes, I guess she was. More or less. She was a very easy woman, Rita was—"

"Good-looking?"

"I suppose she was, when she was all fixed up. We sat her when she was working around the place mostly—"

"When did you see her when she was fixed up and looking her best, then? When she was with Carver?"

"I don't remember, I just don't remember."

"And you're not worried?"

"About Carver? Hell, no. . . ."

"Besides Carver. You're not worried?"

"What about?"

"What about?" I repeated. "My God, two men have been murdered and another killed himself. . . . Somebody seems to be wiping out the jolly boys, Mr. Crocker, and you're a card-carrying jolly boy—"

"General Goode told me you'd say that," he said knowingly, "and the answer is simply that there's no connecting the two killings—"

"You actually believe that? Two apparently motiveless murders of two longtime friends, two sets of snapshots taken . . . and you don't think there's a connection? Nobody, but nobody, could really believe that . . . not you, not Goode, not Bernstein, nobody." I was grinning at him beneath the crying birds, which he didn't seem to notice. The street level was far away below us and we were thirty yards from the top of the hill his machinery was ripping to bits. "Tell me, can't you remember something more about Blankenship— does he fit the pattern? Is his suicide linked to the murders? To Carver and Rita? In any way? Why the hell don't you just tell me?"

He walked on, breathing hard, and I put my hand out to stop him and he struck at it, quickly, heavily, with a paw.

"Tim, Marty, Blankenship, Rita, Carver, Kim," he repeated angrily, eyes straight ahead. "I don't know who's doing all these new killings, they've nothing to do with me. . . ."

"What about the old killings? What did they have to do with you?"

His head snapped toward me.

"What the hell do you mean, old killings? I don't know what you're talking about."

"You said something about these new killings . . . that implies there were some old ones—"

"New, recent—Jesus, you sure know how to piss me off."

We were almost to the top.

"Somebody else is more pissed off than you are," I said. "Somebody else is killing people . . . unless you are the killer."

"Okay, Cavanaugh, I don't care if your father is an old friend, I've had it with you. I'm telling you—" His teeth were grinding and a vein pulsed in the block of his large square forehead. "I'm telling you, drop this whole thing—just drop it. I'm not asking, I'm telling. There are ways to make you drop it but I don't want to do that if I don't have to—just use your common sense. It's none of your business. None of your business." He scowled at me.

"Well, if it isn't Primal Man doing his club-waving number. . . . Once the paralysis leaves my lower limbs, I shall run and tell my daddy. . . . Honest to God, you make me sick. What are you going to do, send goons on bulldozers up to my floor and then scrape me up and dump me in a corner?"

"Mister, you're not too far wrong. . . ."

"What I can't figure out is why you and Goode aren't worried about getting killed. It doesn't make any sense—"

I never finished that simple thought and never got what would have doubtless been another threat because one of Crocker's cat jockeys came running toward us from the top of the hill, yelling Crocker's name, telling him to hurry.

I went with them and what I saw was a delirium tremens attack come to life in the sunshine, indescribable, terrifying, hypnotizing. On the top of the hill and on the other side, the earthmovers had dropped their blades and scraped the roof off a civilization of rats. I'd heard about such things but only half believed them, but it was real. The earth, the beautiful green park, had been cut open like a Washington Avenue abortion and several of the superficial tears had collapsed inward, leaving abscesslike craters on the surface of the grass. And the abscesses were moving, trembling, quivering as we watched. A stench rose in almost palpable columns from the openings and the wind carried it like epidemic disease in all directions. The quivering became, at closer look, with our hands over our mouths and noses, the twitching noses and plump scurrying bodies of brown rats whose lives were being nastily interrupted. Not many at first, just a few, maybe forty or fifty brave enough to dare the sun's awful brightness and the terrifying, unexpected blasts of wind, both foreign to a subterranean world.

Moving quickly, the man with the machine closest to the crest of the hill slid dirt down over the opening and with a god-awful grinding of gears and thrashing of threads, he dug his blade down and began to push toward the rats. But the crust of earth over the rat colony was too fragile. Slowly but very surely the grass surrounding the huge yellow machine began to grow scraggly fissures as it sagged inward, leaving the man and the countless pounds of yellow steel alone like a mechanical island surrounded by rats and putrescent refuse. The rats looked myopically from their lunches, took a squint or two, and began to burrow backward into their hill; some daring fellows scampered toward the machine, making squeaking sounds. The driver looked over at us, saw that no suggestions were forthcoming, and climbed slowly down from his perch. He made the mistake of trying to run to safety. After three strides his boot and then his leg up to the knee smashed down through the next layer and as he tried to brace himself to pull the leg out, his hand descended on the head of a large, somnolent-seeming rat who awoke with a terrified start and clamped its teeth into the peculiar white hand which had attacked him. The man screamed and as he jerked his hand into the air, the rat came with it and in a paroxysm of horror the man looked up and saw the brown thing with its long, serpentine tail swinging and whipping in the air, teeth sunk deep into the flesh, hanging on for dear life, and the screaming rose an octave as the man desperately swung the arm, hand, and rat, all three of which were now being covered with spraying blood. In time the rat, choking on flesh and blood, let go to avoid suffocation and took an amazingly large chunk of the hand with him. The victim, struggling in the pulsating sea of garbage and rats, got his leg free of the hole and slowly, bloodily, dragged himself out of the mess. Two rats were attached to his leg and ankle, and Crocker kicked them off, frantically yelling into his walkie-talkie, trying to make himself understood. "Rats, an infestation of them," he cried into the machine, commanding his men to call the fire department and sanitation department for help.

At least at the beginning the rats were hesitant about venturing out; they sent their scouts as far as the edge, where the grass firmed up, but soon they would hurry back to their comrades beneath the carpet of green covering the park. Finally we completely abandoned the hill, as the birds had done before us, gagging with the lingering fetid stench. Crocker was beyond my reach now, conferring with his operations manager, public-relations executives, and fire-department officials. I talked with a sanitation-department officer while we waited.

"Well, it had to happen eventually, I guess," he said, worried but excited. "We knew they were there, of course, they had to be, their infestations are as old as the country. Lots of rats were brought in from Europe—funny, Norway was one of the biggest suppliers of rats to this country. You Norwegian?"

"No," I said.

"Whew." He laughed, anxious to inform me. The wounded man had been taken into the trailer. "You gotta be careful around here, what you say about Norwegians and Swedes. Anyway, I was in New York studying the rat problem they've got—more rats there than people—my God, you wouldn't believe what they've got . . . alligators and crocodiles and beavers and rats and who the hell knows what else lives in the sewers, probably things we don't even know about, mutants. . . . Central Park's full of rats like these here, big, eighteen inches, weigh two or three pounds, came over from Norway in 1775. They like tunnels, construction sites, sewers, parks where people leave food—now, that's what you got here, this park's probably a hundred years old, more or less, and these rats

generation after generation, have probably lived here
all that time—just beneath the surface, bringing in
garbage to eat, burying the passing generations,
Christ, no wonder it smells like it does, particularly
on a hot day. . . . No, you got yourself a pretty siz-
able rat population here by now. . . ."

"So what happens now?"

"Well, we'll have to kill 'em one way or another,
won't we? Course, some of 'em we'll just drive out
into the neighborhood and there are terrible risks
there, rabid rats are pretty damned mean . . . but we
can't just leave 'em, can we? I mean, this construction's gotta go on, so we gotta get 'em the hell out of
here, don't we?" He sighed, pushed his glasses up
on his snub nose, and ran a hand through thinning
sandy hair. "Well, I'm sure as hell glad it's not my
problem. We usually use warfarin to kill 'em over
the long haul—it's an anticoagulant rat poison—
though in time they build up an immunity to it—then
you got yourself a superrat, and they are really tough.
There are some rats the scientists just ain't quite
sure how the hell to kill. Pretty thought, ain't it?" He
chuckled bleakly. "I suppose we'll wind up going after
them with chemicals, pump something into the hill and
hope it stays in the hill and doesn't kill everybody who
lives hereabouts." He looked at me solemnly and
laughed abruptly. "There's always fire and water,
too. Remember the Black Death? The bubonic
plague? Wiped out whole goddamn countries in olden
times. . . . That was rats. Well, I'd better report for
duty here. . . . This is gonna take days, I expect."
He shook his head. "Think of it, the plague. . . .
Now, how the hell would the Chamber of Commerce
handle that one? Play hell with the Quality of Life
boys, hunh?" He thought that was wonderfully amusing.

I stayed until the middle of the afternoon; it was
like watching a military operation and the television
crews arrived and every so often several men would
wheel canisters up the hill. The temperature passed
ninety, and hundreds, then thousands of people began
to line the streets, numbly, quietly watching. There

was nothing funny about it. They lived on the edges of the park, many of them, and rats weren't something you laughed at. From time to time a shriek would come from the crowd as a rat began to move down the hill toward the people. Beaters moved them back up, but if the rats had gotten moving *en masse* toward the people, there'd have been a lot of dead bodies in the aftermath, little brown ones and big white and black ones. I stayed until I just couldn't take the heat and the increasing putrescence and the dull faces of the crowd anymore. The whole thing was too much for me.

Ole Kronstrom called me a few minutes after I climbed into my shower; twice in one day, very possibly a new American League record for right-handed overweight critics. He wondered if he could stop by for a chat in half an hour. I scrubbed the smell of rats for about twenty minutes, doused myself with Yardley, and received him wrapped in my terry-cloth robe, drinking a Pimm's Cup, trying to forget the little brown things digging in for the gas attack on the North Side.

I fixed Ole Kronstrom a glass of iced tea and we sat in the cool, dark living room. I sat at my desk as I always did and Ole sat where Kim had sat the night before. It seemed longer ago than that but it was less than a full day. Ole squeezed his lemon slice and took a long drink; his hand hid the glass. He wore a seersucker jacket, a bow tie, and gray slacks, the picture of someone who wasn't about to be done in by the heat. I asked him what I could do for him.

"I'm a little hesitant about getting into this," he said softly, having a hard time looking me in the eye. "I don't want you to think I'm being presumptuous or protective . . . or just plain nosy. I abhor people who are any of those things. But I've spoken with Kim today and she had a good deal to say about you. . . ." He took another long nervous drink, insofar as he could possibly reflect a case of nerves in his stolid, white-haired presence.

I'd known this was coming; it was inevitable. No

matter how you cut it, I was muscling in on his girlfriend, whether he thought of her as his daughter or Ann-Margret. It didn't really matter what their relationship was; since I'd turned up, it was less. Less friendship, less companionship, less everything and he was too nice a man to just bear down on me, threaten muscle as Crocker had done. I watched him set his iced tea down and fumble with his tobacco pouch and pipe. If he asked me to stand back from Kim, I wasn't going to be able to do it. So what the hell could I say?

"What was it she had to say?"

"It was very personal," he said, stuffing tobacco into the bowl of a battered old pipe. "It amounts to the fact that she has grown very close to you, at least by her standards. You know by now that she is not free and relaxed with anyone, but particularly not with men. You and I aren't really concerned with her rationale, not at the moment. But you see, she feels. . . ." He stopped and lit the tobacco, drawing softly and slowly. "She feels a sense of guilt—about me, that is. She has a very peculiar conscience, she cannot bear the idea of betrayal, the business of using other people. . . . And she's afraid her feelings about you—and they are by no means clear and simple—will make me feel that she has used me." He puffed again, dotting the air before him with clouds of blue smoke.

"What do you think?" I asked. "About the whole thing."

He massaged the pipe with his huge hands, smiling to himself.

"I'm concerned about Kim. She is, in fact, the only real concern I have in life. I want things to go well for her, she's had a very difficult time in many ways, and she's the kind of person—and they're quite exceedingly rare, in my experience—who lives very deeply, whose emotions are so tender and raw to the touch that they must be almost hidden, even from herself. . . ." He looked up at me, had no trouble connecting with my eyes this time. "I can see that you're worried, Mr. Cavanaugh, worried about what I'm going to say about you, about your effect on Kim—"

"It had crossed my mind," I said.

"I understand your interest in Kim. I don't know if it's wise on your part, I don't know if you're up to coping with such a person . . . but I always respected your father and I enjoyed our discussion the other day. The important thing, of course, is not that you are interested in Kim. What is significant is that, at least to some degree, Kim returns your interest . . . and I would say *interest* is the precise word. Her attitude is one of interest, no more than that—perhaps a feeling that you are a sympathetic person, someone who seems to want to understand her." He sipped some tea, evidently more relaxed now. "She's still frightened of you. And she's terribly frightened of herself, her reactions to you. She's both drawn toward you . . . and repelled by what you represent—a possibly intimate relationship. She's not ready for that. . . ."

"I know," I said.

"And you must realize that she may never be ready for what most of us might think of as a normal relationship between a man and a woman. Can you cope with that?"

"I'm not awash with confidence, no. I've not been overly lucky with women. They always turn out to be more complex than I am. But, yes, I want to reach into her, get hold of her from the inside. I lie in bed at night and I wonder, is it an ego thing? Do I want to do it because it's hard to do? I really don't know. . . ."

"Well, all I wanted to do was set your mind at ease so far as I'm concerned. She's like a daughter to me, not a captive. I've given her what I could, she's given me a daughter's love and companionship . . . but I'm not interested in sealing her off. She was concerned about what I might think and perhaps you were too—there's no need to be. But be careful. That's just a friendly word of caution." He leaned back and sighed, relieved, and I fixed him another iced tea. He didn't seem inclined to leave and mentioned that Kim had told him about the events of the night before.

"Both at the Guthrie and at the park," he said.

"It was a gruesome evening," I said.

"She's very stoic at times. She wondered if she should report hitting the boy and take the consequences. Perhaps I was wrong but I advised her against it. Then I called the police myself to see if there'd been any such accident brought to their attention—there hadn't been, of course."

"She could have killed the guy," I said.

"She sees red sometimes, it's a complex reaction. She strikes out, acts when other people only think about it—"

"Exactly."

"It's her sense of morality," he said after a lengthy pause. "She is a fundamentalist, rather like me, only she's got more muscles in her principles. . . . She believes in right and wrong, in loyalty for those who earn it, punishment for those who deserve it." He stared at me from behind those heavy black plastic glasses, taking my measure, adding me up.

"I have my doubts about right and wrong," I said. "Whether moral abstractions exist at all in the real world."

"It's not an easy business, is it?" he said enigmatically. "But she's one of those who believe in individual responsibility. Personal accountability."

"You said the same thing about Tim Dierker," I said, remembering the phrase.

"Did I? Well, I suppose I was right both times. Tim believed in paying for his mistakes."

"Is that what he was doing when he went off the roof?"

"Maybe," he said calmly, puffing slowly. "Who knows?"

I let the idea go and told him what I'd seen at the construction site. He shrunk into the couch when I described the rats, the man trapped with the rats clinging to him, the stench, the faces of the onlookers. I told him Crocker had threatened me in the matter of Carver Maxvill.

"Are you sure you don't know why Maxvill gets to them all so badly . . . and not to you? Not to Archie? What has Maxvill to do with them and not with you?"

"Well, don't forget that your father and I are very marginal figures in terms of our involvement with the club. It would be very simple for there to have been something we didn't know about . . . but my feeling is that probably, no matter how unlikely it may seem to you, they're telling you the truth . . . their motivations may not be good, but they fit the men we're talking about." He tamped the ash down into the bowl and applied a match to the remains.

"Do you think somebody's killing the club members? I mean, systematically? Or do you buy the coincidence theory?"

"Oh," he said, "I don't have much in the way of theories—"

"But you're one of them, you could be on the list."

He gave me a surprised look and slid a huge hand back along the stiff white hair. "My gosh, I don't think I'm on anybody's list. I think people who are in danger of being murdered must know why, don't you? Nobody would want to kill me, I'm very sure of that."

"I'm convinced that there is a pattern, though," I said, "and I'm also convinced that General Goode and Crocker are in it. . . . Let me try this one on you. What if Maxvill is still alive? Maybe he has a reason for killing them. . . . It popped into my mind and now I can't quite get rid of it. No body was ever found, no indication that he's dead . . . and why did he disappear? No one has ever figured that out either. And the mention of his name drives Goode and Crocker and Boyle and even Hub Anthony crazy." I chewed up an apple slice from the slush in the bottom of the Pimm's Cup. "Working from those suppositions, I could be right . . . if his disappearance was somehow the result of something the clubbies did to him, if they drove him out of town, out of sight, then mightn't he have waited, his anger festering, until now, thirty years later, he's having his revenge . . . taking target practice on his old chums?"

"He'd be very hard to catch, wouldn't he?" he asked innocently. "If he's the man who doesn't exist . . . I've read that most murders are never solved. This could be one of those, I suppose." He sighed and got up from the couch. "It bothers me, everything about Minneapolis seems to bother me. . . . Sometimes I think the people are fooling themselves, trying to convince themselves that they're different, better, cleaner, purer than people in other places. I'm old enough to know it's not true, not at bedrock—down there it's just like any place else. But when something rotten works its way to the surface it seems all the worse because so many of us have convinced ourselves that nothing bad can happen here. Maybe it's simple hypocrisy, but I think it's deeper, I think it's an ingrown self-delusion, smugness, self-congratulation. . . . But it's a hobby-horse of mine and nobody much agrees with me. Well, don't let me bore you. I've been thinking about Norway as a place to spend my declining years. . . . Oslo or maybe Bergen, a quiet life where I'll have time to add up my life, find out what it's been about and if I've made any sense of it, learned anything. . . ." He let that thought trail off. A police siren wailed on the freeway and the wind took a gratuitous whack at the remaining geraniums. He knocked his pipe into an ashtray and smiled at me. "Are you planning to keep after this business?"

"Until I hit a dead end, I suppose."

"Why?"

"I'm beginning to think I've forgotten. It's self-propelling now."

"Well, don't let it do something bad to you, Paul. It's deep and I believe it's dangerous . . . but you don't need advice from me. I'm out of the battle now and I ought to mind my own business." He stuffed the pipe and tobacco pouch into a bulging pocket and I followed him down the hallway to the door. He turned with his hand on the knob. "Forgive me, but what I really came to talk about was Kim and I must be blunt. What are your feelings about her?"

"Did she ask you to find out?"

"Oh, no, no, she wouldn't want me talking to you about her at all. It's just that I can't help myself, my fatherly instincts. I'm curious. I want to know. But you don't have any obligation to tell me, I realize that."

"I don't know," I said. "I've never known anyone like her, never reacted to anyone this way. She frightens me at times because I think she could hurt me badly . . . but I can't stop thinking about her. I can't seem to control my feelings about her. . . . I'm making no sense, she does that to me."

"She said she thought you were rather alike. And confound it, you are. I guess it'll just work itself out, one way or the other." We shook hands and he left. I felt as if I were drifting in an open boat, no sight of land, my ship long sunk, at the mercy of the sea. The more I thought about Kim, the more confused I became. But it was encouraging to know that she'd spoken to Ole about me, that I did mean something to her. I went to the kitchen and made another Pimm's Cup and sat down at my desk again. I'd gone over it all so many times: Larry, Tim, Father Boyle, Carver Maxvill, and Rita. Harriet Dierker and Kim and Ole. You try to fit it all together in different ways, hoping like hell it will finally, accidentally make sense. But it was always a forlorn hope.

Who was Larry Blankenship and why did he cry when he talked with Kim in the parking lot and finally put a bullet in his head?

Why were Tim and Father Boyle killed?

Why did Carver Maxvill and Rita Hook disappear on the same day? Why did they disappear at all? And did they go together?

What was it about Maxvill that scared Goode and Crocker?

Why did Goode lie about being in Minneapolis when Maxvill disappeared?

Why did someone steal the file and the snapshots?

Why did I feel that Billy Whitefoot knew more about the goings-on at the lodge than he was telling?

And where did Kim really fit in? Was she just a bystander or did that role ring false? I thought about the boy on the bicycle . . . Then I figured, the hell with it. Too complex.

It was dark and the wind was whipping at the swing on my balcony, moving it like a ghost rider, making it squeak. I was just going to begin listing in my mind what I actually knew about the case when I realized how much my head ached and my eyes hurt. I popped three Excedrin, glared at my empty refrigerator, opened *The Baseball Encyclopedia* and closed it listlessly, turned on the Twins game just in time to hear a windblown fly ball by Danny Thompson go for a home run. Thompson was, to my knowledge, the only shortstop with leukemia ever to play in the big leagues—not an enviable distinction but a reflection on the kind of guy he was. I paced out onto the balcony, shielding my eyes against the microscope debris swirling upward, sucked toward Heaven.

The telephone rang at the other end, rang and rang and rang, and when she answered it, I could hear music and people laughing and talking. She had a hard time hearing me.

"Paul," I said. "Paul, the guy who took you to the fights last night, then on to the porno show and the demolition derby—"

"Oh, *that* Paul. . . . Hold on, let me take this in the bedroom. *To* the bedroom, thirty-foot cord, I'm walking down the hall now, past the cheering throng and the lasagna cooks in the kitchen, around the corner past the bathroom's tuneful flushing . . . and into the inviolate chamber itself, the virgin queen's very own bedroom. . . . Hi, Paul, how's tricks?"

"Is this the featherweight champion of the Guthrie Lobby?"

"In the flesh, throwing a victory party. *Body and Soul,* Canada Lee getting socked in the head once too often and getting those awful headaches, and John Garfield telling George Macready that he's not afraid because everybody dies. . . ."

"My God," I said.

"Oh, there are sides to me you've never dreamed

of, Critic. It's the only movie I know but I really know it. . . . Fatalistic Flicks of the Forties. . . ."

"You're nice but you may be drunk," I said.

"Not really but I'm having a party. This is what comes out when I push the phony, awful, rotten, giddy hostess button. You have my apologies. I did so want to keep this face a secret—"

"You've wanted to keep them all secret, Champ."

"Not true. Not the up-to-date me." She turned her mouth away from the telephone and said, "Okay, okay, I'll be out in just a minute. Personal call." Then she turned back. "You haven't told me. . . ."

"What?"

"Tricks—how are they?"

"You really want to know?"

"I don't know, do I?"

"I'm lonely and I'm getting scared—"

"Of being lonely?"

"No, of becoming dependent."

"On?"

"You."

"Oho, you were right, I didn't want to know."

"Why didn't you ask me to your party?"

"Well, two reasons. You're not a university person, a colleague, so to speak. And to the best of my recollection, you're not a war-gamer. So you'd be hopelessly out of place on my guest list, which is made of university war-gamers. We are fighting the Battle of the Bulge right in the living room—"

"To Led Zeppelin?"

"Not my fault. A guest is using it for inspiration."

"Well, much to your surprise, I wouldn't be at all out of place. Not a bit."

"You're a war-gamer? You astound me. . . ."

"No, no. But I am a world class lasagna eater. Heh, heh, that's my little joke."

"Can you bear it, then?"

"What?"

"Coming down, seeing me at my worst, putting on five pounds of lasagna?"

"Yeah, I can."

"Well . . . hurry, then."

As it turned out, it wasn't the Battle of the Bulge but the German invasion of Russia that was going on when I got to Kim's apartment. The game was called Panzer Blitz and all it needed for that last soupçon of verisimilitude was Anne standing in a corner hurling gasoline-powered Messerschmitts on the players' heads. It was a casually dressed, heavily bearded, low-breasted group deeply involved in the specifics of blocking roads, getting tanks out of swamps, training artillery from hilltops, and trying to move troops in trucks. Led Zeppelin had given way to the Beatles and the volume was down; it was apparently time to think and conversations were carried on in hushed tones. There were maybe twenty people clustered around the table, some nibbling on lasagna and salad and debating the finer points of what seemed to be a set of rules more involved than the Treaty of Brest-Litovsk. Kim came from the kitchen to meet me, wearing Levi's and a red-and-blue-striped rugby shirt with a white collar. It was awkward; we didn't know whether to kiss, hug, or nod. She settled for smiling and taking me by the hand and leading me into the kitchen, which looked and smelled like a rather good Italian restaurant.

"I'm glad you called," she said, chopping out a square of lasagna and dishing salad onto a white plate. "I was thinking about you, about what an awful night I gave you . . . wondering if you thought I'd gone mad, hitting old ladies and running down perverts. Here, try this white Chianti, it's perfect with lasagna. . . . Did you think I'd gone mad?"

"No, I didn't really. But I thought you were being put to a pretty severe test."

"Well, I don't normally behave so violently." She shrugged, put an end to it. She looked at her watch and I munched, more or less content. "This thing may go on forever, once they get started. You want to go watch? I'm not really playing—I've done Panzer Blitz so many times I just don't think there are many variations I haven't tried. . . ." We went in together and watched. She couldn't help herself; in a few minutes she was arguing with a dark, very heavy man wearing what appeared to be a fright wig. They couldn't agree on strategy and I leaned back against the wall to finish my dinner. The wine was dry and sharp and cold. I watched her; it occurred to me that in the eyes of anyone who might have noticed, she must have seemed my girl, my girlfriend. I wanted her badly; seeing her with other people, people who knew her in everyday life, murderless and nonviolent—seeing her rubbing shoulders and arguing and laughing animatedly and picking up dirty dishes and whispering confidentially to one of the women, seeing her lean forward to get a better view of the game, straining against the Levi's, catching a glimpse of her tiny brassiered breasts beneath the heavy material of the rugby shirt, it all worked on me, hammered at the distance we'd both been keeping between us. I finally cut it out, turned the record over to "Oobladi, Ooblada," and took my dishes to the kitchen. A small man with a pointed beard and horn-rimmed spectacles was eating a piece of lasagna with his fingers. He looked up and smiled at me.

"You have to hand it to her," he said, his mouth full.

"Right, good food."

"Not the food, man," he said with a puzzled expression. "Lasagna's just lasagna as far as I'm concerned . . . but the way she gets her guns on top of the hills, I mean, she's a methodical one. . . . She analyzes the situation, sees what will work and what won't, and doesn't spend time fucking around with the stuff that's not gonna do it. She has a way of seeing to the heart of the problem. Not very feminine, if you know what I mean—she doesn't follow the feminine stereotype —got a mind like we used to think only men had. Now, of course, we all know better. . . ." He licked tomato sauce off his fingertips. "Because Gloria Steinem told us so." He drank some of the Chianti and stuck out a sticky hand. "Baxter, mathematics," he said.

"Cavanaugh," I said. "Befuddlement."

"That's good." He laughed. "Me, too. Say, I got

your hand all sticky . . . son of a bitch, sorry about that. . . ."

She found me later and smiled ruefully. "You must be horribly bored. I really am sorry, I shouldn't have let you come. But I wanted to see you. Selfish. Do you want to leave?"

I told her about my unsettling day with Crocker and the rats, how I hadn't been able to get unwound since seeing it happen. She said she'd heard something about it on the television news but had been up to her elbows in the kitchen at the time.

"I've been thinking I might run up there and take a look yet tonight. If the rats break out they're going to need more than heavy artillery on the surrounding hills."

"Would you take me? They'll never miss me here, they'll be playing all night, at least some of them, until every last calorie of food and wine is gone. . . . Come on, let's go." She looked up expectantly.

The night had turned brisk and chilly and the wind blew papers and dust along the empty streets as I headed up into the alternately garish and dowdy North Side. She huddled inside her arms and I told her about the man with the rats hanging on him. And I told her that Crocker had given me a pretty harsh warning.

"You're really very foolhardy," she said. "I don't know what's going to become of you." She spoke with a dying fall, as if something rather sorrowful had occurred to her.

Floodlights had been set up in the park, the beams trained on the hill. Two fire trucks stood gleaming on the grass, police patrolled the perimeters, and several of Crocker's workmen lounged against earthmovers smoking, talking. A canteen of sorts had been set up near the trailer and the strong aroma of coffee mingled with the smell from the hill. The night's cold had toned down the fetid odor and we sat and watched from the Porsche. An ambulance pulled up beside the Crocker trailer and two white-outfitted men went over to the coffee.

We levered ourselves out of the car and headed toward the maroon-and-gold trailer. Crocker himself was standing sipping coffee, filling the doorway, his face drawn and dirty. He didn't seem to focus on me properly, then gave a sour crunch to his mouth as I became clear. He'd taken off the hard hat and his thick white hair was plastered against his head; he rubbed his eyes with his knuckles, the University of Minnesota ring catching the dim light in its red stone. He started to speak to me.

"Haven't you had enough for one—"

Then he saw Kim behind me and stopped abruptly, his mouth cocked open and locked in place. He covered his surprise reflex by knocking back some coffee; when he looked up he was grinning almost boyishly, erasing for a moment the years and the tiredness. He must have been a ladies' man, the football hero.

"Kim," he rumbled. "What are you doing here? No place for a girl—"

"Hello, Mr. Crocker," she said very quietly, casting a glance at the ground, almost as if she were suddenly reverting to the days when she took orders at Norway Creek. "Paul wanted to come up and see if it was under control. . . ." She shrugged. "So I came with him. I had no idea you'd be here."

"Well, it's my responsibility, it was my machinery that broke it open and set the damn things loose. I'd better be here until we know what's going to happen with them—"

"What's the status?" I asked.

"Christ, it's a mess. They haven't come out yet, not in large numbers anyway, that's why they rigged up those lights up on top. Somebody's figured that'd keep them blinded, keep them underground. . . . I sure as hell don't know. I've heard about things like this, but I've never seen it happen. They're up there now, took canisters of gas . . . but it's not easy, tough to control. They keep talking about a rat stampede. . . . You'd have a hell of a panic then."

"What happened to the guy who got bitten?"

"Another mess. Rat bit damn near clear through his hand, they bit through arteries in his hand and leg, I guess . . . he's in the hospital. . . . I don't know what's gonna happen, that's all I know for sure."

Kim edged away from us, toward the coffee maker. Crocker leaned toward me, glowering, speaking from behind tight lips.

"What the hell do you think you're doing? Can't you see I've got enough trouble here? Just take your goddamn questions and your insinuations and get the hell out of here. . . ." His voice cracked, from exhaustion and frustration. "You heard what I told you this morning. You need a lesson taught you, son. Take the girl and move out." He gripped my arm until it hurt, an old man who scared me. "You've made a hell of a mistake, you've pushed me at just the wrong goddamn time. And I'm pushing back." He drew himself up and threw the barrel chest my way. "And don't go dragging that girl into all this crap you keep shoveling—just leave her out of it. Kim would never —ah, just leave her the hell out of it."

"What would she never?"

"Are you seeing her? Seeing, I mean, seeing her. . . ."

"Shove it, Sunny Jim," I snapped. "Just shove it where the sun don't shine. And stop threatening me, either get hard with me or shut the fuck up."

He stared at me wearily as if he'd broken better and bigger men than me over his goddamn knee.

"Just you remember one thing," he said quietly. "You gave the order."

I'd once thought him gruff and kindly, doting on his grandchildren, presiding over the dynasty he'd begun. But he was a different man now. Everybody kept changing just when I thought I was getting hold of them.

"Do you think you should have spoken to him like that?" She hooked an arm through mine.

"Probably not," I said. "But eventually you get tired of having people lie to you, lead you astray, jockey you around, threaten you. Then you press the button."

We climbed back into the Porsche and I got it started. Crocker was still standing in the doorway watching us. I was sure he was a dead man but he didn't seem to believe it. None of them believed it. I drove around the park, watching the hill, which lay in peculiar, mottled shadows from the floodlights. Men paced the hillside like sentries and there was no sign of the little brown fellows. Somewhere under the hill their world was being poisoned, generations were dying, choking, wilting, and all they had done was build in the wrong place. The wrong place at the wrong time and it was an old story, a rat tragedy. All bullshit.

"But what if Mr. Crocker pushes the button? His button?" She was half turned to face me, sitting with one leg under her. "He sounded angry enough . . . to kill somebody. You."

"I don't know," I said, and we drove back to the Riverfront Towers in complete quiet but for the continuing agonies of the car. I looked at her when the car was stopped and she was staring at her lap. I leaned over clumsily and tilted her head up, kissed her dry lips.

"I wonder if they've finished with the Eastern Front," she said, her lips moving against mine.

"We could check, I suppose," I said.

She was a different person, too: normal, not herself. I didn't trust it, but I wanted to. I came close. She leaned against me in the elevator and I tried to be satisfied with whatever blessing came my way.

There was a note scotch-taped to the kitchen wall: "Russkies held out longer than usual. But not long enough. Great party. And good night, Kim-O, wherever you are."

"They are gone," she sighed, her voice unnaturally cheery. "It's hard to believe."

"Well, here we are," I said. "Alone at last."

"We've been alone before," she said.

"This is a little different. . . ."

"I thought so. I thought maybe—"

I reached out and took her, held her against me, hoping she was ready.

"Paul," she said, her voice trembling.

I kissed her again, wanting her to be pliant, yielding. I moved my hand from the small of her back down to her hips, pulling her against me so she'd know. And she tried.

I've got to give her that. She tried; she had several reasons for wanting it to work, one of which may even have been instinctual and spontaneous. She held herself against me and returned my kiss with a kind of pathetic manufactured fervor, her body stiffening as she tried to make it softer, melt, lubricate. Mind and matter were at it and I knew it and finally she knew I knew it. She stopped pressing, stopped the movement of her lips on mine, and sighed deeply, clinging, with her arms around my neck, leaning on me. It was exhausting, fighting toward such a commonplace goal so far from her grasp, and she clung like a child. She was sweating and I don't remember ever feeling any closer to anyone. For most people in my life it had been so easy, so natural; for her it was so terribly difficult, so consigned to failure's hollow bin. . . . Shared failure can bring two people closer together: The ragged edges of character and breeding show through and you get close. The toughest, rawest kind of failure is the dispiriting failure of the body. She couldn't make her body work for her and in the darkened, private rooms where she lived she was of no use to me; it wasn't true, but she felt it, backed away, shaking her head, fists clenched.

"I'm sorry," she said. Her lips were pressed together, everything about her was tight, clamped shut. "I really wanted to . . . you don't know what it's like, but I can't, I can't let go. When you go, I'll be able to satisfy myself—it doesn't bother me to tell you that, I don't feel as if I have any secrets from you— when I'm alone I'll take a hot bath and I'll be all right, I'll make it happen, but now it's hopeless . . . sometimes I think I'm the only sexual partner I can trust, I can use myself and I won't betray me. . . ." She opened her refrigerator and popped a can of beer, sipped from the rim and handed it to me. "God," she whispered, "I can't believe the things I let myself tell you. . . ." The can was cold against my mouth. "Are you angry?"

"No," I said. "I love you."

"I wish you didn't," she said. "It's because you haven't been able to have me. . . ."

"I don't know anything about reasons."

"I'm so distracted, my mind is splintered—maybe that's why I'm so far away so much of the time. I really tried tonight, from the moment you called. I wanted to be light and easy, but I couldn't do it. I'm in the middle of so many things, so incomplete, I wish I could tell you . . . how my mind works, the way I think and what I have to do. . . ." She came back to me and took my hand.

"But I can't and if you're fed up, I don't blame you. If you want to leave and never come back, I'd understand. . . ."

"I'm not done yet," I said. "I can wait. . . ."

"I hope you don't have to wait forever, that's too long."

It was well past one o'clock when I left Kim and I didn't really take my mind with me. She had completely occupied my thinking process, doubtless because I'd decided that it was only a matter of time before she felt secure enough with me to let whatever there was between us take root, flower. I drove rather aimlessly, trying to imagine exactly what she would be like when I finally took her to bed, and I didn't pay any attention to the car behind me. But it was there, patient, determined, waiting for me to get away from the lights of the downtown loop. They must have thought I was crazy, cruising the deserted, bright, windswept streets, but they stayed with it. Up Hennepin, all the way to Franklin, where I turned right and bumped westward to the northern end of Lake of the Isles. In the bright moonlight the tennis courts in the park had a gray glow about them and the heavy trees on the gentle slope of Kenwood Park were navy blue. The surface of the lake moved in the wind, lapped at the shores with a faint sucking sound; the wind in the treetops made noises like a train rushing out of a darkened tunnel.

I stopped the Porsche and crossed the street, walked through the shadows and stood by a tree which angled out over the water. I thought I was alone and I felt like a poet, shivering in the wind, watching the

white plate of moon flicker and ripple in the water. I
don't often feel like a poet but I did then, drifting
on the youthful hope of love and warmth and affection which I'd given up as lost causes a long time
ago. It was back, that sense of humanity which springs
only from the pulse of love, eager and glowing first
love. What I felt, felt new, unlike whatever I'd known
before, and I stood for a long time leaning on that
tree feeling pleased, even proud, as if I'd dragged
life out of the cold ashes and made it spark and catch
fire again. A miracle.

I'd almost gotten back to the car when I noticed
what appeared to be a pickup truck a hundred yards
or so away. That was just registering as a curiosity
when they stepped out from the shadow of an immense oak near my car. They moved neither quickly
nor slowly, just calmly, wordlessly, around my car,
one on either side of me. Nobody said anything. One
pinned my arms behind me and the other hit me with
a methodical left and right, burying his fists in my
stomach. Lasagna and Chianti backed up in my throat
and the fellow behind me let me slide to the ground.
I could hear myself gagging and gasping, the grinding
of their shoes on the pavement. I was desperately
sucking at air and I got some dirt and pebbles in my
mouth. I drew my knees up toward my chest, bracing
myself, protecting myself from the boots which were
sure to start tattooing my ribs, kidneys, groin.

But the kicks didn't come. One of the men leaned
over me, turned me face up.

"Can you breathe through your mouth?" He was
talking to me and my addled brain wondered what
the hell was going on.

I groaned some animal sound, an affirmative, and
he leaned down beside me, tilted my face so that I
was staring straight up, seeing the moon through a
pattern of leaves. Involuntary tears blurred my vision. I couldn't see his face, only a darkened, bleary
shadow, but he was staring at my face. Then, like the
blade of a guillotine descending, the side of his hand
dropped down and smashed across the bridge of my
nose. I heard something crunch in my head, waited,

and was then engulfed in a circular, swirling sort of pain, inescapable and acute. I brought my hands up to my face and felt the stickiness of blood smearing down my cheek. I choked on blood running into my throat, turned my head, spit it out with a nasty gurgling sound.

"He gets the message," the observer said tonelessly. He yawned audibly, bored.

"You'd better see about that nose," the hitter said.

They went away and I lay in the roadway beside the car for a while, trying to get a grip on reality. I'd been beaten up, a novel experience. My stomach hurt and my nose was surely broken. So I lay there taking stock, breathing through my mouth. I got the message all right: Crocker wanted me to keep my nose out of his business. When the truck had cruised past me, I'd seen it in the moonlight, maroon and gold with the lettering across the door: CROCKER CONSTRUCTION COMPANY.

16

WHEN I woke up the next morning, I wondered for a moment if it had been a nightmare. I lay in bed, hanging like a spider at the end of his filament between sleep and consciousness, pondering my condition, curious as to the noise I was hearing, a whistling, scraping rattle. When I began moving, I knew it hadn't been a dream: Little darts of pain across my abdomen quickly became great awful arrows and the peculiar sound was coming from my mouth, which tasted like the inside of the Porsche's carburetor. When I stood up, my head fell off and rolled under the bed. I tripped over it when it rolled on out the other side, gingerly replaced it, and, peering at it in the bathroom mirror, disowned it altogether. My eyes were swollen and red; spreading outward from the bridge of my nose was a pale purple bruise seeping away almost to the outside corners of my eyes. I didn't even try to inhale through what had in the old days been a usable, if undistinguished, nose.

I soaked my face with ice cubes wrapped in a hand towel, achieving a certain numbing of facial pain. My gut felt as if I had been sawed in half by an especially clumsy magician and inadequately stuck back together. I found a package of Q-tips and tentatively inserted one in a nostril, wiping out blood and mucus and some other stuff gentlemen would never imagine discussing. It was clearly no time for home remedies so I called Max Condon, my only doctor friend, and when I finally got to his office, he repaired what was reparable, packed my nostrils, clucked at my nocturnal habits, droned on about some goddamn fish he'd caught on a trip to Acapulco and was having stuffed, and put a symbolic bandage across my nose.

"You look like Jack Nicholson in *Chinatown*," his nurse said with irritating good humor. I mentally gave them both the finger and went home, called Kim without any answer, and crawled back into bed hugging my bloodstained pillow.

It was dark when I woke up and I'd lost a day. I did a couple of four-minute eggs and amused myself for half an hour trying to pick off the recalcitrant bits of shell.

The telephone scared me half to death. It was Archie. He said he had some news so I struggled into the Porsche and headed back out on Highway 12. I had dropped four Excedrin into the eggs and my tummy now felt funny both inside and out.

We settled in Archie's study, as we were doing with considerable regularity these days. It was cozy and I held the stage for a telling of how I'd come to resemble the Swedish Angel following a tough match during which Man Mountain Dean sat on his head. Archie humphed, gnawing on his cheroot, when I revealed my assailants as mugs from the Crocker Construction Company. Julia was amused. "Man of his word," she said. "And no waiting. Just a good thrashing—plenty macho! Frontier justice." She patted my arm, poured coffee. "Don't despair." Then, to Archie: "Does this mean that Jim Crocker is the murderer, dear? I'd never had thought *that* of him. . . . Unless it's some kind of vigilante thing, righting wrongs and whatnot, I can see him taking matters into his own hands if he believed it *had* to be done. . . ."

"I don't know," Archie mused. "Crocker's deeper than people think. And he's used to having his own way. . . . I can see him killing somebody, no doubt of that, but not dropping them off buildings . . . and not stealing snapshot albums and rifling the newspaper files. Hell, he'd just sock 'em with a big fist and wait for the cops. How's your nose, Paul?"

"It hurts. Now, what's your news?"

Archie had been moving fast since the previous morning and everything had been dropping into place. He'd begun his search for Larry Blankenship—"who the hell he was, that might give us an idea of why he killed himself"—with an old friend of his who was the president of the advertising agency where Larry had worked briefly before being laid off. On his job application and insurance forms Larry had listed as his parents a Mr. and Mrs. Clyde Blankenship of Bemidji, Minnesota. Archie hired a private pilot to get him up to Bemidji and wait while he found the Blankenship home, a humble but respectable Depression bungalow where scientology had been practiced since the fifties by Mr. Blankenship, a bookkeeper for a large hardware store, and Mrs. Blankenship, a substitute elementary-school teacher. They were both quiet, uncommunicative people, solemn, put-upon by life but bearing up nicely, thank you.

Larry Blankenship was not their natural child and they had been very happy to get him through an adoption service, even though he'd been rather old—twelve years old, actually—and hard to place. He'd been a conscientious boy, hard-working, quiet; he had been an average student; "high average," Mrs. Blankenship had corrected Clyde, with a nice way of talking to grown-ups, very respectful.

The difficult part of the interview had been the fact that they had not known of his death. There were no tears: He'd been gone for some time, had written only a few letters a year, a card at Christmas. "And always a remembrance on Mother's Day and Father's Day," Mrs. Blankenship, Edna, had said, dry-eyed. "They were amazing people," Archie had said, "simultaneously dead and alive, no smiles, no tears, nothing. Could Bemidji do that to people? Or scientology?" Remembering that he was trying to trace Larry back as far as he could, Archie had kept digging. Larry had come to the Blankenships from the Sacred Heart Orphanage in Duluth in the fall of 1945. Archie left them on the front stoop of the little bungalow with its neatly trimmed lawn and precise flower beds and the concrete birdbath which had become a planter a quarter of a century ago. That had been Larry's idea his senior year in high school. He loved geraniums, bright-red geraniums, his favorite flower. No, they knew nothing of the family Larry'd come from, of course not. "It was none of our business, was it?" Edna said. "He may have been twelve, but he was our baby. We even named him . . . I always favored the name Larry, such a happy name. He was our Larry for a while. Then he left. Children grow up, leave the nest, that's the way of life, isn't it?"

By midafternoon Archie was in Duluth, finding out that the Sacred Heart Orphanage was a dead end. The old orphanage building had burned to the ground in 1958, shortly after the move to a new building on the northern outskirts of town. No great damage had been done by the fire, the children and staff having moved out the week before. But the great mass of records had been lost and were irreplaceable. It was all a long time ago as far as the present staff was concerned. But when Archie was leaving, one of the sisters had a thought: She remembered that Sister Mary Margaret, who had been in charge of admissions in the forties, was now residing in a convent rest home near Dubuque, Iowa. Archie got the name of the residence and was told not to expect too much:

Sister Mary Margaret must be close to ninety. He could imagine the chances of her remembering a certain lad, someone from thirty years before, one from among so many.

While I was being beaten on the nose beside Lake of the Isles, Archie was sleeping soundly in the Julian Motor Hotel in Dubuque. His pilot, intrigued by the adventure, had the room next door, marveling at the eccentricities of the famous mystery novelist. In the morning Archie had found Sister Mary Margaret, hard of hearing, but sharp-eyed, watching a game show on television in the residence common room.

After two hours of shouting Archie sagged in his chair, grinned weakly at Sister Mary Margaret, and let her return to the television: The soap operas were beginning. She had remembered the boy, he was there in the cupboard of her memory, darting into view for an instant, then retreating, wiped away by time. But she did remember, in the first place because so few children came to Sacred Heart at such an advanced age. She remembered the name of the family he went to, the Blankenships, once Archie mentioned it, but not the boy's own name. She remembered him as a lethargic boy, puffy, always eating when he shouldn't have been, tending toward the sullen, but not an outright complainer, resentful, but easily led, one who did what he was told to do . . . yes, he'd gone to Bemidji, and she remembered that there had been something sad, something unusual about that—something about the boy. . . .

But she couldn't remember what it was. A blank.

Still, we knew a good deal more about Larry than we had before. He had simply *appeared;* Maxvill and Rita had *disappeared.* He had been added, they had been subtracted. He had no beginning, they had no end. Archie smiled at the symmetry of it, wondered if it was all part of some glorious plot concocted by some celestial novelist. He liked it.

"We don't quite know where the puffy lad who became Larry Blankenship actually fits but we're closing in on him," Archie said. "We're closing, I can feel it. It's working just like it does on paper for Fenton

Carey. . . . I'm really quite amazed, life imitating art, don't you see?"

Julia turned to face us from the French door, hand on hip, smoothing her hair with the other hand. "Kim and her cousin, the boy, were in an orphanage in Duluth. Weren't they? Yes, we've established that. . . . Could it have been the same one?" Her eyes roamed between us. "Don't you see, don't you see how beautiful it is? What if Kim, age four or five, had actually known this twelve-year-old orphan boy? Maybe all three were friends. . . . And all those years later, all grown up, Kim and Larry found each other again . . . and fell in love. . . "

"Sounds like an opera," Archie growled. "She was only four. Even if it was the same orphanage and she did know him, they'd never recognize each other twenty-five or thirty years later. . . . Impossible. You've got to keep to the path of reason, dear Julia, eschew flights of fancy." He smiled benignly.

"I know, I know," she admitted, fingering her lower lip, "but it does make a lovely story. If you forget the ending, anyway. A fairy tale, I know."

"It is a nice story," I said consolingly. "And I'd believe almost anything about her . . . she hasn't led the most conventional of lives. She seems drawn to the irregular, the dramatic, as if she were being controlled by an astrological destiny. Seems fated, if you know what I mean." I let it trail off since it made no sense and caught Archie peering at me over his Ben Franklin spectacles.

"Could we return to reality, girls?" he said. "Fiction Writing One is excused, Advanced Criminology is called to order. Let's consider our killer." He stood up, rolled the blackboard out, wiped away some accumulated scribbles, and with red chalk printed the name MAXVILL in capitals. "I see a couple of possibilities, each of which has something to recommend it. Personally, instinctively, I'm being seduced by the Maxvill theory. . . . Why the devil should we for a moment assume he's dead? No logical reason for it. No, I reckon he's alive—and he's my number one candidate . . . the more I think about it, the better it looks. It all fits. I can make it at least a working hypothesis.

"It begins way to hell and gone back there, with Carver Maxvill and Rita Hook." He chalked her first name in capitals across from his. "There was Maxvill up at the lodge and in Grand Rouge, sort of on the prowl sexually. He takes up with Rita Hook, true to his form—she's someone of a distinctly lower class —just his meat, so we've heard. And he flaunts this relationship among the other members, maybe makes his pals jealous . . . in some way, somehow, this relationship threatens or irritates the group. And the group responds by expelling him and her with him—" He held up his hand to still objections. "It's a hypothesis, Paul, so relax. I grant it's heavy going in here, looking for specifics, but I have some ideas. In any case, the group exerted pressure on him to leave, call it expulsion or something else. They may even have paid him off to take his wench and beat it, become a nonperson, an anonymity, *disappear*. . . . So he and Rita leave, with some of the group's money, presumably given to them, but just possibly extorted in some way. . . . The years go by." Archie stopped and lit a cheroot with a wooden match and clouded his head in smoke. "The years go by and in his hiding place something happens to Carver Maxvill, perhaps his mind snaps, that seems a possibility when you think of the enormity of what our killer is perpetrating here, and he surveys the wreckage of his life, his nonpersonhood, and he decides to revenge himself on the men who had the power and the fortune to erase him from the book of life. . . . He could prove his continued existence by these violent acts. The last things his victims would know would be the fact of his endurance. . . ."

"My God," I said, "that might even account in a crazy way for the stealing of the photo albums, the file from the newspaper—he's making sure, he's symbolically drawing attention to himself!"

"Oh, such heavy thinking," Julia said, but there was a sense of excitement in her voice, as if we were coming upon the truth more or less by surprise.

"Revenge or love," Archie said triumphantly, pacing back and forth before the blackboard, clutching the red chalk and gesturing with it. "The most likely motives by far for an instance of *homicidim seriatim* . . . . Stop and think, any serial murder must involve a group, an alliance of individuals, who have somehow, whether in reality or in a demented imagination, injured or threatened someone so terribly, so unforgivably that the only possible response is the systematic elimination of the offenders. Think how the world must appear to the killer, a crimson smear . . . he is beset and hounded by these people, these monsters who have despoiled his life." Archie took a deep breath, excited by the onrushing ideas which seemed to make so much sense. "Consumed by this need for revenge, our man Maxvill comes out of the woodwork—maybe he's alone now, maybe Rita is dead by this time, maybe there's nothing left of his life and he broods on the ruins, looks at what it has all come to . . . and he sees how much of it these men have stolen from him. . . ."

I was intrigued by it but I had questions.

"But why, really, why would the group give them money—enough money to kick over the traces of their lives for good? And what could have made Carver go for it in the first place? Why didn't he just tell them to go to hell? He and Rita would have had all the money Rita wound up leaving in the bank—and where did that come from? Where could she have gotten all that money? So why don't we turn it around? Let's take the extortion thing. . . . Maybe Maxvill and Rita had something on the group."

Archie sighted down the slim brown cylinder of cheroot, which had gone cold as he talked.

"You mean," he said deliberately, "Carver and Rita *chose* to disappear, it was *their* idea? And they were financed by the group. . . . Blackmail, then, plain and simple. 'We'll leave,' quoth Rita and Carver, 'and we won't blow the whistle on youse guys' —whatever their sins might have been—'but you gotta pay us off. . . .' Or words to that effect." He mused over that one, stared at the blackboard, absentmindedly drew multiple slashes beneath the two names. "That's good," he said at last, "I like it. God only knows, though, what they'd be blackmailing the members about . . . but it accounts for the group's not wanting the Maxvill thing brought up now all these years later, for fear that it might bring this nameless skeleton out of the closet." He nodded slowly.

My nose ached dully and the flesh was tender to the touch all the way out to the cheekbones. My eyes were tired and burned. Julia brought us coffee and Danish and I munched hungrily, very nearly suffocating myself in the process. Archie sat behind his desk, eyes a little glassy, thinking his way through the complexities of the thing. I was trying not to: When I tried to unravel it, my head ached. Finally I said, "So what's your second theory?" There was something nasty nibbling at the back of my mind like one of Crocker's rats peering down from the hilltop, blinking, teeth gleaming in the spotlights. I pushed it away, it had no name and I didn't want to give it one.

Archie jerked up out of his meditation.

"Oh, yes . . . that it's someone inside the club, someone afraid that something the club was involved in may be revealed. . . . I'm just groping in on this, but if Maxvill doesn't really figure in it, if he did die or just went the hell away, then our best bet is a club member." He sighed and took off his glasses, rubbed knuckles into his eyes. "I reckon that most serial murders, rare as they are, are committed by members of the group which is actually being eradicated—so just maybe one of our friends is killing the others. Oh, sure, it's bizarre as hell, I know that, but Jesus, any way you cut it, it's insanely bizarre. Real people are getting killed . . . so what the hell, if it's not Crocker—and I don't believe he's anything like subtle enough—maybe it's Jon Goode, hell, he's spent most of his adult life trying to figure new ways of killing people. . . ." My father peeled an eye my way. "You know that better than anyone, *you* of all people . . . Goode's a fine candidate but"—he sighed deeply—"but I think, I *think*—maybe because I don't know him—old Carver's our boy."

The wind blew the curtains inward, toward us, as if a ghost were entering the room.

"Where do you fit in, Dad?" I said. "Level with me, you were in the club. . . ."

"Look, you miss the point," he said. "I'm not involved, any more than you and Julia are. The time frame is wrong. Let's say the club members were being blackmailed—but I know for a fact that I wasn't. Obviously the ones who got murdered must have know why they were murdered, something they all had in common.

"Now, they must have had something in common with one another that they didn't have in common with me . . . because, Paul, I'm telling you, no one has got a reason to kill me. Just believe me, take my word for it."

"But what," I asked, "if Maxvill is insane? He wouldn't need an actual reason, only an imagined one. . . ."

"So you're buying the Maxvill thing? As a real possibility?"

"Yes, aren't you?"

"I don't know. I wanted to try it out on you to read your reaction. I admit it has a ring to it." He grinned puckishly.

"Well, say it *is* Maxvill. What the hell do we do now?"

"If you corner him in a dark alley," Julia offered quietly from the folds of her needlepoint, "don't lead with your nose." She chuckled.

I ignored her; she didn't know how much it hurt. "Are we done now?" I asked. "We'll never find him. . . ."

Archie leaned forward and chewed on a prune roll.

"I don't know that that's necessarily the case," he said, sounding a trifle disappointed in me. "If he's killing people, he is here, among us. Watching, waiting. We might be able to find him . . . but the first thing we'd better do—it rubs me the wrong way, God knows—but we'd better at least talk it over with

Bernstein. We've done his thinking for him . . .
now we give him the benefit of our ruminations."

"That's a detective-story word," I said.

My face and head ached too much to drive back
into town so I wearily climbed the stairs, returning to
a makeshift womb, wounded and exhausted. Alone,
the bone of doubt in the shrubbery of my mind
gleamed like ivory. The drive of coincidence, life's
strong, renegade engine running its own course, was
eating at me. Larry Blankenship, Kim (Shirley)
Hook, and Kim's older cousin, Robert—they all had
found their childhoods tied and knotted at an orphanage in Duluth. Possibly the same orphanage. The
three of them; the two boys about the same age, Kim
almost a decade younger. We knew what happened
to Larry: He grew up and fate brought him back to
Kim, the little girl he'd probably never even noticed as a lad of twelve. And he killed himself. We
knew what happened to Kim. But her old cousin—
the fat quiet kid who walked Grande Rouge's barren
streets with his head down—we had no idea what
happened to him. The blank made me curious.

On the small black-and-white television set in the
guest room I watched the ten o'clock news and Dave
Moore reassured the Twin Cities that there was no
evidence of a rat stampede on the Crocker construction site. Not yet, anyway. He interviewed Crocker,
who looked sunken and tired and professed a dogged
optimism. On film a scientist tried to explain what
chemical steps were being taken beneath the surface
of the clean, perfect, self-satisfied city where to want
was to have. Now the city wanted those rats dead.
From the hilltop itself, the last bit of film footage
gave us a look at a bewildered rat silhouetted in
the kliegs, looking out at the rest of us like an under-
study who'd neglected the learning of his lines.
That's show biz, baby.

I turned it off before they got to the Twins' score
—that's how disoriented I was. I called Kim and she
answered on the eighth ring. She'd almost fallen
asleep reading one of Fenton Carey's adventures. I

couldn't tell if she was in one of her remote moods or just tired. Her interest quickened when I told her about my object lesson at the hands of Crocker's goons the night before; she clucked over me almost protectively, hardly her customary role. We chatted in the manner of two people who have developed a relationship, however tenuous and imprecise, based on having confessed inner weaknesses and surface affections, such as they were. I was setting her up and my devious intent made me squirm against my pillow. She was right the first time, she couldn't really trust me: I kept probing. But it didn't keep me from loving her. I worked us around to childhood, memories, the haunts of youth.

"What was it like at the orphanage?" I asked logically. "Was it like Dickens or were the sisters nice ladies?"

"They were all right," she said. "I was awfully young."

"Time sure as hell flies," I mused. "I was up in Duluth, I can't remember why anymore, when the old Sacred Heart burned down."

"Well, I was long gone by then," she said.

"I suppose it was tougher on Robert than on you, being so much older . . . twelve, thirteen, that's a pretty impressionable age. I guess unless it's happened to you, you can't know. . . ."

"He wasn't there long." She patted a yawn.

"Don't you ever wonder what happened to him?"

"No," she said quietly. "Not really. I grew up thinking of myself as an only child. Look, I've go to get some sleep. I played tennis all day. . . . I'm sorry about your nose. Consider it kissed and made well."

"I love you," I said.

"Oh, God," she said tiredly. "I think I love you, too. Now good night, Paul."

We were right. *All three of them had been there at the same orphanage*. I hadn't had the nerve to ask her if she'd known the one who became Larry Blankenship.

17

ARCHIE AND I were in Bernstein's office by eight thirty and the Candidate was all in off-white, prompting me to make a smart crack about his virginity. He retaliated by being terribly amusing about the condition of my face. When he got serious, wanting to know why it happened, I said my face had gotten between the wall and a squash ball; he gave that a fishy look but he was too busy to pursue it. We filled him in on our night's theorizing and he took it calmly, endlessly clicking the top of a ball-point pen. He admitted it was as good as any scenario he'd concocted and said he'd start two of his two-headed lads checking hotels for recent arrivals. He got a description of the young Maxvill from Archie, chewed on the pen for a while, and shook his head.

"Well," he said finally, "I'm not the only guy in town with his dick in a wringer. Your friend Crocker is up to here in rats. . . . I don't know who's worse off." He sighed and propped his white shoes up on the desk, a vision of pristine otherworldliness in the generally swinish confines of his cubicle.

"The voters of Minneapolis," I said. "They're worse off."

"That's good, Paul," he said. "That's a good one, all right."

We left Bernstein straightening his bright-red tie in a tiny makeup mirror on his desk. Outside Archie shoved his hands into his hip pockets and rocked on his heels. "I'll never understand how the cops ever get anything done right. I won't deny that they do—they do. But how?"

He headed for the Minneapolis Club and I headed up toward the North Side to check on the rats. The sun had burned through an early cloud cover and it was getting hot early. I could smell Crocker's Folly a couple of blocks away and there was plenty of activity when I got there. A couple of television cameramen were wandering around with gear resting on their shoulders, stockpiling footage for voice-overs. The white-coated mad scientists were doing Karloff and Chaney bits but behind them stood rows of sinister white canisters. The crowds hadn't changed; they looked as if they'd all been hypnotized by some sort of hovering ray gun whipped up twenty years ago by George Pal's special-effects unit. Perhaps that was how the rats had gotten there in the first place, lowered on little rope ladders from ominous, whirring Martian spaceships. . . . The pain in my nose was obviously affecting my brain. I trudged through the dust and came upon a large young man who caught my eye and looked quickly away; he was wearing a maroon-and-gold Crocker Construction shirt and surprisingly enough, I recognized him. I'd have thought it had been too dark, but I knew him. I followed him across the worn-down, browned-out remains of the grass and caught up in front of the main maroon-and-gold trailer. He was bending over a tool case pretending to be busy. He looked up because I was very nearly standing on him.

"Hi, champ," I said.

"What?" He squinted upward, dust in the tanned creases of his face.

"I said hi," I said. "Nice to see you again."

"What are you talking about?"

"Just wanted you to know that if I ever get the chance I'm going to pick me out a nice two-by-four and make jelly out of your face. I'll probably never get the chance, though." I tried to keep it conversational but I was getting a nasty acid drip going in my stomach. "But you ought to know when somebody bears you ill will. Who knows, maybe I'll hire a couple of gorillas to do it for me. Think about it . . . and when you get home at night and it's dark and you have to park your car, you'd better check the bushes, baby."

He stood up and walked away. Crocker was piling out of a Crocker pickup and did a double take when he saw me and my bandaged face.

"I was just talking to the creep who does your hitting for you," I said, closing on him. There was a deep glimmer of distrust in his eyes, almost fear. He brought his hands up to his belt as if preparing to ward off a suicide charge. I grinned at him.

"You're so scared," I said, "that I've stopped worrying about you. You really disgust me. I'm not easily disgusted, but you do the trick. You see my face, Crocker? I made a point not to tell Bernstein about how it happened. . . . I didn't want him to start thinking about you. He might have put protection around you so the killer can't get to you. As far as I'm concerned, you look good as a target."

He stared at my bandage, his mouth working behind tight lips. His massive, rough-hewn head shook as if taken by a palsy. The fists clenched, relaxed, clenched. He couldn't bring himself to speak.

"Are you working yourself up to a conniption or just pretending? What have you got to be mad about? I'm the one with the smashed face. . . ."

"Get away from me," he said at last, forcing it out between teeth like millstones. His hands swept across in front of his thick chest, as if the breeze would take me away.

"What are you going to do? Have one of the lads beat me up? Christ, you're so stupid, Crocker. You could save your life and get the killer caught if you'd just go to Bernstein. . . . You smell of fear. And cowardice."

"I am sorry," he said suddenly, "about your face. There's no point in denying it. It's not easy for me to apologize . . . but I couldn't think of what else to do. You don't understand, Cavanaugh, and there's no real reason you should. . . ." He grunted glumly, the anger completely gone. He amazed me; it was the last thing I'd expected. The color had left his face as surely as if a vampire's shadow had flitted across his jugular. "I'm a blunt man. But I couldn't order you to drop this thing and get the hell away, to safety—no, it's not cheap melodrama, Critic. You don't believe me, but the closer you get to it, the closer you get to danger for yourself. . . ."

"Your concern is very moving," I said, but the conviction of my sarcasm was as bloodless as his face. A heavy truck ground its gears coming down the hill, its tires shredding the grass. It was carrying a load of brown fur. The aroma of dead rats penetrated even my nose. It reached the bottom of the slope and stopped. White-uniformed sanitation workers tied a canvas tarpaulin tight over the mound of dead things. My stomach slid sweatily and I looked back at Crocker.

"The only danger I've encountered was from you," I said.

"It won't happen again, I promise you. I know, it won't fix your face, will it? There's nothing I can say. I'm sorry." He turned away, leaned a huge hand on the trailer for support.

"You look like hell," I said.

"Just tired." His voice was as gray and lifeless as his face, his lips. "Got to pace myself, that's all. Fucking rats. When I sleep, I dream about them."

"You should go home. They don't need you here."

"You don't understand, I'm the boss. This is my company, my goddamn mess. I belong here. I rest in the van here. . . . I'm staying all night. . . . They tell me we may have it licked by nightfall. I'll stay on tonight." He was almost talking to himself, reassuring himself. "It'll be quiet then. You just get the hell out of here and forget about all of us. . . ."

"Can't forget Carver Maxvill," I said. "Can you?"

"Who? He looked up numbly, trying to get me in clearer focus. "Who did you say?"

"Carver Maxvill. The man who's come back. . . ."

He searched my eyes for several seconds, his broad, weathered face expressionless, and then began doing an old man's death rattle which turned into a throaty, rolling chuckle. He flushed and leaned back against the trailer, where the sun caught him in the eyes.

"You dumb son of a bitch," he said at last, half choking on his quiet, bottled-up laughter.

"You're next on his list," I said with fading authority.

He kept on chuckling, a ruddy look seeping into his face, bringing back his tan.

"What's so funny?"

"Funny?" He wiped his eyes, leaving a dirty smudge. "Nothing, nothing. . . . It's just that I know who the killer is, that's all." He coughed deep in his lungs. "Shit, I guess it is funny . . . I don't know. Just haul your ass off this site, that's all. And say your prayers, Cavanaugh, you poor bastard. . . ."

I went back to my place. My face was on fire and my eyes ached. I popped a couple of the pain pills Condon had prescribed and took a shower, Archie's signal to call. He'd gone home and gotten a telephone call from the little old nun in Dubuque.

"Quite an old lady," he said, measuring his words. "Memory like a damned elephant. She said she remembered what was so sad about Larry's leaving the orphanage. . . ."

"So?"

"Well, the thing was, he had a little sister—she *thinks* it was his sister—a little girl anyway, and this little girl, just a wee thing, who was terribly dependent on him . . . apparently she came unglued when Larry was taken away, or went away, whatever. . . ." He paused, then filled the silence: "Well, I just thought I'd tell you, keep you current. You've got to admit it's a sad story, right?"

"Yeah. Sad." I sat there at my desk, dripping wet, wondering. The pain pills weren't working.

Kim was sunbathing when I called from the lobby and when she opened the door, she'd slipped a pale-yellow shirt over a tan bikini which blended into the color of her smooth flesh. She gave me a quick shy kiss and ten minutes later we were sitting on her balcony eating cantaloupe halves filled with pineapple, strawberries, and cherries, and sipping icy Chablis. A day earlier it would have made me feel happy and cared for, a member of the human race. She murmured concern over my injuries. I nodded. Our normal roles were reversed; she was the one trying to ease the situation and give it warmth while I was off in a world of my own thoughts, disturbed and remote.

She was facing the sun. A fine dew of perspiration stood out on her forehead and when she leaned forward to pour me more wine, the front to the shirt belled open and gravity drew a streak of sweat between her tiny breasts. She was making conversation and I nodded sporadically but I wasn't listening. I was trying to sort out what my priorities were, love or curiosity, and were they in conflict? I didn't want to drive a wedge between us: It had been so difficult to bring it this far. But I had to know the truth.

"All right," she said matter-of-factly, setting down her empty wineglass and dabbing her lips with the lime-green linen. "What's the matter? I can't talk to myself forever, you know. So what's troubling your poor smashed-in face?" She smiled very slightly.

"Are we in love?" I blurted. "I don't mean to lean on you, I don't want to frighten you away . . . but there are a couple of things I have to do and before I do them I want to know what there is between us. One moment, when I'm with you, it seems that we are—in a funny way, sure, but real just the same— then, when I'm alone, I think I'm being foolish." A helicopter swirled past the balcony, roaring angrily, shining like a metallic prehistoric predator in the sun. "Now I guess I've got to know. . . . I'm sorry."

She leaned back, pushing her sunglasses up her moist, straight nose. I couldn't see her eyes and felt as if I were revealed, naked under her gaze.

"Why is it that you suddenly need some definite answer?" she asked. "What are you going to do? Not something foolish that you'll regret, I hope . . . that I'll regret. . . ."

"You're just going to have to trust me. I can't go into it."

"I told you our relationship couldn't be normal. I warned you. I'm not ready, not able . . . you can't say I've led you on."

"No. But the undertow has been one of secrecy,

I've had to pry at you . . . if I hadn't cared about you, I'd have said the hell with you. But I did care, *do* care. I've tried to guess at your feelings, I've accepted bits and pieces and scraps of emotion. And that's all right, it's a small price to pay if I can keep you. You've brought me back to life. . . . I'd reached the point where I couldn't imagine being close to anyone, certainly not a woman, and you've changed all that. I believed that the only woman I could ever love was a woman who could fill my attention, make all others irrelevant, and I was sure that no such woman existed." I took a deep breath, rattled on. "I was wrong. There's you. But that's not enough. . . . I've got to know what's coming back, from you to me. . . ." I waited but she simply stared at me, the sunglasses flat and black against the sun. "There's got to be some kind of honesty and openness between us. Real honesty."

"Don't you believe what I tell you?" she said edgily. "The whole point is that my secrecy has nothing whatever to do with our relationship. I have been honest about everything that counts between us—I haven't ever lied to you about my feelings or kept them secret. I've told you about my personal problems, you know I've told you things about myself that only you know, I've made myself emotionally vulnerable. . . . What more can you want? I'm not an expert on love, I'm not experienced in it. . . . I've only wondered why my past has been so important to you, what it has to do with you. I still don't know why but my feelings for you have even gotten me past that obstacle." She leaned forward and emptied the Chablis into her glass, held the rim to her lower lip. "I think what I feel for you is love, Paul. If it has to be given a name, as you seem to think it does . . . you're great on giving things names. I'm not. Why is it all so important to you— my past, giving what's between us a name? I've never understood that. You're not the only one who's been in the dark. . . ." But even in all this there was a curious quality of circumspection, guardedness, as if there were layers of plot to her life I'd never dreamed of. Instead of making me see reason, she fed my cu-

riosity, the sense of unease in which I'd come to live.
I watched her sip the wine, saw a muscle jump in
her soft, smooth cheek. For a moment, a shadow
across her face, she looked as she had the night she'd
driven into the boy on the bicycle: unrepentant, cool,
a distant arousal as if thrilled sexually by danger and
the threat of death.

"I don't know why," I said, "I've forgotten. . . . I
only know that it's all important to me. I wouldn't
have come here to pursue it otherwise. It was now or
never, maybe."

"Well, I'm sorry if I've disappointed you again."

"What was your mother's name?"

"Rita Hook."

"No, Kim, not your aunt . . . *your mother*."

"Why do you do this to me?" She put her hand to
her mouth, the long fingers quivering. "It makes all
your protestations of love seem false . . . calculated."

"A simple question. What was your mother's
name?"

"Wilson," she said. "Patricia Wilson." The quaking
of her hands had been communicated to her voice.
"But she died when I was born."

I stared off across the city with its landscape of deserted railway terminals, renewal projects, and the
towers of the University of Minnesota in the distance.
When I looked back toward her, she was crying, tears
seeping out beneath the dark lenses. I scraped my
chair back, went and knelt beside her. She wouldn't
turn to face me. I touched her hair, kissed her cheek,
and when I got up and left, she was still sitting on the
balcony, her pretty linen napkin rolled into a tight ball
and held tightly against her lips, tears sliding relentlessly down her beautiful, somber face.

I went back to my apartment, packed an overnight
bag, and just made the two o'clock Northwest flight
to Chicago. By three thirty, thanks to a twenty-five-
dollar cab ride, I'd found the Merrivale Memorial
Hospital on a tree-lined street not far from the University of Chicago. It was small and old and private,
looking more like a discreet residential hotel than

what it was. With my face giving off signals, the lady behind the information desk tried to direct me to the outpatient area but I held firm in search of the records office.

A middle-aged woman, in what used to be described as a severe suit when people still wore them, was watering a split-leaf philodendron in a small office at the end of a long dingy hall. A window gave on a tiny shaded courtyard. I watched a nurse push a bundle of ailing human being around the path in an old wicker-backed wheelchair. The lady in the suit finished with the drooping plant, sighed, and blinked huge watery eyes floating behind thick spectacles. "The problem is, I'm very much afraid, a lack of sunlight in this office and there's not much I can do about that, is there? And what can I do for you?" She checked a large Timex watch on a thin wrist and smiled at me with a mouth that remained oddly pursed. I got the feeling that her philodendron problem was about as close to grief as she got.

I told her I had come all the way from Minneapolis to check on a matter relating to an inheritance, orphans, a bit of quick embroidery which was so old a line that it may not have occurred to her to doubt me. I lied badly but made a show of inspecting the undersides of the plant's leaves as if I knew what I was doing. I implied vaguely that I represented a firm of attorneys.

"It's a question of two sisters," I said, "and two children born in this hospital quite a long time ago. Both children were orphaned and two people have now turned up with claims on an inheritance." I grinned beneath my bandaged nose.

"How very Dickensian," she said, eyes brightening enthusiastically. "Are you a private eye?"

"No, not really." I shrugged diffidently, leaving her in doubt.

"I thought you might be . . . your nose, the bandage. I'm sorry, I sometimes leap before I look." She sat down primly at her desk, her fingers checking the wisps of gray hair dangling from her bun. "Now, precisely what do you need to know?"

It wasn't difficult once I got it rolling. I gave her Patricia Wilson's name first, noting that she presumably had a child, female, at Merrivale in 1940. Would she be good enough to check? The green file cabinets, their tops covered with cactuses in clay pots, lined one wall. It wasn't a big hospital; all the records were in those cabinets. I watched the courtyard, the old men sitting on a slat bench in bathrobes, doling out bread crumbs to pigeons. It was unbearably hot and humid in the tiny office. There were streaks on the inside of the window. I hadn't noticed how uncomfortable I was until I had to wait while she searched. It took forever.

Finally she gave me a perplexed look. "Nothing! No Patricia Wilson, not in 1940, never. We do all our filing by last names—we've got two Patrick Wilsons both deceased, but nary a Patricia. Could she have been admitted under another name, by chance? A maiden name?"

"I don't know and I don't know how to find out," I confessed. "But there's the other sister—let's check her. Name was Rita Hook . . . she was here in 1932, reportedly gave birth to a boy. She was a resident of Grande Rouge, Minnesota, and Patricia Wilson's sister." My voice seemed to be droning on, coming from someone else. I was watching the scene, sweating and feeling light-headed. I was afraid. She knelt down and began flipping through folders. The last fly of summer banged against the window like a machine bent on self-destruction.

"Well, now, that's odd," she said, straightening up, a knee cracking. "Very odd, indeed. This is Rita Hook's file, all right . . . but what we've got here isn't what you've described. How peculiar. . . ."

"What's wrong?" I said, my voice dry.

"Well, your Rita Hook, your resident of Grande Rouge, local next of kin Patricia Wilson, sister, she was here in 1932—gave birth to a boy just as you suggested. Robert, eight pounds, two ounces, father one Ted Hook, Grande Rouge, Minnesota . . . that's all right here. . . ."

"So what's the problem?"

"Well, that was only her first visit," she said slowly.

"Somewhere along the line you've gotten your facts askew. . . . Eight years later, in 1940, it wasn't Patricia Wilson who came here to have a baby . . . it was Mrs. Hook again, Rita Hook, and Patricia Wilson was again listed as local next of kin." She peered up at me over the edge of the tattered manila folder. "Don't you see? Mrs. Wilson was next of kin, not the mother . . . this Rita Hook person was the mother both times, a boy, that was little Robert in 1932, and then little Shirley in 1940. . . ."

"And nobody died?" I asked. "The little girl's mother survived the birth?"

"Oh, my, yes," she said, a faint note of shock in her voice. "You don't look so well, though. Here, sit down. . . ."

"It's my nose. I get flashes of pain—"

"Here, have some water." She handed me a tumbler from a tray on a bookcase. The water was warm and dust floated on it. "Can I get you an aspirin?"

"No, no, I'm fine." I took a deep breath.

"Well, at least no one died," she said consolingly. "That's good."

I nodded. She gave me the address listed for Patricia Wilson thirty-four years ago. I thanked her, picked up my overnight bag, and went back out into the wet, steaming afternoon. I wasn't stopping to think. I just wanted to keep moving.

18

I STOPPED at a drugstore on the corner and went to the telephone booth back behind the flea-and-tick spray. The book hung by a chain and appeared to have been chewed on by something with very big teeth. But there was a P. Wilson with the same address as the one in the hospital's records. It had been a long time at the same address. I went back out on the corner and wiped my face as best I could but the sweat got under the bandage and felt as if fire ants were building a nest. A black kid was leaning against a fire hydrant with a portable radio blaring soul at his ear; he watched me from milky caramel-tinted eyes. I walked over to him.

"Hey, how's it goin', man?" he said, rocking his head to the music. "Whatcha lookin' for, man?"

I gave him the address and he said it was only five minutes from where we stood. He gave me explicit directions and I thanked him; he gave me the peace sign and smiled and I wondered why he was so friendly. Friendly people always surprise me. I passed a filling station and popped for a Coke, drank it in the shade watching cars lined up at the gas pumps, a sign of the rotten times. Nixon was a crook, gas was seventy-five cents a gallon, and Ford was a lackey. There were rats crawling around beneath Minnesota's answer to the nastiness of urban sprawl. Bodies were piling up back home and Kim Roderick had quite a surprise in store for her. It had been a long day and the sun was burning a hole in my back as I set off again. The day wasn't done yet.

The row houses must have dated from the turn of the century and leafy old trees threw the street into deep, moist shadows. A tiny green patch of grass lay between a wrought-iron fence and the brick housefront. A Boston fern sat alone and regal in the window, lace curtains at the side. I pushed the doorbell. I saw a movement behind the leaded glass and an elderly woman in a voluminous housecoat opened the door.

"Mrs. Wilson?" I said. She nodded, head forward, leaning on a white cane. She wore tinted glasses, heavy costume rings on gnarled, crooked fingers. I told her I'd come from Minneapolis to ask her about her sister, Rita. She nodded again and beckoned me into the dark hallway, on into an old-fashioned parlor. She didn't seem surprised. She sat down in a Leatherette recliner and motioned me to a straight chair.

"I knew you were coming," she said, her voice high

and almost musical, like a child's. "I've been expecting you."

"I don't understand," I said. "Why? How could you?"

"Oh I've always known you'd turn up," she said, leaning back, her face tilted slightly upward. She was blind or nearly so and she had no fear of a stranger. "Something about Rita. I've always known I hadn't heard the end of Rita. It's just like Donald, my husband, Donald Wilson—I've always known that someday, out of the blue, I'd hear about Donald . . . he was a sailor, a navy man, he went off almost forty years ago and never came back. The Depression got to him, the responsibility of a wife, and he just shipped out one day. I've lived alone ever since. Waiting, you might say. And then little Rita, she's my younger sister, you see, she went off, too. I never knew how they did it, I've spent a lot of time trying to figure it out—I'd have just gone off myself, too, but I never got the hang of it, how you do it. Seems funny now but there was a time when it wasn't funny at all. . . ." She smiled tentatively, squeezing the handle of her cane. "So what have you got to tell me about little Rita, Mr. Cavanaugh?"

"When did you last see her, Mrs. Wilson?"

"That last time she came to Chicago, of course. . . ." She paused, head cocked to one side, listening for the echoes of her past. "The year before the war, 1940 that would be . . . when Shirley was born. I never saw her again." She gave me a vague, good-natured smile, long removed from the battle. "I've been alone ever since. My eyesight began to go about ten years ago . . . thank heavens, Rita had sent me some money and I've been able to make ends meet. It was such a shock, Rita going away and leaving me with no relations at all . . . but she'd taken good care of me. Tell me, Mr. Cavanaugh, has she sent you to me? Is Rita all right? I've always thought she was out there somewhere . . . very bad, a very pitiful woman. . . ." She turned to me again, expectantly, the smile timid, like an animal in a shrub.

"I don't know," I said. "Rita hasn't sent me. I'm very sorry. That's not why I've come."

"I guess I didn't *really* think you had," she said, the grin fixed. "I was just . . . hoping. Just had a feeling." She hooked the handle of the cane over the arm of the chair, folded her hands in her lap, the fingers stroking the bright knobby rings. The light outside was dimming as the sun dropped and the large trees cut out the rays. An air conditioner hummed in the next room. The room was neat, uncluttered, dusted. Her chin sank toward her chest. Hers was the smile of the just.

I was exhausted and felt myself sinking back against the hard wooden chair. I wiped sweat off my forehead. A car screeched to a stop outside, honked, roared away. I looked at the old woman, struck by how everyone seemed to be so alone. It was the human condition, I supposed, but I'd never been more bleakly aware of it than I had in the last couple weeks. It had begun with the loneliness of Larry Blankenship's death and it had just kept growing—the sense of loss. People just kept vanishing; others were left behind, and life struggled on as best it could. Patricia Wilson couldn't see me. I watched her in the dusky early evening, trying to imagine her as a young woman, wrapped up in her sister coming to Chicago to have her babies.

"Well," she said suddenly, emerging from her reverie, "why did you come? You're still here, I can hear you breathing. . . ."

"I wanted to ask you about Rita's babies, Mrs. Wilson . . . we're trying to trace them, trying to get some identification cleared up. They went through an orphanage, went their separate ways. . . . Whatever happened to them, as far as you know? Have you ever heard from them?"

"No, no, I never have. Rita wasn't much for keeping up, letter writing and such. Not her style."

"Was Ted the father? Of both of them? Is that possible?"

"Oh, now, I don't want to speak ill of absent friends," she said primly. "People lead their own lives. I only met this Ted once, he was much older than Rita or me, and he seemed to be in bad health . . . wheezing and coughing all the time. Didn't look strong enough to father any children, but appearances can be deceiving, can't they?"

"But didn't Rita ever confide in you, let slip some clue? It's very important to know if someone else was the father . . . someone Rita may have loved?"

"Let me think," she murmured, "let me try and recollect. . . . Rita was a high liver, a risk taker, don't you know? She was never satisfied with her lot in life, not even as a child, that was why she was willing to marry an old wreck like Ted, for what she hoped would be his money . . . but the joke was on her, Ted never really made much and poor Rita was always looking for a way out—she was a very warm, friendly girl, hot-blooded, too, if the truth's to be told. She always had an eye peeled for something better, she had a roving eye. She met my Donald once and she looked him over pretty carefully . . . and I saw him looking her over, too, I wasn't blind then, but there was no time for them to misbehave. But she was always looking for a way out of the north country . . . she didn't know how to go about it, though. And she had me as a model, I got out and look what it got me, a sailor named Donald Wilson who went away—"

"So there were other men in her life? Somebody besides Ted Hook?"

"I told you, I can't malign the memory of my poor little sister." She peered at me, perplexed, as if she could see. I figured she didn't get the chance to talk much about her past: Who'd want to listen? She was alone. So I waited for the urge to communicate to get the better of her. "But the truth is the truth, isn't it, Mr. Cavanaugh?" I said it was. "And the truth is that Rita was only as good as she had to be, she had a feel for things, sensitive and like that, y'know? I think she liked the menfolks, that's the truth of it, cross my heart."

"What do you think happened to her? Really."

"Went off with a man. What else? Let's face it, that's what Rita would do, isn't it?"

"Are you sure she never let on about who the father might be? Who fathered the children? Who she ran off with? Try to remember, Mrs. Wilson . . . it's not going to hurt Rita now. But it's important to some other people. Try."

"Let's see, once in '32 and once in '40 . . . well, she never let on to me, not directly, but he was a swell, a high-class fellow—I got that impression from her, she was sort of sly about it, little hints here and there, and there was the money she sent me . . . it had to come from somewhere, didn't it? And I always thought to myself that she had a man. It seemed to me, from the kind of a twinkle she had, that it was all part of a plan that was going real well . . . for instance, she was never upset about those babies, never acted like she didn't want them, she never said she wanted an abortion, nothing like that. . . ."

"She must have run off with the father," I said.

"Stands to reason," she said tiredly, the high voice not used to all the talking. "I don't have any facts, mind you, but it stands to reason, the way I see it. It must have been a real love affair, real romantic— why, it started and lasted all those years, until '44 and who knows how long after that?"

It was dark outside. I stood on the stoop and thanked her for her time and her trouble. She smiled her empty smile and as I watched, it faded.

"Rita's dead," she said, bitterness surfacing at last like garbage on a pond. "I feel it, I know it. Rita's dead. She's been dead for a long time. I've always known that. I lied to myself, people do that, don't they?" Her false teeth clicked in the darkness, where she spent all her hours. "Thank you for talking with me, listening to me." Before I could answer she'd closed the door. A threatening breeze rustled the parched leaves. There was rain in the air, the smell and feel of it. It was a quiet street and I headed back toward traffic, my perspiration soaking my clothing, cooling as I walked. There was nothing left to do in Chicago.

I grabbed a sandwich at a joint near the university and caught a cab to O'Hare in time to take the 11:30 flight back to the Twin Cities. The cabin was hot and sticky and my eyes burned. My head ached. My stomach was jumpy and I felt groggy from what I realized I had learned. Or thought I had learned. The cabin was dark while most of the passengers yawned and trusted their lives to fate. I got a gin and tonic in a flat plastic cup, wiped my dirty face with a white napkin that came away gray and smudged. I closed my eyes, took a long sip of the drink, and dared to think for the first time all day.

Larry Blankenship was born in 1932, orphaned in 1944, when he appeared at the Sacred Heart Orphanage in Duluth and went subsequently to the Blankenship family in Bemidji, where he picked up his new name. Those were the facts.

Larry had brought a little sister with him to the Sacred Heart Orphanage, a girl of four or five who could therefore have been born in 1940. She was left behind in the orphanage when Larry went to Bemidji. She was Kim's age, just as Larry was the same age as Kim's never-found male cousin. Those were the facts.

Ted Hook had said that both of his household's children, born in 1932 and 1940, a boy of his own and Rita's and a girl born to Rita's sister in Chicago, had been placed in an orphanage in Duluth—the Sacred Heart Orphanage, acknowledged by Kim herself.

There are crucial moments when possibilities become likelihoods and I was staring at one. There was no hard proof and I knew it, but I'd have wagered a good deal that Larry Blankenship had begun life as Robert Hook, that he and Kim were brother and sister, that there had not been a threesome at the orphanage at all. It fit so handsomely and its facets fired back the kinds of reflections you'd expect in a murder case. Surely Kim and Robert were in fact the son and daughter of Rita Hook, not cousins; little Robert and little Shirley, born eight years apart at Merrivale Memorial Hospital in Chicago while Patricia Wilson paced the hallway outside, thankful for at least the fleeting contact with her risk-taking younger sister who was no better behaved than she had to be. There had never been another boy who became Larry Blankenship, who had also had a little sister. . . . No.

The question of the father took on added significance as I sucked the crescent of lime and listened to the powerful throb and roar of the jet engines. Ted had assumed that the son was his and Rita's, the daughter Patricia Wilson's. He had been fooled on the daughter; why not on the son, as well? Could the father of one also have been the father of the other? Could Carver Maxvill have been the father?

If I could have considered it as a puzzle, from a safe, objective distance, I might have been fascinated. But I loved the little daughter . . . who had become the wife in an incestuous marriage, which had produced a child who was spending her life in an institution because her parents had been brother and sister. . . .

I had another drink and looked out into the moonlit night, occasional clusters of lights blinking at me from the Wisconsin countryside below. If I had been an observer once, even until today, I wasn't anymore. Kim was part of these murders, part of the vast, improbably, immensely human pattern. I remembered the beginning of it, the suicide in the lobby and the birdlike woman telling me that Kim Blankenship/Roderick was a murderer. . . . Well, the information had been inaccurate but it was all tied together somehow and Harriet Dierker had known it.

Time had damaged Larry and Kim (Robert and Shirley, if you prefer; to me they were Larry and Kim), had torn them apart, disguised them, hurled them back at each other a quarter of a century later. By then, with only the Norway Creek Club members in common, they were strangers. . . . Norway Creek—she had worked there and Larry had gone to work for a member and gained entry through the front door. They were strangers when they met, Norway Creek their only common ground. The thought bedeviled me, the irony of Norway Creek's being involved in such goings-on. I was naive to be shocked by that, of course, but the club was like the city, wrapped carefully in a cloak of rectitude and morality and proudly proclaimed goodness, as if morality were something you conferred on yourself cosmetically, to hide your sins.

Kim and Larry obviously had known nothing of their original sibling relationship when they married. Kim didn't know yet. But it seemed to me that I had come up with the reason Larry had killed himself: Somehow he had found out the truth. Life had played him for a chump all along; nothing ever worked out right, not his career, not his marriage, not his childhood . . . and the final belly laugh from above was too much. The empty apartment must have mocked him, the new Thunderbird he couldn't pay for must have jeered, the silent telephone must have hammered his last hopes to pieces, leaving him crying to his ex-wife in the parking lot and the child stashed away out of sight and the lie inherent in his neat summer clothes—it was all a dirge for the end of Larry Blankenship's unsuccessful attempt at living. Then he'd discovered that the woman he'd loved and married and lost was his sister and then he'd written his considerate little note and shot himself to death.

I knew it was true. And there was a connection to the murders of Tim Dierker and Father Boyle; there had to be. There was no sense in half a pattern. The next thing I had to know was the identity of the father or fathers. . . . Was it Ted for Larry and Carver Maxvill for Kim? Or not?

We began our descent through a gray cloud bank which didn't part until the red landing lights jumped up beneath us and the wheels locked down into place.

I was afraid.

If the knowledge of the incest had moved Larry Blankenship to kill himself, what might it do to Kim? And could I bring myself to tell her? Loving her as I did, what the hell was I supposed to do?

By the time I fell into my bed the murderer had extended the serial. . . .

19

I WAS dumbfounded, utterly confused after a night of intermittent dozing. The wind roared at the windows like a hungry beast and the humidity weighed you down; dawn came slowly, gray and windy, but the sun followed, turning the freeway a salmon pink, and the wind and I sat on the balcony staring into the spaces between me and the downtown towers. My mind refused to attack. I called Archie and we arranged to meet at Norway Creek for breakfast.

He was cool and fresh in a seersucker jacket, collar open with some white chest hair curling up toward his throat, mustache trimmed, white hair slicked back, a paisley silk square in his jacket pocket. My nose still throbbed. He listened quietly, carefully operating with knife and fork on his eggs Benedict, as I told him the story of my Chicago adventures and the sad conclusions I'd drawn.

When I lapsed into silence, he motioned toward my plate and told me to eat. Outside a foursome was coming up the fairway and spiked shoes clattered on the veranda. The sun was unnaturally bright. It made my eyes ache.

"Well, you've turned the key, I think, yes, you have." He leaned back and a lit a cheroot. "You've given us some room to move around in, very good work, Paul. . . . I know it's hard on you with this Kim business." He stepped lightly there; Archie looked on romance as something that got in the way of the plot, whether in the coils of fiction or reality. So it surprised me when he forced himself to ask me how serious I really was about her.

"Serious," I said. "I love her. She made me realize

I still had that capability in my bag. . . . It's important to me, she's important to me."

"I see, more or less. You realize that, like most such undertakings, it's exceptionally ill advised. The woman's erratic behavior is not a closely guarded secret."

"I know. I'm not giving her a grade, you know. I'm in love with her."

"Well, there you are, then. You'll have a problem, presumably you realize that. You're an adult. Good luck to you!"

"It's all part of life's rich pageant," I said.

"I expect you're right on the button with the way you're reading things," Archie said, turning from the discomfort of the emotional life to the safety of a puzzle which with luck would yield to intellect and reason. "They've almost *got* to be brother and sister. It'd be a pity—in terms of plot construction only, of course—if they weren't, if there really had been another brother-and-sister act at the same orphanage at the same time Kim and her brother were there. I can't seriously consider the possibility, it makes hash of everything.

"And being brother and sister, it seems that Larry's discovery of incestuous marriage might be enough to drive that unhappy citizen to suicide. Important question is, how did he find out? We'll have to find the answer eventually.

"The matter of the father or fathers—now, that's quite thorny, isn't it? Patricia Wilson says the father of the second child, the girl, was quite probably something of a swell . . . and we know for a fact it wasn't Ted. Ted was told by Rita that it was Patricia Wilson's baby. . . . Was Ted the father of the first child, the son? Who knows? It may not even be important —to anyone other than Kim and Larry. But who fathered the girl? Who was the swell, the ladies' man, Rita's ticket out of Grande Rouge? Pretty damn well jumps out at you, doesn't it, son?"

"Carver Maxvill," I said.

"Right. It's a nice snug fit. Kim is Maxvill's daughter." He signaled for more coffee and when we were alone again, he sighed and used his lips, planning what he was going to say. "It's a tangle," he went on, "but I think I know who the killer is, *know* at least in my guts." He smiled and went on.

"First, start with Rita's money, the hundred and fifty thousand dollars she left behind in the bank for Ted—she may have gotten sentimental about Ted and left him that as a present . . . as long as she had more on the way. But how the devil did she get the first hundred and fifty thousand? Remember we discussed it before? Well, I've worked on it and, Paul, I believe you were on target, there's only one way that makes any sense . . . blackmail. Payoff. Extortion. The club —who else, when you get right down to it?—the club was paying her off . . . it was the only imaginable source of that kind of money she could tap. I don't know *why* they'd pay her. . . . But we don't have to know yet. We can make the assumption that the club coughed up the money. Over quite a lengthy period of time, though I certainly never knew about it in my club days . . . that puzzles me rather, that I could be so close to something, however fleetingly, and not know it . . . it makes me realize how little I actually had in common with them.

"Anyway, what is it that happens to blackmailers? They either connect for the big, final payoff and go away . . . or they get killed by their victims. My bet is that she connected for the big one . . . mainly because I can't see these guys killing her. I suppose it's a blind spot, but they don't seem the type at all. . . . No, they'd pay before they'd kill. With Maxvill, her lover, on her side, she connected for the final installment. By 1944 the lads could well have afforded it . . . who knows how much, another hundred and fifty thousand maybe? She left the first bankroll for Ted and the kids, never knowing he'd farm the kids out to an orphanage, and she and Carver went off free as the breeze. Alone, plenty of money, they had made life pay off for them. . . ." Archie leaned back and stroked his mustache, grinning with a kind of grudging admiration. "Think of it, Paul, think how happy they must have been, imagine how powerful they must have felt, Bonnie and Clyde pulling off the biggest heist of all and no cops in jalopies hot on the trail. You've got to hand it to 'em, don't you? Rita and Carver beat the system. She finally got out of Grande Rouge." He poked his sunglasses down his nose, his eyes twinkling at me over the rims.

"Well, that's the last time something happy happened," I said sourly. I couldn't stop worrying about Kim, what she had in store for her. A man rolled in a long one and did a jig on the eighteenth green. "So how did the happy thief become a murderer, Arch?"

"He got old, his wife, Rita, died, he came back to Minneapolis out of loneliness, a need to return to the scenes of his youth—whatever the reason, it doesn't matter—and what does he find? Think of it, picture the old man who has abandoned his children and lived his life on stolen money . . . he comes back like Rip Van Winkle, life has gone on, his pals have grown old, too, and to his horror he discovers that they have *allowed* his daughter to marry her brother—after all, *they knew,* and they have had their revenge." He was wound up now, rolling. "Pure opera, Paul! The club has punished him for blackmailing them by allowing the incestuous marriage of his daughter . . . for all we know of his son and his daughter, he *could* have fathered both children." He looked at me again. "Showstopper, what? They have blighted not only Maxvill's life, but Larry's and Kim's and their child's as well. Now, if that's the way Maxvill sees it, murder is a very logical response, don't you agree?" He softly tapped the table with his finger. "Mark my words, we've got it figured out, Paul. He's going to kill them all. . . . He's gone off the edge, they're all guilty . . . and it's the incest that's unhinged him."

"It makes sense," I said. "But why does it have to be Maxvill?"

"What do you mean? I've just told you—"

"But why not Rita? Who says it isn't Rita that's come back? Her motive is just as good as his, better . . . they're her babies."

Archie's mouth dropped open and he scowled.

"Well, god damn it," he whispered. "That never occurred to me. . . . I've been absolutely hypnotized by the man in the case." He took a bite of his lower lip. "It could be the woman. . . ."

We drank our coffee in stillness, listening to the chatter of the brunch crowd beginning to gather.

"Crocker said he knew who the murderer is," Archie said.

"Right," I said. "And it could just as easily be one as the other. . . ."

"But the pictures of Maxvill . . . the file being stolen." Archie clung to the idea. "But," he said grudgingly, "I see your point."

We went out toward the pool on the neatly kept path, children and mothers anxiously using up what might be the last good family day at the club for that summer. Voices were higher pitched, as if the tension of the winter's certainty up ahead were getting to them. Leaves were already beginning to drop in places. The hot sunshine was a bonus and there were large white clouds to the west, and who knew when it would begin to squall and turn cold?

There was a club tennis tourney winding up and Darwin McGill sat edgily at the top of the scorer's high chair, He was as dark as an Indian and I remembered he was dying, or said he was, but then, who wasn't? Archie sat at a table with a shade umbrella on the flagstone terrace above the tennis courts. "We'd better talk about Kim," he said shyly, facing up to it. "What are you going to do about her?"

"Well, I'm in for the distance," I said, dropping heavily into a chair beside him. The fringe on the umbrella flapped overhead. "It's not a whim on my part. But God knows, she throws me nothing but curves . . . once in a while a big fastball, a big piece of truth up the middle, almost like a confession, as if I've succeeded in wringing it out of her, she's done it a couple, three times . . . but mainly curves, nipping at the corners, getting strikes but only giving me little edges of truth. It's unsettling, Dad, I don't know who she really is . . . every time I get a

handle on her she slips away, turns out to be somebody else. I don't know how to pin her down."

"She's pretty well pinned down now, I'd say," Archie said, soothing me with the calmness of his voice.
"She's a complex woman who has led a peculiar sort
of life, more changes and uncertainties than most people go through in seventy years. She's had no rest,
Paul, no time to sit and think and put it together. . . . Think about it—who is she most like in
this entire matter? Who would you pair her with, of all
the people we've come across and heard about?"

He toyed with the crease in his slacks, folded his
arms across his chest, and watched the tennis match
and the clouds piling up just beyond the edge of the
city. I sat quietly, confused.

"Her mother," Archie said somberly. "She's got a
lot of Rita Hook in her, Paul. A drive to get rid of
her north country upbringing, the ability to cancel out
one deal and make another, to go from one man to
another, bettering herself. Bettering herself in every
way, by going to school, by broadening her friendships and her knowledge. Think of it, just the facts of
it. . . . She's on her own, she's making her way with
whatever she has at hand. First, there was the need to
get away from Grande Rouge. And she did it. Then
there was Billy Whitefoot so she wasn't all by herself
in the threatening city, then Larry Blankenship and
a full step into middle-class respectability, then Ole
Kronstrom and a world of money and privilege and
leisure. . . . She's got guts, the guts of a burglar, just
like her mother. Now, she's giving you a pretty good
looking over . . . younger, plenty of money, a certain
standing. . . ."

"You sound like Harriet," I said. "You make her
sound like a calculating, cold-blooded monster—"

"Nonsense, I said nothing of the kind and I won't
have you say I did. . . . I was analyzing a character
—that is, a person—in an objective manner from
the evidence at hand. I was making no accusations of
any kind." He tweezed his lips between thumb and
forefinger, tugging on them. "In point of fact, I'm
rather in awe of her. She's obviously got a hell of a

backbone, real gumption. She's strong, Paul, in a way that you and I will never be strong. She's *had* to be strong . . . that's the point of what I'm telling you. Don't worry about her—she's got a lot of sides to her character, you've seen some of them, and she's adaptable. She does what she has to do to survive. She's not going to come apart in the face of the truth. So don't be frightened of what you're afraid is her fragility. If she were fragile, breakable, she'd have gotten broken a long time ago. If you're worried about her learning the truth of her parentage and her relationship to Larry, forget it—she can take it."

"All right," I said, "supposing all that's true, I'm still afraid. . . . I don't quite know what I mean, but I'm afraid that something may happen to her—"

"What's that supposed to mean?"

"I'm afraid that she's in danger, too. Now, damn it, don't look at me that way, I can't help it. She's so elusive, so mysterious, she's connected with the whole thing in such peculiar, convoluted, coincidental ways. I'm afraid she's going to get sucked all the way in. . . . I'm afraid that she's going to become a victim." I looked away at the tennis action; they seemed to be playing faster, trying to beat the threat of rain, but the sun was still hot. "It's just a feeling, that's all."

Archie stood up, put his hand on my shoulder.

"Don't apologize, kiddo," he said. "Same thing occurred to me. I don't know why either."

We were walking back up the grassy hill when a man Archie knew came across the parking lot toward us, a bemused expression on his thick, flat face.

"Did you hear the news just now, Archie?" Archie shook his head. "Well, get ready for the shit to hit the fan again. Ford just granted Nixon a full pardon. . . . Full pardon. That makes me more embarrassed to be a Republican than anything Dick himself ever did. Christ, a full pardon! Can you imagine the hay they're going to make out of this?" He punched Archie's arm. "Well, we live and learn."

"You know it, Walter," Archie said. "Then, you

look at it from another way, we live and never learn a goddamn thing."

"Say, now, you writers have a way with words," Walter said, and trotted off toward the clubhouse to spread the word.

"We'd better go see Kim," Archie said. "Do you mind if I come with you?" I didn't and we climbed into the Porsche. I didn't feel much like talking; my mind was turning over, trying to get a good purchase on things, and things kept crumbling in my grasp. It was the complexity of it that did it to me, the differences between appearance and reality being so pronounced, so awful. Just beneath that tranquil surface, the scuttling and clawing went on and on, the monster was growing hungry and itchy. It was like the rats, all right, taking up residence long ago, foraging in the garbage, making it their home. God only knew what else lay beneath the surface, scratching away at what Tim and Marty and the rest of them had built and valued, wanted at any cost to protect.

Somehow I'd become the bulldozer, ripping and scraping at the mound called 1974, with nothing whatever to gain. I'd become the machine, tearing the seams, gouging away at time, opening it all up and spilling out the rodents of forty years ago. . . . Forty years of garbage and crap that had nothing to do with me, smashing it up and scattering it around, all the vermin and creatures of filth blinking in the light, vague and unsure and newly wakened, terrified by me. I had set them running again, the disease carriers, and the poison was out. And it was none of my business.

"Doesn't surprise me," Archie said.

"What doesn't surprise you?"

"Ford pardoning Nixon. And people worry about the younger generation. . . ." He sniffed contemptuously.

It seemed to me that it all went together beautifully, my problems and the country's. The monster was everywhere. And I didn't know the half of it. There was another body spoiling in the heat but nobody knew it yet.

20

I TOOK the wrong highway trying to beat the crush around Lake Calhoun on a big sunning and boating day and got caught in a traffic jam. There was a rescue-unit truck, an ambulance, and three squad cars and it took several seconds for me to realize where I'd gotten us. It was the Crocker construction site and the first thought across my consciousness was that the rat stampede had started. I reflexively jabbed WCCO to life since they'd be the quickest to comment but they were in the middle of celebrating 1942 and Dinah Shore began a slow, plaintive rendition of "You'd Be So Nice to Come Home To."

Lights flashed, sirens screeched, and we waited in the heat with the top down. Archie swore quietly and tried not to notice the heat and the dust and the noise. There were cops all over the trailer area but nothing much seemed to be going on up on the hill. A couple of sanitation trucks stood mute and four white-coated workmen stood lazily on the hill, confident that the rats were under control. But something had happened at the site. I peered for a glimpse of James Crocker but he didn't seem to be running things at the moment. Suddenly the traffic began to move and I headed on into town. Billy Daniels was singing "That Old Black Magic" on the radio and I was wishing I had some to use on Kim. My stomach had turned over to die and I wasn't used to breathing through my nose. I was trying to rehearse in my mind what I was going to say to her. None of it was very graceful. By the time we left the car with a scowling doorman Sinatra was working on "The Lamplighter's Serenade" and the sun had done the top of my head medium well.

She buzzed us in and when she answered the door, I suddenly remembered how lousy our last conversation had been, how hard she'd tried to make it nice, and how I'd left her. She shook hands with Archie, winked at me cheerily, which made my mission all the worse, and said, "My God, did you hear about Nixon?" She took us in to sit in the chrome-and-glass living room with bright explosions of flowers here and there. Archie gave it all an appreciative glance. He liked to observe women, was intrigued by the messes they got themselves into and the means by which they got themselves out; he just liked to keep his distance. She was wearing a robe of lemon yellow and the hair at the nape of her neck was still wet. A war game called Sniper was strewn about the floor, its distinctive box propped against a chair leg. She looked at the mess and smiled at Archie. "Sorry about this. It's a new one and I was up half the night figuring out the rules . . . they really do approximate life's complexities as best they can. It's the complexity that makes it fun, of course, but you've got to be patient."

"Patience is a rare quality in beautiful women, Miss Roderick." Archie was trying to sound like an author: He'd seen a stack of three Fenton Carey paperbacks on an end table. But it was irritating me because of why we were there.

"Kim," I said, cutting into their repartee, "we're here for a reason. It's pretty serious, Dad, so let's get—"

Archie's face clouded and he clasped his hands in front of him, leaning forward in his chair.

"We're very much afraid that your life may be in danger," he said, wisely choosing the best possible angle for a beginning. "Paul's come into some troubling information and it's going to come as a shock to you, I'm afraid. He's going to tell you and I'll do what I can to help. But remember, nothing is irreparable . . . from what Paul has told me about you, I'm sure you can handle it. . . ." He looked at me.

"I went to Chicago yesterday," I said, wondering

where to look, "and talked with Patricia Wilson."
Kim's eyes widened just a bit and the tip of her
tongue appeared between her lips, waiting, anticipating. "She's not dead and, the thing is, she's not your
mother. Rita Hook was your mother and we believe
Carver Maxvill is your father." I stopped, short of
breath. Her hand jerked upward to cover her mouth.
Her body seemed to shrink, the flesh pressing back
against the bone structure. She made a soft sound,
as if the breath were being forced out of her lungs
by the pressure. Her face bore something in common
with the night at the Guthrie when she'd been set
upon by Harriet, but the anger was missing now, replaced by something a lot like fear, the fear that
comes when you reach out for support and touch
something that's alive and moving.

"That's the good part," I said. I reached for her
hand but she slid away.

"All right," she said from far away, "what's the bad
part?"

While the air conditioning purred and blew cold air
over our heads, while the flowers breathed and quivered and reached out in such desperately slow motion, while Archie clenched his hands on his knobby
knees and the sniper waited quietly on his assigned
hexagon, I told Kim that Larry Blankenship had been
her brother unless she'd been victimized by the most
bizarre coincidence of all time. I told her that the second most bizarre coincidence was their meeting, falling in love, marrying, and having a child, but it had
apparently happened. I told her we believed Larry had
learned the truth and it had been the final blow, had
put the lock on his suicide. I told her that we believed the murder-go-round was balanced on the facts
of her real parentage and her incestuous marriage.

She had gone white, mouth dry, eyes staring; her
carefully constructed life lay in rubble around her
tense bare feet, toes clawed into the carpet. She
clasped herself with both arms, as if there were a
fatal agony in her stomach. She said nothing. I could
hear her trying to swallow. Her eyes had grown large,
stopped staring, darted about the room. The sunshine

made a mirror of the glass door to the balcony and a bottle of suntan lotion stood on another Fenton Carey leaving a greasy circle.

"Which brings us to the danger, Miss Roderick," Archie said, clearing his throat. Her small dark head snapped toward him, nostrils flaring, eyes unblinking, like a terrified animal with its foot in a trap. Archie spoke very slowly, in contrast to the anxious spill of words from me. "Two things have us worried. Let me be very explicit. In the first place, when Larry Blankenship discovered the truth of your relationship —or so we believe—he killed himself. We don't want this to happen to you . . . that's why we decided to come here, to try to provide a buffer between you and the news, the *bad* news. Maybe we can lend some perspective. . . ." He spread his hands and shrugged. "In the second place, if Carver Maxvill has come back to clean up on the old gang, he may very well be insane. *And,* if he's insane, he may hold you as responsible for lousing up the end of his life . . . as the men who let you and Larry get married. A deranged mind is not predictable because no one can be sure how far gone it is and down what path . . . and you may therefore be in danger. For instance, now no one can surprise you with this information. . . ." Archie smiled at her blank gaze, looked at me. "I'm very sorry, Miss Roderick," he said, "but better you hear it from us than from someone who doesn't wish you well—"

"You expect me to just believe this?" She turned from Archie to me. "You tell me this and expect me to just say okay, that's interesting, and what else is new?" There was no feeling in her voice but it was high and skating.

"There's a lot of evidence," I said.

"What do you know about evidence? Tell me, what do you know about it? And who gave you the right? Oh—" She stood up, clutching the robe around her slim body, quaking as if she had a bad chill. Her eyes took aim at me like twin rifle muzzles. "God, you made me trust you! Why? What have I done to you, for God's sake?"

"I love you," I said sappily. "I want to help you out
of this mess . . . make sure nothing bad happens to
you. . . ."

She stalked to the window, staring at the happy
sunny world outside and so far below, an act of bravado in the face of heavy fire. "Carver Maxvill!" She
hissed at the glass. "My father . . . and my husband
my brother. . . ."

"That's the way it looks," Archie said.

"Was there another brother-and-sister combination
at the orphanage," I asked, "same age as you and
your brother?" I was watching the back of her sleek
head, the narrow shoulders beneath the yellow robe,
her feet wide apart and braced as if she saw a tornado
wheeling and spinning toward her.

"How the hell should I know? I was four years old,
you idiot—" She shook her head violently.

"It fits, Kim," I said.

She turned. "It fits," she mimicked. "That's what
appeals to you, isn't it? The fit. God, you're so cold—"
She finally cracked, her face and voice coming apart
at the same moment, tears bubbling over and sobs
convulsing in her throat. Without another word, she
walked across the room and we heard the door to her
bedroom slam.

I looked at Archie. He shook his head. "There was
no easy way. But we had to tell her. . . ."

I didn't know if that was true. Did we have to?
Was it any of our business? Maybe not. If I hadn't
spoken with Harriet Dierker the morning after Blankenship shot himself, I'd never have met Kim, never
have fallen in love with her. . . . But that was an if
and to hell with them. It *was* my business. I was in
love with her, regardless of how abnormal and loused
up our relationship was. I had no choice; it was just
a rotten piece of business.

I looked up at Archie. "There was gray fluff on the
floor of Blankenship's apartment," I said. "Tim
Dierker had been down in Blankenship's apartment. . . . I wonder if Tim told him the true story.
It fits," I added, unthinking.

Archie gave me a sour look. "Yes, Paul, it fits."

We could hear her sobbing through the wall. It was as if someone were being tortured next door and we couldn't stop it. I went to the kitchen and dug a couple of cans of Olympia out of the fridge and brought them back into the living room. I stepped out into the blast of heat on the balcony and drank deeply, looking down at the empty midday streets wavering behind the heat rising from the pavement. Two people in tennis whites batted the ball lazily and there was desultory splashing in the turquoise-blue pool. I heard a siren wailing. Almost any time of night or day there was a siren somewhere in earshot. Everybody had a crisis.

She had stopped crying when I went inside and I went to the bedroom door. Archie was in the living room drinking beer and reading one of his own novels. I knocked and she said I should come in. She was propped up against pillows, knees bent up, painting her toenails. The robe fell open so I could see the backs of her thighs disappearing beneath a fold of yellow terry velour. She didn't look up and I sat in a small flowered reading chair.

"I'm all right now," she said. "I'm probably in shock or something but I feel better. I cried it out. And I'm sorry for taking it out on you. I just haven't had a lot of experience dealing with this kind of news. . . . I can see how ancient rulers used to kill bearers of bad tidings." She wielded the brush expertly, carefully doing each nail, bits of cotton between her toes to hold them apart. I gave a deep, inner sigh of relief; she was back, she wasn't angry, and she wasn't holding it against me. In the midst of all the compounded horrors, that was what I cared about. "Come here," she said. I stood beside her and she finally looked up. "Let me kiss you." I did and she held her mouth to my cheek and then went back to her task. She seemed utterly composed except for her bloodshot eyes. She seemed to sag beneath the robe; she had veered violently from anger and palpable hatred of me to this solemn acceptance, exhaustion. She was probably right: shock. She wasn't quite taking in all the implications of what we'd told her but her strength was showing through.

"Would you like me to stay with you?"

"Do you think Maxvill will contact me?" she asked, ignoring my question. "Is that what you see happening?"

"It wouldn't surprise me . . . we don't know if he saw Larry, but he might have. So, a definite maybe. You may never hear a word from anybody but we can't count on the easiest way out. We've got to expect the worst and hope for the best. But I'll bet somebody told Larry. That somebody might tell you—it could be brutal. It's better to have you prepared."

She nodded and capped the bottle.

"Do you think he's my father?"

"Probably."

"Do you think he murdered Tim and Father Boyle?"

"He's the leading candidate."

"Okay." She stood up. "I'm sorry for the things I said to you."

"Do you want me to stay?"

"No, it's all right. I'm going out on the St. Croix, on Ole's boat. We'll be on the river until later this evening. I'll be all right. Don't worry."

"Call me when you get home," I said. "Please."

"I will."

She went out to the living room and apologized to Archie. She assured us again that she'd be fine, that she'd call me when she got home. I kissed her at the door.

In the elevator, Archie said, "Jesus, I hope Ole's not the killer." I told him I hoped not, too.

Whoever it was, he now had three to his credit and we were just about to find out.

21

ARCHIE suggested that we drive past the Crocker construction site on our way back to the club, just to see what the devil was causing all the commotion.

The area had cleared out and a passerby would have noticed nothing out of the ordinary. There was one police car parked in the shade across the street, an unmarked green sedan behind it, and a *Tribune* reporter I knew by sight was standing by the trailer picking his nose. No fuss; everything smoothed over and the rain holding off in the west. The dehydration of my body and soul informed me that it was ninety. Dust blew in whirlwinds making it a very bad place for Mark Bernstein, who was turned out in a royal-blue polyester blazer suit, a phony crest on the pocket, shiny white shoes and belt. He saw us coming and stood staring at us, shielding his eyes against the sun and the crud blowing around and lousing up his suit. His hair spray wasn't working and a cowlick had exploded out of a twenty-dollar haircut. He was very unhappy.

"I feel like a cop in a movie," he said. "Every time something bad happens I look up and here come the heroes in their rattling crappy old car, full of funny remarks. . . ." He kicked at the dust and dirtied his assistant's black oxfords.

"How's it going, Mark?" I said brightly, but it didn't feel right. It wasn't that kind of day at all. Twenty-four hours before, I'd just decided to go to Chicago and lose my innocence. There hadn't been a lot of laughs since then. "What's going on?" The guy from the *Trib* snapped a picture of the Crocker trailer, edged closer to us.

"Tell him to get the hell outa here," Bernstein snapped to his helper, who marched off to accost the reporter. He swiveled back to us, squinting. "James Crocker, football hero and pillar of the Establishment, got it in the eye last night. In there." He jerked his thumb at the trailer. "Shot in the right eye. Killer locked the body in with Crocker's own key and very neatly left the key under the little steps by the door. Guy named Watson, a veep at Crocker Construction, came down to the site today to check and found his boss in the trailer sitting there with brains splattered all over the wall behind him and dripping down his nose. No, you don't want to go in there, it smells funny and the body's gone now, anyway. . . ."

"Have you found any trace of Maxvill yet?" Archie asked. My mouth fell open. I couldn't help it.

"No. I've got three men combing through the hotels and rooming houses, interviewing anybody who might have sold him that gun or answered any questions, anyone who might have known him . . . lawyers, men he worked with and for, but nothing so far." He coughed in the dust and led us into the shade beneath a big overhanging oak that hadn't been killed yet. "If you're right, if it is Maxvill, he's got hellish nerve, real cool MO. He just sort of comes in the night, plugs 'em, evaporates. Somehow he must have known Crocker was going to be here alone last night . . . we've got that pinned down because there was somebody from Crocker Construction here with him until almost midnight. The killer could have got him anytime after twelve midnight—I'm waiting to get the outer limit but it'll take a little time. Somebody knew he was going to be here alone. . . ."

"Or somebody was watching and waiting," I said.

"Probably the latter," Archie said. "I see Maxvill as a man of great patience, willing to wait his chance and then carry it out in a very orderly way."

"Well, he's beating us, three to zip," Bernstein said tiredly. He patted the full hairdo, delicately trying to squash the errant strands. "Would you believe I've got to speak to Women for a Saner Society on Tuesday? Can you imagine the kind of questions they're gonna ask, can you? 'How can you expect us to vote for you if you can't find the killer of three of our leading citizens?' " He seemed to see the question as something palpable, rising out of the dust to confront him. " 'Shit, madam, we're doing our best but we are handicapped by our lack of intelligence and courage.' The next question will be about the rats and I will point out that to my knowledge no rat has committed a crime." He winced. "That's not true, of course. Several of them apparently ate a good deal of one of Crocker's men right at the beginning . . . that's bad enough, right? Well, this morning the guy died. They're calling it shock, people always buy shock as a cause of death, shock from loss of blood, but . . . the word downtown is that the rats are carriers of something supernasty—no, don't say typhoid and rabies, just don't say it, whatever you think. Because that would be just too god-awful to be true. 'Why?', you ask, I'll tell you why . . . because the sanitation creeps discovered yesterday afternoon that the rats, heh heh, are gone, gentlemen, gone and they did not take Northwest Airlines, they walked out the back door, which we apparently didn't know there was one of—" He took a deep breath and hitched up his natty self-belted trousers. "They are simply out and about, among us, hungry and scared and maybe just a little touchy since we have, after all, unleashed chemical warfare on their mommies and daddies and kiddies. . . . Mad rats, what every politican needs . . . not even Nixon was visited by a plague of rats. He got Gerry Ford and Gerry Ford told him not to worry, he's suffered enough. I get three murders by a ghost and an army of disease-carrying rats. . . ." He walked away to find his helper.

Archie turned to me.

"I'd say our theory looks better than ever. The pattern is just as steady as a rock. It leaves Goode and Hub Anthony as the last two club regulars."

"And you and Ole Kronstrom as associates."

"Mmm. Well, you know what I think about that."

Another unmarked car appeared and a couple of fellows from forensic got out and Bernstein followed them into the trailer.

"It's funny," I said. "I told him he was going to get it next and he said he knew who the murderer was, told me to get out of danger myself. Me. . . ."

"He may have had a point. You're the guy who's been stirring everything up. . . ." Archie was cupping his hands and lighting a cheroot.

"I don't think I'm in any danger," I said, meaning it. "It's too farfetched. I'm a bystander. But I wonder if Crocker was right. I wonder if the murderer came as no surprise."

Archie looked reflective and shrugged.

Bernstein came back out and rejoined us, sat down on a green bench, and stretched his arms along its back.

"I'll know by nightfall if it's the same gun that did for Boyle. I know damn well it is."

"What about Goode and Anthony?"

"I'm putting protection on both of them. It may deter him, it may, but he comes across to me as a pretty determined man. Man with a gun."

"Any sign of a struggle in there?" Archie asked.

"Nope. Just sitting in his chair, a lamb. Just like Boyle. They all three just went willingly, no fuss . . . they must not have been able to believe it, that this person could possibly kill them. It's an odd angle . . . but then the whole thing is nuts!"

Back in the car we sat sweating, trying to find a comfortable position. The Porsche was fresh out of those, sorry. "Unless it's Rita, not Carver," I said. "They might have figured she couldn't kill them. . . ."

"Well, it all adds up to the same thing, doesn't it? Same crimes, method . . . just a different killer. Probably pretty close to the same motive."

"Sure, but the cops are looking for the wrong person. The wrong sex. . . ."

The Porsche gave a mighty wheeze, smashed itself in the carburetor, and trundled forward.

"You've got to get a new car," Archie said pleasantly. "You realize that, of course."

"Anne wants to play with the carburetor."

We shoved our way into the sluggish highway traffic and at a light Archie leaned over and said, "It doesn't make the slightest difference whether they're looking for a man or a woman."

"Why not?"

"They're not going to find the killer, man or woman." Archie chuckled and leaned back, an old man who figured he'd seen it all.

As it turned out, he hadn't.

I went back to my place, turned on the television just in time to see some disgruntled, amazed commentators trying to think of what to say about the pardoning of Richard Nixon. They were having tough sledding, indeed, and kept switching to interviews with American citizens who felt collectively that it was all some sort of bad joke. I congratulated them on their perception and built a pitcher of Pimm's Cup, took a plastic cup and my portable Panasonic and went up to the rooftop swimming pool. I had it almost to myself and turned on the ball game. There was a lot of static and off to the west I had a great view of the blackening sky. The Twins were winning behind Joe Decker and I lay down in one of the plastic chairs, looked toward the sun, and closed my eyes. My new nose bandage was a great improvement and the heat and the constant strong breeze felt fine.

Crocker's murder hadn't been a complete surprise but I felt a jab of guilt about my last conversation with him. My hatred had boiled over, I had as much as wished him dead, and now he wasn't going to preside over the dynasty in which he'd taken such obvious pride. I thought of all the chickens he wasn't going to barbecue and all the sailboat excursions on Long Lake he wasn't going to take, the remembered cheering of the crowd he wasn't going to hear. The sudden death of the old has an entirely different kind of poignancy about it, gentler, more bittersweet, but nonetheless real and affecting. Three old men were gone, one young man. The world wouldn't really miss one any more than another; who, precisely, would the world miss?

Murder. Had the three old men deserved to die? It was entirely possible. Murders were characterized by their motives; murders were as different as the reasons behind them. I was a product of situation ethics. Rigid morality was foreign to my nature. Kim had propounded the same attitude that day up on the North Shore. I had killed the old man in Finland because I was down to the last nub, choosing between extinguishing him or myself. I found it harder to accept forgiveness of myself than of others but objectivity told me that these three old men might have deserved to die. Our theory about Maxvill, whether he was mad or extraordinarily sane, provided him with what might be a hell of a justification for murder. But murder. . . . How far could you ride on situation ethics?

In the end, time outlived us all, left us for dead. Time moved relentlessly forward, the one enemy which looked as if it were insurmountable. Maybe that explained why we were so easily lured into and captured by the past; it was as if we could catch time in a bottle, as Jim Croce had sung before time made off with him, hold it still and keep it from running out. Everywhere you looked people were gazing backward: The chic young things and the somewhat older things were wearing Gatsby white that summer and spending countless millions of hours in darkened theaters where Jack Nicholson and Faye Dunaway were mixing it up in *Chinatown*'s approximation of 1937 Los Angeles. Men were wearing ice-cream suits and women were slinking about with feather boas and gowns with built-up shoulders and blood-red lips and Bette Midler was singing from all the record players at all the parties.

We were all in the middle of a nostalgia craze, longing for a time which we now knew for a fact we'd survived, unlike the present. We'd gotten through the thirties, individually or as a nation, so it must not have been quite so bad, after all.

Well, I wondered, how about that? Everything connected with the murders and suicide I'd been working on . . . everything had begun back in the thirties, that wonderful and simple time everyone was always talking about. There'd been no atomic bomb, they said, and our ambitions had been in the proper scale and we'd not yet been disillusioned by whatever was supposed to have disillusioned us in the past forty years. It had a nice resonant sound to it, instant sociological analysis turned out for cocktail parties where everybody was wearing the right clothes and listening to Bette Midler sing "Boogie Woogie Bugle Boy of Company B."

But it hadn't been quite so wonderful for Rita Hook and Ted, for Carver Maxvill, for all the rest of the lads going up to the lodge to get away from their wives. Maybe they'd all been nostalgic for something, too. Maybe that searching of the past for bits of reassurance was always with us. Maybe it never really made any more sense than it did just then to me.

Something unpleasant had happened back there and all of them, the living and the dead, had been involved in it. Some had been blackmailed, some had disappeared, and some had come all the way to 1974 to keep their appointments. My mind was sorting through it all, ever more slowly, until I gave a hell of a sigh and fell asleep.

It was cold when I woke up, raindrops splashing on a sunburn and sending chills and gooseflesh along my ribs. Tiny waves lapped at the sides of the pool and the sky overhead was almost black, split by stitches of ice-white lightning over the city. Voices floated up to me from people on balconies, ice clinked in tumblers, and laughter swept on from one party to another. I stood up, picked up my pitcher and radio, and headed for the stairway. I stood for a moment where Tim Dierker had taken the fall, shook my head to get rid of the memory of the crumpled body and the dent in the hood of the Pontiac and the wet gray slipper in the rain, and groped my way down the dark stairways. Thunder broke behind me and I flinched, looked back, and saw another jagged slash of electricity rip at the night. I wondered what the hell was coming up next.

I curled up with *The Baseball Encyclopedia* and the old Ray Milland/Charles Laughton thriller, *The*

Big Clock, on the tube. The rain drummed steadily outside and dripped from the balcony above and I didn't think once about any of them, not even Kim. I'd missed the ten o'clock news on purpose so I didn't know how much of the Crocker story had gotten out. Bernstein was probably doing his damnedest to keep the lid on at least overnight.

The telephone scared me half to death.

It was Kim. She was scared half to death, too. I knew it was Kim but I couldn't quite figure out what she was saying; the words came with a rush, interspersed with gasps, and finally I shouted at her to stop. She hung there on the other end of the line, panting.

"Listen to me," I said. "Tell me first, are you all right at this very minute? Right now?"

"Yes," she answered cautiously, her voice shaking. "But. . . ." She was sobbing in her throat and she couldn't get the words out. I'd never heard a human voice so tight, strangled.

"Are you at your apartment?"

"Yes."

"Are you alone?"

"Yes."

"Are you safe?"

"I don't . . . yes, I'm safe."

"All right. Now give it to me slowly—what's the matter?"

"Will you come down here right away, Paul? Please? Right now. . . ."

"Of course, I'm leaving, I'm on my way." My mouth was dry. Curtains whipped in the wind over my bed.

"Paul . . . he's been here. In my apartment."

"Who?"

"That man . . . the man you said was the . . . that man, Maxvill. Oh, God"—she broke off an escalating cry—"he was here. . . ."

Thunder smashed at the city like a mailed fist. You could feel the jolts in your bones and the rain was driven like spikes into the gleaming, slick paving. It bounced on the streets, spraying upward, drumming against the underslung Porsche. The world looked as if it were melting and running out there beyond the windshield and the wipers couldn't make the glass come clear. Cars pulled over to the curbs and storm sewers backed up, making every dip a lake, and the Porsche had to be eased through carefully. By the time I got to Riverfront Towers the brakes were gone.

She buzzed me in while the doorman yawned, looked morosely at the Porsche in the no-parking zone. Wind whistled around his doors like placating, unwanted guests begging entry. She met me at the door. Her face was tear-streaked. Her hands were cold and when the windbreaker fell open, her nipples jutted out like buttons beneath her T-shirt. She hugged herself, shaking, and led me inside. She pointed to the glass coffee table.

Black and dangerous, seeming about to uncoil and strike, a short-barreled Smith and Wesson .38 revolver squatted on the glass. We looked down at it and our reflections framed it.

"It was here when I got home," she whispered. "I haven't touched it. . . . He was here while I was gone. Right here, where I *live,* for God's sake. . . ." She held out her hand, a small sheet of notepaper fluttering. "He left this."

I took it from her, gingerly holding it by the edge. It was a printed message, written with a red Flair pen.

L. KNEW WHAT TO DO. DO YOU?

"It was underneath the gun, I pulled it out. . . . He used my own pen." She pointed to a pot of the fiber-tipped pens in various colors. Thunder shook us with an unholy racket and rain sprayed noisily on the balcony furniture. She clutched at my arm, fingers tightening. "Paul," she said, her voice held way too tightly, about to go wild, "he wants me to kill myself . . . as Larry did." She shook away from me, nervously wiping her face with one hand, sniffling, tears of fright spilling over again. "It's got to be him . . . that man. And he's crazy, Paul, insane." Her body shook. She leaned against the wall, small and terrified, her teeth chattering, her eyes huge and blank. She was trying to get control of herself and the situation. She was failing by inches.

I herded her into the kitchen and pushed her into a chair. She put her feet on a rung and hugged down against her knees, making herself even smaller. Her elegant face, which showed emotion so rarely, remained passive, but everything else about her said she needed help. I poured coffee and she warmed her hands on the cup. Every time the thunder struck she jerked and when the hot coffee ran down her hands, she showed no sign of feeling it.

"You were right. Everything you said was right." She sipped the scalding black coffee. "It's Carver Maxvill and he has gone mad. He knows about Larry and me and he blames us as much as the men in the club. . . . He's killing them. He expects his son and daughter to kill themselves." She gave way and began to cry, making no attempt to hide her face or wipe the tears away. "Oh God, oh God, oh God," she moaned. "He wants me to do what Larry did . . . he's my father."

I held her and she leaned against me, gasping for breath through her tears like a child. I thought about the gun, the carefully printed question, and comforted her when the thunder cracked like doom, applause for Carver Maxvill. He'd been there, in that apartment; he'd killed James Crocker in the dead of night, then vanished for the day, kept watch on all of us, waited until we'd all gone away, then had boldly gotten into the apartment by means of a credit card applied to the easy lock and left his message and the gun.

I knew it was the gun used on Father Boyle and James Crocker. Esthetic consistency demanded it. It was part of a master plan. It was something out of one of Archie's books. The whole business was a perfect setup; he'd counted on her to break, to do what Larry had done, what I'd feared she might do on her own. But Carver Maxvill wasn't leaving anything to chance when he could help it along. He was out there now, waiting for the shot. I couldn't cope with that kind of madness. If anyone had been an innocent victim of chance, it had been Kim, or Shirley, or whatever, *his daughter.* But he didn't see it that way. Unwittingly, she was an accomplice in the crime against nature, against Carver Maxvill's last faint hopes. She had to die. He couldn't pull the trigger on his daughter, but he knew she had to die. . . .

I locked her in the apartment and went downstairs to check with the doorman about any unusual men seen in the lobby area. He hadn't but suggested I check with the underground parking attendants. When I did, I discovered that the garage was a sauna and the doors to the in/out ramps had been locked in the open position to bring some fresh air inside, however hot. Beads of moisture had gathered on the beams and the single uniformed attendant had soaked through his shirt. Anyone could have walked into the area, waited for a legitimate resident, and gotten inside the elevator well with no trouble. No, he hadn't noticed anyone in particular, but that didn't mean there wasn't someone. He was sorry but he'd have passed out if he'd kept the doors closed. I nodded and went back upstairs.

Kim was in the shower and I poured two vodka and tonics and when she came out, we sat and drank them and I told her about Crocker. She took it well, apparently composed and quieted by the shower and the drink and the passage of time. I didn't want to stir her emotions. I kept a lid on everything, didn't touch her or say anything personal, anything about us. Finally she began to fade a bit, eyes drooping, and I followed her as she padded into her bedroom, her bare feet leaving little damp tracks. I insisted on staying the night. I kissed her cheek and she curled on her side beneath the sheet, which settled down, molded around her body.

I went back to the living room, opened the sliding door onto the balcony, and went out feeling the spray of rain. It was still throbbing against the day's heat, sheets of water draped over the city. Lightning lit up the skyline, reflected like the finger of death in the sterile face of the IDS tower. But it was starting to cool off and I left the door open, lay down on the couch facing the rain, and watched it bouncing on the railing until I fell asleep, thinking about Kim, my love, in the next room.

The sun was shining when I woke up; the humidity made me feel like something that had been found at the bottom of a very nasty fishbowl. And when I looked, I discovered that she was gone. The bed was empty, the closet door was open, there was an uncharacteristic hint of disarray which smacked of fear and hurry. . . . She was gone, all right. I walked back out to the balcony and looked down at the city crawling through the September heat down below. I didn't know what to do. She'd gone to ground. . . .

The gun and the note lay on the glass tabletop. I was alone.

22

FEELING numb and lost and deserted, unloved and unwanted, I wearily went up the street to the Sheraton-Ritz for breakfast. It was cool and I read the morning paper, which was a mistake. They were having a fit about the murder of "the third leading citizen of the city in a matter of days." Bernstein went so far as to say the police had several pieces of information and were seeking at least one primary suspect. It all sounded like a stall and the editorial page said as much. There was a biography of Crocker with pictures dating back to the football star in his funny old uniform. It was an exercise in nostalgia as James Crocker marched across the history of the city, parlaying his touchdown days into a thriving construction company which became the city's largest shortly after the end of World War II.

There were sidebars recapitulating the coverage of the Dierker and Boyle murders, but little was made of the connection among the victims. Archie had been right: The hunting and fishing club was what tied them all together, what made it a *homicidim seriatim,* and anyone investigating the murders would have to excavate through forty years of trivia to get to anything that made sense. Archie was right: Barring a fluke, Bernstein was never going to solve it or find Carver Maxvill. It just wasn't part of the pattern.

After breakfast I called Archie, told him that Kim was gone and the circumstances surrounding her departure, and drove out to his house. A thick gray haze hung overhead. You couldn't take a deep breath and I wondered what had happened to the early autumn I'd been complaining about.

The radio told me that the rat scare was over, that all of the little devils had been exterminated on the spot. Would anybody believe it? Sure they would; bad things just didn't happen here and facing up to a mass murderer was putting enough strain on the civic psyche. Meanwhile, the rats were doing some serious house hunting. The lid was on and only one man had died. Of shock. What a way to go.

Archie and I sat in the shade trying not to move. Julia was out and we watched the action on the lake and pondered what to do. Between us, on a wrought-iron table, I'd placed the gun and the note.

"I think we'd better just leave the gun out of this," Archie said, stroking his mustache. "We're on our own. We don't know for sure where it's leading . . . the gun could, undoubtedly would, drag Kim right into the heart of it. Unnecessary, don't you think? Once Bernstein knows she's gone and starts asking questions, who knows what he might get to thinking? Better not to complicate matters. . . ."

"We've got to find her," I said. "She's afraid. She's running for her life . . . and he's after her, he wants her dead." My voice sounded weak, unsure, a particularly accurate representation of my condition.

"You underestimate her, I think. She surveyed the situation and decided she'd be better off out of sight. She's probably quite right . . . But I am rather surprised at Maxvill's going this far. The answer, I sup-

pose, is that he is quite deranged. It's a very Old
Testament kind of idea, the sinner must die, regardless
of surface innocence. . . . 'Nuts' is the word that comes
most quickly to mind, I should think."

"*You* underestimate Maxvill, I think," I said. "If
he wants her dead, he'll find her and kill her. Jesus,
Archie, think of what she's going through, what she's
had to survive to get her life to this point—and now
she's in danger of losing it all. . . ."

"Mmm," Archie murmured. "Well, perhaps you're
right. Where do you think she went?"

"How the hell should I know? Far, I hope, for her
sake."

"I think not. I think she'll stay close. She knows it
has to do with her, she won't leave. She's got to stay
close if she ever wants it to end." He shrugged. "Just a
hunch. Anyway, leave the gun and the note with me."

"I want to find her."

"If she wanted you to find her, she'd have told you
where she was going. Whatever her reasons, she
wants you well out of it . . . she's wanted you out of it
from the beginning. But she let you bully her, let you
force your way into her life. Now she draws the line,
she must go out on her own. She may be trying to
protect you . . . if she loves you. There's a logic to it.
So let's wait. It's all we can do, wait and see what
happens." He wiped his forehead with a white towel.
"Cultivate patience, Paul. There's always a time
when patience is the only answer."

I left Archie working calmly on the notes for his
next book, the gun and the note beside him, birds
twittering in the trees, white sails carving the lake below. I felt hectic and tattered and aimless. When I
got back to town, I pulled into the overgrown tunnel
of leaves and shrubs leading to the turnaround in front
of our old house. Anne was sitting in a front window
smoking a joint and playing in a window box. Without
looking up, she took a hit and said, "My God, I could
hear you a block away. That car could kill you. And
in that vein, who's killing all these people, Paul? I
hear you're nosing around in it."

I stood on the gravel looking up at her.

"Kim tell you?"

"Yup. She was your type, after all, wasn't she?"

"I don't know. I don't know what type she is. I don't know *where* she is at the moment. . . . Have you seen her?"

"Not since last week. We played tennis, talked. . . . She asked me some questions about you. Are you in love with her?"

"What did she say about that?"

She pushed around in the wet dirt with a trowel. She had mud halfway up her arms. Even the joint was muddy. Her hair was tangled; she was sweating through her Viking T-shirt. She grinned faintly.

"She'd never say anything like that. But I fancy I can read her, at least a little. I don't know what she thinks about you, but she sure as hell does think about you. Very unusual for her. Do you love her?"

"You don't know where she is, I take it?"

"Not a clue."

"If she comes to you, keep her there and call me. Will you do that?"

"If you answer my question." I remembered another reason why our marriage went crash.

"Yes," I said. "I do."

I reached Ole Kronstrom at home.

"Why, no, Paul, I haven't heard from her since I dropped her off last night. Is anything wrong?"

I told him she'd gone, omitting the gun and the note.

"She's very independent," he said slowly. "She might have felt—may I be frank?"

"Sure."

"She may have begun feeling claustrophobic, that you were closing in on her. She gets that way, gets to feeling that her options are being taken away. Then she simply gets out for a while, to reestablish her own freedom. . . . My advice is not to worry, not to close in. Let her go, let her know she's free. Do you see my point?"

"I don't think it applies here," I said.

"No, I don't suppose you do," he said calmly. "I

don't blame you. All I can say is not to worry. I trust her judgment, she sees the long view of things, the realities of a situation. She has a way of knowing where the importance of a thing really lies . . . she's better that way than almost anybody I've ever known. She never leaves a job unfinished. She hasn't just left you to stew, she wouldn't do that. When she goes for good, you'll be the first to know. Be patient. All you can do is wait."

I felt like screaming.

The day was interminable. The heat kept shoving, a bully who took the form of a thick, gray film. I took two showers, paced, drank, and sat at my desk looking through the snapshots of Kim playing tennis that Anne had given me so long ago. I fantasized about making love to her and cursed myself for never having forced the issue. What if I never had the chance again? I wanted her and she was gone.

In the evening I tracked Bernstein down. He was sitting in his cubicle drinking iced tea and eating a pasteboard sandwich. He wiped his forehead and the Kleenex came away dirty. I declined a bite of the sandwich, which he tried to pass off as tuna salad. He threw it toward his metal wastebasket and missed.

"Same gun," he said. He sneezed and blew his nose. "Goddamn weather, hot and cold, stormy, I firmly expect a rain of toads tomorrow. Same gun killed Boyle and Crocker." He stared at me, his eyes watering. I sat like a stump so he leaned his head back and poured Murine into each eye. When he faced me, it ran down his cheeks like tears. "Same gun," he muttered. "Smith and Wesson thirty-eight."

I thought about the gun. I wondered what Archie had done with it.

"Gee," he said. "Stop by anytime. You really brighten up the place."

The rain had begun again and felt hot and dirty. No stars, no moon, and the Porsche looked as if it were sweating from the inside. I tried to delay going home. I drove past Riverfront Towers with a dull ache in my chest, slowly up Hennepin, where the hookers had been driven into doorways, where you could catch the flash and glitter of rhinestones on their hot pants. There was a tear in the fabric of the car's top and it dripped incessantly behind me, like a finger tapping to be let out of the rear end, the grave. I was soaked with my own sweat and the rain blowing in the windows. There was no hope in any corner of the city. It twitched in the wetness like something that had forgotten to die and was proving an embarrassment to the tourist board. So I finally made an illegal left across Hennepin and pulled into the driveway to my underground garage. The electric gizmo that opened the door was floating around on the floor. I ducked down to get it, fished it out from beneath the seat, and leaned back tiredly. Streetlights caught the rain like sprays of jewelry. It dripped from the leaves on the trees and coursed in the gutters. I was hypnotizing myself when the passenger window and the front windshield exploded. As the glass flew wildly around inside the remains of the car, I heard the blast of the gun. The remaining sheet of windshield grew a cobweb of minute cracks and slowly fell apart across the hood, down the dashboard, across my legs.

Lights off, a car I'd barely noticed pulled away from the curb about thirty yards up the street, sped past behind me, and was gone in the rush of rain.

I tried to push my way through the back of the seat, my eyes squeezed shut, every muscle screaming in terror. I waited a few seconds, opened my eyes, and everything was quiet. No more shots, the street deserted, only the hissing of tires on the freeway interfering with the drumming of the rain. Wind was blowing rain through the places where the windshield and side window had been and my pants were shaping themselves to my legs. Everything about me was wet. When I got out to inspect my rapidly disintegrating automobile, my shoes squished like waders and I thought very carefully, *Somebody just tried to kill me.* I was shaking and climbed back behind the wheel and got the poor thing into the garage and put it to bed.

There was glass all over and the car looked like a bathtub that had gone wrong.

Somebody just tried to kill me. It had happened in a speck of time, death blowing through my car, and now it was gone with no cries of outrage.

In all probability Carver Maxvill had just tried to kill me. Being beaten up was one thing. This was something else altogether. In the lobby of the building the ancient Pinkerton man was sitting with the hound of the Baskervilles snoozing at his side.

"Did you just hear anything?" I asked. "A back-fire? Sounded like a gunshot?"

He shifted his ample behind and scratched his head. The dog stirred and broke wind. "No, can't say as I did but then, I was making my rounds. Why?" Worry crossed his bland, perplexed face. A couple of months before, a tenant had been mugged outside under the marquee, in a brightly lit area. Fido and his keeper had slept right through it.

"Nothing," I said. "My imagination." I walked to the elevators.

"Say, you got broken glass on your pants there," he called after me, beginning to suspect me of an obscure crime. Was breaking glass a crime? He was following me in the deep carpeting. He bent down and picked up a gleaming sliver. "See? Glass right here. . . ."

I nodded. The elevator came. I got in. He peered after me, the dog sauntering up to him sneezing. I waved good-bye and the doors closed.

Archie was still up and took my call in his study. I told him what had happened and he whistled softly. "Well, well," he said. "We're getting close. I don't think he wanted to kill you. . . . I doubt if he'd kill for self-preservation. He's got a reason to kill and killing you doesn't fit—he's not a criminal, you know, not in any conventional sense. He's an avenging angel. And he wants you to get out of his way. . . . He must be watching very closely. He may have watched you go to Bernstein's office. He can't afford to have the police getting too close—so he tries to scare you off. . . ."

"Cutting it pretty damn close, I'd say." I was still picking glass out of my hair, and my stomach was still clinging to the inside of my chest. "It worked. I'm scared."

"I should hope so," Archie said. "Now go to sleep. I'll try to think of what to do . . . maybe we should back off entirely. There are limits to everything. This isn't worth dying for." Thunder cracked over the lake, a mortal blow, by the sound of it, and it gnashed at my ear across the line.

I lay on the bed with the lights off and waited for sleep. It was a long wait. You didn't survive a murder attempt every night, after all. So I lay there cringing in my bed, frightened out of shape, a perfect example of conditioning.

23

CROCKER'S funeral was a major event, the cortege tying up traffic for half an hour in a heavy mist, headlamps blurring dimly, motorcycle cops holding cross traffic at a standstill. I went to the cemetery, one of several hundred, sticky and uncomfortable and praying for a breeze that refused to come. I was too far from the graveside to hear what was said so I marveled at the size of the crowd, remembered that he'd set his goons on me, and figured he might have a tough time getting in upstairs.

The thought kept gnawing at me: He said he knew who the murderer was . . . so why couldn't he protect himself? Unless it was bravado, unless he hadn't known.

I searched the crowd in the hope that Kim might have come but that was a waste and only made me hotter. Hub Anthony nodded to me from twenty yards away and pointed to a pair of large straight-ahead types on either side of him and winked. Bernstein

was taking no chances. Hub had his protection and
so did General Goode, who looked very small and in-
tense as he bowed his head, flanked by two guys who
could have picked him up and used him for a pipe
cleaner. Archie stood with Ole Kronstrom, both looking cool and composed, almost angelic. Bernstein had
offered them protection but they had adamantly refused. In any case, we were all protected because
the crowd was alive with coppers looking for Carver
Maxvill. They didn't know what he looked like but that
didn't stop them from being obvious, giving out with
a lot of long hard stares and consulting one another
in hushed tones. It was hopeless. Carver Maxvill could
have spoken the eulogy and they wouldn't have recognized him.

But the thought stuck in my mind as I slowly
scanned the crowd: Is there a murderer here somewhere, enjoying the fruit of his labor but with work
still to be done? I hoped Kim had gone absolutely to
ground to wait it out. Otherwise, somehow, he'd find
her. . . .

At lunch Julia wore a perplexed frown and put her
hand over mine. It was past one o'clock and the
crowd at Charlie's was thinned out and we were all
munching on peppered beef and potato salad. Archie
was working on his second martini and it was dark
and quiet and Julia said she understood how I must
feel about Kim's disappearance.

"But she's one of the independent breed," she said.
"She takes care of herself, I expect, and doesn't like
being dependent on men to take care of her. If she's
actually in danger, then she's done the right thing. She's
probably just sorting things out, deciding what to do.
I have a feeling about her—if she believes she must, I
can even see her killing to save herself. . . . I don't
mean that quite the way it sounds, dear."

"That's what I told him," Archie said. "She's a
smart cookie, she saw the flame coming closer. She
backed off."

I asked Julia what she thought the incest revelation
would do to Kim, to any woman.

"There's no point in generalizing about it, Paul.

Different women would react differently. Kim hasn't had an easy time with the men in her life, this thing would just be another blow. . . . If you mean do I think she'd crack, no, I don't. A sheltered woman might go to pieces under the same circumstances, but not this woman—she's toughened. She'd cope with it, one way or another."

"You know, that note Maxvill left for her," Archie said. "That's the only really clumsy thing he's done . . . he obviously can't bring himself to hurt her directly." He leaned back and patted his mustache, sipped at the martini. "It's really quite an awesome pattern he's working on, murders on the one hand, suicides on the other. . . . God, you've got to hand it to him, mad as a hare but what a determined son of a bitch!"

"I'm worried about her all the same," I said.

"Of course you are," Julia said. "It would be wrong if you weren't. But you'll see her again, it's all going to turn out. Just hold on and see what happens. . . . She'll get through all this, mark my words."

"That's what I told him. Patience. It's like being in the eye of the hurricane. . . . Suspense." He smiled. "Suspense is my business but I've never done better than this."

Julia took off in her car and Archie and I went back to my place. In his way, I think he was worried about me. He didn't want me to have to be alone. And the attempt on my life, whether serious or as a warning, was bothering us all. He had encouraged me to stay on the case and now he wondered if we'd gone too far. Diminishing returns and all. What was left for us to gain? What had there ever been in it for us? All I wanted now was to get Kim back.

It was three o'clock when the telephone rang and we were able to stop waiting and get moving again. I didn't recognize the voice at first, though there was something familiar about it. I said yes, I was Paul Cavanaugh.

"This is William Whitefoot. You paid me a visit not long ago. An unsettling visit. It's been on my mind ever since you left." There was no warmth, no humor, no touch of life in his voice, but he seemed slightly short of breath, as if placing the call were making him nervous.

"Is Kim with you?" I blurted. Why else would he call? Archie looked up sharply.

"No, she's not here. Why would she be here, for heaven's sake?" He was genuinely puzzled and my hopes slipped away. I felt myself sag.

"She's gone off," I said. "No problem, I was just curious. What can I do for you, Mr. Whitefoot?"

"You can get in your car and meet me at the lodge tonight. The club's lodge. You can make it in five hours or so. That's what you can do for me."

"Why?" It was my turn to be puzzled.

"I have something to tell you. . . . Look, it's important or, believe me, I wouldn't have . . . called you. As far as I'm concerned, the less I see of you, the better I like it. But it's been eating at me ever since we talked . . . now Crocker's dead, that makes three of them, right? So I'd better get this off my chest and you're the lucky recipient. And don't ask me to tell you over the phone—absolutely out of the question. As far as I'm concerned, every Indian in Minnesota and the Dakotas has got a tap on his phone." He took a breath.

"All right," I said. "I'm bringing my father. He's in this as deep as I am. . . ."

"He was in the club, wasn't he?"

"Not in the inner circle. But he knew the men who were. If I come, he comes."

"Okay. He'll be interested, in any case. I've got a late-afternoon meeting here but I'll get there as soon as I can. If I'm late, just wait. I'll be there."

He hung up and I turned to Archie. I felt alive again.

For Archie our trip north was like a journey backward through time. It was as if the years were falling away and he was going north for a week of fishing forty years ago, when there was no freeway, no pollution, no murders staring you in the face, and you were young. That was the key to it, being young. An ambitious young newspaperman with the idea that he could write books, an ex-football hero, two canny young businessmen figuring they could make it in the paint business, a pair of bright University of Minnesota lawyers, ramrod-straight career army man, a convivial young priest with the knack for putting people at their ease . . . they'd all been young, with the years stretching ahead, a landscape of hope and possibility, a lifetime in which to make their marks and leave their tracks to prove they'd been there. Youth made up for a lot and the Depression was something that hadn't hit them badly at all. They didn't know it then, but they would turn out well in all cases but one. Life would smile and the newspaperman would become a famous mystery novelist, the football player and the businessmen and a lawyer and the priest and the soldier—they would reach those goals that seemed so important forty years before. Only one, the second lawyer, remembered in snapshots as the blond, long-haired one in baggy pants with a tight belt and the handsome rectangular face, only he would be denied his hopes whatever they might have been.

Archie drifted between reminiscing and mute reflection on his life and theirs, how it had all turned out. The freeway swept past as we worked our way toward Duluth. The mist clung to the earth and there were patches of ground fog but traffic was light. I was nervous, tight with anticipation, desperately curious about Billy's message yet afraid to hear it.

"It's funny," Archie was saying, "being so near the end and looking back across your life, being able to think about it as a whole story. I do it, knowing I'm near the end, but I don't *feel* like I'm near the end. . . . I still figure I'm going to live forever, but I've got evidence to the contrary right under my nose, all the experiences of my lifetime. Anyway, I've got news for you, the idea of dying doesn't frighten me at all anymore. . . . I think it's a young man's fear, the fear that you'll miss so much. At my age you don't figure there's much to miss, there's no expectation of terrific things to come—you've done whatever great things you were going to do. Nobody lives much longer than this, there are no precedents for what the hell there is left for you to do . . . so I guess I'll just keep writing books until my mind goes west. . . ." He smiled and grew silent again, content.

Later he said, "You know, as a bunch we were a pretty unimaginative lot. Boring. God, how could we have enjoyed it so much? Thank heavens, I'm not a joiner, I only went up once in a while and then moved away, but think of the ones whose spare time revolved around that goddamn lodge. . . . Whew. Crocker and his idiotic football crap, one locker-room extravaganza after another. And Dierker, he was no prize either— all the sense of humor you'd find in your average turnip. Honest, moral, sober as a young man, churchgoer. . . . And Boyle, always had a dirty joke and a red face, like he'd been caught jacking off in the men's room." Archie made a little face. "Goode, he was always there with all the answers, he could shoot straighter, swim farther, run faster, and who the hell cared? Hub Anthony was always going on about which heiress to which grain or lumber or railroad fortune gave him his last blowjob . . . he kept score, I'm sure, and I'm amazed he never married several million dollars. Maybe all the heiresses were ugly, who knows? I never believed a word of it. So long ago. Doesn't amount to a damn thing now, does it?

"And conservative? Oh, what a bunch of Establishment bastards. They'd take anything but a risk, they hated running risks for fear of making a mess. . . . It happened just once, a real mess, so far as I know. Hub told me about it and it seemed funny to me at the time, though today I'm not sure why. It was that whorehouse business and it really scared hell out of them." Archie laughed, shaking his head, caught in memory's web. "They could just see all their wonderful ambitions getting blown right out of the water, wives beating them with umbrellas and rolling pins, I suppose. You see, apparently one of them had heard quite a bit about this all-Indian-maiden whorehouse way to hell and gone somewhere, beautiful Indian virgins were the stuff of north woods dreams forty years ago, kiddo, and some woman named Helen Littlefeather ran the place—Hub didn't tell me whose idea it was but they apparently went up there *en masse* one night and something nasty happened, somebody got hurt, one of the girls, I mean. One of the lads got a bit overly enthusiastic was the way Hub put it and worked one of the Indian virgins over at some length. . . .

"Well, hysteria reigned and Helen kept some husky, very physical young Indian gentlemen on hand who were about ready to avenge the wrongs of the past century on our boisterous clubmen. Hub stepped into the breach, according to his version, with offers of large sums of money, far exceeding the cost of any repairs to the girl. The young bucks figured they'd take the money and then beat hell out of these arrogant bastards but Helen's cooler head prevailed. . . . They simply bought their way out of what could have been a nasty scrape, might have escalated into a scandal. . . . anything to avoid the consequences, they lived by that. It wasn't that I blamed them or even disagreed with them, but when I heard about it, all I could think was gee, I wish the Injuns had beaten the shit out of 'em! And these guys were my friends!"

The mist had thickened and I turned the headlights on before we got to the crest of the hill that dropped down into Duluth. Then I turned the wipers on and wiped sweat out of my eyes with a Kleenex. It was like driving through a soup caldron.

"You know," he said, continuing along the same line, "I always thought that it was Jon Goode, the one who beat up the girl. He's got a hell of a primitive soul flailing away beneath that buttoned-up surface. He told you man was a predator, well, he ought to know, using himself as an example. He's a killer." He yawned. "If Maxvill goes after Jon, he'd better be prepared. Jonny's not gonna sit there and take it between the eyes." He stretched his legs under the dashboard, shifted position.

We took the dip down into Duluth beside the metallic slab of lake and came out in another country where the light was gone behind the high bluffs, the mist had turned to a stinging spray, and the temperature had dropped thirty degrees. Archie put on his Burberry when we stopped for gasoline and huddled with the collar turned up, quiet, for the remainder of the journey. It was past eight o'clock when I turned left away from Lake Superior and began to wind inward toward the lodge.

The headlamps poked accusingly into the wet darkness and finally brought the building up out of the gloom. We were the first to arrive and I pulled the car through the spongy grass as close to the porch as I could. It was a child's fright dream come to life, the constant dripping of the rain, the wind scuttling where you couldn't see it, the trees rustling and bending in the darkness. The steps creaked. The lights worked inside and I clomped into the living room, as if loud footfalls would frighten off the evil things.

The lamplight was dim and it was cold and damp inside the lodge. Archie wandered around, distracted by the memories being summoned, and I set about building a fire, lost for the moment in my own memories of being there with Kim the day she'd sought me out and brought a picnic with her. I had fallen absolutely in love with her that day. It seemed so long ago. I'd just gotten the logs crackling when Archie called to me from the porch.

"He's here, son."

A Camaro pulled up, doused its lights, and the wiry, athletic figure of Billy Whitefoot dashed across the fifteen feet of rain and mounted the steps. He shook hands with me and I introduced him to Archie.

"Of course," Archie said, "I remember Bill. It's been a long time and Paul tells me you've made good use of the years—it's good to see you again." They shook hands.

"It sure beats hell out of the last time I saw you," Billy said. "I think I was riding my lawn mower." There was a thick irony in his voice but no hostility. He had come on business and he brushed past us, went into the main room, where he hung his jacket across the back of a chair, and went to warm himself by the fire. He was wearing a blue button-down shirt and old Levi's. With his horn-rims and the gray-flecked hair he was a strikingly handsome man, a fact which had passed me by earlier.

"This is going to take a little time, gentlemen," he said abruptly, rubbing his hands together, "and I've got to get back to Jasper tonight. I don't want to leave my daughter alone all night. I think you both better sit down . . . I'm going to need room to pace around. Please, sit down." He gestured toward a couch and we sat down expectantly.

"What has this got to do with the murders?" I asked.

He looked at me impatiently. "This is bound to go a lot faster if you hold back on the questions, all right? It's pretty damned self-explanatory but when I'm done, you can have me fill in the gaps. . . ." I nodded and he began pacing, speaking as he went.

"When you came up to Jasper with all that bullshit about wanting to write a newspaper story, I figured something funny was going on—didn't require a genius. You dragged the Norway Creek connection in, my ex-wife, and then that business about Rita Hook's disappearance, that got me pretty good and I wondered how much you really knew. . . .

"You know how it is when you've got a guilty secret you're carrying around? You figure everybody's watching you, everybody knows . . . well, that's the way I've felt for the last couple years. I have had that kind of secret, a deathbed bequest I've had to live with, not knowing what the hell to do about it. I knew something I had no business knowing but it had all happened so long ago I just sat there being mocked by it . . . no one would care about it anymore and a lot of people might be hurt very badly. Why not let the past stay dead, right? Well, that's what I decided to do . . . but Kim was involved in it, in a horrible way, and that kept eating at me. I hold her in very high regard, she was the injured party in our marriage . . . anyway, I finally got in touch with her about six months after I came into possession of the true story, that'd be toward the end of 1972, the winter of '72–'73." He had come back to stand staring at us. Rain lashed at the windows and cold winds shuffled along the floor.

"I had to tell Kim that Rita Hook wasn't her aunt at all, but her mother. And her father was unknown." He took a deep breath. "And I had to tell her that there was a very good chance that Larry Blankenship was her brother . . . that they had both been born to Rita Hook. . . ." He waited for us to react. I looked at Archie, holding my breath.

"You mean to say," Archie said slowly, "you told Kim all this in 1972? Almost two years ago?"

"That's right. I went to Minneapolis and told her."

"And how did she take it?"

"She was shocked, of course, but she didn't accept it completely. She said she would do some checking of her own. She was that way. She always figured she knew the better way to handle a thing. . . . I'm not saying she was wrong, either."

I said, "How did you ever find this out? We already know it, we discovered it a few days ago . . . but we really had to dig it out. Did you?"

"No. Running Buck told me just before he died. It was the summer of '72 and he was hanging on by a thread and he had this story weighing very heavily on him. He didn't want to die with it on his conscience and I was the only person he had to tell . . . that wasn't all, not by a hell of a way. The part about Kim, that was just an angle, he didn't give a damn about that really, one way or the other. . . ." His eyes flickered in the firelight like doorways to centuries that were long out of reach. His mouth was set in a grim line. "No, he told me the whole story of what happened at the lodge on the night of December 16, 1944."

24

THE winter of 1944 had begun early in Grande Rouge and there had been almost a foot of snow on the ground by mid-December. The cold had come blowing off the lake and the nights froze deep and hard. Willie Running Buck was spending the evening working in Ted Hook's outbuilding, tinkering over odd bits of carpentry and plumbing, a potbellied wood-burning stove sending out dry warmth with the wind fit to be tied outside, sleet rattling on the door. An old Motorola table-model radio was contributing *Inner Sanctum*. It was a good winter night.

Then Rita Hook had come knocking with a burr under her saddle. She had to go out to the lodge. She wasn't drunk but she'd been drinking; she was full of hundred-proof courage, as if she'd been getting herself ready for something. She wanted Willie to drive her in the pickup truck and she wouldn't take no for an answer. He didn't want to go; he'd miss his radio shows, for one thing, and the heater in the truck wasn't worth a damn. But there was no point in arguing.

The drive had taken almost an hour. The temperature was rising unexpectedly and the sleet got wetter and wetter, weighing down the wipers and piling up on the windows, causing him to stop several times and wipe it off with his gloved hand and the arm of his plaid mackinaw. Rita had been nervous, laughing without reason, smoking incessantly, filling the cab of the truck and making Willie cough. She talked constantly, thinking out loud, some of it making sense and some not.

She'd been preoccupied with money, telling Willie

that her ship had really come in this time, that everything was going to be all right after she got through the evening. She went on about what she was going to do, how she was going to get the hell out of Grande Rouge and, once the war was over, she was going to do some traveling. And buy some pretty clothes. See the world and have a good time. Her ship had really come in this time.

Willie was only half listening, mostly because his attention was locked on the road, which seemed to slip and slide beneath the truck—but also because he was an Indian and he'd learned you could say or do anything in front of an Indian, they weren't like real people. Not up in that neck of the woods. He nodded and grunted from time to time and Rita just rattled on, finally produced a bottle of bourbon from her bag and took a swig, smacking her lips. Willie remembered that, the smell of the bourbon mixing with the cigarette smoke. It was making him sick to his stomach and when he had to get out to take care of the mush on the windshield, he did so thankfully, gulping the cold, moist air.

They finally turned off the highway and the tire chains rattled and dug into the snow and gravel. The sleet and rain hung like a wall before them and he edged the truck slowly into the narrow path among the trees. It wasn't until then that Rita began talking directly to him and the slur dropped away from her words. It didn't make much sense to him but she clutched his arm and forced him to pay attention.

She said that she wasn't there to check the pipes and the bottled gas, as she'd originally claimed. She was in fact going to the lodge to meet the members of the club; she rattled off the names, checking them off on her fingers. He knew some of the names; he knew the members of the club by sight but their names were of no account to him. They were white men, they were rich, they were from the Cities; beyond that there was nothing he needed to know about any of them. Rita didn't go any further into why she was meeting them. Willie figured they were giving her money—why was none of his business. He didn't care. White men had their ways and he didn't give a damn one way or the other.

He didn't much care for his role in the evening's activities, however. Her plan was for him to pull the truck up beside the lodge and move off into the thick shrubbery about fifty yards in front of and above the building, where he could see quite clearly but would be hidden from view. When the meeting ended and her visitors left, he would come down and drive her home. It was simple. She even had him walk around the clearing, feeling his way in the darkness so that there would be no telltale tracks across the rapidly disintegrating expanse of snow. He went because she told him to, because he worked for Ted Hook and she was Ted Hook's wife, but he didn't see the point of it, any of it.

Rita went into the lodge and he saw lights go on. He brushed the snow from a rock and sat down, the earflaps of his cap pulled down, huddled behind the windbreak of fir and evergreen. Icicles dripped in the darkness and the wind howled in the trees upland. Sleet and rain blew across the clearing. He was cold. He missed his radio and the aromatic smell of the wood fire but he waited.

After half an hour he heard the first car on the narrow road, saw the fingers of light hooking around the corner as it slid slowly toward the lodge. Two overcoated men got out and hurried, dark shapes, hats pulled low against the night, hands in deep pockets, into the lodge. Smoke was curling up from the chimney, the wind taking it once it reached the proper height and whipping it angrily. Fifteen minutes later another large car, a LaSalle of some years, pulled up behind the other and two men slogged through the slush, up the stairs, and inside. Finally, not long afterward, the third car, with two men, arrived and emptied. Six men in all and Willie waited shivering, nose running, fingers numb.

Shadows moved across the yellow windows but all he could hear was the wind. He was wet and cold and tired. Another hour must have passed; he had dozed off and on. What woke him was the slamming of the

front door as it was thrown open and banged against
the wall. A woman's piercing shriek filled the clearing
and yellow light cut across the porch. Rita was standing silhouetted in the doorway, feet apart, half turned
toward the night. She had screamed at someone inside
and Willie had no idea what was happening. He heard
a deep, commanding voice shout not to let her get
away. . . .

Suddenly she turned to face Willie as if she were
searching for him and made a stumbling dash down
the steps, fell into the snow as she reached the bottom.
As she struggled to her feet, the men filled the doorway, a confusion of voices, like hounds in pursuit of a
fox. On her feet she threaded her way between the
cars, slipping and falling, reaching for a running board
to pull herself back up. They came behind her, one
man falling heavily on the stairs and swearing. They
all moved slowly, hampered by the lack of footing.

As she reached the clearing, only a dark form from
where a frightened Willie crouched, she stopped as if
she knew there was no place to hide. She turned back
to face them. A man in a camel-hair coat broke away
from the group and went to her, spun clumsily to face
them, hands up, shouting something, waving at them,
No, no, no . . . and the commanding voice yelled at
the others to get out of the way, stepped forward, and
with a terrible roar and flash, arm stretched to its full
length, shot the man in the camel coat, who fell sideways to his knees, holding his head, then toppled over
in the snow. By the time he was still Rita had turned
and begun to run again. She got five sliding steps before the roar and flash exploded twice more, slamming her forward, face down into the snow.

Willie said that when the noise died, there was a
silence more complete than any he'd ever known. The
men stood stock-still for an endless time as he
watched, a fist across his mouth to keep him quiet.
Finally, the rain pelting down on them, they moved
closer to the man who'd done the shooting, then on
toward the two bodies, bending down. The man in the
camel-hair coat was turned over, limp, a mound of
clothing in the dark. Rita Hook lay flat; they turned

her over, knelt staring at her. Willie didn't move. He didn't want to die.

In the end, after a certain amount of jabbering among themselves, they carted the two bodies around to the back of the lodge. The largest man carried the body of Rita Hook over his shoulder. Willie was drawn to the ghastly procession; he moved among the trees, keeping them in view as he skirted the ridge of firs, hidden. They trekked up the path toward the ice cave, the last man, the roly-poly one, who had fallen on the stairway, bearing a large packing case from the woodshed. He fell again and someone laughed harshly, the sound carrying over the wind and rain.

Willie wasn't more than a hundred feet above them, rain streaming down his face and soaking his coat, when they reached the entrance to the cave. By flashlight, their faces pale and dripping, they pried back the side of the large case, which screeched as the wires were bent, until it lay open, a huge, square coffin. Willie saw that it had once held a gas range.

They were breathing hard. Willie recognized them but forgot to put names to them. One was the priest —he remembered him—the fat one who carried the case.

They stood resting for a moment, lighting cigarettes, stepping under the cave's overhang, out of Willie's sight, leaving the two bodies and the crate out in the rain. They were talking but he couldn't catch any words. The red tip of a cigarette arced through the rain and disappeared in the snow. They lifted the two bodies and put them in the case, awkwardly crammed together beyond pain or humiliation. Then they closed the lid and wired it shut. With much groaning and swearing, they pulled and pushed it into the cave. Ten minutes later they straggled back out and went quickly down the path to the lodge. *"Damned good riddance,"* one of them said, *"both of them."* Other voices chimed in. It was agreed.

Willie made his way back to his original outpost and sat back down on the stone, wondering at the behavior of these men. He wasn't really saddened: Rita was no favorite of his, neither were the men.

They were simply white, another race, strange and inexplicable in their ways. But, as he sat and waited for the men to leave, he knew he'd better keep his mouth shut or he'd be up on a murder charge. He thought about that for a time as the rain beat down steadily. The snow in the clearing was washing away, turning to mud.

When they came out at last, there were hurried good-byes, engines turning over, headlamps snapping on, the large automobiles backing and turning, churning the clearing, splashing mud. Once they were gone, Willie ventured down and stood in the rain where Rita Hook had fallen.

He drove slowly back to Grande Rouge. He went to Ted Hook's place, told him that Rita had decided to stay the night, and bought a bottle of apple brandy. Ted groused that that was Rita all over and he hoped the children didn't wake up too early, he was weak and needed his sleep.

It was not his custom but Willie drank himself to sleep. The rain drummed overhead all night.

The fire jumped and spit behind Billy and when he finished, there was a clap of thunder. A prolonged flash of lightning illuminated the clearing outside with an icy white glare. It was raining hard. We all looked, we all saw the spot where Carver Maxvill and Rita Hook had died, where the club had made sure they were dead. Billy turned and went to the window, where he stood with his hands jammed into his pockets. He scowled at us.

"That's the story Running Buck told me. Two days later he was dead and I was the only one who knew . . . well, what the hell was I going to do? It had been almost thirty years, the word of a dead Indian, and the investigation—Jesus, that was quite an investigation . . . but I suppose the rain had washed everything away and they weren't looked for clues in a murder case—the investigation hadn't turned up anything to make anybody suspicious." He threw up his hands and came back toward us. "But it festered in my mind, two people had been shot down in cold blood and nobody

had ever been charged with the crime . . . hell, nobody knew there'd even been a crime! That was one
thing . . . and Willie had also told me about Kim and
her brother—Rita got a little high one other time and
confided that little bit of news to Willie . . . never told
him who the father was. So that ate at me. For about
six months. Then I figured I had to tell Kim. . . ."

I was wrapped in my usual confusion, which was
deeper than usual. If Kim had known the story of her
mother's real identity, the incestuous nature of her
marriage, then why had she gone through the Bern-
hardt routine when we told her our conclusions? The
hysteria had been real enough. I had felt the impact
of shock pass through me on its way from her. But
why? To what end?

"And you told your former wife of the double murder of her mother and Carver Maxvill? He's obviously
the other victim—no one else disappeared that night.
Kim knew the whole story?" Archie smoothed his way
through the questions.

"Everything. Why not? It was all so remote."

"How did she take it?" Archie asked again.

"I couldn't tell, I never could tell what was going on
in her mind. . . . She just listened to me, didn't say
much, took it all very quietly. She had her doubts, as
I said. . . . She made us a pot of coffee and we talked
all afternoon and when I left, she gave me a kiss and
that was that. I knew she was thinking it over but I
had no idea what she thought." He leaned against the
mantel and watched the fire for a moment. "She's a
thinker. I wouldn't be surprised if she'd tried to verify
the story some way. But I don't know."

Why had she gone to the trouble of doing the number on us? Had it been our conclusion that Carver
Maxvill had been her father? Then she'd have realized that both her father and mother were dead. Archie and I hadn't known Carver was dead, nor Rita
. . . that made a kind of sense.

"Now I read about the members of the club getting killed," Billy said, "and you come snooping
around with questions about what happened at the
lodge that night, like maybe Running Buck might have

told me something. . . . Well, hell, at first I figured you actually knew what had happened and were trying it on me to see if I knew. Then I decided I was being paranoid, that I had to take the chance and tell you." He sighed. "That's why I've got a gun in my pocket. If one of you is the killer and wants me out of the way, you're bound for one hell of a problem. . . ."

Archie shook his head. "No, it's not us. And it's not the man we thought it was, either. That's the peculiar part of it. We had the wrong man in mind . . . though I'm sure he was the father of Larry and Kim. That's why he had to die, because he was Rita's lover and tried to protect her from the others. . . ."

The weather was getting worse. It was past ten o'clock. The wind ripped a screen off one of the windows and branches scraped against the house. In the dim light it was easy to think these were ghosts among us.

"So Kim knew from the day you spoke with her in 1972 that the members of the club had killed her mother. . . ." I tried to hold the idea still by saying it aloud. "She knew that one of them was an actual murderer and that the others had acquiesced. And she knew Larry was her brother." I heard my own voice shaking. "It must have terrified her—knowing that she knew what they were and what they had done. The only thing that protected her from them was the fact that they were unaware she knew . . . if they ever found out that she knew, bang-bang, she was dead." I blew out a lungful of tension. "And she lived with that for two years. And that's why she's taken cover now. Now . . . someone knows she knows, thus the note suggesting suicide . . . the note we assumed was from Carver Maxvill. So who the hell wrote her the note?"

"The murderer," Archie said. "Someone who has so far murdered five people and driven another to suicide. Carver Maxvill, Rita Hook, Tim Dierker, Martin Boyle, James Crocker, and Larry Blankenship." He spoke the names slowly, a litany, and we looked at each other. "Assuming, of course, that Willie Running Buck's story was the truth. . . ."

After a while Billy Whitefoot said, "Let's find out."

Billy's flashlight spread an arc of light up the pathway from the back of the lodge. The rain had turned it muddy and we were soaked within minutes. Lightning bursts showed me their wet faces; our breath came hard as we fought to keep our footing in the slippery rivers of mud and slick grass and it was as if we were joined in the rumble of the night by the men who had made the same dread journey so long before us. I slipped and cracked my knee on a jagged rock that slit my trousers and flesh like a blade; the blood trickled inside my pants, warm. Martin Boyle had carried the empty packing case in the rain and sleet and he, too, had fallen.

Archie stopped halfway, leaned against a tree trunk, catching his breath. His eyes searched mine. Had we come too far? Should we have left it alone? Billy called back to us, passing the beam across our faces. Come on, there was no point in dragging it out.

And it still took forever, rain gushing through the leaves, blinding me, running into my eyes and mouth and inside my clothing, cold and chilling my bones. Finally we reached the entrance to the cave and sagged against the rock sides, wiping our faces, looking back down the hill to the lodge with the yellow lights in the windows, smoke rising from the chimney. We gasped, sucking oxygen, legs quivering. Archie was pale as death.

Moss, bits of shrubbery, dead leaves. The cave curled back out of reach of flashlight's beam. I felt my body tensing, rebelling at the idea of going into the depths; the walls were already closing around me. My throat contracted. A furry black family of bats hung from the ceiling and I shrank back, crying out.

But Billy pushed on in and we followed, Archie in the rear. Twenty feet inside, when the first turn came, I began to stoop a bit and felt a shocking blast of cold air in my face. I didn't know the first thing about the workings of an ice cave but there was no doubt about the reality of it. Twenty feet farther and Billy stopped. Our breath hung before us in the cold. He waited for us both to catch up. Then he pushed on. There were no more bats: It was too cold, they couldn't have lived. I smelled a kind of mossy, earthy vegetation, but the primary sensation was one of bitter cold.

We must have been forty yards into the cave when it abruptly came to an end. Ice covered the sides and the back wall of the cave was covered with frost, a dirty gray slipperiness in the beam of the lamp. Billy picked up a rock and scraped at the flat frost, chipping a layer of ice away, sliding his bare hand under the brittle pane of ice, pulling it away, breaking it off in sheets.

I saw pale wood behind the ice.

Heart pounding, I joined him, cracking the ice and pulling it away. It was the packing case, slowly appearing beneath our frenzy, pale and rough and preserved, the wires connected at the side, wires rusting and frozen tight. I grabbed the first one, felt it tear a fingernail, felt my hand finally lose its feeling from the cold. It took us fifteen minutes to pry the wires back and when they were undone, we stood back looking into each other's eyes, afraid at the end to open it.

Archie had been watching. As our energies and courage flagged, he stepped between us, a wet, bedraggled, frail old man. Without a word he reached forward, took hold of the case's lid, and with a mighty tug yanked it open.

They were frozen. Frost clung to them like white moss. Her face was caked with brown blood. The flesh had sunk against the bones. . . .

"It's them," Archie said.

25

THE face of the woman in the case lingered in my mind like childhood's nightmares, the visage of grinning, mocking death. There was no illusion of life, no after-image of the woman she'd been. The flesh, while preserved, had dehydrated as the years had passed and the skin had sunk back against the skull, pulling tight, leaving the dried eyeballs to bulge obscenely from their sockets. The teeth protruded in a travesty of a grin and the dark brown blood on her face had turned dry and flaky. The head had been twisted at an unnatural angle when the bodies were forced to fit in the packing case and Maxvill's face had been buried in the collar of Rita's coat; they formed a heap of clothing and crisscrossed limbs, like a tumbling act that had come suddenly to grief and never been untangled.

Billy was gone. It was well past midnight and the fire had burned low. Archie and I sat quietly, shocked into silence, slowly drying out, scraping caked mud from our shoes and clothing. The rain drummed steadily on. I pitched a parched log into the failing embers and the bark ignited, curling in a burst of flames. I rubbed my eyes and tried to ignore the ache in my bones.

Archie and I had jammed the packing case closed, rewired the fastenings by the light of Billy's torch. The Indian, shrugging in disgust at more of the white man's inexplicable goings-on, had left us, gone to the entrance of the cave to wait while we reburied the dead. Then the three of us slipped and slid back down from the ice cave and took some time to recover by the fire. Billy washed his hands of the whole mess. He said his conscience was clear; it was up to us what was done about it. He left without shaking hands but there had been no particular malice. He just wanted to be rid of us and our vile little night games. I didn't blame him. His face seemed to say that if we wanted to cover it all up again, that was our business. White man's business. . . .

I kept thinking of the thing in the packing case as Rita Hook . . . wife of Ted, sister of Patricia, mother of Kim and Larry, lover of Carver Maxvill. She had never gotten away from Grande Rouge after all. She'd been waiting on ice for thirty years to be found and now that we had come there was nothing for us to do. No recourse, no justice, no way of extracting payment for her mean, solitary going. She had gone to the trouble of posting a lookout, a witness in case anything bad happened to her, and he had seen the worst happen, had watched her run for her life and not make it, had called it white man's business. And he had kept his secret to himself.

We finally left the place of ghosts, climbed into Archie's big car, and slowly wheeled through the mud back toward the real world. I didn't even look back at it. I knew what it looked like. I drove across the killing ground, where the bodies had fallen, and I didn't figure I was coming back.

We were making the right turn at Grande Rouge, still in the middle of the night, when Archie finally spoke.

"Well, we were wrong. Carver Maxvill was an innocent man. Innocent and dead the whole damned time!" His voice crackled, anger spilling over. "It fit, it was so perfect. . . . Jesus, I'd have sworn we had it. It *should* have happened that way. I don't care . . . plots are my business, for God's sake!"

"We'd better rethink," I said. "There's still a killer loose. . . ."

He grunted assent.

"I figure Kim told Larry the truth about their relationship, that they were brother and sister, and that's why she instigated the divorce. Makes sense, right?" I was exercising all my self-control when I spoke of Kim; inside me there was a long wail of fear for her safety, the wish that I'd made her understand more clearly, deeply, what I felt for her. But Archie wouldn't have been impressed and I'd have gone to pieces had it come out. And it would have done her no good. The best I could do was keep as clear a mind as I could.

"She told him that much of it," I went on. "No one in the club knew that anyone had witnessed what they did that night. . . . Almost thirty years had come and gone, it must have nearly passed from their memories . . . but suppose Larry listened to Kim and didn't like what he heard, argued with her, refused to believe her—and to convince him she let him have the rest of it, the story that the group had murdered their mother. You can imagine what that must have done to his poor, downtrodden soul. So, as one last attempt at normality, say he went to one of the club, hoping against hope to be told that it wasn't true, of course it wasn't true; just the ravings of a dying Indian. . . . He tries to talk Kim out of it in the parking lot, where Bill Oliver sees them, but she's adamant—that's her nature, facing up to the blows that come your way, overcoming them. . . .

"But it's not Larry's way. He wants to be told they're not the blows they appear to be. So who would he naturally go to to corroborate or disprove what Kim had said?"

Archie stirred. "Tim Dierker. He lived in the same building."

"Of course, Tim Dierker. Thoughtfully, Larry doesn't want to run the risk of disturbing Harriet, so he asks Tim to come to his apartment. The gray fluff on the floor. . . . Tim leaves it when he visits Larry. And Larry puts it to him. He may not tell Tim where he heard the story, but he asks him if it's true. . . . Are he and Kim brother and sister? And did the club kill Rita and Maxvill?

"I can see it now, Dad. Old Tim is a dying man, he's in an alcoholic fog most of the time, he's been sitting around looking at his scrapbooks, remembering the way it was . . . the *good* times . . . and now this specter arises, like a messenger of God, asking him to confess his sins . . . giving him the *opportunity* to confess, to leave with a clean slate. So the old man breaks down—

yes, he says, yes, we did it, we thought we had our reasons, and we killed them and we hid the bodies where they'd never be found. . . . And yes, we knew that all we could do was see to it that Rita's children were taken care of, we kept track of both of you, we sent money for your education, we knew who you were, where you were . . . and when chance brought Kim and Larry together, as strangers, it wasn't just a coincidence. Kim naturally went to them at Norway Creek, her benefactors . . . and maybe the story Tim told Harriet about Larry just showing up one day was just plain bullshit—a man like Tim could have arranged for Larry to hear there was a good job at the paint company. And hiring Larry would have been another way of salving what must have been a pretty beaten-up conscience. . . ."

The road unwound through the dark like a tape. The rain blew in gusts across my vision and we were utterly alone. The smell of the lake seeped in everywhere, like a fragrant gas, keeping us alert.

"When Kim and Larry met and, against the odds, fell for each other, what the hell could Tim do? What could any of them do?

"Well, we know what Tim did. Harriet told us—he did everything he could to dissuade Larry from marrying her, he went into a decline when he failed, but he couldn't actually tell Larry the truth. So he sat by and let it happen. . . . And now Larry's worst fears have been confirmed, his life is a ruin, as he sees it, and it finally drives him to suicide." I looked over at Archie, who was nodding slowly. "So that makes three lives Tim's got on his conscience. . . . He in turn unburdens himself to the group, tells them that Larry knew. What do the members of the club do? Say they all know, say they all go into a kind of collective shock—they don't know what to do but they're afraid, they're old men, one of them may spill the beans . . . perhaps Tim actually blithers on about it, says he's got to tell, that there's been enough death, that they can never escape the guilt of what happened thirty years before. . . . Now they're all in a moral quandary, the atmosphere is such that the truth might actually come out . . . All of them but one. One knows damn well how he feels, he doesn't want any nonsensical, sentimental idiot telling the truth. They could all still be ruined, the scandal would stand Minneapolis upside down. And one of them cannot even bear the possibility of such disclosures. So he kills Tim when the pressure gets to be too much. And having killed one, it becomes easier to eliminate the others—something has damn well snapped inside his head, he sees his old pals weakening, loosening their grip, so he kills them. He figures there's less danger in that than in letting them live. All it takes is one to tell the truth, to show the authorities where the bodies are buried. . . . The question is, which one? Does he have to kill them all?"

Archie said, "Who's left? We know it's not Tim, it's not Boyle, and it's not Crocker. . . . You take Ole and me out of it and it leaves Jon Goode and Hub Anthony. Simple elimination. They're both under protective guard. One of them is a killer and the other is the next scheduled victim—can you imagine what's going through their minds? The killer must be frantic. He's got to get loose, penetrate the other's protection, kill him . . . and he's got to pray to God the other one hasn't told the whole story. Good Lord, talk about desperation!"

"Which one is it?" I asked. "Who's got the most to lose?"

"I think that's the wrong angle," Archie said. "Which one has the killer mentality? That's the man we want."

"Dierker was killed because he was a dying man with nothing to lose by telling the truth," I said. "Boyle was killed because he was religious and who knows what a priest might do in this kind of squeeze? Crocker knew who the killer was, yet he wasn't worried —this man surely wouldn't kill him, Crocker figured he was as tough as the killer, figured the killer knew he wasn't going to tell and was therefore safe. So much for Crocker's belief in friendship and being chums together. . . ."

"It's Goode, of course," Archie said tonelessly.

"Obviously," I said. "Born killer."

We drove quietly through the small, dark towns, past the all-night filling stations with their lonely, desolate gas pumps, the single light bulbs dangling behind rain-spattered windows. Deep night, a steady cold rain, northern Minnesota; just about the end of the world. A kind of loneliness all its own and it matched what was going on inside me.

Kim wasn't going to kill herself. But Goode was going to go after her. I knew it. Larry had had to find out the truth from someone and Jon Goode was no fool. He'd figured it out. He'd left the note and the gun. And if he figured out that much, he'd know she wasn't going to kill herself. She was no Larry, no weakling. He was going to have to hit her.

We should have had the son of a bitch pegged from the beginning. Of all people, I should have known. Goode was a killer, up close or by remote control. People dying was his way of life. Mercy wasn't among his qualities. Never had been.

"Goode was the one who did the shooting," Archie said, as if he were reading my mind. "They were all guilty, of course, but Goode was the only one with the guts to pull the trigger on Maxvill and Rita. Probably enjoyed it."

Poor Rita. The blackmailer. But what in the world did she have on them? Why had they paid so long? Were we ever going to know? Carver and she, the lovers—they were blackmailers together. What in the world had the lads done?

We put the movements of General Jon Goode together from evidence that became available later. This is what he was doing as we stopped for breakfast at a small town off the freeway north of the Twin Cities. The rain had slackened to a heavy mist and the morning at six o'clock was a murky gray. Fog hovered a few feet above the fields stretching flatly away on either side of the roadway. We settled tiredly into a wooden booth. Archie's face was gray and lined, his eyelids drooped, he sipped anxiously at his hot coffee.

General Goode arose early that same morning, moved stealthily around the master bedroom, which ran the length of his home on the second floor. A window and small balcony faced Lake Harriet. At the other end of the bedroom French windows with translucent curtains stretched at top and bottom on antique brass rods opened onto a sun deck which had a fine view of his backyard rock garden and faded flowers.

Downstairs a plainclothes detective dozed lightly before a television set. *Sunrise Semester* was providing a low background din and every few minutes the detective's eyelids fluttered open to prove to himself that he wasn't asleep. The aroma of hot freshly perked coffee saturated the first floor, and the detective, who had brewed it at five o'clock, when the danger of sleeping was greatest, roused himself to work at his second cup. He wasn't asleep but he wasn't awake either and if Jon Goode made any noise, the cop didn't hear it.

Another police officer was stationed in a patrol car parked directly in front of Goode's house. He was wide awake reading a Ross Macdonald novel, *The Zebra-Striped Hearse,* and spent several moments chatting with the newspaper boy at six forty-five. He did not see any movement from the house and certainly was unaware that General Goode had left the premises.

Which wasn't surprising, considering the fog growing thick with the coming of morning and the fact that the general made his exit down the fire escape ladder from the rear sun deck. He wore Addidas running shoes, gray sweat pants and sweat shirt, a yellow nylon jacket with a string-tied hood. He dropped softly to the wet grass, crossed the yard, went through a break in the privet hedge, traversed the back lawns of two neighbors, and appeared three hundred yards down the street from the parked police patrol car. He was hidden by three hundred yards of nearly palpable fog.

In his right hand he carried a small gray canvas bag with a tan leather strap. The bag contained a .45-

caliber service revolver with grips of inlaid ivory. Set against the ivory was an engraved plate on which a message could still be read: FOR JON GOODE . . . MY KIND OF SOLDIER . . . GEORGE S. PATTON. The gun was loaded. General Goode meant business.

Walking briskly, he reached the lake and began to jog. He was following his usual pattern, a creature of discipline and habit. He tucked the canvas bag under his arm. The waves sucked at the shore. He felt the tension leaving his body as his feet lightly hit the path. He was in perfect condition, in body and mind. Twice around the lake would do it. Then to business. So concentrated was he on the blending of muscle and lungs and brain, beating out the rhythm of his step, that he failed to notice the large automobile which slid past him in the fog, its headlights blurred, its shape moving like a dream just beyond consciousness. He didn't notice that it pulled down off the road into the parking lot by the curved shell where the bands of summer played so merrily. The lights snapped off. The general kept running, coming closer to the green benches, the shuttered popcorn stand. He heard his own breath, sensed the dinghies bobbing on the water to his right. He was watching the ground, enjoying the hint of tiredness he knew he could overcome. There was no end to his confidence. He squeezed the canvas bag with the revolver close to his body.

For some reason we'll never know, he glanced up.

Someone in a raincoat was standing in the path ahead of him. Someone with a gun.

26

"So MUCH for that theory," Archie muttered into the turned-up collar of his Burberry. He was beside himself, powerless, mystified by the continuing demolition of his theories. It was cold by the lake. Bernstein had called us at eleven o'clock; we were trying to nap at my apartment. Now he was slouched over the body lying on the path. One bullet had been fired into the center of Jon Goode's face and gone out the back of his neat little head, which was conspicuously less neat now. He lay on his back in the path, arms flung out at his sides as if at the last moment someone had decided not to crucify him after all and had drilled him instead. The canvas bag had already been taken away to the police laboratory. Bernstein lit a cigarette and threw the match into a puddle.

"Detective Bernard Schultz went upstairs to check on the general at nine o'clock, having heard no action from the bedroom." He paused for dramatic effect. "The general was not only gone, he was probably already dead. Officer Hathaway hadn't seen anything at the front of the house. The goddamn fog was just about impenetrable but it finally occurred to them that the old bastard might have sneaked out to do his roadwork. They found him about an hour ago. I called you out of habit. If I had to go look at a murder victim without you, I'd be lonesome."

Archie and I were so far into concealing evidence by now that we couldn't open our mouths for fear of saying the wrong thing. I shrugged. "What do you make of it?"

Bernstein made a hopeless hand gesture.

"Looks like your Carver Maxvill got his limit early

369

today. It's funny. The son of a bitch is just invisible
. . . we've rousted all the elderly tourists and traveling
salesmen in the Twin Cities and all we've got is a
bunch of old bastards who hate us. I don't know,
maybe it's somebody else . . . but who?" He kicked
at a bench leg and looked over at the body with its
crowd of cops and a coroner and a photographer. Fog
lapped across the parking lot, fuzzing all the edges.

"Anyway, we'd better take pretty damn good care of
Judge Anthony—he's the only survivor if you're right
about you and Ole not counting—Christ, a judge!
Bjornstad is calling out to his place now, just making
sure he's still there. . . ."

Archie nodded. "I'm sure we're not in it. But Hub
. . . yes, you'd better keep checking, keep him closely
guarded." He clamped his jaw shut, running a finger
across his mustache, smoothing it down. Bags under
his eyes looked as if they were packed for a world
cruise.

"No bright ideas, Paul?" Bernstein favored me
with a quirky, slanted smile. "No smartass remarks?"

"No," I said.

"Well, I've got one other happy bit of news. A four-
year-old boy was bitten by a rat yesterday, eight
blocks from the sight of Crocker's fucking folly. . . .
Try and put the lid on that.'" He coughed hard, bending over his hand. "I've got another one for you, I
went to the doctor this morning. My cold, you know?
It's not a cold. He called it walking pneumonia." He
glared at me from bloodshot eyes. "Kiss me, you
fool." Then he walked away and forgot about us.

I went to the car, thankful that it wasn't the
Porsche, and Archie followed me. Inside, the heater
on, he chewed on the lower fringe of his mustache
and rubbed his eye.

"Well," he said, "we couldn't tell him . . . how the
devil could we have explained it all? And as far as
Kim goes, even if he could find her, his protection
isn't worth a tinker's damn."

"Do you want to check in with a new theory?" I
asked. He lit a cheroot and blew smoke out the win-

dow. Bernstein and his men were just shadows behind the fog.

"It's no longer a theory," he said. "It's over. You were right—it was the man with the most to lose, not the man with a killer streak. It's Hub . . . there's nobody left."

"I played tennis with him the day Larry—"

"Don't be fatuous and don't try to reconstruct everything the man's ever said to you. . . . It's Hub. Process of elimination. All that remains is to see how he plays it out. Does he pretend to be the terrified next victim or—"

"Does he go after Kim?"

Archie looked at me sideways. There was no twinkle left in his eyes, only weariness.

"He's not safe as long as she's alive and the note he left in her apartment proves he knows it." Archie licked his lips, adjusted the cheroot. "I'd say he gets loose and goes after her."

I was sick to my stomach from lack of sleep and worry. Now there was no time to rest. We had to find Kim before Hubbard Anthony did.

My last angry meeting with General Goode crossed my mind as we left the scene of his murder. His killer had gotten him right about where I had spoken with him as he materialized out of another morning's wet fog. He was the only man in the world I actually hated, the blank-faced kind of hatred that isn't very demonstrative but never lessens or changes or dies. He had stunted my life, made me one of his tools, and looking at his corpse and the shredded opening in the back of his head, I was very glad that he was dead. He deserved to die violently and the world was a measurably better place without him. He had called all men predators: Right or wrong, it was one of the predators who got him.

But the extent of the carnage was outside my ken. How, in a rational world, could all these men have been killed, men I'd spoken with, whose eyes I'd seen and voices I'd heard, whose lives I'd briefly peered into? They didn't exist anymore, yet only a short time before, they'd been there—rotters and scoundrels, perhaps, but alive. . . . Murderers, but alive. . . .

Their faces flashed before me. I was tired and it was like seeing an old movie, a reprise of the faces of the dead, laughing and smiling in better days. . . . They hadn't been able to escape the past; the thought read like something very near an immutable law. You cannot outrun the past, and as Tim Dierker had believed, in the end you are finally accountable for your life and deeds. In the end, one way or another, you paid up.

After all the poking around I'd done, the conversations that had seemed to me to have so little point at the time, after all the time wasting and finding a woman to love and catching the Twins' broadcasts and running back and forth to Archie's and discovering I was still capable of loving and worrying about someone —after all that, it all seemed to be spinning away from me, too fast, uncontrollable. There didn't seem to be any time to think. We knew the story now, what had been there behind the countless veils of subterfuge and evasion and lies. We knew who everyone really was and what they were trying to hide and we knew it was worse than we could ever have imagined. We knew that lives had been built on the decay and corruption of what men had done, that lives had been forever tainted and had finally rotted through and split open and the putrescence had seeped out. And it was lethal and the rats had been sent scurrying. There was no time to shift it, grab hold and cope with it. . . .

"Hub," I said. "For Christ's sake, Hub—how could it be Hub? I remember how shaken he was the day Larry killed himself, how shocked when he realized who it was. . . ." I remembered the sunny, perfect end-of-summer day, how he'd waited me out and worn me down, beaten me on the shade-dappled tennis courts at Norway Creek. I hadn't known Kim then. I hadn't even begun. But he was also the one who'd later told me to lay off, to stop picking at the past and scaring Father Boyle and Crocker and Goode. Then he'd had to kill them: They were too shaken; he couldn't trust them to pull themselves together, close ranks. So he had to kill them all, even the one who had been a killer himself and was George Patton's kind of soldier.

"It's Hub," Archie said sourly. "So stop nattering away about it. It won't change. Keep your mind on finding Kim."

"I know, I know."

The fog never did lift completely. From my balcony it stretched away like an inhospitable sea washing across Minneapolis, swallowing it. Archie drank coffee and I waited while the telephone rang in Grande Rouge. It was finally answered by a woman with a short temper.

"May I speak with Ted Hook?" I asked.

"You gotta be kidding," she snorted. "He can't hear on the phone, he won't talk on the phone atall. Anyway, he's taken to his bed—maybe for the last time, too, wheezin' and coughin'."

"Perhaps you can help me, then?"

"You'd better hurry it up, then. We're gettin' ready for a banquet. Whattaya want?" she snapped. If she were one of Ted's relatives, I shared his disgust.

"It's about Mr. Hook's daughter, or niece. . . . Does she happen to be there? Visiting Ted?"

"Would that be the snotty one from the Cities? What's her name?"

"Kim," I said. "Is she there?"

"Nope and thank God for that. I don't mind telling you, she's a pain, always yelling at us about not taking care of the old man. . . . No, she ain't here—"

I hung up, looked at Archie, shook my head.

I called her apartment. Nothing.

I called Anne. Nothing.

I was about to dial another number when the telephone rang. It was Mark Bernstein and he was coughing, his voice muffled. He was calling from Hub

Anthony's library and he sounded as if he'd had enough.

"He's gone." His voice whistled through stuffed nasal passages. "He found out about Goode an hour or so ago and so help me God he got away from here in the meantime. How many Excedrin can you take at a time, anyway? I've taken eight since I got up and my head's killing me. . . . So we've got to find him——"

"How did he do it? You had men there, didn't you?"

"Jesus, what difference does it make? I can't get a straight story out of these guys. . . . One of them was in the john with an upset stomach, the other was off diddling himself, I don't know. I've got a bulletin out on his car but I'm not much counting on it. Anyway, I thought you might like to know. . . . If Archie gets any ideas about where he might go to hide, get hold of me." He coughed. "Poor bastard's probably scared to death. I should be in the hospital. Walking pneumonia, bullshit. I'm half dead. Good-bye, Paul. Good-bye forever and when you think of me in years to come, smile. . . ." The line went dead.

Archie said, "Don't tell me. Hub's gone."

"That's right."

"Figures. Hope blooms eternal . . . *escape*. And it's hopeless, Hub." I couldn't look at him.

I called Ole Kronstrom at his office. I asked to see him. He told us to come down. He'd be in later, at four o'clock.

The day was dripping away and Archie and I stayed awake by fueling up with lunch, force-feeding ourselves at Charlie's, washing it down with gallons of coffee. We got to Ole's office on the dot and he was alone, unwinding a muffler and hanging up his wet raincoat. He looked as tired as we did. I told him about General Goode and about Hub Anthony's disappearing act. Archie revived, now that he was on the scent, and told Ole that we had reason to believe that Hub Anthony would be the final victim if we didn't find him at once. He was so convincing that I almost believed him. We alone knew Hub was a murderer, not the final victim.

Ole looked up, leaned back in his desk chair, said nothing.

"We also have reason to believe that Kim may be in some danger," I said.

"Oh, you do?" Ole Kronstrom closed his eyes and made a bridge with his fingers. "Kim in danger," he mused. "May I ask from whom?"

"The man who killed everyone else."

"Any names come to mind?"

"No names," Archie said quickly. "Whoever it is, he must be stopped. That's all."

"But why would Kim be in danger? What has she to do with all this?" Ole opened his eyes slowly. "I'm confused. . . ."

"Are you?" Archie asked. "How confused are you, Ole?"

Ole leaned forward in his chair, picked up a pipe, and began to fill it from a humidor. He smiled slyly, slowly shaking his head. He said, "Well, let's say just slightly confused."

"We've got to find her," I said, watching them being obscure with each other. "You're more likely to have an idea where she might be than anyone else . . . think, where does she go when she gets away from it all? She goes off by herself habitually, you told me that. . . . But where?"

He lit the pipe and I smelled the thick latakia. He tamped the ash down with a stubby, calloused forefinger. While we waited, he pushed out of his chair and stood before the window. He was broad and powerfully built; age had made him settle on his foundation, not wither.

"I suppose she could have gone to the boat," he said doubtfully. "She *could* be there, I suppose . . . she might feel safe there. She likes it there." He nodded, agreeing with himself.

Archie stood up. "Has Hub ever been on your boat?"

Ole nodded glumly. "Yes, he loves it. Fancies himself quite a good sailor. . . ."

"Has he ever been there when Kim was there?" I asked.

Ole nodded again.

"I'm coming with you," he said. "It's my boat."

We were fed irrepressibly into the rush-hour traffic made worse by the fog and the beginnings of an oily rain. It was dark by six o'clock and we'd come upon a three-car accident which cut the traffic flow to one lane. An ambulance was taking on a stretcher. Another mile ahead a semitrailer had jackknifed against the median fence and again only a single lane was passable. Faces contorted in anger and frustration behind clouded windows, wheels spun on the wet pavement, a purple gasoline spill spread out from the truck. Three police cars, red lights spinning, stopped us entirely while a tow truck slid and burned rubber trying to right the leaking behemoth.

It was another hour before we had gotten free and were heading into the rain toward the St. Croix. Cooper's Falls, where the boat docked, was almost another hour's drive under the wet conditions and we listened to WCCO as we pushed on. The story of General Jonathan Goode's murder was on the news but they didn't really have much. There was a tape of Mark Bernstein saying that there really was no comment he could make at present and no, he didn't know if there were going to be any more prominent citizens murdered but he certainly hoped not. Then he coughed.

By Stillwater traffic had all but disappeared and we dropped down the long hill into the town, past the neon lights glowing through the fog, back onto the highway, where visibility was cut to almost nothing. I couldn't get it over thirty because I just couldn't see, so we sweated it out, silent, listening to the Twins at Tiger Stadium in Detroit. *Be safe,* I thought to myself, *be safe and be on that goddamn boat*. Hub was out there, too, fighting the fog, looking for her. Had he thought of the boat? I speeded up at the thought, felt the right rear tire slide off onto a muddy shoulder when I nearly missed a turn, and fought myself to slow back down. I opened my window and felt spray hit my face. Willie Horton hit a three-run homer for the Tigers in the bottom of the third when I was ten miles from the Cooper's Falls marina.

"Here it is," Ole said a bit later from the backseat. Archie jerked, came up from a snoring doze. "Take this gravel road."

I felt the change in the surface of the road. The lights picked up high grass at the side of the road, barbed-wire fencing above a gully. Gravel flew up underneath the car. Archie leaned forward. "Slow down, for God's sake. . . . I think those are fresh tracks ahead of us. . . . What am I saying? What do I know about fresh tracks?"

There was a light glowing at the entrance to the marina. I stopped when Ole gave me the word, turned off the engine. We got out and stood still in the fog. You could sense the boats, smell them and hear them moan as they moved in the water, waves slapping at the hulls. We made our way slowly out the slip beside the forty-foot Chris-Craft cabin cruiser with its gleaming brass and white paint and polished wood reflecting the blurred light from the fog lantern hanging on a post. There was a light glowing from the cabin.

"Kim," I called. "Kim, are you there?"

We waited, then Ole climbed aboard. The boat swayed gently in the water; rain sifted against us.

"Somebody's here or has been here. I don't leave lights on."

I was afraid and fear was passing through all three of us like a blade. All we had to do was open the door and step down into the cabin where the light burned. I was frantic to find Kim, to reach her before Hub Anthony did, yet I hesitated, looked from Ole to my father.

Archie pushed his hands down into the Burberry's commodious pockets. When he took his right hand out, it was filled with the revolver the killer had left for Kim.

"And what do you plan to do with that?" Ole asked softly.

27

PEERING into the eye of the barrel, I felt time drawn up tight, standing still, the deck shifting slowly beneath us. I braced myself, searched out my father's face. Archie returned my gaze, eyes flat and hard.

"If Kim Roderick is in there," he said, "I'll put this thing away and we can all breathe a sigh of relief and have a beer. If it's somebody else, I want a gun."

"All right," Ole said. "But I'd just as soon you didn't shoot up my ship."

We'd hung back as long as we could. Archie leaned forward and opened the door to the main cabin and let it swing back. There was a funny, harsh smell in the enclosure and someone was sitting on the upholstered bench at one side, leaning against the bulkhead next to the stairway that went down to the galley. The light hung from the ceiling and cast shadows which moved ominously with the rocking of the boat. The light brushed across the face looking at us. It wasn't Kim.

"Hub!" Archie exclaimed, clutching the revolver. He took a step forward, stopped nervously as Hub Anthony slowly raised a limp hand in greeting. He made a sibilant moaning sound. As we stepped closer, we saw why.

It looked like another theory shot to hell. The front of his wheat-colored boating sweater was soaked with the blood. He had been shot by somebody who had failed to kill quickly for the first time.

We drew close, Archie muttering under his breath, and it was obvious that there was nothing we could do. Blood had soaked into his khaki slacks, welling up around the belt line. As you got closer, you sniffed the sweetish blood. We stood over him. "Sit down," he croaked softly, "you make it dark, too dark. . . ." His arm dropped.

"Who did this to you?" Archie said.

"Oh, no," he said, "none of that. It's over now, it's better this way, much better, nothing left to worry about, doesn't make any difference anymore—"

"Who?" Archie repeated. "How long have you been sitting here like this?"

"Long enough," he rasped, "long enough to know I'm not leaving here . . . this is it for me. What a joke! I'm sorry, Ole, sorry about the mess. . . ."

"Hub," Ole said slowly, "Hub, who shot you?"

"What difference does it make?" Hub said, his hand fluttering at his chest, blood clotting on his fingers. "I can't tell you, it's right, it's all right. . . . I'm the last, no more killing now. . . . It's over at last. . . ."

"We know," Archie said. "We know about what happened at the lodge, about Rita and Maxvill."

Hub Anthony nodded.

"Goode actually killed them—" He broke off, coughing wetly, his body quaking, his handsome aristocratic features knotting in pain. "But we all went along with it . . . collective guilt, all willing accessories, hid the bodies in the goddamn ice cave . . . what a night that was . . . How did you find out, for Christ's sake?"

"Rita wasn't alone that night," I said, and his eyes shifted to me as if he were seeing me for the first time. "She had Running Buck watch the whole thing . . . but he never told, not until he was dying, then he got it off his conscience and told Billy Whitefoot. Billy told us. . . ."

A dreadful grin flickered on his pain-distended face. "Jesus, he knew all the time, that's rich, that's a good one. . . . Billy, Billy . . ."

"She was blackmailing you, wasn't she? She and Carver, that's why you killed them—" I stopped: His face bore a puzzled, confused grin.

"Carver? Carver blackmailing us? No, no, no, you haven't got it right at all. . . ."

Ole passed him a hammered silver flask; Hub

washed it across his mouth and immediately began coughing. Pinkish foam collected in the corners of his mouth. He shook his head violently, wiped his hand across the lips, glared at the watery stain on his tan fingers as if it offended him. He tried to straighten his back against the bulkhead, exerting himself, Archie's arm helping to steady him, but it was too much, he was wounded too badly. As he strained upward, something seemed to break inside his chest, and thick dark blood gushed out of his mouth, poured down his chin, and soaked into the sweater. Ole groaned behind me and the sleeve of Archie's Burberry went dark.

There was a terrible obscenity in seeing Hubbard Anthony's natural grace and elegance awash in his own gore. My premier tennis partner, Christ's sake, a murderer murdered, leaking like something in a packing plant, his chest pumping blood, foaming like surf on his chin, his life draining away. Who had shot him? If the killing wasn't done, I thought again of myself. The killer had had a crack at me and missed. And maybe it wasn't over, after all.

The hemorrhaging had stopped finally and Hub was laughing without making a sound, his even white teeth dark red with gouts of blood clinging like leeches.

"Not Carver," he whispered, vastly amused now that the end was at hand and we'd made a joke. "Not old Carver . . . she was blackmailing all of us, Carver, too, all of us . . . aw, hell, it was a long time ago, Arch, people were different then, they cared about the way things looked . . . we were very young, naïve, didn't know what the hell was going on. . . . And Rita. . . ." A smile crossed the blood-streaked face. Ole was edging toward the door, groping for a handhold, his face ashen. "Rita was a woman of the world, she knew how to use us . . . how to make us pay. . . ."

I leaned forward, ignoring the fresh smell of blood. His fingers were sunk into the folds of his sweater, clutching his chest.

"But what did she have on you, Hub?" I cleared my throat. I looked into his eyes, squinting in pain, sunk deep into his face. "What did she know?"

He looked away, grimacing, moaning. Archie had tried to look at the wound but it was hidden, secret. It was swamped in blood, matted, much too far along. Archie stared at his hands, dismay on his face.

"Oh, God," Hub said, a haze of delirium shielding him from reality, "oh, God, I'm going to die and I'm so damned hungry. . . . I haven't eaten for two days, too scared. . . . I knew I was going to get it, but I didn't know who was going to do it. . . . Jon, I thought. . . ." Tears began to slide down his cheeks. He didn't want to say good-bye, was fighting it. "Shit, now I'm done for and all I can think is I'm never going to have another sandwich, another Reuben . . . another hot pastrami on an onion roll and some cole-slaw. . . ." He looked up at me and winked slowly. "I know, Paul, I know, I'm sounding crazy, no great last words. . . . You've got to lose some weight and shape up your backhand, learn to hit through on your backhand, don't be afraid to hit it hard. . . . Oh, God, I'm so hungry. . . ."

Archie was sobbing to himself, wiping tears away and bloodying his face in the process.

"Why was she blackmailing you, Hub?" I had to know. I had to know what Rita knew. It was like picking a dead friend's pocket but I kept at it.

"Christ, you're so dense," he whispered wetly. "She was our woman. . . . Rita was our whore, we all used to screw her . . . all the time, passing her around, some weekends she'd never have a stitch on from Friday night till Monday morning . . . we'd take turns, I don't think we ever satisfied her . . . we'd have her till we dropped. . . ." He chuckled; it stuck in his throat. "That was our deal, we paid her plenty, gave her bonuses, she salted away a lot of money over those twelve, thirteen years . . . we were paying her a thousand a month, Tim and Jim and Jon and Marty and Carver—fifty a week from each of us, we got our money's worth . . . it was the Depression, a lot of money for her. . . ." His eyes were closed now, he was quiet, hands still, voice droning on. He was composing himself for wherever he was going.

"She had two children and we increased the money

each time, we wanted to be fair with her . . . somebody's rubber broke or didn't get put on. . . ." There was more bubbling red laughter, eyes squeezed shut.

"My God," I said, "who was the father? Larry's father? Kim's?"

"That's life's little joke, isn't it? Who could tell? How would we ever be able to know? We used her all the time, somebody was always running up and having her. . . ."

I shrank back, exhausted. I felt myself falling away in disgust. Was it what they had done? Or was it that I loved Kim, that I knew what it had done to her, how it had shaped her life? I wasn't a big believer in tragedy among the common folk, but it struck me that there was tragedy in this, fate working itself out, winding like a snake around an innocent, a child.

"But you killed her," Archie said. "You were paying her. Why kill her?"

"She wanted more, another hundred and fifty thousand, in one lump . . . we couldn't handle that, it was too much . . . she threatened us, she had pictures she'd taken of us and we'd taken of her . . . it was the old story, our wives would get sets of the pictures, our friends, our enemies, she was really sticking it to us . . . well, Jon had a bellyful, he'd brought this gun Patton had given him, he killed them. . . . Carver tried to protect her, he thought killing her was nuts . . . so Jon shot him and then he shot Rita . . . we all went along with it. What the hell else were we going to do?"

"So who shot you?" It was Ole.

"There's been enough killing . . . it'll stop here. Let it all die with me. . . . We got about what we deserved. It all just caught up with us. . . ."

"Who killed you?" Archie asked, insistent, badgering. "Who?"

"Aha, I'm not killed yet . . . but I sure am hungry. . . ."

That was all. Hubbard Anthony was dead.

Archie and I had grown accustomed to death and Ole Kronstrom was not the type to panic. Together, with the awful relief of those left alive, we went down to the galley and Ole brewed coffee and spiked it with brandy. It steamed in the tight quarters and we drank it silently, avoiding one another's eyes.

Finally Archie said into his cup, under his breath, "Another theory, my last, down the drain. Wrong on all counts. Nothing but victims . . . no killer." He sighed and inspected the blood all over his raincoat. "And now we find out that, no matter how you cut it, they deserved to die. Where does that leave us, then?"

"Not wanting to find a murderer," Ole said, clinking his spoon against the cup. "Executioner, I should say."

"But he's still loose, whatever the hell you call him," I said. "Don't forget, he tried to kill me. . . ." I looked from one to the other. The old men were worn thin. "The thing is, who is it? There's nobody left. . . . But Kim's still in danger. If he hasn't found her yet."

"Maybe," Archie said. The enthusiasm was gone. He was through.

"Give me the gun," I said to Archie. He fished it out of his pocket and I put it in mine.

We decided to leave the boat and report the death of Hub Anthony the next day. Ole would simply go out to work on his boat and discover the body, stiff and cold. We finished the coffee, went past the remains, turned out the light, and climbed back on deck. A biting cold was coming with the fog and rain. We were carrying on the obfuscation the club had begun forty years ago when they began making their deals with Rita. I swung over the side and felt solid ground again.

We drove back to Minneapolis and dropped Ole at his darkened parking lot. It was midnight and the city was quiet in the cold rain.

"I've got to find Kim," I said.

"You're the one to do it, Paul. You're the one now. . . ." Ole shook my hand.

I drove Archie back to my place. I got him bundled up under blankets. I made him a hot toddy and told him to go to sleep. He looked like an old man. He smiled halfheartedly and accepted the toddy.

"I've got to find her, Dad, you know that. I love her. . . ."

"It's over, Paul," he said sleepily. "It's over for me, anyway, the ones who had to die are dead. Very nicely rounded off. . . . Take the gun, go find Kim, but I think the killing is over. . . . Just find the woman, that's all. That's all that's left. . . . You see, Billy— we forgot about Billy. And he doesn't know Kim's gone. . . . He wouldn't kill her, would he? What they did to her . . . that's why he killed them." He ran his tongue over dry lips, closed his eyes. Tired.

I kissed my father impulsively and went downstairs to his car. There was someone standing in the shadows outside in visitors' parking. The rain splattered on the tarmac and I felt the hair on my neck stiffen. The shadowy figure moved, came toward me. I flattened myself against the wall, rain dripping in my face. I felt for the gun. The figure stepped into the light. It was the Pinkerton man. He smiled and went inside.

I knew where I was going. I knew where Kim was and I was trying to arrange the whole story in my weary mind. I had to drive north and there was so little time.

28

I HEADED out on the freeway toward Duluth in the dead of the cold, wet night, wipers working methodically across the vast expanse of glass fronting Archie's automobile. The rain spit out of the darkness and I drove twenty-mile stretches without seeing another pair of headlamps. Franklin Hobbs was cooing his way through the night on WCCO. Frank Sinatra sang

"Time After Time" and I remembered the words from high school romances. Al Hibbler sang "Unchained Melody" and I let the huge car take over. I felt oddly peaceful, alone, free of surprises and things I could neither control nor understand. I still wasn't having much success at getting a moral fix on what had been going on but I realized with a sense of ironic detachment that I was at least able to be calm while considering it. My nose didn't hurt much anymore. I was tired but I wasn't dead and that put me ahead of the game.

As the invisible night slipped past outside, I hummed to the music and thought about it all, calmly, rationally, analytically. There was, in the first place, the enormity of what the lads had done to Rita and Carver that night at the lodge. Frightened, frustrated —but also arrogant, full of the certainty that they could kill and get away with it. Why? What made them so sure, so confident? I was no psychologist; I made no pretense of knowing the answer. The fact was they'd done it and they had gotten away with it, almost. . . . A quirk, a freak had brought them to grief, an old man who might just as well have taken his secret to the grave. And even if he'd only made his deathbed confession, it took the unlikely marriage of Kim to *both* Billy and Larry to crystalize the mordant joke.

In the second place there was the awesome retribution visited on the lads from thirty years' distance. They had sat on their guilt so long, had let the insulation of time cut them off from the unpleasantness; it must almost have passed into misty legend, even for them. Remembered like wartime experiences, heroics and cowardice, the moral imperative of the act long since bled dry. It had happened and there was nothing to be done; there would be no summons from the icy grave.

But they had been unfortunate: Someone had not been quite so willing to let bygones be bygones, someone had carried the past inside, the seeds of retribution, someone whose morality demanded an accounting. And so had waited for them at the end.

At some sticking point, in one determined, unforgiving soul, the caldron had finally boiled over. *You will not go free,* an inner voice had said, authority echoing, *You will pay for your sins.* I shook my head and wiped my eyes; too Biblical. Still, the idea was about right.

But who had known it all? And why had it come so long after the fact?

The Maxvill theory had fit so beautifully: Back from the chasm of anonymity, life in shambles and nearing the end, he had struck back and finished them off. But he'd been dead for thirty years.

The Goode theory had made sense, too. He'd been a killer all his life and now, in a spasm of fear, he saw his comrades threatening to clear the fields of their consciences. . . . A collective conscience or only one, it made no difference: The truth from whatever source was working its way back to the surface after all those years of safety. . . . But then someone killed him, too.

The Hub Anthony theory made a kind of sense as well as seeming to be the only one left: Everyone else was dead, *ergo* the one remaining . . . etc. The judge, the man with the most to lose, the final irony of elegance and style driven to foulest murder; he had fit the killer-from-within-the-group scenario. And at that point you took whoever happened to be left and made the facts fit. But he was shot to death, too.

They were all dead and Agatha Christie would have loved it. Their lives had gone rotten early on and yet they had lived them out, trying to hide the truth with respectability. Martin Boyle . . . I remembered our discussion of evil, cast now in an entirely different light. A *priest.* . . . A football hero, a soldier, a judge, a businessman. . . .

Someone hadn't forgotten. Someone hadn't let them off the hook.

Billy. Why had he never really crossed my mind? Because he was an Indian, because I was a part of Minnesota, because an Indian was our invisible man? Because a motive never occurred to me . . . because he wasn't one of *us,* those of us who seemed a part of the present? Because he had seemed to help, because he'd finally been the one who had revealed the most to us, most dramatically?

What did I know about him, after all?

For one thing, he still loved Kim. He held nothing against her, found her guilty of nothing. He lived with their daughter—the image of Kim—always before him. He hadn't remarried. And he knew what they'd done to her mother, to her life . . . he knew about Larry, the fact that Larry was Kim's brother. If he loved Kim still, he didn't need more of a motive than that. . . .

And he knew about death. He knew what had happened to his father; any Indian in Minnesota had had his brush with death. And he probably honored a code of behavior; he felt certain compulsions. He may have accepted the necessity for retribution. And who knew what he felt about the overall justification for killing some rich white men? Surely he knew the story of the club's raid on the Indian whorehouse.

Once you made the assumption that he could kill, it all made sense. A motive of love and hate. And nobody had ever checked his alibi. From Jasper he could easily have made his forays into Minneapolis, made his kill and gotten out . . . the invisible man. He could even tell us the story of the club's murders without fear. In the first place, it stood to reason that no killer would make such a revelation, drawing himself into matters when he might have stayed clear, and, in the second place, by telling us Running Buck's story he was able to put into words the justification for his actions—proving once again, if only to himself, that he was an executioner, not a murderer. . . .

Billy. The idea played in my mind, darting here, there, like a figure in a shooting gallery, the one you could never quite hit.

I wasn't altogether sure I was safe. I might still be a candidate for the role of Last Victim. But I knew that I would rather have it be me than Kim, which is, I suppose, a commentary on what rediscovering love can do to your mind. It wouldn't be Kim, not if I could help it.

Perhaps I was slow to see the truth of it, the only

pattern that made sense. I've trekked back and forth over the same ground hundreds of times since that night, trying to discern an alarum, a flare in the night which might have warned me . . . but hindsight is irrelevant. I don't know if it should have occurred to me earlier or not; in any case, it hadn't, not until I was north of Duluth and it was a dark-gray five o'clock in the morning. That was when I finally realized who had been killing these old men. . . . I almost smiled at it. Not quite, but almost. It had a very pure, cold kind of beauty to it. It chilled me. I felt as if icy water were closing all around me, numbing and tightening off all feeling, all sensibility, all ideas of right and wrong. I had to get to Kim before something awful happened.

I left Archie's car in the shelter of some high, ragged brush and picked my way along the wet, sandy path toward the miniature castle she'd shown me. The rain had stopped and a stiff breeze strafed the beach, whipping the whitecaps on the steel-gray lake. I trudged on, head down, hands pushed into pockets, the gun feeling cold and alive, like a docile reptile. I was out of breath when I slid across the wet stone shingle and reached the castle. There was a fire going under a pot of coffee and two cups were placed neatly on a flat rock.

I stood beside the wall, sheltering from the wind, and saw the bronze Mark IV above on the level of the narrow roadway. I could see them down past the edge of the rock slabs, standing on the beach looking out at the vicious, swirling lake. She wore Levi's, her army jacket, and her hair was loose, blowing in the wind. Her arms were crossed across her chest and she strode slowly along the sand, gulls swooping around her, water advancing toward her. He walked beside her, watching the sand.

She was still alive and I felt a long sigh escape me, my body relaxing. I watched her pace slowly along the rock shelf, spray exploding as she moved. Fog banks a mile out were moving inland.

She looked up finally and saw me, walked toward me, across the seventy yards of rock and beach. He

stood alone, watched her moving away. I took her in
as she came nearer; the flat gaze of her eyes, the pur-
poseful walk, the slender boyish body I'd never known.
When she was near, I stepped forward and held her;
her arms went around me, her face beside mine, her
grip strong and lingering.

"You're all right," I said. "I was so afraid I'd be
too late, you'd be dead and that would be all there
was. . . ." I heard her breathing, felt the rise and fall
of her in my arms, "Oh, God, I love you," I said. "I
love you and I don't know what to do about it. . . ."
My emotions were being turned inside and out. I
felt raw, exposed, cheated, fooled, finished. I was in
over my head, had been from the beginning, and now
it was too late. I knew too much not to know all of
it.

I kissed her and she finally pulled her head away,
looking away toward where he stood, straight, far
away with gray water beyond.

"I knew you'd come. I asked Billy to come wait
with me," she said, watching my eyes. "I knew you'd
find me if I came here and waited . . . but I didn't
want to be alone." She smiled, looked away, rubbed
her nose in the wind. "You're like an extra side of
myself—I wish I knew what that meant, for better or
worse. . . . I knew I'd never be able to hide from you
. . . or hide anything from you." She took a few steps
past me, turned at the entrance to the tiny castle. "I've
made us coffee, Paul." I followed her inside. She
stripped off the army jacket. She wore a heavy blue
oiled wool sweater and knelt by the fire, poured me a
cup of steaming black coffee. I wanted her near me
forever. It was all unspeakably sad. "Well," she said,
"is it time to talk it through?"

"Yes." I sat down on the rock ledge so I could look
down at her small, perfect face, watched as she pursed
her lips and sipped the coffee. She was perfect. There
was color in her cheek, a glitter in her eyes, her dark
hair shone. "You might as well tell me the whole
truth this time. They're all dead now. . . . You and
I are the only ones left, kiddo. Two survivors. And
him." I nodded toward the lake.

"Is the killing over?" she asked.

"Oh, I think so. Unless you or I get it in the denouement. What do you think? Is it over?"

"We'll see, I suppose. It's like everything else in life. Game's never over till the last man's out. Isn't that what you baseball fans say? Till the last man is out?"

I nodded. "Take me through it. . . . You've never told me all you know, Kim. And I realized a couple of hours ago that you know it all. Don't you?"

When she had finished telling me the story, she stood up and stepped outside. There was a yellow haze in the sky over the lake and the breeze was warmer. I smelled the lake and the wet sand and the beach grass. She looked back at me, took a deep breath, and strolled back down toward the water's edge. I stared after her, then sank back down beside the fire, filled my cup with the coffee's dregs, and went outside. The sun was struggling to burn a hole through the fog. I saw my shadow on the castle wall and leaned there, watching her get smaller. My hand wasn't shaking and I wasn't breathing hard. I wondered if Billy was still there, waiting. It didn't make any difference anymore.

She knew the whole story and laid it out for me with the kind of precision that was her custom. She had put it together herself. It was, like everyone else's theory, perfect.

In 1931 the hunting and fishing club had been formed and the lodge near Grande Rouge had been built. That same year Rita married Ted Hook, bar owner and disabled veteran of the Great War, many years her senior. During the winter of 1931–1932 the club hired Rita Hook to run their lodge for them, do the cooking, keep it shipshape and attended year round. At the same time, she struck a bargain with the well-reared young blades from Minneapolis: She would serve as a ready and willing sexual partner for the entire group; it was a package deal for the enterprising Mrs. Hook, for which she was paid the handsome sum of one thousand dollars per month.

Late in 1932 Rita Hook gave birth to a son, Robert,

and it was assumed that Ted Hook, not so frail as he appeared, was the father. In fact, Kim later learned, the father was a member of the group, though it was quite impossible to say which member. The group, as far as Rita's services were concerned, consisted of Timothy Dierker, James Crocker, Father Martin Boyle, Jonathan Goode, Hubbard Anthony, and Carver Maxvill.

Eight years passed and life in Grande Rouge proceeded nicely. Rita was saving her money, laying countless plans, toying with the thoughts of her future as if they were moving-picture scenarios; a small-town girl who knew there was a great world and was doing what she could to reach it. But in 1940 she discovered she was again pregnant, a victim of either urgency or carelessness. She had no idea which one might be the father but knew that Ted could not be taken in again: Their sexual relationship, pitiful as it had been in the best of times, had ended not long after the birth of little Robert.

Always quick with a scheme, she concealed her own pregnancy, telling Ted that her sister in Chicago, who was not particularly robust, was pregnant by her sailor husband, who was off at sea as usual. Since she was alone and puny, she had written to ask Rita to visit her until the baby was born. Ted Hook didn't really care one way or the other. Rita went. She lived with her sister, who wasn't pregnant but was alone, and had her second child, a girl called Shirley. Rita brought the girl back to Grande Rouge, relating the sad events of her sister Patricia's death in childbirth. It never occurred to anyone in Grande Rouge that something might be amiss. Chicago was awfully far away and, besides, who was there to care?

The members of the club accepted Rita's request for an increase in her monthly check. After all, she had had two children by them and had been useful; she had retained her looks and her sexual performance remained quite unlike anything they were likely to find at home. But by 1944, with Robert twelve and Shirley four, Rita Hook had begun to feel that it was now or never. The years were gathering a weight of their own. If she wanted to escape, she would have to do it. The club members by then had grown prosperous and prominent. They could, she surmised, afford one final payoff and a good-bye kiss.

She arranged for them all to visit the lodge the night of December 16, 1944. Without precisely threatening them, she flexed her muscles a bit, made sure they understood that attendance was mandatory. With Running Buck to drive her and watch the goings-on, she went to the lodge that dreadful night. She trusted Running Buck: He was mute when it came to blabbing white people's affairs. She trusted him; she had told him most of the truth of her relationship with the club members, secure in the knowledge that he would never tell. She had needed to tell *someone*. . . .

Her suggestion of a final payoff had not gone over well with her employers. She had moved on to overt blackmail threats. General Goode snapped, chased her out into the snow with a gun in his hand. Carver Maxvill had tried to intervene, to protect her. General Goode shot and killed them both and the entire group joined in burying the bodies in the ice cave. Running Buck never told what he had seen. The two orphans, Robert and Shirley, were clearly too much for Ted Hook. He arranged, in the aftermath of his wife's "disappearance" (she was never found—neither was Maxvill; the investigation at the lodge was cursory, without evidence of foul play), for the children to go to an orphanage, the Sacred Heart, in Duluth. They moved on to new homes. Robert becomes Larry Blankenship in Bemidji and Shirley becomes Kim Roderick in Duluth. With the power of their positions and Martin Boyle's Catholic connections, the club keeps track of their two children. A sense of duty which in the end was the proof that sealed their unhappy fates. The year was 1945.

Larry Blankenship never returned to Grande Rouge. He had no interest in learning of his father's life or in what had happened to little Shirley. He rejected his past, blacked it out; at twelve he had been wounded too deeply by his "father's" refusal to keep him. He washed his hands of the whole thing. He became Larry Blankenship.

But Kim, or Shirley, had retained a relationship with Ted Hook. By 1956, when she was sixteen, she was visiting him regularly in the summer, helping out in the roadhouse/motel Ted had built with the $150,000 Rita had saved from her monthly checks. Again, in another time and place, that $150,000 might have led to involved, finally incriminating investigations . . . but not in Grande Rouge. Ted had blinked hard and gotten his hands on the money. He had lived in Grande Rouge a long time. He knew the right people. He got the money.

While working in the restaurant, Kim at sixteen met Running Buck's putative nephew, Billy Whitefoot, a handsome Indian boy with nice manners and a gentle way about him. Nature, as it will, took its course. During the summer of 1957 they became lovers. In 1958, having graduated from high school in Duluth, Kim went to Minneapolis and applied for a job at the Norway Creek Club, the city's most impressive old-line country club. Why Norway Creek? Because she had come briefly to know the members of the hunting and fishing club during the summers she'd worked at Ted's. Though she couldn't have known it then, they had sent money for her expenses to the Rodericks in Duluth, explaining their generosity in terms of concern for the unfortunate child of a devoted servant who had run off leaving her children and ailing husband to fend for themselves. Kim did, of course, know who the men were when she met them in Grande Rouge at Ted's. They spoke highly of "poor" Rita, expressed regret about her disappearance, and seemed nice . . . that was her word. Nice. She knew them only fleetingly but, yes, they were nice well-to-do men.

Which was what brought her to Norway Creek in 1958. They were the only people she knew in Minneapolis but they were enough. In eighteen years, the first eighteen years of her life, she'd gotten to Minneapolis. Her mother had never made it. Each generation, she learned, betters itself. She was trying. But the city frightened her.

To combat the fear of being alone in the city, she urged Billy Whitefoot to come to Norway Creek as well. Her friends at Norway Creek, the nice gentlemen from the lodge, made sure that Billy was hired as a groundkeeper and general maintenance man. The nice gentlemen never realized that Billy had been close to Running Buck and if they had, it would have made no difference. They had no way of knowing that Running Buck had been watching the night they committed two murders.

It was 1959. Kim Roderick married the Indian boy, who was one year her senior. She was pregnant. Their daughter was born in 1960 and by that time she realized that the marriage had been a terrible mistake. She had seen some of what life could provide and Billy, so far as she could tell, wasn't part of it. Realizing her disinterest, he began drinking and finally left Norway Creek more or less in disgrace. He took his child with him and fled back to the north, where he was safe, where he could think and recover from Kim Roderick, who was moving on, perfecting her tennis game, catching the eye of a well-off gentleman who had been a peripheral member of the hunting and fishing club—sufficiently peripheral that he knew nothing of the arrangement the other members had with Rita Hook, that Kim was the club's daughter. . . . His name was Ole Kronstrom. He was a partner of Tim Dierker, who was a core club member, and his wife, Helga, didn't understand him. He befriended Kim; he enjoyed her company; he didn't really care what others thought of him or of his behavior—and he liked the girl. He asked nothing of her. He cared for her. He began to believe he loved her. She began to believe she loved him. Ole Kronstrom was a replacement for her father and her husband, and he was the first substantial, solid human being she had ever known. As a friend.

Her divorce from Billy Whitefoot was final in 1961. She was twenty-one and she was being looked after by Ole Kronstrom. She played tennis, she led a life of relative leisure; he was giving her time to find herself, an old-fashioned notion but not particularly unwise. It made them both happy. Ole's pals at Norway Creek, without letting him hear the slightest whisper, found it mildly amusing—that Ole had fallen for their daughter. Of course, they completely misjudged the relationship, assuming it reflected their own inclinations.

Kim Roderick was happy. And she remained happy when she met a new man who had gone to work for Tim Dierker, a promising salesman of thirty, Larry Blankenship. Tim had given him the job with the approval of his fellow club members: After all, Larry was their son. They had even made it known to Larry, obliquely, of course, that there was a position at Dierker's firm. They were still managing lives, still controlling, chuckling over their power and the means they possessed to assuage their collective guilt. They were taking care of Rita's children. They were pretty good damn fellows, after all. They'd just been pushed a wee bit too far that night so long ago. . . .

But they were unhappy, indeed, when it became obvious that Kim Roderick's relationship with Ole Kronstrom was not what it seemed. It did not preclude her becoming involved with Larry Blankenship; involved quickly became too mild a term. Larry and Kim fell in love. The club members didn't like it. Tim Dierker was horrified. Brother and sister, it was beyond accepting on any level, but when he put it to his fellows, they clucked, admitted it was an unhappy turn, but not quite so ghastly as it might appear. After all, while they had the same mother there was no proof at all they had the same father. And having murdered two people, including their mother, they were hardly well advised to develop excessive squeamishness over what was nothing more than the *possibility* of incest. Total incest, that was.

Dierker was an old-line moralist. The killings had eaten away at his heart, soul, and entrails for years; he had subscribed to the gestures they'd made toward the children in the intervening years with devout enthusiasm. Relief. Now they were failing to stop another moral horror. And try as he might, Tim failed to stop the marriage; he hadn't the courage to deal with the truth in the face of his friends' determination that he remain quiet. Quite logically they believed that to open up the brother/sister business again might run them a terrible risk. The chances of a disaster were too great. Dierker buckled. Brother and sister were married. It was 1964.

In 1966 Kim Blankenship gave birth to a child with congenital brain damage. Ole Kronstrom, always her reliable, trusted friend, saw her through it. Larry, weak and willing and eager to please and an inveterate loser, very nearly suffered a nervous breakdown. He considered the child a result of his own inadequacy. It was the sort of judgment which defined his nature. Kim was twenty-six.

Her marriage to Larry ground along, now together, now apart, half functioning but never successful. His mental condition veered this way and that. He left Dierker's firm, tried to find himself in a series of dead-end jobs, grew smaller and smaller in his own eyes. And in his wife's, as well. She grew increasingly dependent on Ole. She went to the University of Minnesota, she developed her natural intelligence, gloried in the newly glimpsed complexities of life and the mind. She took herself too seriously at first; she was not unlike anyone else who discovers in himself the existence of a brain. It is a wonderful discovery. And Ole let her flourish.

She lived apart from Larry most of the time, the exceptions being his desperate attempts at reconciliation. She appeared for these sorrowful occasions but she could not truly lend herself to them. They failed. Larry diminished further still.

It was 1972 and Kim Blankenship was thirty-two years old. Larry Blankenship was forty. She was inevitably moving toward a final dissolution of their marriage. She was living on Ole Kronstrom's money; Larry was scraping by as best he could. The marriage was dead. Then, far away in Grande Rouge, Running Buck took to his deathbed and told his secrets to young Billy, who was now thirty-three, with a doctorate and a noteworthy career in sociology and Indian affairs and personal friendships with Russell Means, Dennis Banks, and Marlon Brando. The old man spilled the whole thing, everything Rita had ever told him—the sexual relationship with the club members, the two children by them, everything. And the story of the night of December 16, 1944.

Billy Whitefoot was stunned. He believed what the old man told him. He faced the fact that he had once loved Kim, one of Rita's children, and had in his own mind treated her badly by leaving her, taking their daughter with him. He felt a sense of responsibility to her . . . even love, the remembered sort. And he also knew that she had married Larry Blankenship . . . Running Buck had learned even that at the lodge, again the invisible man attending to his chores while the members argued it out by the fireplace. Running Buck had heard them say that Larry was Kim's brother and that, too, he'd told Billy as he lay dying.

For six months Billy had fought it out in his own mind. Should he tell Kim the truth? Or, as Running Buck had done, should he stay clear of white man's business? In the end, he remembered Kim. And he went to Minneapolis to see her. He was outraged at what the club members had done. He had never felt such violence in himself; it was new, it was awesome. He knew he could kill. He knew these men deserved to die. . . .

So, not quite sure where events were leading him, Billy took his story to Kim and spent an afternoon telling it, wrapping it around them, drawing them closer than they'd been since they'd been kids in love. It had shocked her, of course, but it hadn't been a surprise, not a surprise because somewhere in the back of her mind she'd feared the faceless thing that haunts childhood dreams. She had taken it well, heard him out, shrugged in the face of the bogeyman come true, coming to stand in the doorway of her life with his shadow erasing the color and falling across her hopes. There hadn't been much she could say; it was all in the past, she told him, and her marriage to

Larry was finished and she couldn't bring her mother back from the grave, from the ice cave. Billy hadn't known what to think. Kim had always been a mystery to him, deep, impossible to fathom. He had felt uncomfortable with her quiet, downplayed reaction. He knew she was thinking. But he didn't know what. In the end, he fell back on the knowledge that he'd done what he could. The rest of it was up to her. That night he prowled the city, the thought of what the men had done festering in his psyche. Could they possibly get away with it? Could they escape punishment forever? He grabbed a cab to Lake Harriet and stood before General Goode's home, staring, hating him with an Indian's atavistic resentment of the white man. He walked all the way around the lake that night, struggling with the givens of his life and this situation. He knew he could make it a good deal more complex by inserting himself; he could make it simpler, too. Finally he heaved a defeated sigh, took a last look at the general's house, and made it simpler. He went back north to Jasper, to his daughter, to the rhythms of life he'd worked so hard to attain.

Kim faced the truth of Billy's story without the slightest doubt. It made sense, there was nothing of a dying man's ravings in them. She tried to measure her response but it was impossible. She felt no particular emotion once the shock had died. She didn't hate the men at first; disgust, yes, but not an active hatred. Her marriage to Larry left her weak when she thought about it and as time went by she thought about it more and more. How could they have let it happen? And she thought about the child who had resulted from their marriage. She couldn't turn to Ole. She had no one. And when she thought about the child, she cried. It was the first thing she cried about in a long time. Ole was solicitous but he didn't understand.

It was 1973 and Larry Blankenship, groping around in his sorry failure's vacuum, never understanding the forces at work in his life, approached Kim about a reconciliation. He had a good job, a new car, a smattering of hope. Kim couldn't bring herself to turn him off with the truth; humanely, trying to deal gently with the fragility of his world, she explained that there was no future for them together, only separately. She tried to make him see that he could push on with his life while she went ahead with her own. They would always be friends. It was a hackneyed bit of business, she was aware of that, but it was all she could offer. The truth would destroy him; murder and incest she could handle because her emotions were so pallid by then. They would kill Larry.

Losing her had very nearly done him in as it was. But a nervous breakdown wasn't the worst that could happen. Nervous breakdowns, even severe ones, you survived. She saw him through it as best she could but she believed it was important to keep herself at a distance, to keep him from leaning on her. It was difficult but she managed it. Ole had helped her through it. His instincts were good. She trusted him. He loved her.

Larry slowly came out of the pit but it was a bad year, in or out of the pit, if you were trying to catch on with an advertising agency. Even if Tim Dierker had pulled some strings to get you the job. It was 1974 and admen were tripping over one another in the unemployment lines. A new man, Larry was the first to go. Alone, he waited for the telephone to ring. He tried to tell Kim his problems but she was tired of his problems. Finally, living in the same building, he took his problems to Tim Dierker. Several times they talked, each adrift in his own hopelessness. Larry had lost his wife and his career wasn't worthy of the name; he was forty-two years old, had just gone through a nervous breakdown, and had a new Thunderbird he couldn't pay for. Tim Dierker had just found out he was going to die; he had an inoperable brain tumor and he hadn't been able to tell Harriet. He told Larry down in Larry's empty, skeletal apartment and they got drunk together. Like Running Buck, Tim Dierker hadn't been able to take his guilt to his grave unspoken. In a spasm of premortem confession, fired with liquor, Tim Dierker told him the tale of murder and incest.

Bludgeoned by shock, Larry Blankenship went to Kim and told her the story, begging her to refute it. She couldn't. That was the end for Larry. For several days he composed himself, sitting alone in the apartment. Then he completed his plan, wrote a note to Bill Oliver, and shot himself in the lobby of the apartment building. It was, he felt sure, the only sane response to the banshee cry of his life.

Which was where I came in from my tennis match.

"Larry's suicide," I had said. "Was that when you decided to kill them all?"

She nodded soberly, her eyes cast up toward me, intelligent and calm eyes, pragmatic eyes that saw life as it was.

"Yes," she'd said. "There was never any real question in my mind after that. If he'd never found out, if he hadn't ended the way he did . . . then I don't suppose I'd ever have done anything about it. But with Larry's death their outrages became part of the present, part of my life—my observable life. It was too much for me to ignore. . . . So I decided to kill them all since they were equally guilty so far as I could tell. I didn't want to get so enmeshed in a huge plan. I just wanted them dead in full knowledge of why they were dying. . . ."

She called Tim Dierker and asked to see him. Harriet was out and Tim was trying to outlive his grief at Larry's suicide. His guilt had almost killed him already. It was stifling in the apartment when she arrived; Tim had been going through his scrapbook. She suggested they go to the roof and he went willingly, babbling about how cool it would be in the rain. Once they were alone in the wind and rain she told him that she knew the story of her mother, her brother. He cowered toward the wall. She pushed him hard at the shoulders, he dropped the scrapbook, she shoved him again, he tried to scramble away. She struck him across the shoulders, wrestled his almost dead weight over the low cement wall. She watched him struggle to his feet on the four-foot graveled extension of the roof. As he came back toward her, she lunged at him. He recoiled and fell backward over the edge. She picked up the scrapbook and left.

She went through the scrapbook carefully, saving the

with the awful relief of those left alive, we went down to the galley and Ole brewed coffee and spiked it with brandy. It steamed in the tight quarters and we drank it silently, avoiding one another's eyes.

Finally Archie said into his cup, under his breath, "Another theory, my last, down the drain. Wrong on all counts. Nothing but victims . . . no killer." He sighed and inspected the blood all over his raincoat. "And now we find out that, no matter how you cut it, they deserved to die. Where does that leave us, then?"

"Not wanting to find a murderer," Ole said, clinking his spoon against the cup. "Executioner, I should say."

"But he's still loose, whatever the hell you call him," I said. "Don't forget, he tried to kill me. . . ." I looked from one to the other. The old men were worn thin. "The thing is, who is it? There's nobody left. . . . But Kim's still in danger. If he hasn't found her yet."

"Maybe," Archie said. The enthusiasm was gone. He was through.

"Give me the gun," I said to Archie. He fished it out of his pocket and I put it in mine.

We decided to leave the boat and report the death of Hub Anthony the next day. Ole would simply go out to work on his boat and discover the body, stiff and cold. We finished the coffee, went past the remains, turned out the light, and climbed back on deck. A biting cold was coming with the fog and rain. We were carrying on the obfuscation the club had begun forty years ago when they began making their deals with Rita. I swung over the side and felt solid ground again.

We drove back to Minneapolis and dropped Ole at his darkened parking lot. It was midnight and the city was quiet in the cold rain.

"I've got to find Kim," I said.

"You're the one to do it, Paul. You're the one now. . . ." Ole shook my hand.

I drove Archie back to my place. I got him bundled up under blankets. I made him a hot toddy and told him to go to sleep. He looked like an old man. He smiled halfheartedly and accepted the toddy.

"I've got to find her, Dad, you know that. I love her. . . ."

"It's over, Paul," he said sleepily. "It's over for me, anyway, the ones who had to die are dead. Very nicely rounded off. . . . Take the gun, go find Kim, but I think the killing is over. . . . Just find the woman, that's all. That's all that's left. . . . You see, Billy— we forgot about Billy. And he doesn't know Kim's gone. . . . He wouldn't kill her, would he? What they did to her . . . that's why he killed them." He ran his tongue over dry lips, closed his eyes. Tired.

I kissed my father impulsively and went downstairs to his car. There was someone standing in the shadows outside in visitors' parking. The rain splattered on the tarmac and I felt the hair on my neck stiffen. The shadowy figure moved, came toward me. I flattened myself against the wall, rain dripping in my face. I felt for the gun. The figure stepped into the light. It was the Pinkerton man. He smiled and went inside.

I knew where I was going. I knew where Kim was and I was trying to arrange the whole story in my weary mind. I had to drive north and there was so little time.

28

I HEADED out on the freeway toward Duluth in the dead of the cold, wet night, wipers working methodically across the vast expanse of glass fronting Archie's automobile. The rain spit out of the darkness and I drove twenty-mile stretches without seeing another pair of headlamps. Franklin Hobbs was cooing his way through the night on WCCO. Frank Sinatra sang fired once into the windshield of my car, hoping to frighten me off. . . . Coming back from the lodge, Archie and I had cobbled together our Goode theory. He was the logical bet and we assumed he'd get loose from his police protection and go hunting for Kim.

We were half right, about our norm. He got loose from his protection. Kim, however, had made the same assumption. Knowing he was both resourceful and a creature of habit, she went to meet him in the fog on the jogging path. Only one remained and time was growing short. The fog which blanketed the Cities was her ally and she used it.

Again she was forced to rely on the predictability of her quarry. She waited on a side road, concealed by the gray wetness, watching his house. Trusting him to escape from the one place he was sure she could find him, she hadn't long to wait. His car swirled out of the fog and she followed him through the rain, knowing almost immediately where he was going. Ole's boat. It was a panic reaction on Hub's part but he must have thought she'd never strike so close to her own preserve. Like the rest of them, he misjudged her. It was no great problem to board the boat undetected in the storm. He had seemed almost relieved when the door swung open and he saw her.

They talked for a bit. He was almost noble in his decay and guilt and sorrow. He did not ask to be spared. He was the only one she regretted having to kill. When she pulled the trigger, she, not Hub, flinched, sending the slug slightly astray. She did not stop to see if he was dead. She simply left the boat, threw the gun onto the passenger's seat of the bronze Mark IV, and drove north, where she somehow was sure I'd find her. She called Billy at a filling station, asked him to meet her. She felt obligated to tell him what she had done.

I squinted up at the mustard-colored sky, shielding my eyes. Kim was far along the shelf, sitting on the edge above the lake. She had pulled her knees up and was hugging them to her chest. The sun was growing warm, drying the sand in patches. I went back inside the castle and felt the pockets of her army jacket. I found the pistol she'd used to kill Jon Goode and Hub Anthony. I took the other gun from my jacket pocket, the one she'd used on Boyle and Crocker. I went back into the sunshine holding the guns. She hadn't moved. Billy was gone. He'd left her to me.

I should have been thinking long thoughts as I walked across the expanse of layered stone. I couldn't. I felt the breeze and the sunshine filtering through and the shelf beneath my feet. I loved her but that was at least a world away.

She didn't look up when I stood beside her.

"Two-gun Cavanaugh," she said distinctly.

"What are you going to do now?"

"That depends on you, doesn't it?"

She might have been a character on the screen. I had somehow stumbled into her screenplay. It was up to me to handle the props.

"You don't seem quite real anymore," I said. "I don't know how to talk to you . . . what to say. I had an uncle once who was dying and when I knew it, I couldn't think of anything to say to him."

She brushed a hand across her eyes. "Do you still love me?" Her mouth turned up at the corners. She might have been laughing at me. She had gone so far beyond me. She seemed full, rich, in control. I felt hollow. The longer I looked at her, the more I felt as if I were floating away, a man in a balloon going away.

I tried to speak but there was nothing. I nodded, yes, yes. . . .

She stood beside me, squeezed my arm. She walked away. I knelt by the edge of the shelf and looked into the blank face of the lake. I dropped the two pistols into thirty feet of water. It might as well have been to the center of the earth.

When I finally turned back, she was out of sight. I walked back up to the castle. Her car was gone. She had taken the coffee things, kicked the coals into the dirt. I got back into Archie's car and moved slowly along the narrow path until I reached the highway. I took my time getting back to Minneapolis. It was over. The end.

Epilogue

THE murders of the five prominent Minneapolitans remain unsolved, though the files are still open. The search for Carver Maxvill continues. Halfheartedly.

Kim and Ole Kronstrom live in Oslo near Frogner Park, where they are much taken by the heroic statuary of Adolf Gustav Vigeland.

Mark Bernstein did not become mayor of Minneapolis.

At Christmas of 1975 Archie Cavanaugh delivered the manuscript of his new Fenton Carey thriller, *Homicidim Seriatim.*